Gateways

BRIAN GOTTHEIL

DEDICATION

To my mother, Joanne,
who was Caryn's inspiration,
and mine.

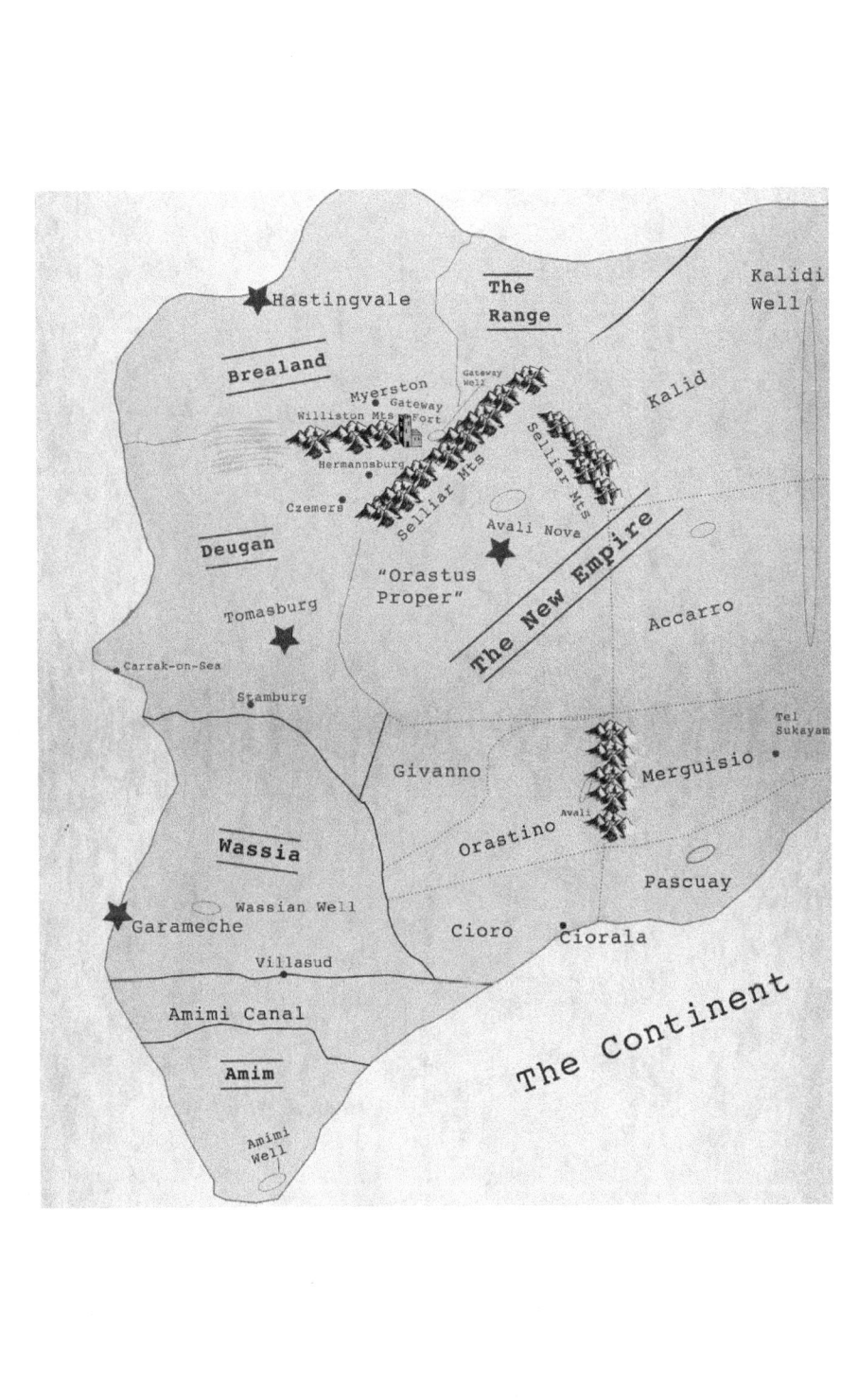

CHAPTER ONE

In the popular imagination, the Great War lives on as a spectacle. Each year, as autumn is threatening to give way to winter, hundreds converge on the Maxalo Pass in Wassia, in the southwest of the Continent, to re-enact the battle that was fought there in 1693 (all dates refer to the Imperial calendar). The mood is festive: vendors hawk sugary drinks, horns and trumpets blow, and women and men march proudly in the brightly coloured uniforms of a bygone era. The day belongs not to the long-suffering veterans, but to a celebration of homespun southern hospitality.

Indeed, the conflict is remembered by many as a distinctively southern war. Certainly, the greater part of the fighting took place in Wassia, where massive graveyards now stand testament to the many who lost their lives in its meadows and valleys. Is it surprising, then, that it is the southern front which has persisted in the cultural memory of the Continent? That schoolchildren, filmmakers and even military historians have been drawn to its cascading offensives and desperate stands?

When, however, the war is considered from a broader historical perspective — not merely as a series of battles, but as a phenomenon that influenced the future course of a Continent — then it is the northern front, the confrontation between the Realm of Breland and the Republic of Deugan, where our focus is inexorably drawn. It is hardly an exaggeration to claim that the Continent entered the modern era through the Gateway, that region which links the two combatants; and a study of wartime Deugan and Breland reveals not only a clearer portrait of the war, but also a glimpse at its more delicate and elusive cousin: Peace.

—Rothwell, Hering et al., *Perspectives on the Great War: The Northern Front* (1745)

It was an old memory, the kind that lies concealed in the corners of the mind until it emerges in times of tension. A dirt floor, a boy, and a night sky filled with so many stars that it almost seemed white.

The stars were a surprise she'd prepared for Brenner. The boy had been moody ever since she met him, but his malaise was darker now. He had set himself apart from Jayla and the professor, brooding, barely speaking. But as she led him out from the room where he slept and as the stars came into view overhead, his harsh expression melted and he hugged her with more warmth than she'd thought possible.

Now they were lying side by side on the ground, staring up at the stars and talking about dogs. "How can you not like dogs?" Jayla demanded. "What's wrong with you?"

"Hey, I have nothing against them," Brenner said. "They're cute and all. But you never really know what they're going to do."

"Well, yeah, they're alive," Jayla said. "They've got brains. Sometimes they'll surprise you. But dogs are awfully predictable. He sees a smaller animal, he'll chase it. He smells food, he'll come running." She grinned. "My little brother was like that."

"But you could reason with your little brother," Brenner said.

"Not when it came to food. Or chasing smaller animals. Besides, you can train a dog."

"Sure," Brenner said, "and that's why I'm okay with them. At least you can figure them out and use that. Seems a bit manipulative, that's all."

Jayla grinned again. "Brenner Halloway! Is the strong, silent specimen who has sulked sullenly the past six span so seduced by this splendid starry sky that he's sorry about manipulating a canine?"

He laughed, a deep belly laugh that echoed off the stone walls. Then his voice turned serious. "How do you do that? I haven't laughed since we got in here. And you just say a bunch of words that start with the same letter and it's like none of it ever happened."

Jayla glanced over at him. He was lying on his side, looking back at her. His brow was furrowed. He was a handsome boy, moody as he was. He was thin without being skinny, tall without being overpowering. His brown hair was still combed over neatly, a curious attention to fashion considering the circumstances. Lacking any shaving supplies, he had grown a fierce brown beard that nearly hid the faint discolouration on the right side of his chin and neck. And while he hardly looked an athlete, there was some definition in his arms as he propped himself up from the ground.

"How I do it?" Jayla repeated. She shrugged. "I really don't know what to say."

"Not a problem I ever thought you'd have," Brenner teased.

"Look, I'm scared and angry too," Jayla said. "I'm just trying to make the best of it. We might still get out of here. The Guard might still come."

"Oh, open your eyes," Brenner snapped. "The Guard isn't coming. Nobody's coming, they're the ones who —"

"Oh, open *your* eyes," Jayla interrupted him, "and look at those stars."

The night sky was gorgeous. Jayla had grown up in Villasud, the city known throughout Wassia as the Light of the South. Its nickname had never been more fitting. Since wide-scale electric lighting was introduced to Villasud a few years before Jayla's birth, its commercial and industrial centres were constantly lit, hiding most of the night's stars. Jayla's father, who had made his fortune purchasing and managing many of Villasud's factories, called it "progress."

"I wish I could take you to the manor," Brenner said. "Show you some real stars."

"Hey!" Jayla shouted, pointing at the sky. "These ones are real."

"What do you mean?"

"Do you think I created an entire sky?" Jayla said. "If I was that good, we'd be out of here by now." She looked around the cavern. At one end of the room, she could still see the green rocks and the dust that had collapsed there, trapping them inside when the avalanche had hit. There were several small holes in the barricade, allowing in the air that kept them alive, but they lacked any tools with which to expand the holes and escape. Throughout the rest of the cave, the walls were not green but orange, strange, rough and glowing. They jutted up from the hard dirt floor, but instead of curving around to form a ceiling, their tops appeared suspended in the air, like the ancient walls of the Raolin Temple ruins in Villasud or the famous arches of the Old Empire, waiting to collapse.

"What did you do, then?" Brenner asked.

"I spoke to the rocks," Jayla said. "The ceiling, I mean. It wouldn't move aside to let us out. But I got it to hide itself. To turn invisible. So we could see the sky through it." She glared at him. "The *real* sky."

Brenner sat up and looked at her. He frowned and rubbed his new beard. "You spoke to the ceiling?"

"Not with words." It was so hard to explain. As a child, Jayla had always been good with people. She'd had to be, to survive at home. Her father was a gruff man whose pride and joy was his business. He was rarely away from his desk, and when he was, its stresses still consumed him. Jayla's mother came from an old but heavily indebted family that had sacrificed much in the way of pride to arrange her marriage to an industrialist. She often felt torn between her new family and her old one, and felt lonely and isolated in the city. Two tired, ragged people who belonged apart had been thrown together, and their arguments were fierce. Jayla had learned from an early age to mediate, to make peace — and that meant she had learned to understand them.

Jayla was concentrating on the orange rocks and on the power that coursed through her, trying to reach out to both at the same time, when suddenly she felt the air shimmer and a wave of warmth rushed through her body, starting at her feet and shooting past her ankles and up through her legs, her centre, her chest. She saw a vision then, a jagged grey boulder jolted with a flash of lightning. She raised a hand to steady herself, but faster than a blink, the warmth was gone and the image faded.

"Have you ever thought about what it would feel like to be a rock in a place like this?" she asked Brenner.

"Rocks don't feel anything."

"I know. It's just a thought." She had thought for several minutes about the vision. Something cold and lifeless suddenly seeing a surge of power rush through it. Unpleasant. Jarring. Then she imagined the feeling continuing, non-stop, like spending hours at that carnival game that tested how long you could stand an electric shock pulsing in your hands.

And the power responded. Flash — a huge mass, breaking apart, its pieces melting — and flash, the vision gone. Jayla focused on physical changes, on no longer being the shape you once were. This was one Jayla really could understand. After a month and a half in this Well, her own body was no longer the sixteen-year-old one she remembered.

"I've used the magic," Brenner said. He said it grudgingly, as though the very word were shameful. "Or the *power* or the *energy* or whatever we're supposed to call it to make it sound less childish.

There's no rhyme or reason to when it works. Sometimes you just think about something, and boom. Other times it happens when you *don't* think about it. Once I was desperate for water, and I bent my whole mind to finding some, and I felt it stir in me and I heard raindrops. My entire room was raining and I stuck my tongue out and drank it straight out of the air. But I tried the exact same thing two days later and nothing happened."

"Well, this one worked because I somehow understood the rocks," Jayla said. "Don't ask me how. Just like your rainstorm, it probably won't work again two days from now. All I know is that I tried to understand them, and the power kept giving me clues, and after awhile it felt like I was talking to the rocks themselves — and I knew I could turn them off, fade them out. Without knowing how I knew it."

Brenner grimaced. "I don't like this."

"Neither do I," Jayla admitted.

"I do like your sky, though," Brenner added. He smiled. "Thanks."

She remembered watching him as he left that day. She'd pulled the moody, brooding Brenner out of his shell, briefly. She'd felt the incredible warmth of his hug and the strange tingling that swept through her stomach. She'd felt something else, a sense of partnership or friendship, as they watched the stars together from the dirt floor of the cavern. But then she'd felt a very different Brenner, a cold one, aloof and untrusting as he withdrew from the room.

Jayla reached out to the Well's power, but not with much hope that she would ever truly understand him.

*

It was an old memory, but it was not the time for old memories.

Caryn Hallom gripped the railing of the carriage as it rumbled along the cobblestones. The streets of the capital were deserted. Its people, those who weren't dragging themselves through gruelling work in the munitions factories, were huddled in their homes, grieving lost relatives or waiting anxiously for news from the fronts. Tension had settled on the city like a blanket.

Strange, Caryn thought, that a memory would surface now of another life in another time. She had stopped using the name Jayla more than fourteen years ago, when she had escaped the Well and fled Wassia for its northern neighbour, the Republic of Deugan. Her life had changed so profoundly that her past as Jayla Sullivan was difficult to believe. It was difficult even to remember.

The driver eyed her curiously as she pointed to the spot where she wanted him to stop. "Here, my lady?"

"Yes. Right here."

"Will you be in need of transportation when your duties here are complete, my lady?"

"No, my friend. Thank you." She produced four coins from her purse and allowed Hans to help her from the carriage, hating the way her knee twinged as she set her weight down.

The sun was beginning to set, a furious orange against the darkening sky. Hans adjusted the rifle he had slung over his shoulder and knocked on the door of the grey stone building ahead of them. After a few seconds, the door opened a crack and a rifle peeked through. Then the door opened wide. "Minister Hallom." A stiff bow. "We've been expecting you."

They were led through the prison, past the intake area and the visitors' waiting room to the entrance to the cells. The warden met them there, a tall, thin man with greying hair. "Minister," he greeted her with a bow. "I must apologize for intruding upon your time today. I am certain you have more urgent matters to attend to."

"Where is he?" Caryn asked. She still half felt she was wasting her time here, and she had long since learned that bluntness was the only way to accomplish things in the Deugan bureaucracy.

"This way," the warden replied, and led them down a corridor. "He insisted on speaking to you personally and said he would give us a full confession if he did. We know he's planning something in Tomasburg, but unless you can get it out of him, we don't have enough to keep him."

"You say that with some chagrin," Caryn observed.

"Not about the laws," the warden said quickly. "Twenty-four hours till you have to charge, well, it makes us civilized. But if there is going to be an attack in the capital — I just hate feeling powerless."

Caryn gave him a rueful smile. "I know that feeling well. Why would he confess, then?"

"Because he doesn't know how little we have," the warden replied. "And there's nothing in the laws says we have to tell him."

The warden led them into a small square room. A wooden desk sat in its centre, with two chairs on either side. The Steffian was sitting on the far side of the desk, rocking back and forth.

He stood when he saw Caryn enter. "The Sorceress herself!" he exclaimed.

"Sit down," the warden said, unamused. "You'll treat the foreign minister with respect."

"I would never dream of disrespecting a sorceress," the man said.

Caryn caught Hans' eye. The sorceress label had been coined years ago by a journalist reporting on Caryn's quick rise through Deugan's National Treasury Department. It was brilliant because it was so rife with implication, and her enemies had latched onto it for just that reason. It wasn't only the sense of mystery and danger, though that was part of it. Sorcery suggested the Wells, and the Wells suggested an association with the Steifar religion, or with the Steffians who followed it. It suggested the witch hunts of eras past, the categories developed by society to define the enemy lurking within.

"Can I be alone with the foreign minister?" the Steffian asked.

The warden opened his mouth to argue, but Caryn intervened. "The warden and the prison guards will wait outside. My personal bodyguard will stay." She gestured to Hans.

"Fair enough." The Steffian was smiling, his attitude cocky. He didn't look about to confess anything.

Caryn's mind ran through everything she knew about the Steffian organization. In broad strokes, she had learned much in the last two years. She knew their philosophies, their history, some patterns behind their attacks and operations, which Steifar populations embraced them and which rejected them. In details, though, the entire government knew depressingly little. The Steffians were skilled at nothing if not secrecy, and their governance and internal hierarchy were mysteries. Due to Deugan's policy of refusing to negotiate with the organization, Caryn had never met its leadership. The names Pellor Amad, Brenth Nono and Bashar Gamoy were well known to her, but as far as she knew, only a photograph of Amad had ever been seen.

"Why have you asked for me?" Caryn demanded.

"I'm a Deugan," the Steffian replied. "Tomasburg, born and raised. Are you surprised?" The man leaned into the light cast by the room's lone electric bulb. His look was Deugan, lithe and dark. Hans stared back at him, impassive. "You people always think a Steffian's going to be whitewashed, some foreigner from Wassia or the Fringes. You think we'll look like Caryn Hallom."

Caryn remained carefully silent. That was something else the sorceress label suggested: Caryn's own months in the Wassian Well, and her childhood in Wassia, where their own boys were now dying. No Deugan would take that kindly if they knew. But they didn't. Her pale skin was not uncommon along the Deugan coast, where she claimed to have been born. Neither was her blonde hair, now well on its way to grey, which she kept cropped short, just above her neck. They were Wassian features, but the Wassians had once occupied that region of Deugan, and the two peoples had been intermingling ever since.

"That's the first message I wanted to give you," the Steffian continued. "We're here. We're Deugans. We're citizens like everybody else."

"Of course you are," Caryn said, wondering what game the man was playing. "Which means that you have to follow the law. I'm told that when they searched your house, they found everything a Steffian would need to build a bomb."

"The Steifar are second class citizens in Deugan," the man said. "Third class, even, behind the atheists. Now that we have the Hallom Doctrine..." He trailed off, allowing the words to linger, the policy initiative that bore Caryn's name. The symbol of her failure. "We all know that if Deugan wins this war, it's the Hallom Doctrine that will be imposed on the Fringes," he continued. "Trading the New Empire's occupation for a made-in-Deugan model."

"I did not come here to argue about politics," Caryn said. She kept her voice calm, but she felt her nerves start to rise. A vision of Jayla flashed before her eyes, rocks surrounding her, trapped. "My doctrine was not meant to undermine the Steifar. Only the Steffians." Caryn glanced at Hans from the corner of her eye and saw that he was at his ready. She took a deep breath. There was no need to be afraid. "Your friends are terrorists and fundamentalists," she told the Steffian. "My doctrine was meant to lift the New Empire's occupation. And to do it without a war. Without bombs. Even homemade ones. So I ask you again: why did you want to see me?"

"Because I know now that I will not be able to send you a message any other way," the Steffian told her. "I meant to send a message through a bomb that would explode at Grunvell Block. The home of your foreign affairs department. There is my confession. I can no longer do so, so I am sending you a message in another way." The man leaned forward, his eyes slits, his expression dark. "I love my country. I refuse to allow it to be ruined. I refuse to allow the Steifar to have anything less than all of the rights Deugan promises. That is my message, Caryn Hallom. The Steffians are coming."

*

It was dark when they left the prison, and Caryn's heart was heavy in her chest. She had known for some time that the Steffians hated her but had thought it no more than rhetoric and propaganda. Knowing that her department had been specifically targeted, that the police had barely managed to stop it —

"Do not concern yourself with that man, my lady," Hans said. He kept one hand on his rifle, as always. The other he offered to steady her steps along the cobblestones. She was not tall, but Hans had always been good about slowing his strides to match hers.

"I was a target," she said.

"You've been a target your entire career. That is what makes you who you are."

"It's also what keeps you employed," Caryn told him. They turned a corner and headed for a small square, less deserted than the area around the prison.

"The Steffians are like gnats," Hans declared. "They bite at you and they pinch at you, and when you swat them away they come back. But they're only an irritation. I would gladly take in a thousand Steffian terrorists to have Brealand out of this war."

Caryn grimaced, though whether at the war or at the twinge in her knee, she couldn't say. The mood in the capital had indeed been bleak ever since Brealand had declared. The war was supposed to be nothing more than a little skirmish with Wassia, they had been told. Wassia had already committed an act of war by closing the Amimi Canal, so really, Deugan wasn't even the aggressor. Faced with no other choice, Deugan would invade northern Wassia, then trade its land back to it to get the Canal reopened. It would all be over in a matter of a few span.

Or so the nation was told.

Months had passed. In the south, Deugan was picking up chunks of Wassian territory, but the going was slow, far too slow. In the east, the New Empire had joined the war on the Wassians' side, forcing Deugan's army into an embarrassing retreat from its eastern border. Now Breland had declared, opening up a third front in the north. And that changed everything.

That, no doubt, was why the president himself had asked Caryn to see him, tonight, after dark, and Caryn could only guess what he had in mind.

Caryn and Hans passed through the square into the Hall of Columns.

It was a transformation that continued to capture Caryn's heart after all this time. While Villasud had its historic district and Carrak-on-Sea its fascinating mix of three cultures' architecture, Tomasburg was the only city Caryn had ever lived in where the ancient world came to life before her, flowing and melding into the modern one. From the grey stones of the prison, the concrete of office towers and the polished wood-and-glass of merchants' shops, she needed only turn one corner to be transported to the days of the Old Empire, immersed in its rows upon rows of sculpted marble pillars. The roof of the palace had long since collapsed, and the walls had been pulled down, but the pillars still stood just as they had so many centuries ago.

The Hall of Columns opened up onto Scheil Square. The garden in the centre was quiet, a testament to the mood in the capital. Tomas Scheil, clad in stone, towered over the garden as always, but while he was normally surrounded by boys playing and women chatting and lovers strolling, tonight he looked wistful to Caryn, and sad, and alone.

Across the square from the Hall of Columns was a building twice its age and twice its height. It mingled with the marble columns of the Old Empire and the glass and wood of modern Deugan so effortlessly that it seemed to be part of them, but it was not. It was a different beauty entirely.

The giant pyramid was a monolith, a testament to the culture of their ancients that the Old Empire had failed to crush. Its twenty-nine landings were an incredible foreshadowing — some even said a prophecy — of the twenty-nine chiefdoms, kingdoms and city-states that Tomas Scheil would later cobble together to create Deugan.

To the right of the pyramid stood Government House, a much smaller building but a beautiful one in its own right. Although it was built within the last century, it had been designed cleverly, to give the impression that it was made of the same ancient stone as the pyramid.

Government House was where Caryn and Hans were headed. They walked through a long entranceway lined with statues of Deugan heroes, then passed underneath a massive pointed archway. One did not, Caryn had learned long ago, build rounded arches in Tomasburg.

Once they had passed through the main security checkpoint, Caryn took her leave of Hans. "Double-check the precautions at Grunvell Block," she told him. "That Steffian may have had others working with him. Thank you for your service, as always."

Hans smiled and bowed. "A pleasure as always, my lady. I will return within the hour."

And there was nothing to do but see the president.

She couldn't understand why she was nervous. Caryn and the president had been friends and allies for years. He had helped get her the Treasury Chief post that had catapulted her to fame — or infamy, depending who you asked — and she had campaigned harder than anyone for his own election. It was the war, Caryn told herself. That was why nothing felt quite right, not even old friendships. It was the war.

She knocked on his door and bowed to him as he opened it. He gave her a terse bow in return and motioned her to a chair. She sat as he closed the door behind her.

The president looked terrible. There were dark bags under his eyes, and he grimaced as he walked to his desk, keeping a hand to his head. He'd been drinking, Caryn realized with dismay. He had gained several pounds, too, and it was starting to show in his face. Not a year ago the president had looked a fighter and acted that part too, but the war was tiring him, and the declaration from Brealand had hit him like a fist in the gut.

He sat down across from her. "You were right," he said without introduction. "Out of all my advisors, all the generals — you have no military background. Only a couple years in foreign affairs. How did you know?"

"I have been giving you my reasons all along, Mr. President," she answered.

"You know you don't need to call me that, Caryn," he said. He tried to smile but only succeeded in twisting his face sickly. "We're friends. Remember?"

"I do remember," Caryn said softly, but the feeling in her gut grew more intense, not less. She felt as though she was sitting across from the Steffian again. The president had called her here for a reason, and dread, unspoken, hung in the air.

"Do you remember when you first applied here?" the president asked. "The financial superstar? You had the reputation, all right, but they still called old Dieter crazy. A woman, in charge of the treasury." He managed a real smile this time. "Dieter was brilliant, the way he spun it. If you're against Caryn Hallom you're against democracy, he said! You're against equality, freedom! But I told Dieter, you can't take a person whose every move is already being scrutinized and try to make her into some sort of symbol. It's too much pressure."

"I appreciated your concern," was all Caryn said. Careful. An old friend he might be, but he was the president now.

"You proved Dieter right, damn you," the president said. "You handled it. And maybe you never were a symbol. But you handled his trying to make you one. So now I have to give you a job that has even more pressure, because I don't know anybody else who can do it." He stopped, leaned across his desk and said softly, "or who I can trust."

Caryn tensed in spite of herself. He had often said, since the war began, that she should have been president instead of him. Of course she never would have been elected. The president and his predecessor Dieter had had enough trouble making the public accept a woman in unelected positions. When Dieter first stuck his neck out to give her the treasury job, one of the religious parties had stormed out of his coalition, forcing an election that Dieter nearly lost. There had been scathing newspaper columns, mad ravings against her in Senate debates, even death threats. If the president did something rash, like appointing a woman with no military experience to an army oversight post, the people would rebel. She had heard stories of the front lines, of the trenches, of the artillery barrages that lasted days without pause, of the machine gun fire, of the step-by-step, position-by-position advancements in Wassia. The parents and friends of the boys on the front had no doubt heard these stories too. The president had to maintain their confidence.

Caryn took a deep breath and waited.

"You told me Brealand entering the war was inevitable," the president said. "Maybe you were right. But all of my senior advisors and all of the top generals told me Brealand would stay out. Why? Caryn, hundreds of thousands of the New Empire's soldiers are stationed within my borders, and there's a fleet of Brea warships massing in the north harbours, but what keeps me awake at night is the thought that my own generals have been lying to me. If I can be crass, I wonder if they wanted to measure their cocks against Brealand's and fooled me into letting them."

"Do you really believe that?" Caryn forgot formality for a moment. She had been against this war from the start, but the president's accusation was startling. Suddenly the Tomasburg dusk seemed even darker.

"The generals are fighting this war now for their own reasons," the president said. "I don't know what those reasons are, and at this point it doesn't really matter. What matters is that I am the commander-in-chief of Deugan's armed forces, and I can't trust what my own generals tell me about what's happening on the front. But I do trust you." The president sighed and looked away. "I need you to go to the Gateway Fort and see it for yourself."

"Excuse me?"

"General Freed's turned the Gateway into his personal little fiefdom," the president spat. "I need to know what's going on."

"And you're asking me?" Caryn said incredulously. "To inspect a military fort? You know I don't know anything about —"

"You're intelligent," the president interrupted. "You're wise. You're kind. You're loyal. You're the last person in Deugan I would want to send somewhere dangerous. Which is why I have to, may the Gods forgive me."

Caryn stared at this man who had been her friend. Who was still her friend. Who was being killed by this war just as surely as the boys in Wassia.

"Mr. President," Caryn said. "I'm your foreign minister. There is a lot of diplomatic work still to be done in the Fringes, to put pressure on the New Empire. The Wassians may be willing to talk now too. That's where I should be. Not on the front lines."

"I know that," the president said. "Gods forgive me, I know that. But if I don't know the facts, if I can't trust General Freed, then how do I negotiate? How do I know what to demand and what to concede? Caryn, how do we build a peace if we're at war with ourselves?"

The feeling in the pit of her stomach was growing. She felt herself tensing. But all she could think to say was, "I don't know, Georg."

He smiled. "Nobody calls me by my real name anymore."

"I'll help you, Georg. We'll get through this. We'll get Deugan through this."

"Thank you," the president replied. Then he paused, and the look on his face was sheepish. For a brief moment he was young. "I've already assembled a team for you. You can meet them in the morning."

*

Caryn couldn't sleep that night. She'd said yes. Why had she said yes? It was difficult to refuse the president, but all the same...

She sighed and tried to turn her mind away from the Gateway. She thought instead about her old memory, and Jayla, and how Jayla had invoked her parents to explain how she used the Well's power. If Caryn rarely thought about the cavern and her life as Jayla, she thought about her parents still less. Funny, she now mused, how her father was always so busy and anxious, her mother so sad and lonely. Neither of them had seen any real problems in their lives; neither one had been trapped in a Well; neither one had been to a war zone. Her father with his fortune, her mother with her name and connections, they had nothing of any consequence to fight over. Yet they had fought constantly, and Caryn, even as a child, had understood why.

That was her real mission now, she knew, no matter what the president said. She wasn't just meeting General Freed to see the defences at the fort. She was meeting him to try to understand why he was fighting.

She was meeting him to stop this war.

CHAPTER TWO

The weather grew hotter as they pushed further north, and the train car was stifling. Whether from the heat or from the tensions in Tomasburg, Caryn felt tiredness wash over her. She was just starting to doze when she felt the train shudder and then grind to a halt. Nearby, she saw Janusz's head jerk upward; Lana laid a bundle of papers into a briefcase and pressed her face against the window.

They had stopped in what appeared to be a small town, though the view from Caryn's window did not allow her to guess which one. There were not supposed to be any stops before they reached the Fort.

Caryn glanced from Hans to Reimund. "A fighter almost as fierce as myself," Hans had described the other guard when they'd met back in Tomasburg. "I would trust him with my life, and with things more valuable still, like yours." Reimund rarely spoke, and Caryn had yet to get the measure of the man, but Hans had been her bodyguard for half a decade. If he trusted Reimund, so could she.

Just now, though, Reimund looked as confused and wary as any of them. Caryn took it as a bad sign. Hans' face, on the other hand, was impassive as usual.

"Marwin," Caryn said. The boy was sitting just in front of her. He wheeled around at the sound of his name. "Do you know why we've stopped?"

Marwin shook his head. "We've passed the junction at Czemers, which means we must be up in Gateway Province."

"Has the Gateway been attacked? Or is there a problem with the train?"

"I've had no more word than you, my lady," Marwin replied.

"Then find word," Caryn said. The boy was clever, Caryn had discovered, but he lacked initiative. She needed to guide him by the hand. "Ask the conductor, and find out the name of this town. Go."

A span had passed since her meeting with the president, and she could not recall hearing a shred of good news in all that time. The New Empire had pushed back a section of Deugan's trenches in the east; the Wassians had stalled their offensive in the south; and in the north, Brealand loomed. Nobody knew which rumours about the Breas were true. Caryn could safely reject some of the more outlandish — that they had steel in their bones which could deflect bullets, that their airplanes could carry tons of explosives across long distances to drop on enemy positions — but whether they were planning an amphibious assault, a build-up in the northwest, or a headlong charge through the Gateway where Caryn was headed, was anybody's guess.

When Marwin was gone, Caryn turned to Janusz and Lana. They were her team, such as it was, and they were not the team Caryn would have chosen on her own. "I had to be subtle about this, Caryn, you must see that," the president had told her the morning after their meeting. He had become happier overnight, almost giddy. "I needed to find people on the political side who would still know enough about the military to be useful to you. They'll be great. Trust me."

Janusz was a tall man in his early thirties. He had the dark complexion so typical in Deugan, a shaved head and a closely cropped black beard. He was a big man, too. Janusz had told her that before his foray into political life he had worked ten years excavating oil in Deugan's northwest. It made him more muscular than a political aide had any right to be.

Lana was the opposite, a slender girl several years younger than Janusz, who looked like a strong gust of wind might blow her away. She had long, straight brown hair with the bangs cut to curl around the top of her forehead. Her face was plain and her dress formal, but she fanned herself with a gaudy multicoloured fan that had no doubt been imported from across the ocean.

Caryn wished she had a fan. Since they'd stopped moving, the train was getting even hotter, if anything. She wiped a bead of sweat from her brow. "Can you believe Amim had a blizzard last span?" she found herself asking. Amim, at the southwestern tip of the Continent, had been Wassia's most prized colony until it declared independence at the outset of the war. Deugan needed what allies it could find, and with Amim, they could press the Wassians from north and south at once.

"I heard the storm broke up a Wassian attack," Janusz put in. "They had to abandon thirty pieces of artillery when the Amimi countered. Thanks to the Gods," he added, and Lana nodded, biting her lip.

Lana was always quiet in public. They had met three years earlier, when Caryn was the head of the Treasury Department and Lana had been assigned there on a college internship. Even then, years after Caryn and some of her contemporaries had broken the ground, Lana remained one of the few women in the Treasury, and she had turned to Caryn as a guide and mentor. As soon as she had a chance, Lana had transferred to Foreign Affairs, perhaps to follow her. In a way, Caryn was glad she had someone with her she knew and trusted, but she would have been far more comfortable had the girl remained in Tomasburg. The capital was well defended, and the Gateway ... well, if the president hadn't had serious doubts, he wouldn't have sent Caryn on this inspection in the first place. Caryn had no idea why the president had assigned Lana to accompany her to a military fort and had a sneaking suspicion Lana had been foolish enough to request the opportunity.

Now she looked scared. "Do you really think the Gateway's been attacked, my lady?"

"I don't know," Caryn said. "Last we heard, Brealand was building up its forces in the west. But that might have been a ruse."

"They'll attack in the west," Janusz declared. "Their strength is on the sea and they'll want to hit our oil. Why would they come through the Gateway in the northeast?"

"What if they do both?" Lana asked uneasily.

"Let's all calm down," Caryn said. "It's probably just a mechanical problem with the train."

They sat in silence for some time, sweating in the northern heat, straining to make out the muffled voices that they could now hear from outside the train. Finally Marwin returned, dragging the conductor with him. "No attack," the boy announced, breathless.

"No train problems either. We've stopped here because our own soldiers have blocked us."

"Our own soldiers?" Janusz demanded angrily. "Don't they know the foreign minister is onboard?"

"They're digging trenches," Marwin replied.

"Trenches?" Caryn said, incredulous. "Why would we need trenches this far from the front? Unless we *have* been attacked?"

"The captain said there was no attack," Marwin insisted hotly. Then, suddenly remembering, he added a mumbled, "My lady."

"I can explain, my lady," the conductor jumped in. He was a short, portly man. "This town is called Hermannsburg. It lies in the centre of the Hermann Gap." He pointed out the window. "Do you see those mountains, my lady?"

Caryn looked. In the distance, beyond the train station, they rose in a smooth line, their reddish-brown peaks jutting toward the sky. "That way is north, so they can only be the Williston Mountains," she said. "The Selliar range is to the southeast."

The conductor nodded. "As you know, my lady, the Gateway is a path linking Brealand to Deugan, bounded by the two mountain ranges. The Gateway Fort guards one end of path, and the Hermann Gap lies across the other. A trench line across the gap is a precautionary measure. In the event the fort falls, we can still keep the enemy bottled up in the Gateway."

Caryn looked back to Marwin. "Is that your understanding?"

Marwin nodded excitedly. "That's what I was told. They've been ordered to set it up now. They say it'll be impregnable."

"Nothing is impregnable," Janusz snorted.

"It's on high ground and the Hermann Gap is tiny," Marwin shot back. "Half of the trench is in the foothills of the mountains already."

"You're exaggerating. That gap's a lot wider than —"

"Never mind all that," Caryn interrupted. "How soon can we be moving again?"

"The captain in charge has given orders to remove the obstruction at once," the conductor replied. "It will take some time, though." He fanned himself with his hand. "There was a pleasant breeze out in Hermannsburg."

"I want to see the trench," Marwin said excitedly.

"Then go," Caryn said. "I wouldn't mind stretching my legs and seeing the town." Janusz and Lana both murmured their approval.

"Reimund, please remain here. Hans, come with us."

Hermannsburg proved to be a larger town than Caryn expected. A grand cobblestone plaza spread before the train station. Large marble statues of men on horseback overlooked the square's two main entrances. Townsfolk were milling about, some standing and chatting, some carrying baskets of fruits or trade goods, others leading horses or, in one case, a goat and a donkey that did not seem to enjoy each other's company. At the centre of the square stood a large fountain, and Caryn heard the shouts of children splashing in it to avoid the heat. Gazing at the scene, she would never have guessed that trenches were being dug outside the town's limits.

At the far end of the square stood the town hall, an elaborate structure of brick, clay and sandstone. A pair of stone tigers guarded the doors. From the edges of its roof flew a series of small yellow flags with a black device on them that Caryn could not make out. The banners were triangles, their points fluttering in the mountain breeze.

Janusz noticed them too. "Pre-Unification flags," he warned in his gruff voice. "These people may not be happy to see politicians from Tomasburg."

"The regions enjoy showing off their local pride," Caryn said softly. "I wouldn't think anything of those flags. They fly the Wheel in its rightful place, high above the others."

It was true. The roof of the town hall sloped up on all four sides to reach a single point, from which emerged a tall flagpole bearing an enormous blue banner. In white print in its centre was a circle, divided like a pie into twenty-nine equal slices. The central point where the slices met was emphasized with a dash of red, giving the false impression that the device was meant to depict a giant wheel. In fact, Deugan's flag was symbolic, the traditional triangular banners of the myriad pre-Unification states, all come together to form a unified whole.

Janusz was unimpressed. "Local pride is one thing in peacetime," he muttered. "Those differences have to be put aside now." He gave Caryn a strange look as he said it, as though challenging her to disagree.

Carefully, she rose to his bait. "I believe that if we suppressed our differences, we would be no better than Brealand. Or the Steffians."

The big man shrugged. "Anyhow, I barely notice the breeze out here, and I think I see a temple down that street, past the statue.

Perhaps we can move our explorations out of the sun."

Lana nodded excitedly at that idea, fanning herself vigorously, so they took off in the direction Janusz had pointed. The cobblestones ended as soon as they left the square. The roads here were packed dirt, and narrow. Squat, single-storey buildings lined them, some made of brick, most of wood. Above the buildings the mountains towered. Their red-brown peaks formed Deugan's border with Brealand, and where they tapered off in the west they were replaced by a vast, unyielding desert. Although maps showed that the two neighbours shared a lengthy land border, for all practical purposes the Gateway was the only overland route for more than three hundred leagues.

The temple was larger than any other building they had seen in Hermannsburg, with a lengthy antechamber leading into a wide five-sided hall. It did not look like much from the outside, but the interior had been decorated with polished wood and stone statues, with golden embroidery and muralled walls, high windows and stained glass.

The main hall of the temple was empty but for a handful of people kneeling on cushions that had been set below each of the chamber's five walls. Janusz strode immediately to the wall painted for Eolanis, the god of justice. The god's likeness itself would never be painted, but the gold and purple themes and the depictions of thrones and staffs left no doubt. She saw Lana hesitate, then turn toward Seppina's wall and kneel.

Caryn wandered instead to the centre of the hall, where a raised platform stood, surrounded by rows upon rows of benches. She stood there for some time, gazing at the beauty of the temple and marvelling at its wealth. Her homeland of Wassia had no need for gods, and the Deugan obsession with their temples continued to fascinate her.

"Will your next career be as a preacher, my lady?"

Caryn started, but it was just Lana, grinning as she brushed her hair from her face. Caryn smiled back. "After years as a politician, it might be a pleasant alternative. I'd love to speak to a roomful of people and have them actually believe me," she joked. "I don't think this is my place, though."

"Lessandro makes a place for everyone," Lana said.

"Yet you knelt before Seppina just now."

Lana shrugged. "I can't go to Lessandro all the time. The others would feel left out." She winked. Then her eyes settled on a wall painted with the silvery sheen of iron and steel, and the red-brown of brick and earth. "Truth be told, I usually visit Carmel. She's an inspiration. The woman who creates. Who gets her hands dirty. The one who men fear, for whatever she builds, she may also destroy. The divine representation of a woman's strength." Lana grinned again. "I heard that somewhere. Can't quite place it..."

Caryn laughed. "Yes, yes. Please, go on, quote me the wise words of Caryn Hallom." She didn't have to believe in their religion to see how useful its imagery could be. "You're aware I don't actually write my own speeches, right?"

"Well, aides have to stay employed somehow," Lana replied lightly. Then her tone grew more sombre. "I will pray to Carmel tonight," she said. "In the coming days, we may need someone who can destroy."

"No," Caryn said. "We have enough of those. We need one who can build."

As if on cue, Hans appeared at their side wearing a dark look. "My lady, we should leave," he said. "Now."

A crowd was forming as they emerged onto the front steps of the temple. It was small, only a dozen people, but they began shouting as soon as they glimpsed her. "It *is* her," one said, and another added angrily, "The sorceress."

Caryn was suddenly nervous, and she struggled to hide the shallowness of her breathing. Hans pushed in front of her. "Make way for the foreign minister," he shouted.

"Piss on the sorceress," a man in the crowd shouted back. There was grumbling, and Lana gripped Caryn's arm.

Hans moved his hand to his rifle, subtly, a warning. Some of the townsfolk drew back. Others stood their ground. Caryn took a deep breath. Jayla would know what to say now, she thought. Jayla had a way of defusing tension, of smoothing things over, but Caryn was lost. You're supposed to grow wiser as you get older, she thought, so why did it seem like her younger self had so many more answers than she did?

"Sorceress?" She tried to sound amiable, nonchalant. "There's no need for that. I'm happy to talk about whatever's troubling you."

"And hoodwink us too," a man said, "like you did to get this job."

"If we had someone strong in the Foreign Ministry, there wouldn't be a war going on two leagues from Hermannsburg," another added with venom.

Hans had had enough. He grasped his rifle in both hands and pushed forward, the others following behind him. One look at his eyes was enough to part the townsfolk. They were almost clear when the first man shouted again.

"She's a Steffian," he spat.

Caryn froze, and blood rushed to her head. Hans, Lana and Janusz pushed on, but a madness took her, and she turned to face her accuser. "Excuse me?"

"Nobody ever sees you in a temple," the man said, moving closer. "When you're there, you don't pray. And you use sorcery. I call you a Steffian."

There were angry murmurs around him. *Turn around and run*, Caryn told herself, yet she did not. Instead she took a step toward him until his face was inches from her own. "We may not agree on much," she told him, "but we agree on this. I hate cowards who hide in shadows and hatch secret plots to murder innocent people." *Who threaten to murder me. Who kill women in the Fringes for displeasing their fathers.* "I may be many things, but I am not one of them."

"And what if I say you are?" the man said, reaching for her —

— and he shouted and fell handily to the ground as Janusz's shoulder drove into him. Janusz's hand closed around hers, strong but strangely gentle. He looked at her, a look that held neither friendship nor enmity, just puzzlement. They took off down the street, and Hans fired a round into the air to dissuade the townsfolk from following.

The train had moved far beyond Hermannsburg before any of them felt ready to speak, but at last Caryn broke the silence. Some of Jayla had come back to her, and she wanted to conciliate, to make peace. It would not be easy. Lana still looked terrified, and Janusz sat sullenly, glancing sideways at her with a look she could not read. She focused her gaze at his hands, to avoid seeing his face.

"I apologize for my madness," she said softly. "The stress of these times is affecting all of us. We will only get through if we stick together. If we trust each other."

Lana closed her eyes, and Marwin nodded gravely. Janusz's expression did not change, but he turned to look at her. "I certainly trust everybody here," he said in a tone that suggested otherwise, "but in this spirit of openness, my lady, is our mission here truly just to inspect a military fort? Something that, meaning no offence, none of us are qualified to do?"

"That's it, Janusz. It puzzles me too." Caryn sighed. "You probably ought to know that there has been a theory circulating around Tomasburg recently. It says that we're fighting the war because the generals provoked it, so the military —"

"Can't be trusted?" Marwin said, shocked. "That's treason! They should hang whoever's saying that!"

Even the president? Caryn wanted to ask. She was exhausted. "Why do you think we're fighting, Marwin?"

"To liberate Amim from Wassia," Marwin said at once. "Wassia has been occupying Amim for centuries, and squeezing them tighter and tighter. Wresting away control of the Canal was meant to bury the Amimi independence movements. Somebody needed to do something."

Caryn held back a laugh. Their propaganda was working on somebody, at least. That was comforting. "Why Brealand, then?" she asked.

"Well, they declared on us," Marwin said. "We don't want to fight them, but —"

"Why did they declare?" Caryn pressed. "Do we have any resources they need?"

"Not really, with their island colonies."

"Any defensive positions?"

"No," Marwin said. "The Gateway protects them as much as us, and the west will just be a salient."

"So why?"

Marwin struggled for a few moments. "Look, they don't believe in the Gods. Or in *any* gods. How are we supposed to understand anything they do?"

That was predictable, Caryn supposed. "What do you think, Lana? Why did Brealand enter the war?"

Lana's eyes flung open and surprise spread across her face. She looked around as though Caryn might have intended the question for another Lana sitting behind her. Finally, she said, "My lady, you always say, about the cultural differences, Brealand needing the great powers strong to counterbalance us."

"I know what I always say," Caryn said. "What's your opinion?"

Lana hesitated again. "I — I suppose you're probably right, my lady," she managed, and started fanning herself more vigorously.

Caryn decided not to press the point further. She leaned back in her seat, and Lana did the same. Marwin, sensing that the conversation was over, turned toward the window.

Janusz was still looking at Caryn with an expression she couldn't read. It wasn't exactly respectful, but it seemed genuinely curious. Caryn looked from his hands to his eyes, and then his chest. He was a year or two older than she was, but Caryn was painfully aware that after her time in the Well, she looked as though she could be his mother.

"Well, you're the one I haven't asked yet," she said, in what she hoped was a light tone. "Why are we fighting this war, Janusz?"

He paused, thought. "I think Marwin's stumbled on the answer in spite of himself," he replied. "Religion."

"Religion?"

"Look at who our enemies are," Janusz shrugged. "Wassia. The New Empire. Now Brealand, for Lessandro's sake. You have to admit, my lady, there are some strange parallels to the ancient wars. Wassia against the Old Empire, the Raolin religion against the Five, sorcerers stationed in their Wells —"

"Sorcerers?" He was testing her. Probing her. But for what? "The Old Empire used magic to learn prophecies, I'll grant you that, even if we call it *power* or *energy* instead of *magic* these days. Rumour even has it that the prophecies never failed to come true. But the old wars were fought with swords and shields, pikes and arrows. There weren't any Wells on the front lines —"

And a wave of panic rushed over Caryn, suddenly and out of nowhere. She gripped the armrest of her seat, hoping that Janusz hadn't noticed. The angry crowd in Hermannsburg had frightened her more than she realized, the sorcery rumours, the witch hunt — but that wasn't it. No, it was something more sinister. It was the full force of the past rushing up to meet her.

There *was* a Well on the front line between Deugan and Brealand. Just east of the Fort, scarcely within Deugan's borders, stood the Gateway Well. For the first time in fourteen years, Jayla was returning to a place that had changed her life forever.

But that was a different Well, Caryn reminded herself, in a different country and a different time, and the Gateway Well was separate from the fort besides. This mission wouldn't even require her to go near it.

Having named the source of her panic, she found that it quickly subsided. She gave Janusz a smile. "The Old Empire's sorcery was nothing more than politics, I think. There was no substance to it. But politics is everything. As long as there is political gain in it, sorcery will never die."

CHAPTER THREE

The purpose of the Energize Project was to generate electricity using the power of the Gateway Well in northeastern Deugan. It was a complete failure.

The basic principles have been known for centuries. The Energy is bound to the Wells, and can never travel or be used outside their borders. The Energy will infect any person who remains in a Well for more than 24 consecutive hours — that's approximate, you understand, some people certainly hold out longer — and the infection is dramatic and irreversible. It allows the infected person to use the Well's power while inside the Well's bounds, but it causes sickness, unnatural aging, potentially even death.

In order for the Project to succeed, we needed to either discover a method for removing Energy from the Well, or design a generation plant that could be located inside the Well and harness its power mechanically. Mechanism was essential. Otherwise, large numbers of humans would need to infect themselves, station themselves inside the Well, and channel the Energy through their bodies to power the generators. Even if anyone was crazy enough to volunteer, their lifespan would drop to a few years and we'd soon need to find someone crazy enough to replace them.

Frankly, I wasn't surprised when CADS [the Council for the Advancement of Deugan Sciences] cut our funding and ended the project. In five years we hadn't made a hint of progress. Not even a single minor discovery that could propel future work. The only thing I learned from the entire Project was that the Power has its own agenda — and it doesn't want to be understood.

— Excerpts from an interview (1692) with Dr. Albrecht Dreidger, professor at the University of Czemers-Broden and former head of the Energize Project

"Jayla."

She blinked and looked up from her papers. Brenner was standing at the edge of her desk, a crude construction built from stones they'd found lying around the cavern. She smiled at him. "Hey, Brenner," she said. "Can we talk in a little while? I'm working on my essay and I'm just starting to get a good flow going."

After their first span trapped in the Well, Professor Terial had insisted on teaching classes and assigning work. They were here on a university assignment, he declared, and they were damn well going to continue their education. Though the cavern could get dark, the orange glow off the walls was more than enough for them to study by. Jayla was actually glad for the schoolwork. It gave them all something useful to do and helped take their minds off their predicament.

The essay was topical, too. It was about the reasons for the Wassian government's newfound interest in studying the Wells, years after abandoning the project as a lost cause. Jayla remembered her father ranting about the idiocy of pouring money into such a useless endeavour. "Can you believe all this talk about military applications?" he'd shouted. "How can there be a military application if the power can't leave the Well, and the Well is hundreds of leagues from the Orastan or the Deugan borders?" The professor, as far as Jayla could tell, seemed to agree. The government wasn't actually trying to use the Well's power. Only to understand it, to explain it scientifically, and so to undermine the Steifar, who revered it as a gift from their god — and who were spearheading the Amimi independence movement.

"Let me give you a hint," Brenner said to Jayla, laying his hand on the desk. "There's a bell curve in this class, and I'm the only other student. All you need to do to get your 'A' is to beat me. And I'm not working on the essay."

"Wow," Jayla teased. "You just said a whole bunch of words all in a row."

"Hey, I'm not *that* quiet, am I?"

"Brenner Halloway! I barely got a word out of you for the whole first month we were in here!" Jayla said.

"Okay, I know, but this whole thing was a shock and that's just how I reacted," he said. "I've been a lot better since — well, since that night you showed me the stars. I don't think you understand how much that meant to me."

She blushed. "Brenner, I — I just —"

"I wanted to pay you back," Brenner said. "Do something nice like that for you. Come on. I've got something to show you." He turned and started walking toward the large room of the main cavern, where they'd watched the stars together. Jayla hesitated, then quickly scribbled two more sentences of her essay and ran to follow him.

When she caught up with Brenner, he was kneeling on the ground in the main cavern. His face was screwed up in concentration, and he was muttering to himself and gesturing strangely. She stood silently, watching him work. He seemed to be getting frustrated, but just when it looked like he might be about to give up, the cavern was suddenly plunged into darkness —

— and a split second later, it erupted into colour. A column of shimmering white light burst from the ground inches from where Jayla was standing, and she jumped backward, startled. She heard Brenner let out a whoop of joy, and then she saw him, bathed in another column of purple light. New columns started bursting up all around them, red and green and orange and silver. She saw Brenner start to run without any direction, his arms raised in the air, joy lighting up his face. He passed through two of the columns and they seemed to explode into fountains, streams of coloured light cascading down like the tails of fireworks. It was the most beautiful sight Jayla had ever seen.

She started to run too, and as she passed through a column of light, she suddenly felt the power reaching out to her, and she seized it and spun it around. The lights started drifting in a slow circle, the fountains spraying their sparks out in waves. She reached out again, and this time the lights started drifting away from them and new lights, fainter, showed up to replace them. Soon the scenery had changed entirely. Instead of darkness interspersed with columns and fountains, the entire room was suddenly bathed in lights that were all the colours of a rainbow.

Then Jayla felt strong arms wrap around her from behind, and she shrieked as Brenner lifted her off the ground and spun her around. The rainbow lights shimmered around her feet as they flew through the air. She started prying at his hands, and he was still trying to lift her, and somehow they both ended up on the ground. Jayla pushed herself up to her knees —

And the scenery shifted again. Brenner had tapped into the energy too, she realized, just as she had. The old columns were blazing streaks of light as they rushed back to meet them.

When their surroundings settled, Jayla and Brenner were kneeling together inside a fountain of golden light that erupted and cascaded all around them. Brenner reached out and took Jayla's hands in his. "I know I'm not as good with words as you are," he said, "but this is my way of saying thank you."

Jayla squeezed his hands. "Brenner, this is so unbelievably beautiful."

"And so are you," Brenner said, and he leaned in toward her, and he kissed her as the fireworks exploded —

*

No, Caryn thought. *That was wrong.* The golden light was right, and the cascading fountain, and his strong hands taking hers, and the kiss — but there were no fireworks then, no explosions. That was the present creeping into her memories.

The shelling had begun within twelve hours of their arrival at the Gateway Fort. It was brutal and frightening, and it never ceased. The concrete walls of the Fort dulled the sounds of the shells, but Caryn was still constantly aware of them, aware that any one of them had the power to end her life. Did the garrisons at these forts ever grow accustomed to it, she wondered, the way she slowly learned to accept her life in the Well? Did they find ways to laugh or joke about it? Could the terrifying become normal — and wasn't *that* terrifying?

"There's a lot of sorceress talk going around," Lana informed her as they sat together in the quarters they shared. The fort had two and a half corridors dedicated to officers' quarters, but even so, General Freed had declared that the politicians could only be accommodated if they slept two to a room. Caryn shared her space with Lana, while Marwin shared with Janusz. Hans and Reimund had quarters in the centre of the corridor, where they could easily respond to any threat.

The Gateway Fort was a massive concrete labyrinth of twisting paths and tunnels. That morning, as a young captain by the name of Willem Toppel led her on a tour through the fortress, she found herself glad to have Marwin by her side. Though still somewhat impetuous, the fair-skinned boy with the freckles and light brown hair had surprised her with his knowledge of military construction. He had been raised in a military family and had read voraciously about armaments, fortifications and tactics. His great-grandfather had served in the Unification Wars, and his grandfather in the Wassian Intervention. His father, in addition to being a reservist, had worked on the construction of several forts that protected a vital highway in Deugan's southeast. Caryn was pleased. The president had chosen well in assigning Marwin to this particular mission.

Marwin had reported the same thing to her, though. He'd taken his lunch in the mess hall that afternoon, and he had overheard the soldiers asking each other whether it was truly a coincidence that the shelling had begun just after the sorceress arrived.

"If I were really a sorceress, I'd stop the shelling, not start it," Caryn said.

Lana grinned. "I hoped you would say that. People can be ridiculous sometimes. Of course they're shelling us because some sorceress made them, and not because *we're at war*."

Caryn laughed too. It felt good to laugh; it hadn't happened too often recently. "Maybe my sorcery muddled the brain of the King of Brealand and forced him to declare war on us in the first place," she suggested. "Or maybe my sorcery caused his pen to slip when he was writing the declaration. He actually meant to attack the New Empire." Lana grinned again. "I have been wondering one thing, though. Yesterday, on the train, I was asking you that exact question, why you thought Brealand entered the war. Why were you so shy about answering?"

Lana sighed. "Marwin had just been openly disrespectful of you, and I know from experience how hard it is for a woman to get respect in government. I know Marwin is young, but if young people keep those attitudes, what hope do the rest of us have? I didn't want to undermine you in front of him."

Caryn was taken aback. Lana's answer, while touching, was not the one she had expected. Caryn groped for words. "Thank you," she finally managed.

Jayla had never had to grope for words, Caryn remembered. She could carry on conversations effortlessly. But she was more carefree then, and younger, so much younger, even in the Well when her skin started to wrinkle and her hair started to grey.

"My lady, my answer yesterday was honest," Lana said. "I do think you're probably right about cultures and counter-balancing and all of that."

"That doesn't matter," Caryn said. "Whether you think I'm right or wrong, I just want you to feel comfortable enough to speak your mind. Don't let Janusz or Marwin shut you up." She sighed. "If I'd let people like that shut me up, I might still be scraping by as a number cruncher in the treasury and counting myself lucky."

"Whereas now you really *are* lucky." Lana grinned. "You're at a military fort that's been hit by four hundred shells since breakfast, and you're meeting this evening with a general who hates your closest political ally."

"Which is why I need your help," Caryn told her. She changed her tone, all business now. "What has your research uncovered?"

"Unfortunately, my lady, I could not find a great deal that we did not already know," Lana said. She was quick on the uptake; she had dropped her informal speech instantly. "We already have the general's family background, his education, his military career." She pulled out a piece of paper from the bundle of materials on her lap. "Here is something you may not have known, my lady. The general actually requested Northern Command. It was two years ago, around the time you became foreign minister. You may recall that tensions with Wassia were high then."

"I do," Caryn said. In fact, she remembered feeling that the president was playing a sick joke on her by thrusting her into the position in the middle of an international crisis. Deugan and Wassia had already been to war twice in the previous century. The more recent occasion had been just thirty-eight years before Caryn's appointment to foreign minister, when Wassia had invaded Deugan in support of a group of rebels fighting for the secession of the coastlands from the nation Tomas Scheil had united. Deugan had beaten back the Wassian Intervention, but Caryn was under no illusion that tensions had subsided. "The Wassians had frozen some Deugan-owned accounts in Wassian banks. They accused us of using them to fund Amimi independence groups. I brokered a compromise where the allegations would be reviewed by a joint committee of Wassian and Deugan officials." It was her first foreign policy triumph, Caryn remembered fondly, a breakthrough that had silenced many of the critics who said a woman could never be taken seriously on the international stage.

"My lady, do you not find it strange that at a time of increasing tensions with Wassia, when many wondered if war would break out in the south, General Freed specifically requested *northern* command? A move to our calmest border?"

Lana was right, Caryn realized. That was bizarre, and it might be useful. "What does it mean?" Caryn asked. "Was the general looking for an easy assignment? Or were there personal motivations?"

"The general was born in central Deugan, my lady. He has no family in the north, save a single cousin living by the coast, hundreds of leagues from the Gateway."

"I know that you have a theory about this," Caryn said. "What is it?"

"My lady," Lana replied, "this is purely guesswork, but I suspect General Freed recognized that Wassia was already suffering from severe economic stress and unyielding political rigidity." Caryn hid a smile. Having grown up in Wassia herself, she knew both to be true. "Wassia would never have the resources or industrial capacity to compete with us in an extended conflict," Lana continued. "The New Empire, meanwhile, was already struggling with Steffian terrorists and independence movements throughout the Fringes, and was at risk of losing the empire entirely. General Freed would have known that, since he spent many years gathering intelligence on the Fringes. My lady, I think that the general was looking to the future and saw Brealand as the true threat looming on the horizon. A large population, a brutal but efficient dictatorship, and enormous naval capabilities that we cannot match. This was not a request born of cowardice, I think. It was a remarkably prescient move that the general took because he wanted to be on the front lines, organizing our defence against what he believed would be a menace to Deugan's very existence."

"Interesting," Caryn said. She was mulling it over and thought that the younger woman was almost certainly right.

"What is most interesting about it," Lana continued, "is that it means you and the general have something in common. Both of you looked to the future and saw that Brealand would join in the next war against us. Nobody else did."

"Sorceresses were always good with prophecy," Caryn said with a grim smile. "Lana, you have a brilliant mind. Please don't let anybody silence you. Not Janusz or Marwin, not your bosses in Foreign Affairs, not anybody. Promise me that."

Lana blushed, but she smiled. "I promise, my lady."

*

Although the general's quarters were only one corridor down from her own, he maintained a separate office near the communications hub in the centre of the fort. Caryn set off well in advance of their scheduled meeting, hoping she would be able to navigate the maze of concrete corridors and tunnels.

The Gateway Fort was not a single structure, Caryn had learned during her tour that morning. There was a large main fortress, but just as important were the five satellite forts arranged in a semicircle to the north. Each of the satellites was connected to the main fort by underground tunnels. The satellites were armed to the teeth with an assortment of 100- and 150-millimetre guns on rotating turrets, as well as smaller artillery pieces and machine guns. The main fort's gunnery housed even larger weapons, 210-millimetre howitzers as well as more conventional artillery with significant range. An army attacking any satellite could be fired on by at least one other satellite and by the large guns on the main fort. As if that weren't enough, a dry moat protected by barbed wire guarded the northern boundary of the emplacement.

Inside the main fort, Caryn had been guided past barrack halls large enough to support a garrison of five thousand soldiers. She was told that the satellites could accommodate another thousand men each, for a total garrison of ten thousand. Captain Toppel, however, had said that only half that number was stationed there. "We will have new recruits within the month," Toppel promised, "but the declaration from Brealand caught us by surprise, and the other fronts are being given priority."

The tour had next taken them underground, where they'd passed vast storerooms of food, arms and ammunition that seemed to run on forever. Caryn was impressed at the extent of the refrigeration units the fort had acquired, extending from wall to wall across two long rooms, although the majority of the food was either tinned or salted or both.

Back above ground was a five-sided chapel overseen by a jovial old chaplain, and a medical bay staffed by two military doctors and a team of nurses, the only women besides Lana that Caryn had seen since arriving at the Fort. Finally, Toppel showed her the communications hub, where Caryn was headed now. It was a large room with rows upon rows of telegraph machines resting on wooden tables. Wires ran from the telegraphs to a large metallic board on the wall that contained a number of knobs and dials. "We are connected by wire directly to Tomasburg, and from there throughout Deugan," her guide had explained. "We also have wireless telegraphy capabilities, but we avoid it when we can because it's less secure. We do have encryption machines, but codes can be broken."

When Caryn arrived at General Freed's office, he was looking over a thick black dossier. He closed it when he heard Caryn knock on his open door. "Minister Hallom," he said. "Please. Come in."

The general was a tall man of perhaps sixty years. His hair had gone grey, but it gave him a stately, distinguished look. He stood behind his desk and bowed to her when she entered, causing his numerous medals to jingle softly. Caryn gave a quick bow in return, then sat herself in a chair across from him.

"General, let me begin by thanking you for your hospitality," she said. "I trust we have not been too great an interference."

"Not at all," the general said, but his tone was cold and his eyes piercing. Caryn took a deep breath. In years past she had hoped that with enough experience, these meetings would stop terrifying her. As a girl she'd been great with people. Jayla had a way of putting everybody at ease, of mediating the fights between her parents, of drawing Brenner out of his shell. It wasn't that she'd lost the skill, but she felt less at ease now when using it. Or maybe, she considered, there was just more at stake.

She waited patiently for her initial fear to subside. When it did, as it always did, she found herself perfectly on edge, the type of anxiety that would make her perform.

"General, as you know, the president has asked me to report to him on the state of the Fort. Not just our defences, but also anything else I might learn about the northern front."

The general's voice remained cold. "Northern Command sends

daily reports by telegraph to Joint Staff Headquarters in Tomasburg. Headquarters reports directly to the Office of the President. The president is the president, and I'm not denying he can send his foreign minister wherever he wants, even if she doesn't know the first thing about military tactics. But quite frankly, I don't know what information I can give you that he doesn't already have."

"I realize I don't have a background in military tactics," Caryn said politely. It was a trick she'd learned many years ago when dealing with difficult bosses in the Treasury. Agreeing with your opponent would often throw him off balance, and sometimes that was just what you needed. "What I would like to know, General, are your personal thoughts on this war. The sorts of things that might not make it into your daily reports."

"Minister Hallom, I don't know if you politicians go around Tomasburg talking about your personal feelings, but I'm a soldier. What I think is irrelevant."

"I didn't say a word about feelings," Caryn shot back. Men could be so predictable. "I'm talking about the shelling today and what you think it means. Is it a prelude to an attack on the Gateway? Is it a diversion for an attack elsewhere?"

"We are preparing for either contingency," the general said, "but a full strength garrison would help us immensely."

Caryn smiled. The general had started by trying to intimidate her, but now he was changing his tune. There were things he wanted, he was hinting, and he might be willing to help her in order to get them.

"I will certainly stress the need to supplement our garrison when I report to the president," she promised. She still needed a way to push back at him, though. The president thought the military was being dishonest, but how could she test that? "General, in preparation for my current assignment, I read the reports from Joint Staff Headquarters going back several months. I don't know if you've seen how Tomasburg edits your reports, but you would find it striking how little bad news we receive."

"Perhaps you should thank your generals for doing such a good job." For the first time, Caryn saw a hint of a smile.

"You have done an excellent job," she assured him. "Northern Wassia is ours and we continue to make southward progress. The eastern front has stabilized and we have been throwing back the New Empire's attacks at a fraction of our enemy's casualties." She smiled.

"Or so we are told. We have no way to verify the military's casualty numbers. We have no way to judge how strong our grip is in Wassia. Do you understand our predicament, General?"

"I do," Freed snapped. "Your predicament is that you have a president who refuses to trust his advisers. With all due respect, the solution isn't to send a former treasury chief to look over our shoulders. I suppose what the president really ought to do is fire the lot of us and replace us all with people he trusts more. You can suggest that to him in your report, if you'd like." He took a deep breath, and when he spoke again, his voice was calmer. "Minister, our reports are genuine. I'm sitting on the front lines, telling him what I'm seeing and thinking and planning, and I get nothing back from Tomasburg but suspicion."

Caryn eyed him carefully across his desk. Could she trust him? Was the president really paranoid? The two men were political enemies, after all. The general had publicly supported the president's chief opponent in the last campaign.

But the general's optimism just didn't fit with all of the news that had been flooding Tomasburg. They were fighting a war on three fronts, for Lessandro's sake, and most of their armies were in the south and the east. Who would they send to the northern front to fight the greatest threat of them all? Brealand had the finest navies on the Continent. Its armies were supremely disciplined. With so much of Deugan's strength tied up elsewhere ... the more Caryn thought about it, the more hopeless it seemed.

What would Jayla do? Ever since that vivid memory had come to Caryn back in Tomasburg, she had been asking herself the question more and more often. Jayla would do what Jayla always did, she decided. Standing up to bullies, refusing to back down from intimidation, that was the way of Caryn Hallom, the so-called trailblazer. Jayla Sullivan's way was mediation. Calming two warring parties, whether they be parents or politicians. She would find a way to make the peace that they desperately needed.

"General," Caryn said, "perhaps if you explain your opinion to me, I can take it back to the president and try to build some trust. You may not realize it sitting in the Gateway, but the mood in Tomasburg is grim. We need hope. You're saying you can give it to us. I'm asking you to help me by telling me, how?"

The general thought for a long moment. Then he said, "I take your point. What you need to realize is that Wassia and the New Empire aren't threats. They're using old tactics, like we're still in the Unification Wars. The Wassians just don't have the technology we have. Sooner or later they'll collapse, I promise you. The New Empire does have modern weapons, but no clue how to use them. We've developed defensive tactics that are as close to flawless as you can get. Double or triple trench lines, barbed wire, machine guns, heavy artillery. Their offensive is effectively over." He grimaced. "But your president still doesn't trust us."

She ignored the last bit. "What about the north? What about an attack through the Gateway? I understand we have a whole string of forts in the northwest, but here there's only the one. And it seems to me that with the satellites all arranged to the north, there isn't much protection against an attack through the Gateway Well."

Freed looked at her incredulously. "Have you ever been in a Well, Minister?"

"Of course not," Caryn lied. She was so practiced at hiding her past now that her indignation was almost reflexive.

"The Well is not an open expanse of ground," the general told her. "It's a maze of ridges and caverns. It would be difficult to manoeuvre an army through and coalesce it into a legitimate attack at the other end. Bringing large artillery pieces along would be next to impossible. In any event, if an attack did materialize out of the Well, it would run straight into fire from the main fort and Seppina, at least."

"Seppina?" Caryn asked, confused. Then she realized. "Oh, you mean the satellite fort that's farthest east. I'd wondered if you chose five satellites for the five Gods. Let me guess," she said in the sort of teasing tone Jayla might have used on Brenner. "The one smack in the centre, with the largest arsenal, is Armano. The fiery God of War leading Deugan's charge against the atheist Breas."

Freed's reaction was not at all what Caryn expected. He pursed his lips and stared at her across his desk before softly saying, "Actually, Minister, you're wrong."

The general hesitated, and when he spoke again, it was with unexpected emotion. "No doubt you would have been right if this fort had been built by the Old Empire, the Orastan Empire, which scarcely knew a year of peace in all its centuries. The empire thrived on war and conquest — but Deugan grew out of its experience as a colony of Orastus. We may still speak the Orastan language to this day, we may still follow the old Orastan gods, but we do not believe what the Orastans believed. Our values are liberty, and equality, and democracy, and justice. Justice most of all. That is what Brealand threatens, those very foundations of our society. And that, Minister, is why the central satellite is named for Eolanis, God of Justice, and why Armano sits at his right hand side. Because power should serve the cause of justice, not the other way around."

"I apologize," Caryn said quietly when Freed's speech was done. "I did not mean to offend."

"No offence was taken," Freed said. "The simple point I am trying to convey to you is that you and I should not be enemies. The only problem here, as far as I am concerned, is that the president doesn't trust me. Only the Gods know why. We're on the same side." He pounded the desk with his fist to punctuate his words. "We have the same values. Justice. Freedom."

"Peace?"

"No," Freed responded frankly. "I certainly want peace, but not at the expense of our true values. Some things are worth fighting for. Besides, you and I both know that the only reason the president wants peace is that he doesn't think we can win."

"Excuse me," Caryn said with indignation. The colour was rising in her face. She knew that the general would try to intimidate her, and she had weathered the storm so far, but suddenly she was furious. Sometimes Jayla's way didn't work. Sometimes bullies needed to be confronted. "In one single day at Japata in Wassia we suffered 30,000 casualties. In the last nine months we've lost more than 500,000 men on the southern front alone. Entire villages and towns were razed to the ground and their people slaughtered when the New Empire broke through our lines. These men are dying in the most horrific ways, explosions with shrapnel and machine gun fire. On the eastern front the New Empire has sent toxic chemical gas into our trenches, and the men have been forced to cover their faces with rags soaked in their own urine. And you dare tell me the only reason I want peace is because I don't think we can win?"

"That's not what I told you," General Freed said calmly. "I said that's why the *president* wants peace." Caryn froze. As much as it pained her to admit it, that just might be true. "I know nothing about your own motivations, Minister Hallom, but your passion just now speaks volumes. You strike me as a very honest person. It's refreshing in a politician."

"I will take that as a compliment," she said stiffly. She was still angry at the callousness of his response. The horror of the stories was weighing on her, and here she was on the front lines herself, the dull thud of the constant shelling still ringing in her ears. She was too old for this, Caryn thought suddenly. It was not a thought she often had, having spent just more than thirty years in this life, but sometimes she felt as old as her body was after its months in the Well, as old as the aches and the pains, as old as the tiredness that tended to come on faster than ever before.

It was flooding her now. Her burst of anger at the general's words was subsiding, leaving behind only emptiness. Caryn wondered if General Freed ever felt the same way. His body was older than hers by half a decade, she guessed, though his transition to middle age had come far more gradually.

"If I am honest, General, perhaps you will indulge me with your own honesty," Caryn said. She was certain that her exhaustion had come through in her voice. "No jockeying or politicking. We are on the same side, after all." She thought about her conversation with Lana, and decided to use it. "Like you, I thought Brealand would be a threat before anybody else did. Like you, I urged the powers that be to pay attention and prepare, and to avoid any wars we were not yet ready to fight. Now I must know."

The general leaned forward in his chair and looked her in the eyes for several moments. Finally he said, "You're asking me whether the president is right. Whether we really can win this war."

Slowly, Caryn nodded. "I am only asking, of course, for your honest opinion."

The general returned her nod and ran a hand over his face. Suddenly he too seemed older than his years. "In my opinion, Minister, it all depends on what you mean by winning."

Caryn smiled. "A politician's answer."

"Yet an honest one. If by winning you mean that we will dominate Brealand and force the king to sue for peace, then the answer is no. We cannot win that way." He sat up taller in his chair. "What we can do is to defeat Wassia and the New Empire, while stalemating the Breas and negotiating a peace with them that's fair for both sides — and that recognizes the facts on the ground in the south. Amimi independence. Access to the Canal. Some practical concessions from the New Empire. I would call that a win."

"How likely is that?"

"Likely enough," Freed said, the harshness back in his voice. "How many times do I need to tell you that I'm being perfectly honest with you? I can deliver this victory, but I need the government behind me. I need Deugan behind me."

"How do you expect me to get behind you when after all this talk, you still won't give me straight answers to the simplest of questions?"

"I can deliver this victory," the general repeated. His voice was a blade. "I can deliver it with trenches and tactics, with the defensive schemes we've learned from fighting the New Empire. I can deliver it with submarines, to harry Brealand's food supplies and distract her navies. I can deliver it with men to staff this fort, and all of the forts of the north. And I can deliver it with Givanno."

Caryn started. "Givanno?"

The general smiled, a full smile, and his face was transformed. For that split second he was no longer grizzled and angry, but kind, almost grandfatherly. Caryn found herself wondering whether he had grandchildren back in Tomasburg, or in the south of Deugan, or out by the coast. Whether he had a life he hoped to return to once this war was over.

General Freed opened a drawer, pulled out a leaf of paper, and slid it across his desk to Caryn. "I only received it this morning, so don't tell me the military's been hiding anything from you. I am pleased to report that as of 0900 hours, Deugan has a new ally."

Caryn grabbed the cable and read it quickly, then read it again slowly to make sure she had gotten it right. As the words sank in, it was as though a weight the size of the Gateway Fort had been lifted from her shoulders. Givanno was the smallest of the New Empire's colonies, the fringe of the Fringes. Largely ignored by the rest of the Continent, it was a beautiful stretch of fertile land that separated Deugan from what used to be the Old Empire. "Givanno has declared independence."

"Indeed," Freed replied, "and its first act as an independent state was to issue a formal declaration of war against the New Empire." Caryn smiled. Givanno itself was barely significant, but if its bold move could convince the other Fringes to follow, then maybe this war wasn't hopeless after all. "Minister," Freed continued, "you may know that I was a vocal critic of the Hallom Doctrine. But now it seems that it might actually be starting to pay off, and not a moment too soon. So I've decided to give you something to help you celebrate." He opened another drawer in his desk and pulled out two bottles of wine. "A fine vintage from northern Wassia, or as I now refer to it, southern Deugan."

"Thank you," Caryn said, taking the bottles from him. There was no point arguing about the Hallom Doctrine, she decided. She had come as close as she was likely to get to a true appraisal of their war efforts, despite the general's hostility. Freed's optimism and his plea for trust were genuine, Caryn realized. He truly believed that they could win.

She rose from her seat and turned to leave, and Freed bade her farewell, but for some reason she would never understand, she turned around to face the general again. He had reopened the dossier that he had been examining before her arrival, and front and centre on his desk was a full-page photograph.

A lump rose in Caryn's throat and she struggled to keep calm. Her stomach felt like insects were crawling around inside. She moved slowly, deliberately back to Freed's desk. The general looked at her with annoyance. "Is there something more I can help you with, Minister?"

Caryn nodded. Those cheeks. Those eyes. That jawline. And then, as if there could be any doubt, there was the birthmark —

"Who is that man?" Caryn asked weakly. She already knew the answer, of course, yet the answer shocked her.

"He is a Steffian. His name is Brenth Nono."

It can't be, Caryn thought, *it can't be*. From Brenner to Brenth was not a great stretch, but a Steffian? Caryn had heard Nono's name several times, but there had never been a photograph before. "What does he do for them?" she found herself asking.

"He is one of their highest-ranking members and has a seat on their governing council," Freed replied. "I am told he is their Master of Secrets."

"Secrets?"

"Energy. Power. Wells." He gave Caryn a strange look, as though he was seeing her for the first time. "Sorcery."

CHAPTER FOUR

Matthias remembered his first visit to Ciorala.

He had come with his father in a tiny steamship cabin that they shared with three other men. The others were also from the colony of Pascuay, deep in the Fringes of the New Empire, and they had engaged Matthias' father in lengthy conversations about home, the crops and the weather, and the opportunities that lay ahead. Matthias lay listening on his bunk, trying to imagine what this adventure would be like. He was only a boy then.

He remembered stepping off the steamship and into another world, the likes of which he had never imagined. Ciorala was resplendent with marble pillars, massive stone arches, and sturdy brick houses. High on a hilltop overlooking the ocean was the largest building Matthias had seen in his life. It looked like a castle, stone and imposing, but it had five towers evenly spaced around its outside walls. Four of the towers had turrets that gleamed gold in the sunlight; the fifth was encrusted with glittering green emeralds. "Is that where the Emperor sits?" Matthias asked his father.

His father laughed. He was a large, burly man with a round belly and a mat of orange hair that matched Matthias's own. "No, my son," he said. "Far from it. This isn't Orastus proper at all. That's the Temple of the Gods. You remember what you learned about the gods of the Old Empire."

Matthias nodded. "There are five of them."

"And that's why there are five towers," his father said. "Do you know why one of them is green like the sea?"

Matthias thought. "Lessandro?"

"Who was Lessandro?" his father quizzed.

"He was the last god. There used to only be four, before him. He could control the sea and the storms, and call rain down from the sky, and bring fish in to the coast where men could catch them. But nobody believed he could. The people all thought he was insulting the other four gods by pretending to be like them. So they chased him and he ran away until they all cornered him on a cliff overlooking the water, and he had nowhere else to go so he jumped off. But since he could control the sea, he landed softly on it and ran on the waves. And since he could control the storms, he made a strong storm to break up the ships that went to chase after him."

"That's right," his father said. "But he returned when there was a drought and the people were starving. Lessandro brought the rains that they needed to survive. When the other four gods saw him use his power to help his fellows, even those who had once tried to kill him, they finally invited him to join them." He ruffled Matthias's hair. "Or so the story goes. They say that's the cliff Lessandro jumped from. Right where the temple is, overlooking the water."

Matthias's eyes grew wide. "Is the story real, then?"

His father ruffled his hair again. "We may never know," he said. "But even if it is, Good Steif can do more than bringing rain or running on waves. Do not forget that."

"I won't," Matthias promised — but tonight, as he strained to manoeuvre the skiff silently past the Imperial Navy's cordon, he whispered prayers to Lessandro nonetheless.

That was also done silently. The others would not take kindly if they heard.

It was a calm night but a cold one, and Matthias shivered. There had been a huge snowstorm in Amim last span, he had heard. That was further south, but not by much. The cold weather would be moving northward, he had no doubt, and the Council would want to take action before it did. Otherwise it might be too late.

They tied up the skiff in a cove just outside of Ciorala harbour. The land there was thickly forested, and the trees shielded them from the gaze of the city and its guards. Quietly they parceled out equipment: rifles, fuses, powders. Their people on the inside were already in position, Matthias knew, and the team would have to hurry to reach them.

They emerged from the forest into the district known as the village, a sprawling tent city that dominated Ciorala's east end. Matthias gazed around the darkened streets, lost in memory. It was years since he had lived here, but it did not seem to have changed. There were still more huts and shacks and tents packed into the tiny area than Matthias could believe. People had thrown up ramshackle dwellings in the middle of roads, nestled against fences, even above other villagers' tents. The smell was just as Matthias remembered it, too, acrid, smoke and fire from the nearby factories mixed with the stink of a mass of humanity, mean, angry and poor. The only benefit to living in the village was that Ciorala's policemen were generally too frightened to enter after dark, making it the perfect staging ground for an operation.

Matthias counted himself lucky that he had only lived six months in the village, from the time he and his father were kicked out of their tiny apartment for non-payment of rent until the day his father declared, "We're leaving this town. They said there'd be plenty of work here, and there is, but only for locals. They don't like colonials like us, so we're going to hop the first ship back east."

"What do you mean, they don't like colonials?" Matthias asked, confused. "I thought they were colonials themselves! Didn't you say Ciorala is still in the Fringes?"

His father flashed him a knowing look. "It is," the big man said, "but there are Fringes and then there are Fringes, son."

It was true even here. There was the magnificence of central Ciorala which had enthralled Matthias that first day he stepped off the boat, immortalizing the ancient grandeur of the Old Empire — and then there was the village.

Their safe house was little more than a few planks of wood thrown up against a fence. As the team filed past him and into the shack, Jakim touched Matthias lightly on the arm and pointed to a tent across the way.

Matthias followed his gaze. There was a poster sitting outside the tent that they could barely make out in the darkness. Matthias crept closer to look at it, and Jakim followed. "That won't stay there too long," Jakim whispered.

"Nor will whoever put it up," Matthias whispered back. "Poor bastards. It's damn brave of them, but they'll end up in a dungeon for their troubles."

"Or worse," Jakim said ominously. He clasped both hands to his heart and whispered a prayer.

The poster was a cheap reprint of Fernando's masterpiece, "The Fall of the Old Empire," with its epic depiction of a battle that took place in Ciorala over 700 years ago. In the foreground was a handsome, blond Wassian raising a sword in triumph over the body of a fallen Old Empire soldier. In the background, Lessandro's emerald tower in the Temple of the Gods was bowed over as though it was weeping.

On the sign, beneath the reprint of the painting, were the words, "This has happened before."

Matthias and Jakim shared a look and moved into the safe house.

It was already bustling. The old woman who lived there was handing out bowls of soup. The soup was cold, since lighting a fire this late at night would have raised suspicions, but the men welcomed it nonetheless and expressed their thanks. The woman hobbled over to the newcomers. "You two were looking at Maria's sign, were you?"

"It was quite bold," Matthias said.

"By which you mean stupid," the woman replied, "but be that as it may, she's right. Orastus fell the first time when it went on adventures in Deugan and damned the people in the colonies. And now it'll fall again for the same mistake, praise to Steif."

Matthias took a breath and kept his expression carefully blank. "Praise to Steif," he repeated.

Matthias had studied the fall of the Orastus Empire as a boy, and he could admit there were some similarities. Through two centuries of occupation, Orastus had never quite managed to quell the resistance of the Deugan city-states it had conquered. Maintaining the occupation had demanded so many resources and conscripts from its nearer colonies that they started to revolt, and that had opened the door for the empire's other enemies to plunge through its borders. In the east it had been barbarians, savage hordes who ran roughshod over the imperial heartland, looting and burning and plundering until only scattered ruins proclaimed that a great empire had once stood there. In the west it had been the empire's traditional rival, the Wassian Empire, annexing its lands and claiming Ciorala's magnificence as its own.

But Orastus's leaders hadn't given up the fight. They had

regrouped north of their heartland, in their most prized colony, and there turned back the barbarians and proclaimed that the empire would continue. The victorious Wassians scoffed, describing Orastus as an "old" empire, dying as its heartland burned. The cabal in the northern colony, they said disparagingly, could only be forming some sort of "new" empire. Both names stuck.

But the New Empire stuck too, Matthias reflected, rising powerfully from the ashes of the Old. It preserved the science and the culture of Orastus, and taught them to its people. Within 150 years the empire had become secure enough to again venture outside its borders and begin to re-colonize much of its former territory, and beyond. The old imperial heartland welcomed the northerners with open arms, and though it was relegated to the rank of a colony, it was treated better than most. The former heartland was given special tax treatment, leadership appointments in other colonies and infrastructure projects — but there were Fringes and then there were Fringes.

In a few minutes some of that infrastructure would be demolished by warriors from the deeper Fringes, the poorer Fringes. Their plan called for simultaneous attacks on four factories in east Ciorala that produced much of the arms and ammunition that were now being shipped to the front with Deugan.

When they were done with the meal, they split off into teams of two, each heading for a different factory. All were within easy walking distance of the village. Matthias and Jakim were to remain at the safe house, watching for patrols both here and along their route back to the cove where their escape lay. They had flares with which to warn the others of danger, but they would try not to use them. The Imperial troops could see flares just as well as the Steffians.

The old woman went to sleep soon after the others left, leaving Matthias and Jakim alone, their eyes darting around the mean shack and outside it into the village. Matthias now had trouble keeping his eyes off the Fall of the Old Empire, though he could barely see it in the darkness.

"What will you do when this war is won?" he asked Jakim, mostly to pass the time.

Jakim laughed. "You know the Council. Will our war ever be over? When the empire falls there will be peace for a time, but soon we will be on the march again. Steif's good word must reach beyond the Fringes."

Matthias nodded. He still agreed with that sentiment, because he still believed that Steif's good word was the truth, and the code to a moral life, and truth and morals were in short supply on this Continent. A life in the Fringes would teach you that. He would always remain a Steifar, a follower of the one god, but the fear and anger that had drawn Matthias to the Steffian organization had ebbed, and after some of the things he had seen, he did not want to march again.

"Deugan must be next," Jakim said. "That's how I see it. They're dangerous."

"Perhaps. But they will never be worse than the New Empire."

Jakim took a breath. "True," he replied. "I doubt anybody will be worse than the New Empire."

And there was the rub, the one connection that kept Matthias with the Steffians through all of the horrors of the operations, through the random gunshots, the bombs targeting dance halls and cafes, the burning of homes and the looting of shops. Through what they were doing now, destroying the factories that gave employment to the poorest of Ciorala's poor, just because it would hurt the empire's war effort. He survived it because he knew that whatever terrible things the Steffians might do, the New Empire was worse.

It wasn't just the burning of Matthias's home village in Pascuay. Life anywhere in the Fringes was marked by starvation, squalor, oppression. Orastus's iron grip on its colonies had to be lifted, and the Steffians were the only ones who seemed willing to do anything about it.

So Matthias stayed through operation after operation, and his stomach turned again and again, and he prayed to Good Steif for guidance and forgiveness, and the one god was silent.

Matthias had not always had these quandaries. Once, his poverty in Pascuay could rile up such anger in him that he wanted nothing more than to lash out at the New Empire, to smash the round arches, to tear down its buildings brick by brick. The local Steffian chapter in Pascuay had given him an outlet for his anger, and had also fuelled it. He had immersed himself in the teachings of Good Steif and sank deeper and deeper into the chapter's political wing. After Steif allowed their brazen attack on the Pascuay governor's complex to succeed, Matthias was so elated that he declared he would take the ultimate step in his faith. He would forego longer life and the gift of children in order to study Secrets, to fully explore the wonder that Good Steif had introduced to the world. For the one question that no atheist had ever been able to answer was how to account for the Wells and their power.

But there were more and more operations. More and more innocent deaths. More and more things Matthias had to see...

The line had been crossed, he realized, and there was no turning back. It terrified him, yet he knew it to be true. He had already betrayed the Steffians, in thought if not in deed. He had already doubted their methods, questioned that their path was the one Good Steif intended. He had done so silently, but he had done so, and he knew that was enough.

Yet there did not seem to be any other option. He supposed he could travel to Orastus with his tail between his legs. He knew enough about the inner workings of the Steffian organization that he was certain they would accept him and pardon his crimes. But the thought of working for Orastus raised bile in his throat and brought his old anger surging back through his chest.

No, that was impossible. He would never help the New Empire to survive. But after the empire was gone, he would begin his search anew. He would ask Good Steif for guidance until he found a way to escape the grip of the Steffians once and for all.

"We will win this war, my friend," Jakim said softly. "As the great powers destroy each other in the northwest, Good Steif will guide us to victory."

"Praise to Steif," Matthias said.

And they heard a distant explosion, and another and another, and through the blackness of the night sky they made out several plumes of smoke drifting toward the heavens. Jakim clasped his hands to his heart again and whispered a quick prayer, and Matthias did the same. Then they started off down the path toward the skiff and got to work untying it and readying it to leave. The others would be back soon, and they would need to make haste to vanish under the cover of nightfall.

CHAPTER FIVE

"Southern Deugan," Janusz scoffed through a gulp of wine. The glass looked comically small in his large hands. "A bit cocky, don't you think?"

"That's our general," Caryn said. "One minute he's waxing eloquent about justice and liberty. The next he's bragging about his conquests. He's as much a mystery as — well, every other man I've known." Lana and Janusz laughed at that; Marwin just looked confused.

"Well, at least he's let us do our jobs," Janusz said. "I was afraid he'd run more interference. My lady, what did you say to him that first night?"

"I made it clear that he wouldn't intimidate me, and then I hinted that if he cooperated, we'd get him what he wanted — more troops for his garrison," Caryn said. "That's how you deal with people. You find out what they want."

"It'll be easy for you to deal with me, then," Janusz announced. "All I want is more wine." Lana grinned and passed him the bottle. His hand brushed hers as he took it.

Their work had indeed gone smoothly. The day after Caryn met with the general, they'd started inspections in earnest. They worked in teams of three, Caryn travelling with Marwin and Reimund while Lana and Janusz were escorted by Hans. Caryn was getting to like Marwin. He was bright, and his military knowledge made him a good person to bounce ideas off. She had also started to admire his enthusiasm. So many of the people she met in government were jaded, even the young ones. It was refreshing to work with someone who truly seemed to care.

"I can't wait to see the northwest tomorrow," he was saying now, excitement flashing in his eyes. The telegraph from Tomasburg had arrived the previous day, telling them that a train had been booked for them to continue onward and inspect their defences in the northwest, on the other side of the mountains and the desert. A day of furious writing and revising had ensued; Caryn had insisted on completing their report to the president before their departure. When she finally pronounced that their product was strong enough to cable back to Tomasburg, Caryn invited the entire team to Janusz and Marwin's quarters, where she broke out the general's wine in celebration. "I've never been to the northwest before," Marwin said.

"I've lived there all my life," Janusz told him. "There isn't much to see. Some rich people out by the coast and a lot of poorer villages inland, working the oil wells or the mines."

"I've heard the desert's amazing," Marwin continued. "They say the sand shifts and rolls as if the earth itself is alive."

"The desert is beautiful," Caryn agreed. She had travelled throughout Deugan in her public life. "I've always lived in large cities, but something draws me to that wilderness. That emptiness where all you see for leagues around are hills and valleys, and shadows playing with the golden light that reflects off the sand."

Marwin nodded vigorously. "I went to Givanno once with my family. It was like that, without the sand. Rolling hills and valleys, and lights and shadows. We stayed in a tiny little town built into a hilltop, with stone steps and narrow, winding roads. It was incredible."

"That sounds lovely," Lana agreed. She was quiet among the men, as usual. Caryn wondered whether she and Janusz had found much to talk about while circling the satellites and storerooms of the Fort. Caryn found it difficult to carry on a conversation with the man. He always seemed to be testing her, or searching for something, something she could never identify.

"I'm glad Givanno's on our side now," Marwin added.

It was all the fort had talked about for days, and Caryn, thirsting for accurate news, had often sent Marwin to wait by the communications hub and demand to see reports as they came in. From what he had told her, Givanno's declaration of independence from the New Empire had had an immediate impact. Trainloads of grain were rushing into Deugan from the southeast. Imperial soldiers and guns were streaming away from their trenches in Deugan, though enough remained behind to maintain the empire's numerical superiority. The forts along the highway that linked Deugan to Givanno were being shelled intensely, but as Marwin liked to boast, his father had built them well and they were holding fast.

"Are you sure you don't want any?" Janusz asked Marwin, gesturing at the wine. The boy shook his head, and Janusz shrugged. "More for me, I suppose." He poured himself another glass. "My lady?"

"I'm fine, thank you."

"I'll take some before you finish it," Hans shouted from the corner of the room where he and Reimund had broken out a deck of cards. Janusz passed him the bottle and Hans poured it. "There's enough for one more glass," Hans announced. "Reimund?"

"No way," the other guard said. "You want me drunk so you can win your money back."

"Nobody's getting too drunk," Caryn announced. "We still have work to do before we leave tomorrow morning."

"I thought the report was done," Marwin complained.

"Almost," Caryn said. "I'm still concerned about a potential attack through the Well. I thought we might have another look at it."

Marwin groaned, but Lana leapt to her feet. "Janusz and I have been inspecting the satellites all along, my lady. We can take another tour of Seppina."

"Good," Caryn said. "Marwin and I will do another run through the gun batteries in the main fort. The large howitzers are on rotating turrets but I can't recall whether they will rotate quite far enough. It would be problematic if Seppina were left to fight on her own."

Janusz stretched out on his bunk. Lana glanced at him, and then turned to Caryn. "My lady, if we must complete our inspections before the train departs, then perhaps it is time to turn in."

"Very wise," Caryn said. "We'll see you all bright and early tomorrow."

*

When the women were back in their own quarters with the door closed, Lana dropped her formal speech and flashed Caryn one of her mischievous grins. "That was wicked of you."

Caryn was taken aback. "What was?"

Lana grinned again. "Janusz obviously had a thirst, and so did Hans. Yet you didn't once mention that the general had given us a second bottle." She pulled it out from under her bunk and found two glasses near the sink. "Shall we?"

"With pleasure." Alcohol had been rationed for months now, and wine was a rare luxury. Lana poured and they both sipped slowly, savouring the taste. From outside, they could still hear the distant thudding as the shells crashed against the concrete walls of the fort. Caryn had started to get used to it, she noticed, even as it picked up in intensity. It was background noise. Normal. She brushed the thought aside, took another sip of wine, and commented, "I noticed you looking at Janusz."

Lana hesitated and blushed. Then she started laughing. "I suppose that's all the answer you need."

"I suppose so." Caryn drank again. She had been careful to pace herself in front of the men, but now, sitting here, all of her tensions were flowing away. She drank deeper and coughed.

"I know he's a strange one," Lana said, sounding embarrassed. "He is very competent, though."

"And very handsome."

"That too." Lana took a sip of wine. "My lady —"

"Please, call me Caryn now."

"It's not a bad thing to sneak some glances at an attractive man," Lana said. "Especially when there's not much else to look at. Marwin's a kid but the soldiers are only a year or two older than he is. They're kids too. It's ridiculous, them all being out here. Going through all of this."

"I know." Caryn sighed. "I can't believe *we're* out here. And I've snuck my share of glances at Janusz myself." It was embarrassing, but the man *was* good-looking, and it had been a very long time. "There's nothing wrong with looking, but — I worry about you, Lana. I know you two have been spending a lot of time together, and I just don't trust him."

"Why not?"

"Do you remember how I told him that the key to diplomacy is finding out what the other person wants?" Lana nodded and looked at Caryn over her wine glass. "I feel that Janusz wants something. I sense it every time I look at him. But I can't put my finger on what it is."

"There's one thing men usually want," Lana suggested.

"Not with women who look like their mothers," Caryn said bluntly. She took another drink. The glass was surprisingly close to emptiness. She refilled it. "Doesn't he have a wife, anyhow?"

"That wouldn't stop some men," Lana replied, "but no. He told me that he did once, a daughter of a migrant worker from the northern continent. Her father returned home when his work visa expired, but she'd fallen in love with Janusz and stayed. Eventually she even got citizenship. Yet they still had trouble finding a temple that would marry them. The skin tone and all of that."

"I can't believe those sorts of things are still happening in Deugan," Caryn said ruefully. What she really couldn't believe was that while those things were happening, the entire country's energy was being spent hurling shells and crawling through trenches, in the name of "liberating" Amim and the Fringes. Caryn knew firsthand that there was a great deal of work still to be done at home. They needed a peace, she thought for the thousandth time, but she had no idea how to achieve it.

"Janusz was away from home for several span at a time. That's the nature of the oil business," Lana explained. "They lived in a small town in the northwest where everybody looked like each other and looked down on her. She was alone with no friends and the constant stares. Finally she had enough, and she left him and went home."

"A sad story," Caryn said. "I wonder how much of it is true."

Lana glared at her. "He's really not that bad."

"You can't be blinded by those muscles."

"Why not?" Lana asked. "I'm nearing twenty-five years in this life, most of my childhood friends have been married for ages, and it's impossible to get anybody to take you seriously when you say that no, you're not just going to give up this 'politics phase' when you settle down. To actually respect that this is important. It's so damn depressing never to be taken seriously even when you try so hard to always be professional and competent, all the time, never show weakness. What is so wrong about doing something stupid and frivolous like pining for someone who's really and truly gorgeous, at least on the outside? Sure, he's probably hiding something, but these days who isn't?"

Caryn took a long drink from her glass. "You're right," she said finally. "We're all hiding something." Lana froze and gave her a curious look. "I know better than most how hard it is to be taken seriously in this country. Eventually I learned not to mind. Some people will at least give you a chance, and that's all you need. Who cares what the rest of them think? Pushing back is what makes them learn."

"Sometimes," Lana agreed. "It's just so damn hard. I saw how they treated your policy. Not like how they argued the president's tax increases or Dieter's social programs. That was politicking and rhetoric and sometimes even personal attacks, but it wasn't the ridicule that your doctrine had. They never would have done that to a male politician. And you were right, besides. Trying to broker a deal between the Fringes and the New Empire, pushing independence in some kind of commonwealth so the economic relationships don't collapse? Getting the Fringes home rule through negotiation, to take all of the wind out of the Steffian movement? It was brilliant. Orastus should have jumped at the chance."

"You're too kind to me, Lana."

"I'm not," Lana insisted. "You were right, and you were ridiculed. Doesn't it get to be too much? I mean, I know that you have that fire, that drive, to prove them wrong, to prove that a woman can do all this, that Deugan actually needs to mean something. But where does that come from? Were you just born with it?"

"Born with it?" Caryn started laughing, and soon she was laughing so hard she started coughing. "Lessandro's name, no, it was exactly the opposite. I didn't want this. Any of this." She gulped down some more wine. The glass was almost empty again, and she felt it starting to go to her head. "My parents were very traditional. I grew up with their values. It's all I knew and I was ready to do it all. Have the kids, take care of the house, find a good husband, everything they tell you about in the stories."

"What made you change your mind?"

Caryn paused. *You're too relaxed*, she told herself, *you have to be careful. It's dangerous to give too much away.* "I didn't, at first."

"But the newspapers say you were never married," Lana said.

"They were wrong," Caryn said simply. "I was married, briefly." It was a lie, but only a white one. She and Brenner — but he wasn't

Brenner anymore. He was Brenth, and a Steffian, and he probably hated her as most Steffians did.

"What happened?"

Caryn had definitely drunk too quickly. The room was starting to wave before her eyes. *Stick to the story*, she told herself. "I couldn't have children," she said. "Finally a doctor told me I was infertile." In fact, after six months in a Well there was no need to go to a doctor, but she had anyway, just to be certain. She'd asked innocently whether it would still be possible for a woman her age. She'd been told it had probably never been possible for her in the first place.

"He left me then," Caryn continued, "and I was too old to remarry, and I was barren, and despoiled at that." Except that he hadn't left her — she had left him. They had finally escaped from the cavern, they were finally free, and she had left him, his pleas for her to stay echoing through her heart. "No man would ever want me, would ever look at me. Those things were taken seriously back then. In a lot of places they still are." In Wassia, for instance. In ancient, backwards Wassia, she couldn't have been raised any other way.

Lana nodded but stayed silent, waiting for Caryn to continue. Caryn took another sip of wine. A million thoughts chased themselves through her mind as she tried to keep the younger woman in focus. "My father ran a business," she said. "My mother made him teach me about it, and he agreed, in his words, 'in case you need to help your brothers.' I became strong at accounting and finance. Then my mother insisted he send me to university. He agreed again, but only because it would let me make connections, let me meet boys from wealthy families." That part was true. Caryn remembered the fights, the screaming matches, the sleepless nights. She did want to go to university, she remembered. Even before the Well and everything else, Jayla wanted that experience. But she'd accepted that it would be a one-time adventure, that the rest of her life would be as she and her parents had always planned.

"My mother did that for me too," Lana said softly. "She made him send me to school. At first my dad would have none of it, but my mother believed that it was important, and she talked him into it. She didn't back down."

"You admire her, don't you," Caryn said, and Lana nodded.

"She'd have done it herself, if it was acceptable in her day," Lana said. "If she'd been able to convince any of them that she could actually use an education."

"The marriage cut short my education," Caryn said. *The Well cut short my education* was what she thought. "After it ended, I started back up where I'd left off."

It was a move born of desperation. Caryn was newly arrived in a strange country, with nowhere to go, no prospects and no childhood. She'd wanted that traditional life, or at least she thought she did, but no boy her age would look twice at her, and the men who did find her attractive seemed wrinkled and ancient to her young eyes. She had only lived seventeen years, and then eighteen, and nineteen, but she looked as though she'd lived forty or more, and she was alone. Those years were the hardest, learning to accept her aging body, to assume her new identity, to understand that Brenner would probably be the closest she would come to love. Over time, Caryn had learned to forget about family and marriage and the things that had seemed so important during her Wassian childhood. There was no use harping on things like that.

In those early years, though, Caryn had only been able to do what she'd done in the cavern: she used study to distract herself, and she immersed herself in it completely. A note from Professor Terial had convinced a Deugan university to admit her in the great coastal city of Carrak-on-Sea, and if it hadn't, she shuddered to think what she would have done.

"Then one day it finally came to me," Caryn whispered, and Lana moved closer to hear her. This was true, Caryn thought, the rest of her story could be told true. "I finally said to myself, why should my life be over just because I happened to be infertile? What sort of asinine, archaic society would tell me I was a useless human being because of one single thing I couldn't do? Wassia, maybe, or Brealand, but this was Deugan. Deugan! Democracy and equality and opportunity and all of those buzzwords they write into all of their speeches. It would mean nothing if I couldn't do this. So I swore that I would." Not to be a trailblazer, or a groundbreaker, or a symbol. Not for power or prestige or political gain. Just to keep herself sane. Just to give life some meaning, in Lessandro's name, some Gods-damned meaning. And this war — the war was destroying meaning. It was destroying hope.

"My lady — I —"

"Don't apologize," Caryn said, "and don't ask me for advice either. Each person has to decide what's right for herself. I had nothing else in my life but politics and I was damn well not going to let a bunch of traditionalists or religious airheads keep me out of it. But you may have something else in your life, something even more important."

Lana shook her head. "No. This is what's important. And I will stay strong. I promise you that."

"That's not why I told you this story," Caryn said. The room was still spinning and she was fading toward exhaustion. She closed her eyes for a moment, then opened them to see Lana grinning, the grin Caryn was learning to love.

"With respect, my lady, this isn't about what you want," Lana said sweetly. "It's about the choice I'll have to make for myself, and you've helped me make it. I'll be careful, but I'll also be strong."

"And you'll continue to be a friend, and listen to a middle-aged woman's drunken ramblings?"

"With complete fascination," Lana grinned. "Goodnight, Caryn."

"Goodnight."

CHAPTER SIX

Caryn awoke the next morning with a dull throbbing in her forehead. As she groaned and rolled out of bed, the muffled thud of the shelling seemed louder, each blast resonating through her temples. She rubbed her head painfully and looked around the room. Lana was gone. Someone had left breakfast for her, but she didn't feel like eating. Instead she dressed beneath the flickering electric light, then pushed open the door of her quarters.

Caryn found Reimund standing guard in the centre of the corridor. He bowed when he saw her approach. "A good night's sleep, Minister?"

"Indeed," Caryn replied. "Where are the others?"

"Lana, Janusz and Hans set out for Seppina half an hour ago," the guard reported. "Marwin is taking breakfast in the mess."

"Let's go find him," Caryn said.

Caryn's head throbbed with each step she took, and she wondered if she had always been this sensitive to wine. Alcohol had been strictly forbidden in her father's household. Caryn had taken her first sips while away at university, and she didn't remember it being this painful, but whether it was the Well that had changed her or merely age, she could never tell.

The mess hall was buzzing with excitement. From the snippets of conversation she overheard, it sounded like the Brea artillery had ripped through parts of the barbed wire that guarded the emplacement from the north, and men were rushing to replace it.

They found Marwin chatting with a boy in uniform who she

judged only a year older than he was. Marwin's plate was nearly empty and he leapt to his feet at the sight of her. "My lady. Shall we proceed?"

Caryn smiled at him. "You were much less excited last night."

"I'm excited to see the outside again," he said. "The concrete is suffocating sometimes, and we have a long train ride ahead this afternoon."

"I can't wait for the train and the chance to sleep," Caryn replied. Their route would take them back through the Hermann Gap to Czemers, then due west past the desert and out toward the sea. "Well, we don't have all day. We may as well get started."

Marwin led their way out of the mess hall, past the barracks to a series of winding staircases. As they climbed the steps, the shelling seemed to get louder and more intense. The main artillery batteries were stationed near the top of the fort, and the walls here had several slits open to the outside air, allowing the barrels of the guns to poke through. The wind was howling through the cracks and across the staircases, and the enemy shells, no longer dampened by the fort's thick walls, were screaming and exploding.

The gunnery was a flurry of activity. Through the slits in the concrete Caryn could see the soldiers rushing to repair the barbed wire that had been torn apart overnight. The fort's guns provided covering fire, and soldiers were running to and fro, loading the 75- and 125-millimetre pieces with shell after shell and then firing them with deafening blasts. Enemy shells were exploding around the fort and the repair workers darted around warily, diving into the protective moat when each volley arrived. Caryn grasped the rungs of the ladder that led up to the roof, trying to ignore the pounding in her skull.

At the top of the ladder stood the 210-millimetre howitzers resting on their giant rotating platforms. They stood open to the outside air, but walls of stone and concrete jutted out from the top of the fort just ahead of them. The howitzers could launch their angled, arcing shots over top of the walls while still enjoying a measure of protection from enemy counter-fire.

When she climbed off the ladder and onto the roof, Caryn immediately sensed that something was wrong. There was a team of gunners stationed there, but when Reimund waved to them, only one man gave a cursory nod in their direction. The others were all holding binoculars and staring out over the walls that protected the howitzers. Reimund shrugged and started toward the nearest gun. "They won't want us moving the platform," he called, "but we can measure the angles again, and calculate the arc of fire."

"I'm on it," Marwin said, and rushed to help him. Caryn was still staring at the gunners. She tried to follow their gaze without any binoculars of her own, squinting toward the horizon.

The view from the top of the fort was magnificent. Breland spread out before her, rough mountains to her left, grasslands ahead of her, hints of forests and lakes in the distance. A warm orange glow out of the right corner of her eye told her that the Gateway Well was waiting, its ancient stones a testament to its power. She sensed the grim determination of the gunners, though, saw their heavy breathing, and almost tasted their trepidation.

Then suddenly her eyes picked up the specks darting back and forth, the almost imperceptible motion on the horizon —

There was a roaring blast and Caryn was flung against the wall. Her right shoulder smashed into it and a wave of pain rushed over her. She heard footsteps and men shouting, and then a crack and screams. Caryn pushed herself away from the wall and looked around wildly.

The quiet trepidation had been replaced by pandemonium. A shell had passed over the protective wall and smashed through the wooden platform that held the nearest howitzer. The twisted metal was knocked entirely off its moorings. It slid down the roof as frightened soldiers dove out of its path. One of the gunners leapt down the ladder behind her while the others dropped their binoculars and searched frantically for ropes to rein in the runaway cannon. Marwin had been thrown to his knees by the force of the blast and was struggling to regain his footing. Caryn groped for the nearest pair of binoculars, gazed out over the wall and gasped.

What had seemed only specks on the horizon was in fact a wave of humanity, masses of men darting and crawling as the fort's shells exploded around them, but advancing, ever advancing. Interspersed among them were contraptions that Caryn had never seen before, huge vehicles on treads with cannons mounted on their backs, artillery that moved of its own power.

And there was Reimund, tugging at her arm. With his other hand, he readied the rifle slung over his shoulder. "Minister, it is not safe here. The fort is under attack. We must go."

Caryn couldn't tear her eyes away from the field before her. It was grassland, almost flat, with a slight rise halfway between the fort and the Brea onslaught. The other howitzers and the smaller guns were peppering the army with shells, and she heard shouts, and saw men fall. Still the Breas advanced. They came with covering fire from the stationary guns that had been shelling the fort all span, and with the mobile artillery too, following along ominously. "Minister!" Reimund insisted, shouting to be heard over the screaming of the shells. "We must go!" He grabbed her by the hand and pulled her back toward the ladder.

She was almost back to it when she noticed a group of specks detach itself from the Brea army and break sharply toward the east. She shook off Reimund's hand and held the binoculars up to her eyes. It was a large squadron of the mobile artillery, circling around to the east, past Eolanis satellite, past Armano —

As the volleys from the main thrust grew louder, Caryn saw a group of infantry, hundreds of them, suddenly emerging out of the Gateway Well. They were charging hard for the satellite fort called Seppina while artillery, guns that could not be manoeuvred through the Well, motored along their treads to join them.

Reimund shouted at Caryn again, and she finally relented and made her way down the ladder. Marwin was already at its base, tapping his foot anxiously, his young face full of fear. The gunnery was a madhouse, gunners loading and reloading shells, messengers rushing back and forth carrying orders from General Freed and bringing reports back to him. The guns were so loud that she couldn't hear herself think, and her head felt ready to burst. With Reimund in the lead, they rushed down the winding staircases, brushing past soldiers who paid them no attention as they ran to help man the artillery.

"Seppina!" Caryn shouted when they reached the bottom of the steps, where it was just quiet enough that she could be heard. "They're attacking Seppina!"

"Back to quarters," Reimund insisted, marching forward. "Come."

"No," Caryn shouted. Her head was aching and she could barely think straight, but one thought was burned into her mind. "Lana's in Seppina. Lana's there, we have to get her out!"

Caryn didn't wait for Reimund to reply. She took off down the corridor as fast as her legs could take her, wishing she was a few years younger, wishing that her knees didn't creak and her calves didn't ache so easily. "Marwin! Quarters, now!" She heard Reimund's sharp voice behind her, and she glimpsed Marwin retreating from the corner of her eye. Caryn barely noticed. All she could think about was Lana, her strength, her passion, her devilish grin and her biting wit. She'd warned the general that the Breas might attack through the Well, she'd guessed that Seppina might have to stand alone, and now if Lana was stuck there —

She rounded a corner and bounded toward a staircase leading to the underground tunnel system that made up much of the fort. She could hear Reimund's footsteps pounding behind her, almost as loud as the artillery shells that continued to crash against the concrete walls.

Reimund caught up with her a few paces from the bottom of the stairs. "Minister!" he shouted, racing in front of her and turning to block her path. "Listen to me. Listen. Hans is with Lana. He will keep her safe. It is not safe for you."

Caryn was shaking and couldn't tell whether it was adrenaline or panic. "I can't leave her. Let me go."

"Hans is with her," Reimund repeated.

"Get out of my way, Reimund, that's an order."

"Minister Hallom." It was a new voice, and Caryn started and wheeled around. The man behind her was wearing a full officer's uniform. She had met him once before, though she could not recall his name. He was General Freed's second-in-command.

"Major," she begged, hoping that she'd gotten his rank correct. "Please. My colleague is in Seppina and she's just a young woman."

"And what in Lessandro's name are you going to do for her if you get in there?" he demanded. "Are you going to fight off their tanks with your bare hands?"

"Do not mock me."

"Go back to your quarters," the officer said. "General's orders."

"Now let's get one thing straight," Caryn snapped. "I am here to speak on behalf of the president, who is the commander-in-chief of the armed forces. I do not take orders from General Freed. He ought to take orders from me."

"Be that as it may," the officer said firmly, "there is nothing you can do for your friend."

"He is right, my lady," Reimund said softly, touching her arm. She tensed at his touch but could not bring herself to remove his hand. "I am sorry, my lady, but you are not a soldier. Those who are will protect her."

Caryn sighed. She could see that he was right, that her presence in Seppina would not do anything to help Lana, that she was simply panicking during her first foray into a warzone. Nonetheless, she would not go down without a fight. "No, Reimund, they will not protect her. Neither will Hans. *You* will."

"My lady?"

"You go in there," she told him, "and you bring her back to quarters. You will not allow her to die. Am I understood?"

Reimund looked as if he might still defy her. Then it passed. "I understand, Minister." He went.

The look on the major's face, if he was a major, was more amused than anything. "Now that's sorted out," he said. "Would you like me to escort you back to your quarters, Voice of the President?"

"The president!" Caryn exclaimed. In her panicked rush down the stairs, in her concern for Lana, she had entirely forgotten. "Has he been notified?"

"He will be," the major said, "when the time is right."

"He will be notified now," Caryn said. She drew herself up to her full height. He might still think she was crazy, but she knew that her frenzied reaction to the attack was wearing off. She was starting to think clearly again. "The president needs to know that Deugan's greatest enemy has crossed our border."

"I'm just following the general's orders," the major replied, "but I don't have any more time to argue with you. I have a battle to fight in Seppina. I strongly suggest you return to quarters, but as long as you don't follow me to the battlegrounds, you can go anywhere you damn well please." With that, he turned on his heel and left her.

Caryn shook with fury as the major walked off toward Seppina. The general's orders, were they, to keep this debacle away from the president's ears as long as possible? Panic was seeping back into her mind, though she strove to shove it aside and lock it down. If they really couldn't trust their generals, where was the hope for Deugan? If the president himself was being kept in the dark, how could there be democracy, or principles, or anything? What in Lessandro's name were they fighting for?

The walk seemed to take hours. Caryn's knee was aching from her earlier run, her right shoulder tinged with every step and her head was pounding more from anger than from last night's wine. It seemed that every few feet a messenger would race past her, or a squadron of soldiers would nearly bowl her over on their way to their stations.

Her journey took her past the northern entrance to the fort. The wide doorway was open and soldiers were streaming in, carrying the wounded on stretchers. Caryn saw men screaming as they were raced by her toward the fort's medical bay. One man had a piece of shrapnel lodged in his head and blood rushing down his face. Another's stomach was ripped open, and he was grasping it with bloodstained hands.

Several soldiers were marching in the other direction too, making for the outdoors, for the machine guns in the moat. The moat was so engulfed in smoke that Caryn could barely make out any details through the open doorway, but she saw the flashes as the machine guns fired, saw Brea soldiers collapsing, saw mobile artillery units stopped dead in their tracks. Still the onslaught came. Caryn took another deep breath, tried to suppress the queasiness in her stomach, and pressed onward.

After what felt like an eternity, Caryn stumbled into the communications hub and into yet another scene of chaos. Rows upon rows of soldiers were typing furiously into their telegraphs. Messengers were running in and out, shouting to be heard over the din of the typists and the crashing of the shells.

"Eolanis taking heavy damage!"

"Armano holding!"

"Carmel seeing first action!"

Caryn took a deep breath. Aside from Lessandro, it sounded like all of the satellites were in play.

In the midst of it stood General Freed, looking proper and distinguished as he shouted commands. He ceased for a moment when he saw Caryn. "Minister! What are you doing here? I sent Major Danzig to see you back to your quarters."

So he was a major after all. "I have a duty to inform the president of what's happening here," she said, in the most authoritative voice she could muster. "Surely one of your operators could make himself available for a very brief cable."

The general stared at her in apparent disbelief, but he was spared from answering when another soldier rushed into the room. Caryn recognized him immediately as Captain Toppel, the young officer who had given her a tour of the fort on her first day here. "Seppina's fallen," Toppel blurted out between ragged breaths. He put his hand on one of the telegraph desks to steady himself. "They've taken Seppina."

Caryn staggered backwards as though she had been punched. *No, not Seppina. Please let Lana have made it out*, she thought, *please, Lana, and Hans and Reimund and even Janusz, please let them all have made it out. Please...*

Freed's yelling yanked Caryn back to the present. "Don't just stand there, soldier, find some Gods damn men and take it back."

"Can't," Toppel panted. "All respect, general, but they've bombed the tunnels. Direct hit on the ground above. Reinforcements shattered. We'd have to go outside."

The general look at him as though he was insane. "Soldier, pull yourself together, and that's an order," he barked. Toppel recoiled, then snapped to attention. "Captain Toppel, Seppina contains an array of 75- and 125-millimetre guns as well as mortars, machine guns and stashes of rifles and grenades. If the enemy controls those weapons, he can turn them on the main fort within the space of two hours. I don't care if you take it from the inside, the outside, or any other Gods-damned side, but you will take it back. Do I make myself clear, Captain?"

"Yes, sir."

"Take as many men as you can find. Five hundred at least, more if you can get them. Assemble at Armano and await my command. Go!"

"Yes, sir!" Toppel ran off again, still panting heavily. *Even more people will die in Seppina*, Caryn thought, the nausea in her stomach growing.

"Yaro!" the general shouted, ignoring her. "Tell the main gunnery to give covering fire for the counterattack on Seppina. Howitzers to stay trained on the rise where the enemy's tanks are having trouble. We still want those easy kills. Aside from that, we'll need the other satellites and the machine guns in the trenches to hold their own."

"Yes, sir!"

"And Yaro, when you're done," the general added with a bit of a groan, "send the foreign minister's Gods-damned cable. She looks like she'll be sick otherwise and our medical bay's full enough."

Caryn looked at him, startled, but before she had a chance to thank him, he had turned away to shout new orders. Instead, she made her way to Yaro's telegraph bench and dictated a short cable: FORT UNDER ATTACK STOP ONE SATELLITE FALLEN STOP MAIN FORT HOLDING STOP. *That wasn't so hard, was it, General?*

She took a deep breath and considered what to do next. She was hungry for information about what was happening outside, but she dared not head back to the vulnerable gunnery areas, and she would clearly be a distraction in the communications hub. It was time to head back to quarters, she supposed, much as she despised the thought. She had gotten a cable out to the president. She had done her duty. Now it was up to the soldiers to do theirs.

Thoughts of the battle were racing through her mind, though. Would the satellites be able to hold off the main thrust of the Brea attack without support from the main fort? Would five hundred men be enough to retake Seppina, a fort armed to the teeth and surrounded by enemy — what Freed had called *tanks*? Could they afford to lose such a huge portion of their garrison in a suicide mission? But on the other hand, if Seppina's guns were relocated so they could fire on the rest of the fort, would any of them stand a chance? Or would the entire Gateway fall?

"General!" came a cry from one of the telegraph operators, so close to Caryn that she jumped. "We've lost contact with the guards at entrance B, repeat, lost contact with entrance B."

"Who the hell's at entrance B?" Freed shouted, storming toward them. "That's the south end of the fort."

"I don't know, sir," the operator replied. "Might just be a stray shell landed there. Or might be some Breas snuck around back while we were staring at Seppina."

"Gods!" the general swore. "Last thing we need are Breas inside the fort. I need men, Gods damn it, I need men!" The operator ran from the room to search for some. Caryn started to follow him, but the general put a hand on her shoulder. "Stay a moment, Minister," he said. "I'll be sending a strike team to investigate the area around that entrance and try to lock it down. They'll have to pass by your quarters on their way, so if you're interested you'll have an escort."

"Thank you," Caryn said. She wished that she could argue, but with Seppina in enemy hands and her telegraph to the president sent, she could think of nothing more useful to do — and if Brea soldiers had actually infiltrated the fort, an escort was probably a wise idea.

Soon she and a team of twelve soldiers had stepped into a different world. Where the rest of the fort was a madhouse, the southern end was eerily still. The sounds of the battle were muffled here, a dull methodical thudding. There was also a high-pitched ring in Caryn's ears that she couldn't place. They crept through the fort slowly, carefully, rifles at the ready, squinting through the dimly lit hallways for signs of the enemy.

They reached a staircase and split up, six of the soldiers continuing along the main level of the fort while the other six led Caryn downward into the vast network of underground tunnels. This place felt well and truly abandoned. The battle outside was nearly inaudible, and their footsteps echoed through the narrow corridors. Caryn placed a hand on the wall of the corridor to steady herself, her knees and her shoulder still aching. She tried to keep calm, but her heart was racing and fear rose inside her. The tunnel system was a labyrinth, and the Breas could be anywhere. The high-pitched noise was still bothering her. And that smell, Caryn thought, what was that new smell?

The others smelled it too. They were slowing, sniffing the air, and then their leader crept forward and peered around a corner. "Smoke," he whispered to the others.

They all inched forward to look. The smoke was thick and heavy in the next hallway, and it was drifting toward them. "Shells?" a soldier asked.

"No, shells would never make it down here without busting through the main fort," another said. "It's a fire." Then he added, suddenly realizing, "That's the food storage, damn it all, they've set our food stores on fire!"

"Let's go!" their leader called. "Adel, Karl, stay with the minister. Everybody else, gas masks on, with me."

"Only four men?" Caryn said. She was scared, but she knew she needed to do the right thing. "You don't know how many Breas there are and our food supply is vital. Take Adel and Karl with you."

"And leave you alone?"

"Our food supply is more important than me, and the Breas can't have gotten too far from where the fire is," she said, pointing into the smoke that grew thicker and closer. "I can make my own way back without passing near them." When the man still failed to answer, she put on her best General Freed voice and shouted, "Soldier, our food is burning. Stop arguing with me and go!"

"Yes, sir!" he snapped as if on reflex. "All of you, with me!"

The smoke had reached them and Caryn started to cough. The high-pitched ring in her ears grew louder and more furious. The soldiers donned their masks and disappeared into the smoke, making for the food storage rooms. Before they had gotten far, though, one of them re-emerged and ran back toward her.

Caryn could barely make out the man's shape through the heavy smoke. She could see his black gas mask obscuring his features, and when he got closer, she made out his crisp Deugan uniform and his gloved hands. Caryn took a breath and coughed again. The man held something out to her, metal that glinted under the dim glow of the lone electric light. "If you are to be alone, Minister, you should at least be armed." He was handing her a revolver, Caryn realized with a gasp. She had never fired a gun before, but there were Breas inside the fort — the sharp ringing in her head reached a fever pitch — she reached out her left hand and took it —

Fire shot through her hand where it touched the metal. Caryn screamed and looked around but the soldier had disappeared into the smoke. The wave of pain burned up her forearm, into her elbow. Caryn flailed and tried to fling the gun to the ground, but it wouldn't leave her hand. The pain crawled up her bicep, through her shoulder, then down into her chest. It was going for her heart, she realized in terror, its fiery tendrils reaching toward her ribcage. She screamed again, and struggled — her other hand grasped at the shoulder, her mind zeroed in on the pain, she felt her heart with every desperate beat —

Then another feeling washed over her, a familiar one, and she seized it. She felt the burning tendrils between her ribs and suddenly she could grasp them and force them backward. She struggled and they fought back, trying to wrap around her barrier. She battled furiously, toning her mind to the energy, striving to remember the time years ago when it was in her always, shaping her and changing her, powerful and mysterious and sinister. She summoned all of her strength and made one final push.

The fire streaked back down her arm, blasted out of her hand like a comet and exploded against the wall of the corridor. Caryn was flung from her feet and her head smashed against the opposite wall.

She felt the power fading out of her as the world went black.

CHAPTER SEVEN

The horse treaded gingerly, picking its way across the tangles of roots and branches. The woods were dark, a setting out of the fairy stories of his youth. Ahead Matthias could make out the faint glow of a cookfire. Behind him, barely visible at the crest of the hill, the crumbling walls of Tel Sukayam reflected in the moonlight.

Tel Sukayam was a heap of mud huts joined by roads that were barely more than ruts in the earth. Its main feature was a series of market stalls where farmers from the surrounding countryside came to hawk their produce. Beyond the market, the town felt lost, abandoned. The ancient walls still stood, but nobody knew who had built them or when. The Old Empire had never extended its reach this far; the walls had been discovered, mostly intact, by the New Empire while it was mapping out the boundaries of its Merguisio colony.

Darkness came fast over Merguisio. There had still been daylight in Tel Sukayam when Matthias had arrived, and barefoot children had been playing in the streets and among the rushes that had cropped up between many of the huts. The children were little more than skin and bones, and several had the facial features that Matthias immediately recognized as malnutrition. Though surrounded by productive farms, Tel Sukayam could not feed its own people. The produce of the region was being shipped west to support the burgeoning population centres of Orastus proper — and that was even before the war.

The journey to Tel Sukayam had been painful and tedious. The skiff he had manoeuvred out of Ciorala had made a rendezvous with a steamship heading back to Pascuay several days earlier. From there Matthias had taken a train to the edge of Merguisio, where the track ended and he was forced to bargain with Merguisian traders for a mount. Matthias had grown up in a fishing village and was unused to riding, so it was not long before his thighs and back were aching.

When Matthias reached the clearing in the woods, he looked around and breathed a sigh of relief. The meeting had not yet begun. He tended to his horse by firelight while sneaking glances at the others. Close by the fire sat Harar, the Master of Finances, a slight, devout man with a thick black beard. Just behind him sat two aides whom Matthias recognized, though he could not recall their names. Beside Harar was Gamoy, the Master of War. His face was set grimly, with lines formed around his eyes and his lips. No doubt the man was planning their next operation as he waited for the meeting to begin. Other Council members ringed the fire too, two or three representing each of the seven Fringes of the New Empire.

Directly across the fire from Harar and Gamoy sat Pellor Amad, the Master of Dignity. His title, of course, referred to Steif's dignity and not Amad's own. He was the Steffians' spiritual leader. Marked a terrorist by the empire, Amad had a bounty on his head that was likely worth more than the economy of Merguisio.

Behind him was the man who rarely spoke at all. Brenth Nono, the Master of Secrets, was tall and wiry. His face was gaunt, giving him a haunted look only magnified by the wine-coloured birthmark on his chin. Matthias knew that his hair was grey, though most did not; he kept it covered under a cowl, and he kept his face clean-shaven, one of the few Steffians who did not allow his beard to grow out. The man was certainly old, but he had spent so much time in Wells that nobody could guess his true age.

Matthias left the horse now and took a seat beside his mentor, who gave him the slightest of nods as a welcome. A few more minutes passed before Pellor Amad stood, and the gathering silenced. For a moment, only the crackling of the fire disturbed the chill night air.

Then the Master of Dignity spoke. "My brothers," he said in a soft, deep voice, "we often speak of Good Steif's teachings. Of the sermons of the Triumvirate. Of the importance of prayer and devotion. Yet we rarely speak of the foundations of our faith, the origins of the Steifar, as we ought. There are important lessons to be learned from our history. The past is a torch. It is the light against the darkness that is the future. We must hold it close, lest we scrape blindly through these trying times."

Around the fire, the men leaned closer to better hear the Master's words. Some were nodding; others simply looked on attentively. The only ones who did not seem enraptured by Amad were Master Nono, whose features were largely hidden behind his cowl, and Master Gamoy, who looked bored.

"We all know how the Steifar began," Amad continued. "It came to us as a fable told around campfires. We heard it as a legend from our fathers, and passed it as a tale to our children. Yet it is more than that. It has great truth buried within it.

"It was, as we all know, a time of strife and godlessness, a time not unlike our own. The world had two mighty empires in those days, Wassia and Orastus, and they were the bitterest of rivals. In each empire men were born in sorrow, spent their lives killing the men of the other empire and died in blood, without ever knowing the truth of Good Steif. For sinister forces had conspired to blind them.

"For Steif has created worlds beyond count," Amad said, his voice rising. "And over each world he set a spirit as his lieutenant, to watch and to guard, to love and to protect.

"But our spirit went amiss. Rao, the protector of our realm, turned his back on his creator. He set himself as a god in his own right, and the people of Wassia knelt before him and worshipped him, though he was only a spirit. He blinded them and dealt unjustly with them. And the wars went on.

"It was in the darkest of these times that a band of scholars uncovered ancient texts speaking of a power greater than Rao, a power that not only created worlds and men, but angels and spirits as well. And they understood, in a rush of clarity, that they had been wronged, for Rao had been consumed by vanity and had set himself as a god unto them, and had hidden the truth of the one true god from the world he was meant to protect.

"And the band yearned for the one true god, and strove to find him, and spread their knowledge of him to all who would listen. They assembled a legion of believers who all added their voices and their minds to the search for Good Steif. And Good Steif heard their prayers. He chose the three most devout of them and appeared to them, and told them to assemble the believers at Villasud in Wassia, for in five days' time, he would make a sign of his great power.

"And exactly five days later, Good Steif returned to our world, which he had created at the dawn of time, and before the believers he struck down the false god Rao. And Rao fell to the earth from the heavens, and landed upon his own great temple in Villasud, and crushed it, and left it in ruins.

"And Good Steif rewarded the three men to whom he had appeared, and who had spread his good word and assembled the believers to witness his return. He granted them riches and made them leaders of his people, and when they died he led them to Gramon, the highest and purest of the Worlds that Good Steif had created. For they were the Triumvirate, and the first of the Steifar.

"We all know this history," Amad continued. "The key is to learn its lessons. Many say that it demonstrates the power of prayer and patience. That we all ought to sit on our hands and wail, and ask Good Steif to come to us as he did to the believers of old. Yet that cannot be what Good Steif intends.

"For in the dark days of old, many prayed. And they lived, and they died, and the wars went on. What set the Triumvirate apart? They prayed, yes. But they also *acted*. They rallied their supporters. They travelled throughout the Wassian Empire and preached the word of Good Steif. They found voices to add to their own. And it was only *afterward* that Good Steif listened, and returned to them, and struck down the pretender.

"Prayer is necessary. But the Steffians understand that prayer alone is not enough. Good Steif *listens* to prayer. But he *rewards* action. And we, the Steffians, will receive his reward, at the end of days. The question, my brothers, is not *whether* to act, but *how*." Amad pumped his fist in the air.

Then he grew solemn. "In recent days, brothers, the Hallom Doctrine has begun to take root. Givanno has declared its independence with Deugan's support and has established a provisional government without a single Steifar member. Not one! The New Empire is teetering and may soon fall, yet its demise will do nothing for the people of this Continent if they continue to be ruled by the godless. The Steffians will not sit silently as an empire ruled from Orastus is replaced by another ruled from Tomasburg. We will not content ourselves with powerlessness and oppression. The Steffians must act!"

There were shouts and cheers from the assembled delegates, and Amad pumped his fist again. Matthias stood stiffly, making a show of applauding the sermon while his gaze darted around the fire. Once, he would have been swept up in the emotion of such a speech. Now it only seemed a dire confirmation of what Jakim had told him in Ciorala: their war would not end with the fall of the empire. Nono's face was impassive as always, and Gamoy still wore his characteristic grimace, but Amad had won over the other delegates.

"At this time," Amad said, raising his arms to quiet the gathering, "I would like to call upon our brothers from Pascuay to report on their progress in combatting the Hallom Doctrine."

The delegates from the colony of Pascuay, Matthias's homeland, rose to their feet. "Brothers," their young leader boomed, "I have excellent news to report." He spoke with both the precision and the vigour of a politician, well rehearsed as an orator. "Pascuay has long been at the forefront of the fight against Orastus. It is a bastion of Steffian pride. Many on this great Council began their journeys with our local chapters." He smiled at Matthias, who gave him a polite nod in return. "For many years, the local chapters have been developing a leadership structure capable of transforming into a true shadow government. In recent months we have succeeded in converting our military wing from roving bands to a disciplined militia. We have begun setting our members out on circuits to judge local disputes and try crimes, with wide acceptance of our rulings from the public. In short, brothers, it is the opinion of the Grand Council of Pascuay that the Steffians have in place the structures and institutions that would permit us to form an effective government immediately following a declaration of independence. And what is more, the powerful citizens of Pascuay agree."

Matthias's ears perked up at the last part, and he was not the only one. He found himself leaning forward in anticipation, despite his misgivings.

"Brothers," the Pascuayan continued, "I am pleased to report that as of this span, we have received confirmation from the Magisters of the two largest cities in Pascuay that they intend to swear allegiance to our provisional government. Further, our sources within the colonial military detachment indicate that its members are likely to desert in large numbers should we declare. The time is ripe for an independent Pascuay."

"And an independent Pascuay we shall have!" Pellor Amad boomed. "Yet there are other considerations to bear in mind. Master Gamoy?"

"The Pascuay military can hold its own," the Master of War barked from his seat. "The problem is political, as my brothers know. If they get Givanno and we get Pascuay, it's a pissing match. It doesn't mean anything."

"It means something to the people of Pascuay," their leader objected.

"We're not fighting for the people of Pascuay," Gamoy shot back. "We're fighting for Good Steif. His ends require a victory. We need to turn two colonies at once if we want to make a statement, but nobody else is ready."

"The people of Merguisio will turn," one of the delegates from that colony announced. "There is little love for the empire here. I am certain not one of my brothers saw an Imperial flag in Tel Sukayam."

"I didn't see a brick or a stone building in Tel Sukayam," Gamoy retorted. "I didn't see a child who your people were able to feed properly."

"Which is, of course, the fault of the empire's policies," Master Harar added in a soothing tone since the entire Merguisian delegation had leapt to their feet in anger.

"Of course," Gamoy said, "but the point is, Pascuay is self-sufficient. The Council would have to prop up a Merguisian state, and it would take most of our military to do it. We'd lose the greatest asset we have, our ability to strike anywhere in the empire at a moment's notice."

"We do not have the funds for such an endeavour either," said Harar, the Master of Finances, again cutting off a livid Merguisian delegate. "I am sorry, my brothers, but the colony is poor —"

"And the needs of our continental war are not served by a focus on the most remote of the Fringes," a new voice said softly. The others quieted in surprise, and even the Merguisian delegates momentarily forgot their anger. Matthias was shocked too. It was not often that the Master of Secrets spoke at such gatherings. "My brothers speak of the Fringes and the empire. But the empire is crumbling. Deugan and Breland are the superpowers of our time."

Nono smiled at Master Gamoy, who stared daggers back at him. "The war in the northwest gives us a unique opportunity to influence the future direction of the Continent. Merguisio does not."

Gamoy looked unimpressed. "Master Nono has presented his plan to the other Masters," Gamoy announced. "His idea is to abandon our heartland in order to conduct some desperate operation in the far west, without any thought to supply lines or how we'd hold any gains we make. Meanwhile, the empire has cracked down on Ciorala. There are curfews throughout Accarro. Steifar were burned out of a temple in Kalid. My brothers, we have a war to fight!"

"And what does all this have to do with Pascuay's independence?" the Pascuayan broke in. "If, as you say, the Merguisians aren't ready, why should we have to wait on them?"

"Who is to say we aren't ready?" a Merguisian fired back. "We're no more disorganized and backwards than Givanno was." That brought the delegates from Givanno to their feet —

But Pellor Amad stood, and they quieted. Slowly but surely, all of the regional delegations resumed their seats around the fire. Matthias shared a knowing look with Master Nono. Each of the Fringes had its own history and culture, and its own dialect of Orastan so unique as to make them almost different languages. It was the charisma and personality of Master Amad that kept the disparate Steffian chapters together as a cohesive whole. Without him, Nono had said more than once, their brothers would tear each other apart.

Only when the gathering had reached full silence did the Master of Dignity speak. "Brothers, we must remain united in our love for Good Steif and our pursuit of justice. These regional differences are the legacy of Imperial rule. The empire has deliberately set Merguisio against Pascuay, Kalid against Accarro, Orastino and Cioro against Givanno. It is the strategy of divide and conquer. It is the politics of a brutal dictatorship. We will not allow ourselves to be overcome by these tactics. We will not play into the empire's hands.

"It is my view that we must consolidate our gains and establish a base of power from which to strike at the godless of the Continent. I applaud Master Nono's insight into the politics of the West and his vision of a Steffian Army of Dignity that will come to dominate distant Brealand, that will make Tomasburg quake in fear. Yet first we must provide for our own. As Good Steif taught, 'Only he who has provided for his own kin and blood, and for his servants, and for the poor and desperate who reside in his community, may he turn his riches to the pursuit of greater glory.' Therefore, from this moment onward, Pascuay and Merguisio shall be colonies of Orastus no longer. They shall rise up from the ranks of the downtrodden, throw off the chains of colonial rule, and declare themselves to be free states, subject only to Good Steif and not to any mortal power.

"Masters Gamoy and Harar, you will assist our newly independent allies, both in money and in men, as they defend their borders from the armies of the godless."

"As you say, Master Amad," Harar said, bowing his head.

Gamoy was not so easily cowed. "And what of the troops I will need to carry out operations in Cioro and Orastino and in Orastus proper?"

"Master Gamoy, we will not abandon our war, but neither will we sacrifice our allies," Amad replied firmly. "You say you lack the troops? Find more. This meeting is adjourned."

The Council scattered as quickly as it had formed. Many of the delegates slept in Tel Sukayam, but Nono took Matthias deeper into the forest. They walked slowly, leading their horses, careful not to trip on the tangled roots. The Master of Secrets did not speak, though they were alone. He seemed to be brooding on his defeat at the Council meeting, at Pellor Amad's refusal to countenance an operation in the distant West.

Finally they reached a place that Nono deemed appropriate for a camp. They tied up the horses and pitched their tents in silence. There was not a soul nearby.

Matthias knew better than to start a conversation with the Master. Nono would speak when he was ready. Instead, Matthias took the opportunity to reflect on the Council meeting. He had grown up in Pascuay yearning against all hope that it might one day free itself of the New Empire's shackles. So why now did he only feel a deep foreboding? Was Nono right in saying that true freedom required operations in Deugan and Brealand? Was the real fight only beginning?

Matthias considered Deugan. It did claim to have religious freedom, although its politicians' speeches were peppered with references to the Five Gods. He knew that Steifar practiced in their midst. And its national language was Orastan. It would not be difficult for Matthias to fit in.

It was a foolish thought, he told himself. He was a Steffian terrorist. He had killed unarmed people in cold blood. He had studied Secrets, which were shunned throughout the West. Deugan would never accept him.

Even if it did, how would he possibly get there? He would have to pass through the heart of Orastus proper, where he was a wanted criminal, without the Council's protection. Then he would have to make it across the trench lines into Deugan, all with the Steffians nipping at his heels.

But if Matthias were assigned to an operation in Deugan, that would be different. Then he could travel among a team of trained Steffian warriors, with all the power of the Council protecting him on his journey. Once inside, he could easily lose the others. He could fade into the fabric of Deugan society, change his name, and never be found again. All he needed to do was to persuade the Council to go along with Nono's plan — and since Nono was his mentor, he could make the attempt without arousing any suspicion.

Matthias was so lost in his planning that he barely noticed the soft voice of his master. "Have you been mapping lately?"

Matthias jolted upright. Nono was standing beside him, just outside of their tents. Matthias hadn't even heard him approach. "No, Master," he said quickly. "I have been sent on many operations recently and have not been given the opportunity to make my way to a Well."

Nono snorted. "That's deliberate on Gamoy's part, I don't doubt. He wants to undermine me by taking my student as his own. I am sorry that you have to be a pawn in this game. It's such blatant idiocy, too. Gamoy doesn't understand how desperately he'll need me, if our operations in the west are to succeed."

"I thought the Council rejected any operations in the west," Matthias said carefully.

Nono smiled. "They did. The delegates needed to be shown that the Steffians would not abandon the Fringes. Certain appearances must be maintained. I must admit, Gamoy played his part well."

"Then the Masters have approved a western operation? Behind the Council's back?"

"You heard nothing from me, Matt." Nono smiled again. "However, you may have heard one or two Council members grumbling that their students were turning down operations in order to travel to the Accarro Well, which has slipped almost entirely from the empire's control."

"Come to think of it," Matthias mused, "I have heard a rumour that Gamoy is upset that more and more Steffians are studying under the Master of Secrets instead of the Master of War."

"You may have heard rumours of a weapon being developed in Kalid."

"I have not heard that one, Master."

"That is why I asked whether you had mapped recently," Nono said. "If you had, you would not need a rumour. You would have seen it for yourself." He paused. "Well, go on."

"Here?" From previous mapping, Matthias knew the rough locations of every Well on the Continent. They were leagues from any of them. "I can't use Secrets here."

"Are you certain?" Nono raised his eyebrows. "It seems that I can." He snapped his fingers.

For a moment nothing happened. Then Matthias began to hear the dripping of water on the leaves of the trees that surrounded them. Wet drops splashed onto his arms, then his face. The rain pelted down faster and harder, soaking Matthias's clothes and hair. Matthias had watched the moon through a cloudless sky during the Council meeting, and scarcely an hour had passed ...

Nono snapped his fingers again, and abruptly the storm ceased. Matthias stared at his mentor in amazement. "Try it," Nono said.

Matthias nodded. He knelt to the ground and concentrated, trying to feel a hint of the energy. He opened his mind to it and slowly, almost shyly, it crept to him. He concentrated on the matters Nono had always trained him to think of when he attempted this effect — of love, beauty, selflessness. He thought of his mother, killed by Imperial soldiers when he was young, but without thought of anger or revenge. Just the love he held for her, just the feeling that he would do anything, anything to bring her back.

Slowly the power responded. It touched him with a simple, soothing hand. It felt at once a caregiver's protection and a lover's embrace. It was Matthias and the energy together in the world, with no need for the outside, for the moon or the stars. As he no longer needed them, so the power dimmed them, until the campsite was engulfed in deepest darkness.

Matthias waited patiently until the darkness was complete, as his mentor had trained him to do. Then he carefully turned his mind to a new aspect of the power, not his own connection with it, but his curiosity for its breadth, its bounds. It was the way a newborn first curls his fingers and toes, stares at light and tests his voice with a cry. It was awe in exploration.

As Matthias explored, the energy revealed itself to him. A pillar of purple light stretched from the forest floor to the heavens, and then one of green light, and of gold and of silver. He reached into the nearest pillar and seized the energy, spinning it slowly to orient himself. The two in a line were Pascuay and Accarro, he knew. They'd shown up in gold and teal this time. Once he realized that, he could place the others. Silver was the powerful Well outside of Kalid. Purple was the Gateway, orange Orastino, green Wassia, burgundy southern Amim.

Then, as his eyes became accustomed to the brightness of the columns, he started to see other, dimmer lights that he had never seen before. There was one in between the Pascuay and Accarro Wells that was barely a pinprick, wavering unsteadily. There were three more pinpricks of light barely visible just west of the purple column. More pinpricks were scattered wantonly throughout the Fringes. And then there was a constellation of lights in Kalid, brighter than the others, illuminating the darkness that the silver column could not reach.

"You take my meaning now, I presume," Nono said softly as Matthias withdrew from the power and the moon re-emerged overhead. "In the jungles of Kalid, the Steffians have harnessed a weapon that has never before been seen on this Continent, and it is in the realm of Secrets. Gamoy does not like that. Even though the Masters have spoken, Gamoy remains hostile, and Harar may well follow him." Nono frowned. "It is a dangerous road I walk. I will need you like I have never needed you before, Matt."

Matthias nodded. "I am with you, Master. From the jungles of Kalid to the mountains of Brealand. I will gladly join your operation." *From Tel Sukayam to Tomasburg*, Matthias thought. *From the Steffians to freedom.*

"I know you will," Nono replied. "Now we should rest, my brother. The days ahead will be long and trying, and there is much work to be done. As Master Amad preached today, Good Steif rewards those who act on their beliefs."

"Praise to Steif," Matthias said absently. He was thinking of Pellor Amad's analogy of the past as a torch against the darkness of the future. There was no torch this time, Matthias thought, no past precedent to apply to everything he had learned in the past several hours. They were all blind, he and Nono and Gamoy and Amad and everybody else, and they were charging headlong toward the darkness.

CHAPTER EIGHT

She awoke to the stench of death.

The Gateway Fort sweltered in the northern heat, and the smell settled on Caryn like a blanket. Her left arm prickled painfully and she was unable to move it. As she blinked the dizziness from her eyes, she noticed a man in a faded uniform slumped against a nearby wall. She tried to sit up, but the nausea came on faster than she believed, and she lay back onto her cot.

Around her men were moaning, bleeding and dying. Caryn blinked again and gazed around the room, trying to feel out her surroundings. This was the fort's medical bay, she realized with relief. For a moment she had feared that the fort had been taken. Now she saw doctors and nurses with the Deugan Wheel pinned to their chests, tending to soldiers in Deugan uniforms. They were safe.

She tried to recall how she had gotten here, and failed. She remembered the tendrils of flame reaching through her ribs and toward her heart, and she remembered the energy coursing through her, barring the attack and then forcing it backward. But she remembered nothing further.

A nurse appeared at her side. "Minister, I'm glad that you're awake. No, don't sit up." She didn't, but she propped herself up with her right arm in order to see better. Even that made her feel lightheaded. "Nothing too serious, thank the Gods," the nurse said. "You inhaled a lot of smoke, but there won't be lasting effects. You were also concussed, but only mildly. You may feel some dizziness for the next few days, and I would avoid any physical activity until it is fully clear." She frowned. "I would also avoid any use of your left arm," she added pointedly. Caryn looked down and saw that it was heavily bandaged. "It appears to have been quite badly burned. You should still have use of it, but it will take time to heal."

"Thank you," Caryn said, hoping the nurse was right. It was her arm that troubled her the most. If it had merely been burned, shouldn't Caryn at least be able to move it? How could the nurse know anything about this kind of injury, caused by the energy surging through her? Caryn forced that thought away. "How long have I been asleep?" she asked instead, suddenly curious. The woman didn't hear her. She had already moved on to another patient with wounds more severe than hers.

Caryn stared again at the bandage on her arm. Her *left* arm. Was it some instinct of self-preservation or merely a happy coincidence that she had reached for the revolver with her weaker hand? Many Deugans would call it an intervention from the Gods, though Caryn doubted that. Still, had she known, somehow, that the gun was a trap? Had she sensed the power in it?

The power was even more troubling. Everybody knew that it resided only in the Wells, could never be removed from them, yet Caryn had been attacked far outside the Gateway Well. How was that possible? What did it mean?

She was too weak, and the heat was too stifling, to think it all through. The room blurred and Caryn drifted into sleep.

She was awakened some time later by a chorus of shouts and cheers. She pushed herself up to a sitting position and found to her relief that the medical bay was not spinning half as badly as before. She soon saw the cause of the commotion. Two Deugan soldiers had burst through the door of the bay carrying a third man on a stretcher, and Caryn realized with a start that the injured man was Captain Toppel, who had led the counterattack on the Seppina satellite fort. Suddenly she ached for news of Seppina and the battle, but from the cheers of the men it was clear that the tide had turned in Deugan's favour. Even Toppel, though his skin was pale and one of his legs was twisted at an odd angle, wore a smile and touched the men's hands as he was carried through the ward. Caryn longed to ask someone what had happened, but just then the cheers turned into chants of "Toppel! Toppel!" and any hope of being heard was lost.

Instead, Caryn turned her thoughts back to the attack in the bowels of the fort. She had been targeted, there was no doubt about that. The man who handed her the revolver had taken pains to ensure he could not be recognized; he was masked, and he had disappeared into the smoke as soon as his deed was done. His hands were gloved, no doubt to protect him from the power of the weapon he meant to unleash on her. After years of meaningless death threats that she had learned to ignore, Caryn Hallom had faced a real assassination attempt, and she had survived.

It was a near thing, too. Had Caryn delayed another moment, had she not been able to tap into the energy and take control of it, the attack would have succeeded. She reflected that the six months she had spent trapped in the Wassian Well, learning to feel the Well's power and speak with it, had saved her life.

And the assassin would know it.

A chill ran up her spine. By all rights, Caryn Hallom should be dead. She was not supposed to have spent months in Wells. She was not supposed to be able to defend herself against such an attack. Yet she had.

Now her assassin knew her secret, and she did not even know his name, had not even seen his face.

To be sure, Caryn thought, she could find the names of the six men who had accompanied her into that corridor, but she was not even certain that the assassin had been one of the six. He could have been hiding, or following the group all along, waiting for an opportunity to strike. Even if he was one of the six, he could not have acted alone. They were common infantrymen. Where had the assassin obtained an impossible weapon, an energy-based weapon with power outside of any Well? Someone else had sent the man, Caryn was certain of it, and to obtain a weapon like that, the perpetrator must be a high-ranking officer at the fort. Her heart caught in her throat. Could it have been General Freed himself? He had stopped her from returning to her quarters alone — he had bade her wait, and sent her off with a select team of soldiers...

Her heart was racing, her breathing coming faster and shallower. By now the assassin might have told anybody the secrets of her past, and his master might be waiting for an opportunity to finish the job. Caryn was gripped by terrible fear and took several deep breaths to calm herself. She had to get out. She had to gather her aides and flee the Gateway as quickly as possible for the safety of Tomasburg. She could not trust anybody in the fort, not now, but she knew that the president would protect her. He needed to be told.

Caryn pushed herself off the cot and wavered a moment, unsteady on her feet. Then, with all of the poise she could muster, she placed one foot in front of the other, slowly making her way toward the door. She saw a doctor running toward her, but she called out to him that she was feeling much better and pressed on without breaking her stride.

She had almost reached the door of the medical bay when out of the corner of her eye, she spied Lana.

The girl was lying on a cot near the door, her eyes closed, her face pale. Her white blouse was stained red, and blood had caked around her chest. Caryn hurried to Lana's side and gripped her hand. Despite the northern heat, it was cool to the touch. Fearing the worst, Caryn pressed her finger into Lana's neck, placed her ear on Lana's chest, searching for a breath, a pulse, any sign of the vibrant, mischievous friend Caryn had known.

Then Caryn knelt, rested her head on Lana's cot, and began to weep.

*

She had the story from Hans the next day, while Janusz looked on, his expression haunted. The first shells had trapped them behind a pile of rubble, and they were working to dig themselves out when the Breas breached the walls of Seppina. Reimund had rushed into the fray, oblivious to the firefight circling around them, and had set to work digging them out. "When we caught our first glimpse of him," Hans said, "he was bleeding from his neck and he had a bullet lodged in his shoulder, but he never stopped. He grabbed Lana and made for the main fort faster than Lessandro running from the mob. We were hard on their heels and we saw them disappear into the tunnel just ahead of us, and thought they were safe." Hans shivered, and Janusz slumped lower in his chair, remembering. "Seconds later the tunnel collapsed. Janusz was screaming for us to go after them, but I knew we would never dig through. It would be suicide. I shoved Janusz behind me and found us a hiding place."

Janusz spoke then. Caryn found it strange to hear such a large man, normally so gruff, speak in a voice so thin and hollow. "Hans was a hero, my lady. He kept us hidden while the Breas were searching the satellite, cataloguing our arms and reorienting the guns. He found us hiding places and moved between them unnoticed so he could spy on the Breas. When Captain Toppel counterattacked, Hans killed twelve enemy soldiers before anybody realized there was someone behind them, and at least another three after that. I swear, my lady, we would not have retaken Seppina without him."

Caryn looked to Hans. She was impressed, but she was unable to muster any enthusiasm. Lana's death was a hole inside her.

"Reimund was the true hero, my lady," Hans told her. "When we had secured Seppina and started digging out the collapsed tunnel, we found him lying flat on top of her, shielding her with his body. He was dead, but she was still breathing. He had bought her life with his own." Hans averted his eyes. "Or so we thought," he added. "We brought her to the medical bay as quickly as we could, but though she still breathed weakly when we arrived, the doctor said it was too late to save her. Within an hour she had passed on."

Janusz closed his eyes. Misery was etched on his features. Caryn found his tenderness surprising, and she felt herself drawn to it, but all she said was, "Reimund was a hero nonetheless, as were you, Hans. I will make certain that you are both honoured once we are safely back in Tomasburg."

"Tomasburg?" Janusz looked surprised. "Are we not continuing westward for another inspection?"

"No," Caryn replied. She had not told any of them what had happened to her in the subterranean corridors, and she did not mean to, since she still didn't know who she could trust. "This attack has changed everything," she said instead. "I must see the president personally and obtain new instructions. I've already sent Marwin to make our arrangements." She had found him unscathed in his quarters, and although she did not actually believe in the Gods, she thanked them nonetheless. She had feared that Marwin would ignore Reimund's instructions and insert himself needlessly into the battle.

They had all been exhausted last night, but early this morning he had gone to arrange their train with one of the privates who managed the fort's supplies. He was to phrase it as a routine request, and Caryn hoped that the soldier would see no need to report it to a commanding officer. With luck, it might be days before the general noticed.

"There has been one piece of good news," Hans ventured. "It does not make up for our losses, but we have captured Michael Ravencliffe."

The name sounded familiar to Caryn, but in her present state she couldn't place it. "Who is this Ravencliffe?"

Janusz grimaced. "I did not know him either, until Hans pointed him out to me during the battle. He was the officer who commanded the Brea assault team in Seppina, and he was taken alive by Captain Toppel. A colonel in their military."

"Not only that, my lady, he's a cousin to the queen," Hans said. "One of her favourites, I'm told, and a respected advisor to the king himself. He will be an extraordinarily useful hostage."

He might be at that, Caryn allowed. Would Brealand hesitate to attack them again, for fear of losing a member of the royal family? No, not likely, she decided. The Breas were known as a harsh and unsentimental people. They were said to live for their realm, each individual no more than a cog in the great imperial machine. Brealand was not like Wassia or the New Empire, sometimes cruel but as often romantic, yearning for their glorious pasts. Brealand lived brutally in the present. Yet, Caryn considered, even Deugan pressed its young men to sacrifice themselves for their country, to put the Wheel ahead of its spokes. Perhaps they were not so different.

But Lana wasn't the one who was supposed to die for her country. It was supposed to be others, nameless, faceless ones. Volunteers. Soldiers. Not her.

Caryn felt overwhelmed again, as she had last night. Stepping into the quarters they had shared, seeing Lana's luggage neatly packed for the journey she would never take, was more than Caryn could bear. She broke down again, sobbing as she had in the medical bay. At least in their quarters nobody could hear her.

Caryn lay awake for hours that night staring at the darkness. She tried to remember every detail of Lana's face, her body, the brief times they had spent together, but already memory was fading and recollections were flowing together, and then she was awakening with a start, not remembering having fallen asleep. Caryn had been terrified that she would dream of Lana. Now she felt guilty that she hadn't.

Footsteps on the concrete floor brought Caryn back to the present. *Ravencliffe,* she remembered, *Hans and Janusz were telling her about Ravencliffe,* but when she looked up Hans and Janusz were silent, their eyes on Marwin as he wandered into her quarters. "What happened?" Caryn asked, the anxiety rising in her voice. "Do we have a train?"

"There are no trains," Marwin said flatly. He held out a piece of paper.

It was a telegram. Caryn inspected it, and it looked genuine. She read it once, then twice, her heart sinking with every word. "The enemy has taken the Hermann Gap," she said finally. "Brealand secretly positioned guns in the Williston Mountains overlooking our trenches, and sent elite troops through the mountains to take us by surprise. The New Empire did the same across the Selliar, so they were able to hit our lines from two directions at once. They timed it to coincide with the attack on the fort, so we would not notice until it was too late." She watched their reactions closely. Marwin, who already had the news, merely grimaced, but Janusz punched the wall in anger, and Hans shook his head and swore.

"It gets worse," Caryn continued. "After our trench was secured, they turned our own guns on Hermannsburg and razed it to the ground. Hundreds of civilians were murdered, and the survivors fled southwest, to Czemers and beyond. Brealand now commands the approaches to the Gateway and all of our railroad tracks in the province." She looked at them gravely. "The enemy is behind us, my friends. This fort is under siege. There is no way out."

*

"There is no way out." Professor Terial prodded at the collapsed rocks with his hand. "We lack the tools."

Brenner scowled and turned away, flinging his pick to the ground. He and the professor had been worrying at the rocks for close to twelve hours now without making a dent. The meagre tools they had brought were meant for taking soil samples and scraping rock, not for digging through barricades.

Jayla sat on the floor of the cavern and wrapped her arms around her knees. "There has to be a way out," she said miserably. "There *has* to be." She had screamed and panicked when the avalanche started, had scratched at the rocks with her bare hands like a madwoman after it ended. So many hours later the fear had run its course, leaving only emptiness.

Terial walked over to her. He was a year or two shy of sixty, but his hair was already grey and his gait unsteady. He would not last long once the Well began to accelerate his aging. "Go to sleep, Jayla," he said, not unkindly. "Perhaps we will all think more clearly in the morning."

"They'll send rescuers, won't they?" Jayla asked.

"Who can say? They may decide it's too dangerous. Or they may simply decide that Baron Halloway, Amaro Sullivan and Professor Terial have received their just desserts, and leave it at that."

"You mean you think they did this on purpose?" Brenner asked darkly. He was looking away from Jayla and the professor, staring at the green rocks as though his eyes could burn a path through them. "Because of my father's land reform program and Jayla's father's movement to — what was your father doing, anyway?"

"You think he told me?" Jayla asked. "Mostly just criticizing the government and throwing his money behind campaigns to loosen up some regulations. That I knew about. There could have been more that he kept secret."

There was no need to ask about Terial's sins. Coming from Amim, the vast southern territory to which Wassia had only recently extended home rule, and openly practicing one of the traditional Amimi faiths would have been suspicious enough. Terial's research focus on the Amimi Well, the column of warmth at the frigid southern tip of the Continent, only fuelled his critics. What pushed the government over the edge, though, was his activism for what he referred to as "academic freedom," after the government cracked down on the religious studies department of the university. Not only was Terial defending religion, but he was attempting to carve out academia as an area free from government intervention, just as Jayla's father was trying to do for industry. In Wassia, there were bound to be consequences.

"So they sent us here and set off the avalanche?" Brenner asked.

"No, I would doubt that," Terial replied. "We're useful to them alive. I fancy I know as much about Wells as any man in Wassia, and the government is becoming increasingly interested in them. Some elements are challenging the belief that technology has made the Wells obsolete just because they're immobile. More are concerned with the effort the Steffians are putting into studying them, not to mention the Orastans, and they're wondering what Wassia is missing. Still others fear that in time, the Wells and the Steifar obsession with them will challenge the atheist precepts of the regime. It's created a perfect storm of intrigue that we haven't seen in decades. When they asked me to take two students and conduct field studies here, the request was genuine. I never would have agreed to take you two, despite the government's 'suggestion,' if I hadn't thoroughly believed that." He sighed and bowed his head. "But it's dangerous work, that cannot be denied."

"So they sent people they wouldn't mind losing." It sounded so stark when Jayla said it like that. The government was their enemy. There would be no rescue. She took a deep breath, fearful — and that made her think of something. "My father's been criticizing the government for years," she said, "but he hasn't *done* anything to them, that I know of. Now he'll be so angry — aren't they afraid?"

Professor Terial looked up and laughed. "Oh, they're terrified."

"Then why —"

"Because a terrorist deals in fear. Terror is more than his namesake, it is a way of life that he embraces. The king always feared your father, Jayla. He dislikes the government and he has money, that was enough. But a terrorist doesn't mind being afraid so long as his enemies fear him still more. Now he has shown that he can do with Amaro Sullivan's family as he will. Quite the message to send."

"And the King of Wassia is a terrorist?" she asked, still disbelieving.

The professor only bowed his head again. Jayla looked to Brenner, but his eyes never moved from the green rocks. "All kings are," Brenner muttered.

CHAPTER NINE

In the early autumn of 1693, Deugan's journalists were enjoying the fruit of the nickname they had planted on Caryn Hallom years earlier. "Sorceress Vanishes" — the headlines practically wrote themselves.

The government's silence about Hallom's whereabouts served only to fuel the speculation. It was not until several span had passed, when word got out that she had been spotted in Hermannsburg mere days before Brealand razed the town, that the obvious conclusion was reached. If Hallom hadn't died in the Hermannsburg Massacre, she must have been killed in the nearby Gateway Fort. Nevertheless, the president's stubborn refusal to appoint a replacement foreign minister led several journalists to insist that Hallom must still be alive, and that the president must know it.

This mystery of the Great War has never been conclusively resolved. It is almost certain that Caryn Hallom is still in the Gateway, buried among other war dead in one of the province's many unmarked graves. But the fact remains that her body was never identified, and as a result, some Deugans insist that she is still alive today, however unlikely. It is a testament to the journalist's ability to make people believe the unbelievable.

— Anja Gotthardt, War Stories: Media, Patriotism and the Home Front *(1714)*

Caryn stood near the entrance of the fort's chapel, staring at the murals that covered the five walls and remembering a different temple she had visited with Hans, Janusz and Lana in Hermannsburg.

She and Lana had stood on the dais there and spoken about the Gods and the war. Now she would never see Lana again.

The chapel was packed with men, and some women too, still in their nursing uniforms. Five days after death was the traditional time to offer prayers of mourning, and every man and woman in the fort had lost a friend in the battle five days past. Caryn did not believe in the Gods, but Lana did, and she would have wanted Caryn to pray for her. If only Caryn knew how.

"Are you lost, Minister?" She looked toward the voice. The fort's chaplain smiled kindly. "This chapel knows no boundaries of faith or thought. I am here to serve all who come to me. This has been a difficult time for all of us."

"Difficult is an understatement," Caryn replied. It had been five days of feeling trapped and helpless and lost in a haze. She had not wanted to remain in the quarters that she and Lana had shared, but neither could she wander the fort, when any of the soldiers might be her assassin. It was difficult to ignore the attack. She remembered it each time she tried to dress herself or to turn the page of a report or even to scratch an itch. She had never realized how much she relied on her weaker hand until it was stolen from her. She could only hope she would recover, but there was no sign of improvement so far.

Then there was the general's conference to worry about. Captain Toppel's leg was in a cast and he complained bitterly about manoeuvring his large metal crutches down the stairs to her quarters, yet he had insisted on delivering her invitation himself. "General Freed was not going to include you," Toppel said. "I insisted that you belong there, as the representative of the government, especially after how your man Hans fought at Seppina. 'She knows what she's doing,' I told the general. 'When I gave her that tour she asked all the right questions, and the Hallom Doctrine was a stroke of genius.' Anyway, the general relented, so now you must come." Caryn just didn't know whether she could. Whether she could face all of them, and whether she would be risking her life by trying.

"It may be less difficult if we pray together," the chaplain now said. "Will you do me the honour, my lady?"

"I will," Caryn said, thinking of Lana. She needed his guidance. She needed somebody. "Thank you."

The chaplain stopped before each wall in turn, and Caryn followed him, repeating his words. They began with Eolanis, asking for his wisdom to guide the mourners to deeper faith, and his justice to deal fairly with the deceased. They beseeched Armano to guard and protect the dead as he guided them to the heavens. Of Carmel they sought strength of arm and mind and spirit that they may join her in building a better world. Before Lessandro, of course, their prayers were for mercy for the living and dead alike.

Finally they reached Seppina's wall. The Gods' likenesses were never depicted, but Seppina was portrayed as a bright sun shining on a wood on the banks of a lazy river. The water was teeming with fish and clams and lobsters. Birds of many colours soared overhead, and squirrels chased each other around the trees as other beasts peered out from the bushes. "No God has only a single aspect," the chaplain explained. "As Carmel builds, so does she destroy, and Seppina is no different. She is the goddess of life, so death is also hers to command."

When they had finished their devotions to the goddess of death, the chaplain took his leave of Caryn and went to comfort the other mourners. Caryn stood at the centre of the chapel, feeling lonely and unfulfilled. Maybe it would be better if she could actually believe in the Gods. If she could get real comfort from these words and rituals, from the promise of Armano's protection and Lessandro's mercy. Maybe if she could tap into Eolanis's wisdom, she would know what to do about Toppel's Gods-damned invitation. But then, if Seppina existed, why would she leave Caryn and Freed and all the damn Breas alive, and take Lana?

Caryn knew she needed to attend General Freed's conference. Her fears were baseless. Freed controlled every aspect of the fort; if he wanted her dead, she'd be dead already. Yet *somebody*, somebody *Deugan*, had tried to murder her, and the danger grew with each passing day.

When did I become so scared? Caryn asked herself suddenly. She was thinking back to her Jayla dreams, to her time in the Well. *I held it together there*, she thought. *Better than Brenner did, anyway. What is happening to me?*

Suddenly she was angry. Angry at the soldiers surrounding her, at the Gods for not existing, and angry most of all at herself. The crowded chapel was suffocating. She pushed through the throng toward the door, and there she saw him.

He seemed three inches taller than his true height, just from the way he carried himself. His back was straight, his pose regal, his eyes piercing. Though not a large man, his frame was fit and muscular. He did not have the swarthy complexion so common in Deugan, nor the pale skin that Caryn shared with the Wassians and Amimi, but skin so dark as to be almost black. It marked his ancestry from beyond the mountains and deserts that for centuries southerners could never cross.

"You are Caryn Hallom," the man said when Caryn reached him. "Foreign minister of Deugan, confidante to the president, sometimes called the Sorceress of the South." His voice was deep, measured, impersonal. He spoke Orastan with only the slightest hint of a Brea accent.

"And you are Michael Ravencliffe," Caryn replied. "Colonel in the Armed Power of the Realm, cousin to the queen of Brealand and trusted advisor to the king."

"Just so," the man said. "Yet you knew that Michael Ravencliffe had been a prisoner here these past five days, while I did not expect to find Caryn Hallom in the Gateway." His eyes remained fixed on hers, penetrating. "Your absence from Tomasburg has been noted. I make a habit of reading the Deugan presses. They are so much more interesting than our own."

"That's because we give our publishers the freedom to write whatever they choose," Caryn told him.

"Why, so do we," Ravencliffe said. "Our publishers are simply wise enough that they choose not to write anything unpatriotic. Be that as it may, there has been rampant speculation as to your travels. Some fools, of course, say that you simply cast a spell and vanished in a puff of smoke. Others that you abandoned Deugan like the traitor you always were. Some say that you went on a top-secret diplomatic mission to persuade the Fringes to rebel against the New Empire, or to ask the powers of the northern continent to send their ships against my precious Realm. Yet I do not recall anybody guessing that you had been sent to the Gateway Fort."

"I'm good at keeping secrets," Caryn said shortly.

"As am I," Ravencliffe replied, "but you haven't managed to keep it a secret that your war is hopeless. You are fighting on three fronts. Once this fort falls, the road to Tomasburg will be laid bare. I do hope my good cousin will honour me with another command after they've stormed the fort. I yearn so desperately to redeem myself for my failure here."

"Who's to say you'll live that long?" Caryn demanded. She did not understand why he was telling her these things, but she felt that all-too-common feeling of a man trying to intimidate her, and her reaction was to return the favour. "We've made the king well aware that we will execute you at the first sign of any attack, and it would never serve us to have him doubt whether we are willing to follow through on our threats."

"Yet you will forebear regardless," Ravencliffe said. "That is the nature of Deugans. They *know* that they should follow through on their threats, they *know* that their mercy does not serve them, yet they persist in their feebleness. You call us a harsh and merciless people, and we call you a soft and weak people, but this is war, Minister. We both know which side is best to err on."

"Why are you telling me this?" she asked, but Ravencliffe did not get the chance to answer. Three other soldiers had come up behind Caryn, dragging the chaplain in tow.

"What is he doing here?" one of the soldiers demanded. "Shouldn't he be in a cell?"

"All are welcome in this chapel," the chaplain said calmly. "This visit has been pre-arranged with the colonel's guards. They stand by the door."

"Aren't you all godless atheists up in Brealand?" another soldier spat at Ravencliffe. "The hell do you need to come to a chapel for?"

"Because watching you Deugans devote yourselves to fantasies and fairy tales is so delightfully amusing," Ravencliffe said, though his voice did not sound amused. "The reminder that we Breas are more logical, rational and intelligent than you helps support me through the dark days of my captivity."

The man started toward Ravencliffe as though to attack him, but the chaplain put a hand on his shoulder and he remembered himself. "My children," the chaplain said as Ravencliffe's guards edged closer, "Deugan's army has plenty of young atheists in it, immigrants from Wassia and Orastus and yes, even Brealand. We must accept them. The Wheel has many spokes, but without any one of them it would not turn." Ravencliffe rolled his eyes. The chaplain ignored him and continued. "We have Steifar here too, whose families arrived from the Fringes. There are Amimi immigrants who follow the Spirits of

Wind and Water. There are transplants from the northern continent who keep all manner of strange gods. And of course there are men whose families have lived in Deugan since the days of the Old Empire, but they learned these other traditions from their new neighbours. As an army chaplain, I must embrace all of them, and I have declared that all are welcome in my chapel."

The soldiers glowered, but knew they could not argue. They stormed out of the chapel just before Ravencliffe's guards arrived to tell him he had "worshipped" long enough. Ravencliffe mouthed the word "soft" at Caryn as they led him away.

"My lady," the chaplain said once Ravencliffe was gone, "the chapel I've described is the Deugan you hope to build, is it not?" Caryn nodded. "Then I pray that Carmel will give you the tools to build it." He bowed and took his leave.

Caryn wandered back through the chapel, thinking of Toppel's invitation and Ravencliffe's words, and of what the chaplain had said about Carmel. The goddess of creation was the one Caryn had often invoked in her speeches, but Caryn had never actually believed. She stared at Carmel's wall. No likenesses of the Gods could ever be created, only symbols after signs after hints. How could she ever look to such for guidance? There was nothing concrete, no way of knowing, nothing to do but find faith and submit.

I've never submitted, Caryn thought. She gazed at Carmel's symbols, the red bricks, the chisels and mortar, the barrows and the ramps and the scaffolds. They were arranged in the shape of a map of Deugan, as though the nation itself were bursting forth from the dust. *I've stood strong against fathers and presidents, against fanatics and assassins, against war and society itself. When did it come to be too much, too difficult? When did I start giving in to fear and doubt?*

When there was no other way forward, Caryn realized. *When I became trapped, a hostage, surrounded by enemies, the war swirling around me. When I lost any chance I may have had to continue fighting for the peace that Deugan needs.* The general had said it himself — peace was not his objective, nor even one of his values. Carmel's wall showed bricks and mortar transforming dust into glorious Deugan. *Yet she who builds may also destroy.*

"No God has only a single aspect," the chaplain had told her. Eolanis meted out justice, but he also showed mercy and love. Seppina gave life, but so could she bring death —

And it came to Caryn in that instant. It was fresh air, a glimmer of hope. She circled the chapel, her arm tracing the symbols on the walls, until at last her hand rested on a painted trumpet, golden, set against a cloudy sky. The sun's rays peeked through the clouds, dissecting the field below into even slices, reminiscent of the Deugan Wheel. The mural was the most elaborate of all those in the chapel, showing the wood and iron of chariots, the black and brown of horses, the red of blood and the green of grass and the blue of the Wheel. It was a glorious muster, an inspired call to arms.

Yet if Armano was the god of war, he must also be the god of peace. *War and peace are two sides of the same coin,* Caryn thought, *like creation and destruction, life and death, love and hate, loyalty and betrayal.*

He was here, in this very fort, almost an Armano himself, War embodied. Which meant he was also Peace.

Caryn needed him — and for that she needed the general.

CHAPTER TEN

They were deep underground, in the bowels of the Gateway Fort.

Captain Toppel's tour had not taken Caryn here, and she hardly needed to wonder why. The walls of the fort's sub-basement, a mixture of stone and reinforced concrete, were coated in soot and coal dust that threatened to choke her. The air was filled with the sounds of machinery grinding and clanging. Here was housed the generator that kept the fort's meagre electricity needs supplied, mostly directed to the communications hub and to refrigeration for their food supplies.

Those supplies had dwindled, Caryn had learned, as Janusz and Marwin briefed her in preparation for the general's conference. Only two thirds of their food had survived the fires the Breas had set during the battle. Then again, some of the more cynical officers had pointed out, only two thirds of their garrison had survived, so when it came to withstanding a siege, it was something of a wash.

In Tomasburg, the president and the media would be spinning the battle as a great victory. At the cost of about 1,600 dead, most of them in Seppina, Deugan had thrown back the Brea onslaught. More than ten thousand Breas had been killed in no-man's land, on foot beneath the fort's guns or in the death traps that their tanks had become. Those thousands were only an opening salvo, though. There were many more Breas to come, and many more soldiers on both sides who would die horrifically, roasted in tanks or ripped apart by shrapnel or impaled upon barbed wires. Then there was the loss of the Hermann Gap, and the siege, and the massacre of the civilians in

Hermannsburg. The president wouldn't be highlighting those parts of the battle.

The general had been active in mapping out their strategy to withstand the siege. In addition to cutting back on rations, he had dispatched nearly a thousand soldiers to fourteen towns and villages that lay between the fort and the Hermann Gap. They would perform double duty there, guarding the surrounding farmland from Brea raids and eating the food grown there so they wouldn't need to rely on the fort's stores. Caryn wondered whether it would be enough. Two thousand five hundred men would remain at the fort, and it would be difficult to feed them for any extended period of time.

The general's conference held even more bad news. Two of the Fringes, Pascuay and Merguisio, had declared independence from the New Empire under Steffian-led governments. The New Empire's crackdown affected Givanno too, and Deugan's tiny ally was hard-pressed. As a result, Deugan found itself diverting as many troops away from the eastern front as Orastus did. From the sounds of it, nothing on the ground in Merguisio had changed — the empire still in control, the Steffians still running their guerrilla attacks, the populace still worn down and disengaged — but Pascuay seemed to have descended into an all-out civil war between Imperial troops, Steffians and the pro-democracy movement.

Closer to home, Seppina was not the only satellite fort to have taken heavy damage during the fighting at the Gateway. Eolanis and Armano had also been hit hard, and their soldiers were rushing to repair them before the Breas attacked again. Brealand was reinforcing the siege, too. Troops and supplies were arriving at the Hermann Gap daily, protected by the Brea guns in the mountains, which Deugan had no way to approach. Many of the officers at the conference also expressed concerns about Brealand's tanks, but Caryn soon realized that they were mostly dismayed at how terribly the enemy vehicles had failed. Deugan was just beginning to roll out its own experimental tanks in Wassia, and now it seemed the Deugan models, too, would require expensive modifications.

Everybody at the conference wanted to hit the Hermann Gap from both sides, but the fort's garrison was too depleted to make a convincing attack from the north, and Joint Staff Headquarters in Tomasburg was unwilling to send enough troops from the south. At one point Caryn was afraid General Freed and his second-in-command, Major Danzig, would come to blows over that decision. "They want us to hold the entire Gateway with less than four thousand men?" Danzig shouted. "They're leaving us here to die. Damn it, Ern, if we lose the Gateway we lose the entire north and then the war is over, you know that as well as I do."

"The fort will hold," General Freed snapped in the tone of a man unused to having his authority challenged. "The trenches at Czemers will hold too."

"Like the one at Hermannsburg did?"

"Damn it, Ralf, what in Lessandro's name do you want me to do?" Freed shouted.

"We have the Gods-damned foreign minister here," Danzig shot back, jabbing a finger toward Caryn without looking at her. "Let's put her to some use. Get her on the cable to the president, you know he'll do anything she tells him." Caryn wondered why it was so easy to feel fear and anger at the same time. She hoped Danzig was right, that the president would listen to her. Her entire plan depended on it.

"What would you want her to tell him?" Freed was saying, pounding on his desk. "To pull troops off the eastern front? When our men there have already been shipped out to Givanno? There are *hills* between the Gateway and Tomasburg. We can bleed the Breas at every ridge and rain hell on them in every valley. But if the Orastans break through they're practically in the Hall of Columns."

"Tell the president *something!*" Danzig shouted. "Tell him to put in the Gods-damned draft, get us some more men that way. Who fights on three fronts with *volunteers?* Until then, have him pull men from the northwest. From Givanno, let the bastards fend for themselves. Pull them from Wassia, I don't care. You can't let them ignore us."

"I can and I will," Freed said. His hands were clenched in fists. "Ralf, listen to yourself. Wassia? The whole war is a footrace. Once Wassia's dealt with, we can ship our troops from the southern front up north, and the Breas will be stalemated. The New Empire's already imploding. Just look what's happening in the Fringes; it's a matter of time. If we can hold the Breas off until then, the war's won. But one of these days the Brea fleet's going to leave the north harbours, and their armies are going to batter down the forts in the northwest, and we won't be able to hold them if we still have a southern front."

"And how's the quick win in the south been working out?" Danzig snarled, rising, and Freed leapt to his feet, and soon Toppel was standing and Hans and the other officers too. Only Caryn remained seated, outwardly calm and composed, though her heart was racing and she could barely register her own thoughts.

But her poise, sitting primly and properly in a roomful of standing men, had its desired effect. First Hans' eyes, then Toppel's, and finally even Freed's and Danzig's were drawn to her. "Before I left Tomasburg," she said softly, "the president asked me a question that I've been struggling with ever since. How do we build a peace if we're at war with ourselves? We are all in this room because we love Deugan, and we want her to survive. For that we need peace. Inside and out."

She expected the general to challenge her, but he did not. Instead he picked up on her theme and even carried it along, if not in the direction she would have hoped. "To get peace," he said, "we need a strong enough tactical position that the Breas have some incentive to negotiate. So whatever decisions get made in Tomasburg, we need to do our jobs and see to this fort." With that he sat down, and so did the others, Danzig staring daggers at her.

"Minister Hallom and I had an informal arrangement," the general continued. "I would assist her work for the president, and she would help me get the troops we need to supplement our garrison." He said it politely, as though their first meeting had been amicable, as if their deal had been spoken instead of just implied. Caryn hated being used, and she wondered where Freed was going with this. "Now that we've lost the Hermann Gap, she won't be able to get us any more men. Not without an army massive enough to break through a fortified position, and even then, with the guns the Breas and Orastans have in the mountains, that'll be a hell of a task. So what can she offer us instead?"

So that was it. A trap. She'd already received her end of the bargain, so now she'd be expected to give something up. For nothing. Even though she had nothing to give.

"Men are what we need, and men are what she promised," Danzig said.

"She doesn't have men," Toppel objected.

"Sure she does," Danzig said. "She's got three. One of them's right here."

Caryn's heart caught in her throat. *No, they can't.* Her chest was constricting, her breathing coming shallower. Not her aides. Not her team. Not Hans. The military couldn't steal her only support, the only protection she had. Not after one of their own had tried to murder her. Not after they had taken Lana.

But they could. General Freed controlled the Gateway Fort, completely and utterly. If he wanted her men, he could have them. In fact, as she'd realized that morning, if he wanted her head, he could have that, too.

She realized in that instant that Freed and Danzig weren't asking her to hand over her team. They were telling her. And there was nothing she could do about it.

Or was there? Caryn thought back to her revelation in the chapel that morning, how she had never given up, how a way forward had always opened for her. Suddenly she knew she could stand up to them. Not over Janusz or Marwin, but Hans had been her bodyguard for nearly a decade. He was loyal to her. Without her permission, he would not fight for them, no matter what they did — and what they could do was limited. There was no point in killing or injuring a capable soldier, and in prison Hans would be of no use to anybody. Yet properly engaged, he could be more valuable than ten Marwins put together. Toppel had seen firsthand how Hans had fought in Seppina, and the stories must have reached the general's ears. They wanted him. He was Caryn's bargaining chip.

With another sinking feeling in her stomach, she realized that she had to play him.

"General," she said, trying to stop her voice from shaking, "you did give us free run of the fort for our inspections. We never had a chance to finish our project, though. The part involving the Gateway became moot after the attack. Now we can't leave to continue the project in the northwest. This siege means that neither of us have gotten what we wanted."

Danzig made to respond in anger, but the general silenced him with a glance and looked back attentively to Caryn. It was not out of respect, Caryn realized, but Freed was clever, and perceptive. He was starting to figure Caryn out, on the surface at least. He knew that she cared about being recognized and respected, and he knew how stubborn she could be on matters of principle, but he also knew that in the end she was likely to put her own interests aside for the good of Deugan. Caryn found that she didn't mind, because she was starting to figure him out as well. His conflicting needs to be in charge and to see himself as fair. His desire for frank talk. His quick temper that was almost always a ruse to throw his opponent off guard.

"I realize the fort needs more men," Caryn said, "and I am the last person who would want to stand in the way. I love Deugan as much as any of you. So I am willing to make you a new deal which I'm certain you'll find more than fair." She took a deep breath, steadied herself, and looked General Freed in the eye. "As long as my men agree to enlist: three of mine for one of yours."

*

So it was, not three days later, that Caryn and Hans were trudging through the coal-stained halls of the sub-basement to the fort's prison. To Freed's prisoner. To Michael Ravencliffe.

The prison occupied its own corridor of the sub-basement. It was barely distinguishable from the rest of the fort, a series of cells carved into the walls, with a small team of soldiers nearby standing sentry. Caryn could see at once that the prison was not meant to house this number of men. It was built as a holding cell for prisoners of war waiting to be shipped further south, or for the odd offender among their own garrison. Instead it was packed with Brea soldiers — Brea children. Why would Ravencliffe even want to speak to her under these conditions? What would a Brea colonel care for a Deugan politician and her dream of peace?

Despite the overcrowding of the prison, the general had managed to find Ravencliffe his own cell, a good few yards from those of his countrymen. Captivity did not appear to have dampened his spirits. He leaned casually against the wall, hands on his hips, a smile threaded across his face. He said nothing.

One of his guards unlocked his cell, while the other kept a rifle carefully trained on his heart. Ravencliffe had been treated to a chair, a bed and a low table; Caryn sat on the chair and Hans the table, which creaked under his weight. Caryn felt her anxiety rising. She waited for the adrenaline rush, the familiar sensation that would calm her nerves and set her on edge, ready to fight. It didn't come.

Ravencliffe, on the other hand, did not seem the slightest bit perturbed by their sudden appearance. "I'm afraid I treated you rather rudely at the chapel," he said when his guests were settled. "Normally, any breach of manners on my part would have been deliberate, but in your case it was quite accidental." His eyes flitted to her sling. "I should have shown a great deal more concern for your injuries, Minister. I trust your arm is healing well?"

"Quite well," Caryn lied. She did not like how this had started.

"How might such an injury have come about?" There was humour in Ravencliffe's voice, but not in his eyes. "Surely the Deugan army is not yet so desperate as to put a valuable government official on the front lines?"

"I'll ask you the questions," Caryn said evenly.

"Ask away," Ravencliffe said. "You won't be the first Deugan who's tried. First came some children the general sent down. Then there was a captain or two. I even merited a visit from Ralf Danzig himself, but I'm holding out for Freed."

"Do you ever stop talking, Colonel Ravencliffe?"

"Is that really your first question?"

Caryn shook her head, irritated. Had she lost control already? She'd asked Marwin and Janusz to fill her in on everything they knew about Brealand, about the royal family, anything that might be useful in bringing Ravencliffe onside, and two minutes into their conversation, she was already flummoxed. The panic was starting to set in.

Ravencliffe used her confusion as an opening. "I suppose I'll just have to ask another question, then," he said. "Have you had an opportunity to contemplate what I told you in the chapel?"

Caryn didn't want to play into his hands, but the sirens were sounding in her brain, crowding out thought, strategy. She looked at Hans sitting on the table, and he registered her alarmed expression. No doubt Ravencliffe had as well.

She could do no better than to give Ravencliffe an honest answer. "All you told me was that Deugan would lose the war and that we're all soft and weak," Caryn said. "Oh, and that you'd been following the news about my whereabouts with an almost obsessive intensity."

Ravencliffe spread his hands out before him. "It is the only type of intensity of which I find myself capable." He took a step toward her. Hans reacted instantly, swinging off of the table, rifle at the ready. Ravencliffe took another step forward, ignoring him. "Your friend's rifle does not frighten me, Minister, because death does not frighten me. In the end, I serve the Realm, and the Realm is better served by my death than by answering a single one of your questions." Another step. Hans moved to block his path, but Ravencliffe did not break stride. "So if you want anything from me at all, Minister, start by answering my question. Why is there a sling on your arm?"

Her head was pounding, her mind was going blank, every bone in her body wanted to bolt and run —

Hans lowered his rifle. "Colonel Ravencliffe," he said softly, "you're mistaken."

Ravencliffe stopped in his tracks and turned his head toward Hans, feigning surprise. "The minister's pet has a voice!" he exclaimed in mock delight. "Does he sing?"

"You assume the minister wants information from you," Hans continued. "I know her better than anybody on the Continent. Trust me. She doesn't care. She doesn't want to know where your troops are or when the fleet's leaving the north harbours."

Caryn suddenly realized what Hans was doing, and she seized it eagerly. "That's right," she told Ravencliffe. "It doesn't matter to me what pacts you've made with the northern continent, what you know about the Wassian positions or whether you're funding Steffians in Givanno. I don't care. That's not why I'm here."

For an instant Ravencliffe looked genuinely surprised, which Caryn found gratifying. He quickly composed himself. "I have to admit, Major Danzig didn't have the wit to try that sort of tactic on me."

"Major Danzig barely has the wit to dress himself in the morning!"

Ravencliffe laughed. "I may have misjudged you, Minister Hallom. I find myself genuinely curious, a thing that rarely occurs when it comes to the sorts of savages who inhabit your country." Caryn saw Hans tense at that, but she shot him a look that told him to back down. She knew what to do now.

"Don't pretend I've just piqued your curiosity now," Caryn told Ravencliffe. "You've been reading the news about me. That's what you told me at the chapel, what you wanted me to think on these last few days. That's why you asked me about my arm. You've been curious for months, maybe even years. Why?"

Ravencliffe smiled. He crossed the small cell and lowered himself onto the bed. "You ask a question, yet you stubbornly refuse to answer mine."

"That's because it's none of your Gods-damned business," Hans grunted, but Caryn was already taking a deep breath, preparing for the plunge. Panic was surging back through her, but she had come this far, and she knew she could get it out if only she started.

"I was attacked during the battle," Caryn said shakily. "I was making my way back toward my quarters when I found myself in a corridor filled with smoke. A man in a Deugan uniform emerged from the smoke, wearing a gas mask so I could not see his face." She looked at Hans. His eyes were widening. "This Deugan said something about my need to defend myself. He pressed a revolver into my hand and disappeared." She thought back to the struggle in the hallway, remembering, and she felt the tears start coming and cursed herself and fought to hold them back. "The revolver ... exploded," she finally said in a high voice. "In my hand. There were burns all along my arm."

"Curious," Ravencliffe said. "One would have thought that an assassin would simply shoot you with the revolver and have done with it. But perhaps then he would have been heard, or else the bullet in your body might have been matched to his gun. As it is — I take it the perpetrator has not been caught?" Caryn shook her head. Ravencliffe sighed. "A pity," he said. "It would amuse me to share my captivity with a Deugan prisoner."

"What about my question?" Caryn demanded. "Why are you so interested in me?"

"Because I feel, for reasons I am unable to explain, that unlike most barbarians from outside of the Realm, I may, in time, be able to trust you."

For their first negotiation, Caryn thought, that would have to be enough.

*

"Hans, you were brilliant," Caryn told him as they made their way back toward their quarters. "You absolutely saved me. It was the perfect thing to say."

Hans shrugged. "Everything I know, my lady, I learned from you.

It is exactly what you would have said in that situation, at a better time."

"At a better time we'd never be in that situation," Caryn said, "but I think we have a chance." They rounded the corner into the corridor where their quarters were located. "It will take some time, but I think he'll listen —"

His hands were on her shoulders. Before she knew it, he was shoving her through a doorway and her bad knee was giving out under her. Hans caught her before she fell, but his grip was not gentle. The door slammed shut behind them. He spun her around to face him. "How could you, Caryn?" he demanded.

Caryn panicked, backing away from him. She had never seen Hans this angry. "What are you doing?" she said. Her pitch was an octave higher than she remembered it.

"I have been the shadow by your side for longer than I can remember," Hans hissed. "I have listened to every confidence of yours and told not a soul. I have spent span away from my Marla to better serve you. And you were *attacked under my nose in this fort* and you didn't tell me?"

Caryn's first reaction was relief. She felt almost giddy that this wasn't about something more serious. But one glance at his face stopped her cold. A chill seeped into her chest. "Hans, you are always my strong right hand. You know that. But you're scaring me."

"You could do with some scaring," he said. "Was your plan to pretend that none of this ever happened? That they're not going to, I don't know, try again? My job is to protect you. How am I supposed to do that if you don't tell me anything?"

"Of course I think they might try again," Caryn said. "I don't even know who 'they' are! I was too afraid to tell anybody —"

"Because you didn't think you could trust anybody," Hans finished for her. "Not even me." His anger was fading. He looked hurt now. Worse than hurt. Wounded.

"Hans." She couldn't lose him. Not now, not like this. Not after she had lost Lana and so many others. "Hans, please listen to me. You have been with me long enough to know about my panic attacks. You know how I control them. How I channel them, use them. But you remember the times when I couldn't do that. When I lost sight of who I was and what I was doing. You saw that happen to me downstairs, just now. Please accept that I trust you more than anybody on the Continent. Please don't blame me for this."

His expression softened, but only a touch. "Tell me, then," he demanded. "The part you left out." He looked at her face and scowled. "Don't give me that look. I know you well enough. There was something you didn't tell Ravencliffe. Something that I need to know." When she still didn't answer, he averted his eyes and dropped his arms to his side. "I'm your protector, Caryn. I'm also your friend. I'm trying to help you."

She almost told him then. She felt tears welling up, and she almost let everything spill out, her childhood, her true age, the Wassian Well, the true nature of the attack she'd fended off — but then she thought about the war, and the sorceress slander, and the Steffian associations, and how an explosive secret kept hidden for fourteen years could tear a country apart. How she was the only politician in Deugan working for peace, and how much more distant that dream would be if her veneer of credibility ever washed away. She thought about how Hans had shoved her and slammed his door, and shouted at her.

"You know me too well," Caryn said, trying to force a blush to her cheeks and nearly succeeding. "I can't lie to you, and I wouldn't if I could. But I hope you know me well enough to realize that I'm not undermining how much I trust you when I ask you to let me keep this one secret to myself."

Hans stared at her for a long moment. Finally he nodded. "This one secret," he repeated. "Fine. So what do we do next?"

Caryn sighed. "Thank you, Hans." She took a step backward and thought. "There were six men who accompanied me into that corridor. Our soldiers. They disappeared into the smoke just before the attack."

"Are you sure the soldier who attacked you was one of them?"

"No," Caryn said, "but it's the most likely guess, and anyway, they should have at least seen or heard something."

Hans nodded again. "I'll see what I can find out." He turned and took two brisk steps toward the door, which he grabbed and threw open.

"Hans!" Caryn shouted after him. Hans turned around. *I'm sorry,* she wanted to say, *I'm sorry I didn't trust you, I'm sorry I panicked, I'm sorry I'm such an anxious wreck* ... but he hadn't apologized for shoving her, so she swallowed her words. "The gun," she said instead. "It was rigged, somehow. In a way that doesn't make sense. We should inspect it. If we can find it."

"Understood." He paused as though he was about to say something more. Then he turned again and left.

CHAPTER ELEVEN

Brenner's arms were shaking her when she woke. "Jayla," he was saying. Nothing more. Just her name, softly. "Jayla, Jayla." It was the most beautiful sound in the world.

She snuggled up next to him and laid her left arm across his chest. He pulled her closer. "Jayla. It's okay."

"What is?" she asked sleepily. Then she realized. "Oh no, was I screaming again?"

"No," Brenner said. "Just thrashing around a bit." He gave her a squeeze. "It's okay. I have bad dreams too. You can't — you can't help it here."

Jayla couldn't even remember what she had been dreaming about, but she recognized the exhaustion and the sweat that came with her nightmares. They were growing more frequent, only one of the ways in which the Well was poisoning them. In recent span Jayla had noticed her head pounding, her throat dry, her muscles aching. She was growing weaker by the day.

But with Brenner's arms around her, it was easy to forget all that. His early sullenness lingered when he was around the professor, but he lifted it for her. He was calm, strong and patient.

And tired, she realized. "I can go sleep in my room, if you want," she said. "I feel bad that I keep waking you up."

Brenner's arms only tightened around her. "I don't want you going anywhere."

"Oh really?" Jayla said. This had suddenly become a challenge. She knew Brenner was stronger than her, but when she tickled him, his grip loosened just enough for her to wriggle out of it. He lurched to his feet to chase her, but he was slow from sleep and she danced away. "Come on, come get me."

Brenner came at her, laughing. She twisted to the side, a simple motion, but her body didn't react the way she was used to, and suddenly she was falling. He wasn't fast enough to catch her, and she hit the ground with a thud. Tears welled up, and she blinked them away furiously.

Soon Brenner was beside her on the ground, holding her. "Jayla. Hey." She stared past him at the wall of the cavern. "Jayla. I'm sorry."

"You didn't do anything," Jayla muttered. "This body just gave out on me." *Not my body. This body.* "We're going to die in here."

"We might," Brenner said. It was so much better than if he'd lied and said they wouldn't. "But we might not. We're still alive now." He took her hand and kissed it. "And we're together." He tried to kiss her mouth, but she pushed him away. She couldn't do those things now. Not ... now.

But Brenner misunderstood, and he was looking self-conscious. "Is it this?" He gestured at his receding hairline, the lines on his brow. "I know I must look like — like twenty-eight, or something." He said the number gingerly, as though it were a harbinger of the end of the world.

"What? No, of course not. It's not — wait, is that what you think when you look at me?"

"I've always had a thing for older women," Brenner said slyly. Jayla smacked him in the chest, but at least she found herself smiling again. Brenner had a way of doing that. "You know I don't care about that stuff. It's still you."

"So it's me, so what? You must have been with lots of girls. Girls your own age."

"Jayla Sullivan!" He shouted her name teasingly, the way she always shouted his. "You *are* my age!"

"You know what I mean!"

"And you know what I mean too. There weren't lots of girls. There was one or two, but they weren't you."

"What's so special about me?" Jayla asked. "I get nervous and freak out and I push you away and I wake you up with nightmares and —"

"And you gave me the greatest gift I ever got from anyone."

"Brenner Halloway! If you thank me for those stars one more time..."

"Not stars." Nervousness danced with determination in his eyes. "Hope."

This time it was Jayla who kissed him, and Brenner who kissed her back, and even though they'd kissed before, the sensation was new, more passionate, more urgent. She pressed herself against him and he wrapped an arm around her. They stopped just long enough for her to pull his shirt over his head, and then she pressed him up against a cavern wall, kissing him and stroking his chest and feeling his hands work beneath her shirt and up along the length her body, until his thumbs were brushing her breasts, so lightly, and she gasped. When he froze then, suddenly uncertain, she looked at him and told him not to stop.

Afterward, as they were lying on the cavern floor still wrapped in each other's arms, she asked, "Did you mean that? About me giving you hope?"

"Yeah." Her head was nestled on his chest, so she could feel the vibrations when he spoke. "Yeah, I did."

She could not remember feeling this shy in all her sixteen years. "I need some hope now, too," she whispered.

*

Brenner gave her the hope she'd asked him for, if not in the way she would have preferred. He walked into her room a few days later looking defeated. He hugged her for longer than he needed to, as though he was afraid to let go. He said that he had good news, that he had hope for her. He said that he had proof.

He couldn't show it to her, though, and his mood grew darker and angrier as he tried and failed to replicate the effect. Finally he gave up and said he would have to just explain it. "You know the Old Empire?"

"Not personally."

He was struggling with his words. "Their wars. Their magicians. In Wells. You know what they did. What they were most famous for."

Sudden realization dawned on her. "Brenner, you didn't."

"I did." He clasped her hands in his. "I saw you. Visions of you. They flew by so fast it was hard to follow, but I knew it was you. You older than you are now, by an ocean, on a train, in a city. Jayla, you're going to get out of here."

Jayla shrieked and threw her arms around him, but he was cold and didn't hug her back. "Brenner! This is amazing, we're getting out of here!" When he still didn't answer, she pushed herself back and looked at him. "What's wrong?"

"I didn't see myself," Brenner said. "Anywhere. At all."

Silence fell. Brenner's face was grim. Jayla was torn between exhilaration and foreboding. "That could mean anything," she said warily. "You were trying to find hope for me, like you promised me. So that's what the power showed you. That's all."

"You wouldn't leave without me, would you?"

"Of course not." She squeezed his hand.

"Then I must die before you get out," he said.

"No!" Jayla said firmly. "Don't do that, Brenner. Just don't. You saw what, four visions? Five? Out of my entire lifetime? You won't be standing next to me at those moments. That's all. That's all!"

"You didn't experience it, Jayla! It wasn't just what I saw, it was what I felt. It was like the energy was trying to tell me something. That you're going to get out of this Well and live on the rest of your life. Without me."

"You're not going to die," Jayla snarled, and Caryn, looking back, recognized it as the time the truth had first dawned on her, deep inside, though her conscious mind would spend the next months resisting it. "Brenner," she said softly, hesitantly, "none of this means you're going to die. Maybe we both get out, but — but we just — don't end up together."

Brenner blinked and stared at the floor, his jaw set. "Then what's the point?"

*

The panic arrived with a vengeance as Caryn neared the prison, and she stopped, took several deep breaths and pushed the roaring in her head down to a low rumble. She was pleased at how easy it was, but less impressed with her inability to banish her fear entirely. She was exhausted, she realized. The nightmares and the daytime stresses were taking their toll.

Only a day had passed since her first meeting with Ravencliffe, and she had spent much of that time strategizing with Janusz and Marwin on how to approach the second negotiation. Both had been remarkably helpful, Janusz at guiding her on how to deflect Ravencliffe's taunts, and Marwin in the form of a crash course on the fort's construction and how it compared to their forts in the northwest and the southeast. Marwin said that as a lifelong military officer, Ravencliffe would respect her more if she knew his trade. It wasn't a bad insight, and whatever she learned would at least help her with General Freed. Caryn sensed that Marwin wanted to say even more, but there was no time before he was called away to his army training.

Ravencliffe greeted Caryn with an air of perfect nonchalance that she suspected he had been rehearsing since childhood. "Minister Hallom! I am so pleased you've returned. Captivity is unfathomably dull. I had hoped to be liberated by now."

"Hope can be fickle, Colonel Ravencliffe," Caryn said, propping herself on his table where Hans had sat the day before. Ravencliffe remained standing in the centre of the cell. "Your cousin the queen is focusing on the northwest, from what I hear."

"Not an unsound strategy," Ravencliffe allowed. "Still, based upon our advance plans, I would expect that by now our contingent in the Hermann Gap alone would outnumber your little garrison here. The full might of the Realm is still being mobilized, to be sure, but we could easily send twenty battalions against your — 3,000 men? Maybe 3,500? Your supplies must be running low as well, after that dreadful fire."

"No doubt she means to starve us out," Caryn said, trying to match his casual tone. She and Janusz had talked about how to avoid being goaded. "She realizes, of course, that when food supplies start to run low, it will be our prisoners whose rations are cut first. You'll be a martyr, Colonel Ravencliffe." She channelled Jayla, putting on a teasing smile and closing her good hand into a fist, which she punched in the air. "For the Realm, right?"

To her surprise, Ravencliffe smiled. "It's fascinating what aspects of our Realm you Deugans choose, in your ignorance, to poke fun at." He traced a circle with his hands, then began making chopping motions, as though carving it into pieces. "The great Deugan Wheel," he said. "Twenty-nine states come together to make one. That is your national myth. Your ideal. But you are not one. You are eighteen provinces, and twenty-nine local identities from the pre-unification days, and one hundred senators chosen by four hundred Assembly members elected by tens of millions of voters. You are five gods and ten languages, eight of which are native, but not your official one. Doesn't that grate on you, Minister? That you and I are speaking Orastan, the language of a distant empire that used to own you?"

"Are you finished?" Another thing Caryn and Janusz had discussed was to simply ignore Ravencliffe's tangents.

Ravencliffe ignored her just the same. "The Realm is what you Deugans strive for, but have no hope of achieving. Unity. Solidarity. A single unbroken circle."

Stick to the game plan, Caryn thought. *Get him back on topic*. But how? She racked her brain for anything Janusz or Marwin might have mentioned during their meeting that morning, but she was drawing blanks. Would a direct approach work? It had with General Freed, but here? She swallowed. It was at least worth a try.

"Colonel," she said, "yesterday I told you that I hadn't come here to find out about your tactics or troop movements. Were you curious why I did come?"

"I was," Ravencliffe admitted. "I wondered whether you were expecting a more intimate encounter, which might account for you leaving behind your mindless, but exceptionally pretty, hired gun. But given what I have learned about you, I find that rather unlikely." His voice hardened. "In any event, for the acts I prefer, you would require two hands." He stared pointedly at her sling, and suddenly Caryn felt that she was back in the corridor, the gun sticking in her hand, the tendrils reaching for her heart. Back where he wanted her to be, off-balance. She fought the feeling down.

"Colonel, you and I have an opportunity." She leaned toward him, looking him in the eye. "This is our chance to decide the future of this Continent. Here in this cell. You and I. We can do it without guns, without ships, and without the thousands of dead Breas who littered the Gateway in the aftermath of your attack."

"Or the thousands of dead Deugans who will soon coat the streets of Tomasburg," Ravencliffe replied. "Your instinct for self-preservation is an animal one, but there is no shame in that for a barbarian."

"Are you telling me that Brealand has evolved beyond its will to survive? Let me get a telegraph out to the president. He'll be thrilled."

"Brealand will survive," Ravencliffe said. "Not every Brea will survive, but the Realm will, because it is united. It is one. Your people, millions of ants running around, looking out for themselves, knowing nothing greater —"

"So we should be looking for something greater than ourselves? Colonel Ravencliffe, I'm surprised. For a moment there you sounded almost like a theist."

Ravencliffe laughed. "You're clever, Minister. I like that. You keep my mind agile. It's exactly what I need in — this." He gestured around him, at the cell, the fort, the Gateway. "I do put a certain degree of faith in the Realm, that's fair, but the Realm exists. I know the King and Queen personally. I have met its people. I have seen its architecture. I have lived its culture. You Deugans, putting faith in something that nobody has ever seen, or felt, or touched, and all the while ignoring each other, ignoring what is real ... it's perverse."

"I do believe in my country," Caryn said. "I believe in the things it stands for. And you believe in the things it stands against. That's why we're at war, isn't it?"

Ravencliffe paused, considering. "Do I hear a break from the propaganda? Is the war not about liberating colonies? Or obtaining cheap raw materials from the Fringes? Or revenge for the Wassian Intervention?"

That last probably had some truth to it, Caryn had to admit. The memory of Wassia invading Deugan in support of secessionist rebels had no doubt been top of mind for several Deugan politicians when they decided, forty years later, to invade Wassia in return. But what she said to Ravencliffe was, "We won the Wassian Intervention. Why would we need revenge? Besides, you and I both know what our current dispute is about. Ideas. And ideas can be hashed out in words, in a room like this one. Without wars."

Ravencliffe shook his head. "That's where you're wrong, Minister Hallom." A note of sadness touched his voice. "If the Great Experiment proved anything, it's that ideas are wars unto themselves. Screaming matches in the Assembly, death threats, media blitzes, all to manipulate the masses to believe one idea or another. No real debates, just attacks, propaganda, rhetoric." He grinned. "Funny how they called it the Great Experiment. It sounded almost scientific, but these days the Deugans are clinging to it without even considering the evidence."

Caryn frowned. "What are you asking me to do? Give you a debate?"

"I'm only asking you to examine the data," Ravencliffe said. "Hypothesis: Democracy works. Experiment: Deugan. Observations..." He trailed off and let the shells that exploded against the walls of the fort finish his thought for him.

*

The sounds of the shelling grew louder as Caryn limped back through the sub-basement, up the steps and down the maze of corridors leading to her quarters. She wanted to see the general, but her conversation with Ravencliffe had left her tired and dejected. She had laid it out for him this time, and he wasn't biting. He liked the banter, but he was not interested in real negotiations. Why would he be? He honestly believed that Deugan was on the verge of collapse, and for all Caryn knew, he might be right.

She pushed past her quarters and continued on toward the mess hall. Even if she was not ready to face General Freed again, she might at least find Janusz or Marwin there and learn what the troops were being told about the renewed shelling.

The upper level of the fort was buzzing, though whether with excitement or fear she could not tell. As she moved through the corridors, she passed group after group of soldiers whispering in hushed voices. It wasn't just the shelling, Caryn realized. Something had happened.

The mess was mostly deserted when Caryn arrived. Janusz and Marwin were nowhere to be seen, and Caryn guessed that she was past regular meal times. She did see one familiar face, though, and she made her way toward him. Captain Toppel was sitting on a bench, his broken leg stretched out in front of him, his metal crutches leaning against a nearby table. When he saw Caryn approaching, he rose at once on his good leg, placing a hand on a table to steady himself.

"Captain, please sit," Caryn said. "You're injured."

Toppel remained standing. "Have you heard the news?"

Caryn shook her head. "What happened? It is the Breas? Something bad?"

Toppel shook his head. "The Breas haven't done anything, and it's nothing bad either — depending who you ask." He took a deep breath. "The president's finally done what Freed and Danzig have been asking him to do for months. There's going to be a draft."

CHAPTER TWELVE

Caryn felt like she was drowning, even though she had seen this coming ever since Brealand declared. Ravencliffe had one thing right: Deugans were not Breas, rushing to die for their Realm with reckless abandon. It was not their way. At some point the stream of volunteers would dry up.

Then again, whether reckless abandon was truly the Brea way, Caryn could not know. Brealand had universal service for men and women alike, which would hardly be necessary if all of their people were scrambling to volunteer. The draft in Brealand was an ordinary fact of life.

Soft, she heard Ravencliffe say, and he was right.

Because as Caryn processed this new horror of the war, she knew, with a mixture of hopelessness and pride, that the people would go along with it.

The north would have no choice; it was their lands the Breas would overrun if their defences broke. The east would be thrilled since the New Empire was in their territory already, and more men were needed to throw them out. The centre would support the draft grudgingly; loyalty to Tomasburg had remained part of its culture since Unification, when it had been Tomas Scheil's power base. There might be protests along the coast, but they would be muted. Nobody would want to appear unpatriotic, and nobody knew where the Brea ships would land when they finally left the north harbours.

Captain Toppel was collecting his crutches with a concerned look.

"Come on, Minister," he said. "We need to get you in touch with the president."

Caryn followed him through the fort's narrow hallways. As they walked, Toppel updated her on the status of their repairs. Seppina was still in bad shape, but the other satellites had been restored to good condition. The damage to the main fort's gunnery had been fully repaired. The moat had been reinforced and the barbed wire replaced. More difficult was repairing the landscape north of the fort, where the wreckage of Brea tanks needed to be removed, and the craters left by both sides' shells needed to be filled in. Freed did not want to leave the Brea soldiers any place to take cover from the fort's guns, should they choose to attack again.

When they reached the communications hub, Toppel led Caryn past the rows of telegraph desks to a cranny at the back of the room, where a rusted old piece of equipment had stood abandoned since Caryn arrived. Toppel winked at Caryn, leaned one crutch against a wall, and balancing on his good foot, gave the machine a sharp pull. To Caryn's surprise, it sprang aside easily.

On the ground where it had once stood was a trapdoor and steps leading down below the fort.

Caryn looked at him questioningly. "Go on." Toppel smiled, but an instinct stopped her. She liked Toppel, and he had been kinder to her than any of the fort's other officers, but after the attack she could not risk being alone with any of them. Besides, if he was truly putting her in touch with the president, why would he be leading her away from the telegraphs? "I'd like you to fetch Hans, if you would," she said. "Or Janusz or Marwin, whoever you can find. I'll need their assistance if I'm to contact the president."

Toppel obeyed without hesitation. "I trust you won't be offended if I send somebody else to do the fetching," he said, glancing at his broken leg, and he hobbled over to the nearest telegraph operator to give him the orders. Caryn liked that. He hadn't just yelled at the man like Freed or Danzig would have done. He was a strange breed of officer.

Toppel moved back to Caryn's side and spoke in a low whisper so that the operators couldn't hear. "I don't blame you," he said. "I would never criticize my commanding officer, of course, but I — would have treated you more kindly, were I in General Freed's position. I understand why you have trouble trusting him, or any of us."

Caryn remained carefully silent. She did need allies, but she just couldn't be certain whether to trust him.

Toppel didn't seem certain either. He hesitated. Then something changed in his eyes, as though he'd made up his mind, and suddenly he was leaning even closer to her, speaking directly into her ear. "Tell Hans to be more careful. He's being watched like a hawk."

"By who?" Caryn breathed.

"Whoever Danzig can get. The point is, Hans has only been at it for a few hours and we already know what he's investigating."

Caryn took a deep breath, trying to keep composed. If that were true, the general would be furious that he hadn't been told the details of the attack. But what if it wasn't true? What if Freed and Danzig were merely wondering what Hans was up to, and they had sent Toppel to trick her into letting it slip?

Luckily, she never needed to respond, because just then the telegraph operator reappeared, Janusz and Marwin in tow. "Sergeant Gert has requested a word with you," the operator said to Toppel, who just rolled his eyes.

"I'd better get going," Toppel said. "Set it up for them. A secure line. General's orders," he lied.

Janusz raised his eyebrows at Caryn, as if to ask what that was all about, but she just shrugged, and they made their way down the steps.

At the bottom they found a surprisingly comfortable room, well-lit with a plush chair, writing table, and a luxury that made Caryn and Janusz gasp.

The fort had a telephone.

Caryn had at least seen telephones before, in Government House and in some of the mansions where she had met with wealthy businessmen or senators, though only twice had she ever spoken into one. Janusz just ogled the device. But Marwin surprised Caryn yet again by going straight to the task of helping the operator set up their call. After the operator left, Marwin went back to the telephone and continued fiddling with it for a few more minutes before grinning and placing the receiver into Caryn's hand. "He encrypted it so the Breas couldn't understand it," he explained. "Now the army can't understand it either."

Caryn thanked Marwin, taking joy in the pride etched on his face. Then she told both of them that they could return to their training. Janusz shot her a look — he would probably be in trouble with his sergeant, and she hadn't actually needed him to do anything, as it turned out — but Marwin seemed eager to return, so Janusz just followed him without comment.

The sound of the president's voice, garbled though it was through the strange machinery, was music to Caryn's ears. Their conversation started with the draft and moved to general news of the war, and to Caryn's discussions with Ravencliffe. She had been afraid that the president would laugh at her, but he didn't. He listened carefully, and when she was finished, he said, "You're fighting an uphill battle, Caryn, but if anybody can pull this off it's you."

"I don't know about that," Caryn said, though the president's confidence meant more to her than he could know. "I'm pretty sure General Freed agreed to it just to get me out of the way."

"Who cares why he agreed to it?" The president snorted. "You've built an entire career on having idiots like Ernst Freed underestimate you. Don't stop now."

"Georg, it's impossible," Caryn said. "Ravencliffe hasn't shown any interest in talking, and I'm not surprised. If you were a prisoner, would you negotiate with your captors when they hold all the power? All the information?" She sighed. "We've got to get him some contact with the outside world, to link him up with the king and queen. It's the only way we can legitimately negotiate, well, anything. But Freed will never agree to that."

"Neither would I, in his shoes. Ravencliffe could pass on all sorts of information about the fort and the garrison." The president paused. "I'll give it some thought. Maybe there's some compromise Freed will accept. The Gods know I need my foreign minister doing some diplomacy, and I can't very well send you to the northern continent."

Caryn's first instinct was to angrily point out that it was the president who'd gotten his foreign minister trapped in the Gods-forsaken Gateway in the first place, but that was soon replaced with confusion. "What's the northern continent got to do with this?"

Caryn could almost hear his exasperation over the phone. "It's our big diplomatic push these days. A few banks just have to call in a loan or two and the entire Brea war effort collapses. We're trying to make them an offer that's too good to refuse."

"They'll refuse it," Caryn said at once. The president was right that certain powers on the northern continent had the power to cripple Brealand, but others could cripple Deugan just as easily. With the immense cost of manufacturing ships, airplanes, artillery and ammunition, and keeping millions of men fed, clothed and armed, no government could hope to keep an army in the field for more than five days on general revenues. Domestic banks and war bonds made up the lion's share of the credit available to the warring governments, but foreign banks also played a pivotal role in keeping both Brealand's and Deugan's armies in the field. "Nobody on the northern continent is going to break with their patrons. The interest on those loans is financing the biggest industrial boom their continent has ever seen. It's a balance of power there, and none of them want to be left behind."

"But all of them want to get ahead," the president replied. "If we can offer one of them a significant advantage over its rivals —"

"Then the rivals might take drastic steps to restore the balance," Caryn said. She was growing increasingly alarmed. "It may drag all of them into this war."

"How can you know that?" The president sounded annoyed.

"I'm your foreign minister," Caryn snapped. "You pay me to know this, when I'm not inspecting military forts." She wouldn't normally be sarcastic with the president, but her panic, familiar and hostile, was returning. She was finding it difficult to think of anything but the chain of causation that was slowly revealing itself to her. "The whole economy of the northern continent is propped up by trade across the oceans. Especially now that our own continent's so unstable that they can't do much business here. They need their sea lanes or they suffocate, so an imbalance in naval strength can be catastrophic for any of them. Say we sponsor one country strongly enough that the others feel threatened. The others ask for Brealand's help and get the whole Brea fleet backing them. Anybody who's still on the fence would have no choice. They rely on the same balance of power."

"So they'd enter on our side," the president said. "Wouldn't they?"

Caryn took a deep breath. It sounded like a good thing on the surface, but she could see where it would lead. How could she make him understand? "If half the northern continent's on our side, and the other half's on Brealand's side, it's not going to end there," she explained. "These people rely on trade. They're going to start going after each other's merchant fleets, and that's going to affect their trading partners across the ocean. But each trading partner has sponsors, and those sponsors have their own sponsors. Our continental war is bad enough, but if we don't stop it, now..."

"Qir Ni," the president breathed. "Koltaja."

"Exactly," Caryn said. "The great powers across the ocean could be drawn in. Probably by funding proxies, dozens of them, so that Qir Ni and Koltaja themselves stay strong while our continent weakens. If the overseas powers stir, this war could engulf the entire world."

There was silence on the other end of the line. Caryn waited desperately for a response, for some indication that the president understood, but the silence just stretched on. She imagined him thinking, *Who cares if it becomes a world war, as long as we win?* She started to despair.

"Georg, this is what we have to do, right now. We have to lay all of this out for the Breas, what the implications are. Their culture's been isolationist for centuries, still is, so they won't like it any more than we do. We have to bring them to the table, get them on the official channels —"

"Caryn." The president's voice was weary now, but firm. "There aren't any official channels."

Caryn felt as though she'd been hit by a shell. "What do you mean?"

"Gods, I should never have sent you up there," the president said. "The Breas closed the official channels. They're furious at us."

"What did we do?" Caryn feared the worst.

"Unrestricted submarines," the president said softly. "The powers of the northern continent aren't the only ones who can attack their rivals' merchant fleets."

"They're mad because we've been sinking commercial ships? After they invaded us?"

"Are you going to make me say it?" The president's voice sounded desperately uncomfortable. "You know how Brealand works. They're all mountain and desert. Half of their food is imported from their island colonies. That's what we've been hitting."

"So stop hitting it!" Caryn shouted. "We're talking about a world war! We need those channels open!"

"We can't," the president shouted back. "Our subs are the only things keeping the Brea fleet in the north harbours. They need their ships close to home to escort their food. The second we let up on them, even slightly, we'll have landings all the way down the coast. I will not trade that for the mere possibility that maybe the Breas will *start* negotiating."

"Georg, think about what you're saying," Caryn begged. "This is their civilian food supply. You are starving their women and children."

"They won't starve as long as their ships are escorted," the president said stubbornly. "What other choice do I have?"

"You can choose to do what's right!"

"It's not about what's right anymore," the president replied. "It's about whether Deugan survives."

"If we win this war by starving their kids, then the Deugan I know *hasn't* survived," Caryn argued.

"Enough," the president said. She could feel his anger radiating through the receiver. "I don't like this any more than you do, but for now, formal channels of communication with Brealand are closed. If we want to stop this war from going global, we'll need to find another way. I'll work on it from my end. We'll reorient our push on the northern continent to try to keep them out of the war. We'll keep the diplomatic corps working on all our initiatives in Orastus and Wassia and the Fringes. I'll do everything I can. I promise."

"And what should I do?" Caryn demanded. Her impotence was only fuelling her rage. "Should I sit up here in the Gateway and wait till our food and coal run out, wait for the Breas' next attack, wait here to die?"

The pause on the other end of the line was longer than Caryn expected. When the president spoke again, his tone was strangely formal. "Caryn Hallom, as Foreign Minister of the Republic of Deugan, I hereby authorize you to negotiate a peace treaty with the Realm of Brealand, which will be subject to the ratification of the Assembly and the Senate. Although formal channels of communication are closed," he added pointedly, "you are hereby authorized to utilize any informal channels that you may uncover."

Ravencliffe, of course. Not ten minutes after she explained why that route was impossible, he was sending her back to Ravencliffe. He was telling her that there was no other way.

"In my capacity as commander-in-chief of Deugan's Armed Forces," the president continued, "I also hereby command General Ernst Freed to give you any support and assistance you find necessary to your endeavours." Then, inexplicably, the president laughed. "That ought to twist the old man's briefs in a knot. Take a photograph of his face when he reads my order, will you? I wish I could be there myself."

As though it were all a joke.

As though the president was simply beyond caring.

*

Caryn spent the rest of the afternoon shut in her quarters. For a time she allowed herself the luxury of crying at the impossibility of her task. Lana had talked about how difficult it was to appear strong and confident, always, without fail, and that was the night before the battle, the night before Lana died.

It was just over a span ago, but it felt like months. It felt like Caryn had been locked in the fort for a lifetime.

Caryn Hallom was slowly dying. Not in a way that Freed or Danzig or Toppel would see, or Janusz or Marwin, or even Georg or Hans, who had known her the longest. Not in a way that won battles or made headlines. It was a slow-acting poison. The life was seeping out of her.

Caryn wondered if Lana would have noticed. Then she wondered if Brenner would. Her one-time best friend. Her lover, fourteen long years ago.

She wondered where he was.

That was when she always knew she had hit her lowest points. When she grasped back for the fantasy she'd had all those years previous, that she and Brenner could have stayed together, peacefully, and all would have been well. She knew that it would not have worked. Professor Terial had been right about that, as about so much else. But sometimes she just needed that comfort, that arm around her shoulder, that security. Now she seemed to have angered Hans and Georg and Janusz all at once.

These low points did not come often. Caryn Hallom had built a life for herself in Deugan, and the old doubts and yearnings had been put aside, or at least suppressed. That they were coming back meant that something was terribly, dangerously wrong.

As though she needed to be told that.

Caryn lay on her bed, looking up at the pockmarked concrete on her ceiling. She barely moved, barely thought, just stared. It was already happening, she realized. So soon, and she, too, was finding it difficult to care.

She thought of Ravencliffe, his piercing eyes, his stern, composed face as he insulted and rambled and ridiculed. What had seemed a brilliant insight in the sanctity of the fort's chapel was now a nightmare. *No god has only one aspect,* she thought ruefully. Caryn wondered if she ought to say a prayer to Eolanis. He was the god of wisdom, so he must also be the god of idiocy.

She lounged in her quarters until she was sure it must be nightfall. Even then, she dragged herself out of bed only through a great force of will. She wandered through the fort's corridors alone, not seeking Hans' protection or any other company, although she was well aware that her would-be assassin was still out there. It was another bad sign of how little she could bring herself to care, about anything.

She found herself in Seppina, which looked dark and abandoned. Though she could see the signs of the repair work their soldiers had been conducting there, the satellite still seemed a total mess to Caryn's eyes. She did not like their chances should the Breas attack again.

Why hadn't they? Perhaps Caryn had been right when she told Ravencliffe that they simply didn't have to. The Breas could wait for the fort to starve, then waltz in when its defenders were too weak to lift their rifles. But maybe, Caryn thought, just maybe, they really were more sentimental than their reputation let on. Maybe the queen really did care so much for her favourite cousin that she was not willing to put Michael Ravencliffe's life at risk. Maybe he had already saved all of them.

Soft, he had whispered. In all of their other interactions, he was trying to intimidate her, or entertain himself, or glean information that he could use against her, but that first exchange was different.

When he mouthed the word *soft*, it seemed that he really was trying to tell her something.

Caryn found herself putting one foot in front of the other on instinct. She knew it was unwise. At least a few soldiers would be guarding the entrances to Seppina and the other satellites. If any of them saw her, it would be the end of her reputation, the end of her career and the end of any hope of success with Ravencliffe. Yet she could not seem to stop herself.

As she'd suspected, Seppina's walls had at least one crack large enough for her to climb through, which was far enough from the actual entrances that the guards there would be unlikely to notice her. She stared at it for a long moment before she realized that sooner or later the crack would be repaired. She may not get another chance. She squeezed through it, wishing that she had the figure of her Jayla days, or even of the thirty-year-old that she should be.

The night was dark. There was no moon in the sky, and the stars were barely visible through the clouds. All the better; there was less chance of being seen. Caryn walked slowly, softly. After all her time in the fort, the feeling of grass beneath her shoes and a breeze on her face were heavenly. There was barbed wire to the north, but not to the east. One foot in front of the other, away from the fort, away from her life.

There was no need to draw a marking or a barrier. One step across its threshold and she was transported into a different world, foreign, mysterious. It was more than the heat, the pressure against her skin, the way her muscles tensed. More than any physical sensation. It was just *different*.

Caryn remembered what it was like to feel that for the first time. It was disturbing, as though an alien organism was trying to force itself into her body through the pores. The energy would surround its victims, press at them, probe, and slowly, slowly seep in. The body's natural defences could hold out against it for twenty-four hours — some people even lasted forty-eight — but soon enough the energy became part of them, part of the air in their lungs, the blood in their veins. Once that happened, they could start to access a part of its power while within the Well's bounds, but each day they stayed they grew weaker and sicker, and when they finally emerged they would be unnaturally aged and unrecognizable.

But when Caryn had left, poisonous though the energy was, she'd felt its absence. It wasn't just that she could no longer use the Well's power. It was the difference in the air. It was something intangible that changed when she stepped across the threshold. Having remained in a Well for more than twenty-four hours, she knew that a piece of the energy would always live inside her, so she could return to a Well and use its power again at any time. Having some energy reside with her, though, was very different from the Wells' total immersion.

The Gateway Well was a landscape entirely its own. The ground beneath Caryn's feet was soft like mud. Ahead of her, beneath the open sky, was a collection of brown stone walls, slopes and valleys, cliffs and ridges. She climbed gingerly over and around them, unthinking, exploring. The energy swirled around her, still disturbing and dangerous but also familiar, and she felt its presence with every step.

At length Caryn came to a jut of rock that barely concealed a gentle slope downward, leading her underground. Her chest started to clench up, remembering the cavern where she'd been trapped. She didn't have to go underground now. She could stay outdoors and still remain in the Well for some time; it stretched for leagues until it ended at the Brea border to the north and the Selliar mountains to the east. Nothing would grow in the Well, but there would be other caves and rock formations to explore, stairs to climb and hills to scale.

Instead she plunged forward ferociously, as though by storming this cavern she could erase the last one.

The ramp twisted and turned as it led downward. Along each side of it, the walls of the cavern glowed orange, like the ones of her childhood, but they were cool to the touch. The ramp levelled off into a corridor that was barely wider than the ramp itself. Yellow and blue lights on the floor guided Caryn's path. She walked aimlessly for a while before finding a flat slab that could serve as a bench. She sat there silently, staring at the cavern, absorbing the Well's power.

She could not tell how long she stayed there, but at last she felt her frustration and despair draining out of her, as though the power itself had leeched it from her blood. She began, slowly but surely, to feel like herself again. The task before her was still overwhelming, but she would not give up without a fight. She would at least meet with Ravencliffe again. She would at least try.

But how could she possibly succeed? How could she ever persuade a prisoner as astute as Ravencliffe to negotiate with his captors, blind to the outside world? Even if she could, how would they ever persuade the Brea government to accept a deal that, for all they knew, had come from manipulation, even torture? General Freed might have given her Ravencliffe to get her out from underfoot, but Caryn now knew she had given herself the job for the same reason. She had been so desperate for something useful to do that she had invented a task, even though she knew how pointless it was.

Her inspiration was fading as quickly as it had come. Caryn did not want to return to the fort at all, not like this, a failure. She did not even want to return to Tomasburg, or to Carrak-on-Sea, the great port city where she had lived when she'd first arrived in Deugan, where she claimed to have been born. She needed hope, she needed —

Suddenly she remembered. How Brenner had given her hope the last time. He had found it in a glimpse of the future, in an image of Caryn standing beneath brilliant sunlight, leagues from the Wassian Well.

She also remembered how the prophecy had almost destroyed Brenner when he misinterpreted it, but she pushed that thought aside. She was stronger than Brenner ever was. Whether her future was good or bad, she wanted to see it.

The problem was that she didn't know how. The Old Empire's legions had used the Wells to learn prophecies before all of their battles, and rumour had it that they never failed to come true. The Old Empire's secrets had been lost to time, though, and while Brenner had rediscovered the technique, his experience had been so traumatizing that she had never wanted to try it herself. But Caryn knew what Brenner had been thinking when he saw his prophecy: he was trying to fulfill a promise he'd made to Jayla, to find her hope. Caryn took a deep breath, carefully cleared her mind, and then turned her spirit toward that search. Hope. Love. The promise that the future might bring.

At first nothing happened, but Caryn remained calm, cleared her mind again, and blindly reached out to the power. She felt the wave of warmth wash over her chest as it touched her; she embraced it, drew it into herself. After several minutes, she carefully brought up a hopeful thought, a dream of herself, pen in hand, signing the treaty that would end the war. When she turned her mind back to the cavern, a hazy vision of her dream still remained at the corner of her consciousness, and she knew that the Well had heard.

Whether the Well would respond was up to it, and Caryn knew it would take some time to decide. She stood from her bench and began walking, following the blue and yellow markings further down the narrow corridor.

When she finally reached a corner, she turned, and suddenly the world started spinning. Caryn lost her footing and plummeted to her knees. The cavern wavered before her eyes and she pitched forward, grabbing her head with her good hand. She squeezed her eyes shut to stop the spinning, but behind her eyes she found new images, flashes of colour that burned into her consciousness and then vanished like wisps of smoke.

A dogsled whipping across a sheet of ice. Throngs of people cheering in Scheil Square. With a gasp she was looking at Brenner, his cowl flung back from his face, his horse's hooves churning up the grass beneath him. A Brea lounged casually in the officers' quarters of the Gateway Fort.

Then Caryn saw herself.

She was lying on the ground, which glowed yellow and blue around her. Soldiers in Deugan uniforms held her by the arms and legs, pinning her down. As she struggled feebly against them, General Freed, his stern face illuminated by the orange glow of the rock walls, hesitated — and then threw his fist into her stomach, again and again and again.

Caryn's eyes flew open. She slumped against the wall of the cavern. She blinked, but the vision would not leave her mind.

She started making plans. She would sneak across the Brea border, or cross the Selliar Mountains into the New Empire, or order Hans to kill the general in his sleep. That was before she realized how pointless it all was.

Caryn had seen this for herself. She had reached out to the energy, and felt it respond. This wasn't a storybook, where prophecies came true only because of what people did to avoid them. The Wells' prophecies were a straight reading of the future. They happened, no matter what.

On the other hand, the prophecy hadn't been entirely negative.

The people cheering in the heart of Tomasburg had looked Deugan, not Brea. That probably meant that Tomasburg, at least, would survive the Brea onslaught long enough for some sort of peace to be reached. But if the Breas took over the fort, commanded the Gateway — if Freed had to attack her...

Caryn sat on the floor and hugged herself, shivering. The power was not an old friend after all. It was sinister and its prophecies would destroy her, as they had almost destroyed Brenner. She could not allow herself to sink into despair the way he had. Deugan needed her. She had to find a way to bring herself back from the brink.

Brenner.

Slumped against the glowing rock walls of the Well, hope all but lost, Caryn found herself, without even thinking about it, pulling herself into the place she had shared with him, the special place where they had shared their first kiss, and where he had held her so many times afterward. Where they would retreat together when it all became too much to handle. The rocks stopped glowing. The blue and yellow signposts along the ground faded to black. After a few moments the columns erupted around her, mauve and teal and amber and jade and silver. She reached for them and sent them erupting into sparks and fountains and comets. She wished Brenner were here with her again. She wished she wasn't alone.

But she wasn't.

She sensed the man without seeing him. His presence surrounded her, unmistakeable. Caryn's eyes darted around the corridor. There was nobody there. Caryn stood, wary, her breathing shallow in the warm air of the Well, searching for him, wondering if she had finally gone insane, ready to flee —

An invisible arm closed around her. Caryn screamed and stumbled as its grasp grew tighter. She pressed forward, further on down the corridor, trying to escape. Its grip around her waist loosened, and for a second she thought she was free, until it closed tightly around her right arm. Caryn screamed again and tried to pry herself loose with her left hand, but it was still bound up uselessly in its sling. Caryn scraped her right arm against the wall of the cavern, but her assailant passed through the wall as though it were made of air.

The invisible hand pressed into her arm, once, twice, three times, now shorter, now longer, as Caryn desperately tried to shake it off. She broke into a run. Squeeze, again, again. Repeating, ever repeating.

Caryn's eyes grew wide and she stopped short. She wasn't being attacked at all. She listened, intrigued, to the sequence of squeezes on her arm. There was a pattern to them, and what was more, she recognized it. Professor Terial had drilled sailor's code into her, back in the Wassian Well. "If you're going to pretend to be from the Deugan coast, you need to know this like the back of your hand." Now, panting, Caryn calmed the frantic beating of her heart and waited for the sequence to begin again. A pattern of squeezes, longer and shorter, methodical, spelling out the words, "Who are you?"

What would she answer to that? She took deep breaths, trying not to panic. This was her special place with Brenner. How could some intruder be here, demanding who she was? Brenner had discovered this place. Who else could know of it?

Could it be Brenner himself? Caryn almost threw caution to the wind and declared herself then and there, grasping at the hope that her childhood friend had come back to her in her darkest hour. Caryn was confident Brenner wouldn't harm her, even if he had become a Steffian. But she couldn't know for certain that Brenner was here with her now. Brenner had taught Caryn how to reach this place, and he could just as easily have taught it to someone else. He was the Master of Secrets. Surely this presence was one of his students, a Steffian who would as soon cut her throat as look at her.

The squeezes continued, persistent, but growing fainter. "Who are you?" She couldn't identify herself as Caryn Hallom, or as a Deugan. What could she say that would mean something to Brenner, but nothing to his protégés?

The grip on her arm loosened. She was about to lose her chance. Now she was the one grasping for the other hand, but it slipped away from her, dissolving into sand, running out between her fingers. The columns surrounding her faded and the corridor started to brighten. She stretched with all her might and barely caught a piece of it, a fingertip, clinging weakly, slipping as she coded in a single word.

CHAPTER THIRTEEN

Matthias's head was spinning as he reeled away from the power. Who was she? And how much did she know?

He took a deep breath, then methodically checked his precautions. The door of the room was firmly locked. The lone window was shut and fastened. A wire lay across the windowsill, connected to a small glass bulb that would fall and shatter if the wire was tripped. A rifle, primed and loaded, lay on the ground beside his bed; a pistol was tucked into one of the three belts that encircled his waist. Each of the belts was woven with *acambro*, ready to be unleashed. Matthias could feel the power screaming inside them. It did not enjoy captivity.

That was what made Matthias so uneasy. Not the mysterious woman who had shown up in his mapping, not how vulnerable they would be in the distant west, not even the prospect of traversing Orastus proper, where they were all wanted as terrorists. What scared Matthias more than he could say was that the power might grow to hate him for the *acambro*. That it might abandon him, and that Good Steif might abandon him too, if he hadn't already.

Matthias sat on the bed, staring at the closed door. This was his chance. Not only had he been chosen to go west, he would be protected the entire time. The operation would depend utterly on Secrets, and Matthias, with his years of training under Master Nono, was one of its most skilled users. The Steffians could not afford to lose him. Yet it was difficult to feel hopeful. It was difficult to imagine that this was the route Good Steif would want him to take.

Matthias wished Master Nono was with him. He was not like the other Steffians. He would talk through Matthias's doubts, rather than treating them as a mark of disloyalty. He would know about the woman in the mapping and whether she was a threat. Nono was camped in the jungle, though, beyond the town limits and off any major road. He was not far, but not near enough.

For now the town was silent, but Matthias knew that their operation had already begun. At several drop-offs throughout the colony of Kalid, belts and shirts and sandals interwoven with *acambro* were being packaged into cloth sacks and readied for transit. The stashes had been accumulated over several months, smuggled from a hidden facility on the colony's eastern border. It had been moved little by little, so as not to draw unwanted attention. The New Empire could never know.

It helped that the New Empire's patrols rarely ventured as far into Kalid as the facility. It was, from what Matthias had heard, a place the Imperial troops were wise to avoid. Waves of hot air washed over it incessantly, intensifying the humidity of the Kalidi jungle. Nightmares and visions were said to plague the inhabitants; rashes too, and sicknesses. Matthias had never seen the facility, but he could imagine. It was on the edge of a Well that he knew from his mapping, the one column of light that always shone brighter than the others. The Well stretched for hundreds of leagues on a north-south axis, defining the eastern extremity of the Fringes of the New Empire, and it was there the *acambro* grew.

And there it belonged. Matthias saw that now, clear as day. He stood beside the bed, clasped his hands to his heart and began whispering the prayers he had learned from his father years ago. The ritual was comforting, but too soon it was over, and Matthias was left alone but for the power straining furiously against the *acambro* belts.

"Good Steif, my lord," Matthias whispered, "I come before you humbly, seeking your favour, begging your guidance. I pray you turn your face kindly upon me, for I am your creation and your servant." Those were the traditional words. To go further, Matthias would need to use his own. "My lord, I — I have wasted these last years of my life. I have fought and killed and — and betrayed you. Gone against everything you stand for. I was lost, and confused, and young. I've been trying to find a way out, a way to change." The words started flowing uncontrollably. Matthias was glad the others were too distant to hear. "I was stupid, and I'm no smarter now, but I want —

I need — something. Something safe, something free, but I'm hanging everything on reaching a country that may not even exist anymore by the time I get there."

He felt tears coming to his eyes, and he wiped them away furiously. What would the others think of him? Even Nono would not take kindly to weakness. "Good Steif, my lord, if this operation succeeds, a centuries-long dream will be achieved. The Steifar will have their own country. A land to call our own, which we have never had throughout our entire history. But to do it, to get there, people will die. Many of them. Depending how they all react, we could end the war quickly, but we could also extend it, drag it out, meaning more and more people ... and then, if Nono's right about what the *acambro* can do..."

Matthias trailed off. Was Nono right? And even if he were, would the power cooperate? Or would it be too angry?

And what of the one god? The Wells were sacred. They had been created by Good Steif as a sign of the wonder and mystery with which he had infused the world. His most faithful could learn to understand his Secrets, even to use them, but never to control them. Never, despite Nono's title, to master them. But wasn't confining the power in the *acambro* dangerously close to an attempt at mastery? Matthias's thoughts drifted back to Pellor Amad's speech in the woods outside Tel Sukayam. The Master had spoken of Rao, the spirit sent by Good Steif to guard the world, who had betrayed his lord and set himself up as a god instead. Rao had been struck down and destroyed for his pretensions, his temple in Villasud, in the south of Wassia, smashed and broken. Now the Steffians were trying to own Good Steif's power. Matthias felt deeply uncomfortable.

"My lord," Matthias said softly, "please, I beg of you, guide me, show me the way. Please forgive me for what I have done in the past, and for what I am about to do. I promise that if I can escape the Steffians and the New Empire, I will be a better person, and I will continue to dedicate my life to you, as I have always wanted to do, but never knew how." Matthias thought, but he couldn't find anything more to say. He lay down on the floor beside the bed. Flat on his back, eyes closed. Often he would feel the presence of the one god when he did this, and an answer to his prayers would appear in his thoughts. But this time exhaustion simply overwhelmed him, and he drifted off to sleep.

In his dreams, Matthias was wandering the Kalidi Well, something no man had ever done, ever could do. Flesh, blood, even metals would wither under the unique intensity of its power. That was why the *acambro* plants had remained hidden for so many centuries. They did not grow in any of the Continent's other Wells, and the boundaries of the Kalidi Well could never be breached by a breathing human being. Deugan or Brealand, perhaps, might have been more active in attempting to gain access to the Kalidi Well had it been located in their territories, but instead it was dominated by the New Empire, which controlled several more accessible Wells it could study at will.

It was not until the last few years, with the development of modern steel alloys, mechanical tools that could deploy them from outside the Kalidi Well, and the gathering of all of these tools in a facility that was camouflaged into the jungle to hide it from the New Empire's eyes, that the Steffians could actually manage to extract the *acambro*. Even more years had passed before the *acambro* could be studied and its potential understood.

Yet in Matthias's dream he was wandering the Kalidi Well nonetheless, naked and alone. The heat was oppressive, the sweat rolling down his body in droves. He heard a woman's voice, faintly, but when he moved toward it his arm brushed an *acambro* vine, and it coiled around him and squeezed, again and again, spelling out words in sailor's code that Matthias could not understand. So engrossed was he in puzzling out the meaning of the code that he barely noticed the *acambro* growing tighter around him, vines and leaves intertwined, choking.

A crash of glass.

No sooner had Matthias's eyes flung open than his pistol was in his hand, pointed straight at the window. He heard the sound of gunfire and flattened himself to the ground, sheltering himself behind the bed as he flicked off the safety. He raised his eyes back to the window and fired two shots, just as the soldier tried to swing through. Matthias's second shot took him in the foot and he crashed onto the bed.

The man kept his grip on his gun at first, but before he could get another shot off, Matthias had grabbed his wrist and slammed it into a bedpost. As the soldier's gun clattered to the floor, Matthias fired a shot in the direction of a second soldier who had appeared at the window. He missed but startled the soldier enough to make his shot miss as well. Matthias dove off the bed as he fired another shot at the window. A bullet passed over his head, so close that the wind from it made his hair stand on end. Matthias's next shot caught the soldier in the head, and he stumbled out of view before the one who was already in the room slammed a shoulder into him. Matthias fell heavily to the ground just before the soldier landed on him, pinning him down and wrestling for his pistol. The soldier was stronger than him, and in a better position too, and soon Matthias felt the pistol wrested from his grasp —

— there was a flash of metal, and the soldier pitched forward and shot wildly. He was trying to scream, but when he opened his mouth only blood came out. Khayri strode over casually from the doorway, retrieved the knife from the soldier's neck and slit his throat with it. Matthias stared at him, panting. "A knife?" he asked incredulously.

Khayri shrugged. "Why waste bullets? Come on."

Matthias gathered his rifle and his pack, and they crept out the door, down a hallway and around a corner. They looked over a railing into the common room of the inn. It was pandemonium. Imperial soldiers were pressing through, knocking over tables and shouting, sometimes pushing people up against walls while others ran for the exits. "Where are the others?" Matthias asked Khayri. His friend Jakim from the operation in Ciorala had been with them, and Matthias hoped he was safe.

"They made it out," Khayri said. "They're waiting at the rendezvous. As for us, we'll never get through that common room. We have to get out the fire escapes."

"But the soldiers have the catwalk," Matthias objected. "That's how they got into my room."

"Can't you use some Secrets?" Khayri asked.

"Nono told us not to. Unless it got really desperate. We don't want the empire to know what our weapon is." That was true, but Matthias also worried that the power might not work for him in any event. He hadn't had the presence of mind to try it back in his room, but the energy might have chosen to help him of its own accord, and it hadn't. He thought of the woman again.

Matthias and Khayri rounded the upper level of the inn and came to a door far from the rooms where the Steffians had been staying. Khayri slammed a shoulder into it and it flung open. The room was empty, but the bed was overturned and the drawers were open. The soldiers had been here.

Matthias stepped to the window. "Only two of them on the ground," he said, "and there's a railing we can slide down. As long as nobody else notices us."

Khayri shook his head. "We need Nono and his boys in here. The empire already knows where we are, and the streets are crawling."

"So we need to go, now," Matthias said. Khayri still hesitated. Then Matthias got an idea. "The empire knows we're here, but they don't know how many more of us are in town. For all they know, we have a team two blocks down, ready to take them in the rear." He pointed out the window, at the two soldiers stationed on the street below. "Line them up. You take the one on the left. I've got the right. On my mark."

So desperate was the energy to escape the *acambro* that Matthias had no sooner turned his mind to it than a beam shot into the sky, exploding like a firework two streets away. They heard the commotion almost immediately as soldiers rushed toward the flare. The two men directly below them hadn't moved, but they had turned their heads toward the firework. "Mark!" Matthias shouted. The rifles fired and the two men crumbled, and Khayri and Matthias were racing down the railing and away from the inn, in the opposite direction of the soldiers who were chasing their flare. Matthias could only hope that Nono had seen the flare and would be chasing it too.

The rendezvous was a rickety shed leaned up against a fence at the end of a row of wooden shacks. Matthias saw to his relief that Jakim was there with one other man whose name Matthias couldn't remember. A fifth member of the team was missing. "Where's Ibram?" Khayri demanded.

"Dead," Jakim said. "We ran into a group of soldiers on our way here. Escaped over a fence, but he got shot in the back. We had to leave him."

"Do you know why they stopped chasing us?" the other man asked.

Khayri smiled. "It's a Secret," he said. "What's been happening?"

"No idea," Jakim said, "but the empire's swarming the town. We must have got snitched on."

"If they know about this transfer point, they could know about all of them," Khayri replied.

"Could be," Jakim said. "With all these soldiers around, we can't exactly wait at the town post office for a telegram to come through."

"What about the facility?" Matthias said. That was what worried him.

"Don't know," Jakim said, "but if they've found even three of the transfer points, they'll find the facility soon enough."

"Then our mission's done before it gets started," Matthias said.

"We don't know that yet," Jakim pointed out. "It might take them awhile to find the facility, we can get a lot of *acambro* out before they do. The other drop-off points might still be safe. And maybe we can save this one."

"Right," Khayri said, taking charge. "That's why we're here in the first place. Let's go." Their inn was down the street from the cellar where the *acambro* was being stored, squarely on the route to the jungle hideout where Nono and his troops were waiting. Their mission had been to protect the shipment, in case something exactly like this happened.

"Did you see how many of them were in the streets?" the other man argued. "We're never going to fight them all off."

"We don't have to," Khayri said. "We've gotten a signal off to Nono. We just have to hold them until he can join us."

Khayri led the others out of the shed, and they crept along the streets toward the storage cellar. They had to take a roundabout route to avoid the Imperial soldiers, passing alongside wood cabins with thatched roofs, small wire pens holding pigs or goats, and some places where broad-leaved jungle plants encroached and almost seemed to swallow the settlement. The day was hot, and although the sun was still rising, Matthias was sweaty by the time they reached their destination.

The empire had found the place first. A team of soldiers, thirty or more, ringed a small door set in a large stone building. A firefight had broken out between the soldiers and a few Steffians stationed in the upper levels of the home, and in the alleys on either side of the building.

The men in the alleys were falling fast. Khayri pressed a finger to his lips, then pointed at the roof of a shorter building opposite the home. Matthias saw them at once. Imperial snipers had taken over the roof and were firing down at the Steffians. A wave of anger rushed through him. Their men didn't stand a chance.

It was that shorter building that Khayri, Matthias and the others ran for. They easily dispatched the two soldiers guarding the door, then locked it behind them and thundered up its steps toward the roof. The man whose name Matthias had forgotten was the first one onto the roof; two bullets struck him almost immediately, and he staggered backward, but by then Matthias and Khayri had made it through the breach, guns blazing. Two soldiers went down before a bullet took Khayri in the shoulder, forcing him to drop his rifle. In a fluid motion, he yanked out his knife with his other hand and hurled it at his assailant, burying it in the soldier's throat.

By that time the two snipers had stood, their sniper rifles forgotten but their pistols at the ready. One of their bullets grazed Matthias's arm, which erupted in pain. Khayri was shot again while trying to retrieve his knife, but Jakim was able to take out one of the men while Matthias finished off the other.

Jakim ran over to Khayri, who was lying on his side and groaning. Matthias saw Jakim hovering over the other man, touching him, whispering to him. Khayri tried to respond, but his voice was weak. Matthias placed his hand on his heart and reached out to Good Steif, asking the one god to lend Khayri his strength.

It was not enough. At length Jakim muttered, "He's done." Biting his lip, Jakim lowered his gaze, whispered a prayer, and put his pistol to Khayri's head. Khayri grasped Jakim's hand and thanked him before the trigger was pulled.

While Jakim went looking for the other Steffian who'd been shot, Matthias peered over the edge of the roof. The soldiers on the ground had noticed the commotion above, and some were firing up at him, but most of them were pounding down the door of the stone house. The resistance seemed to have ended, and it was only a matter of time before the door caved in. Matthias flattened himself against the roof to make himself less of a target and fired his rifle into the street below, but he wasn't certain he was actually hitting anything.

The door across the way caved in with a crash, and three of the soldiers had rushed in when an explosion rocked the cellar and the men disappeared. Matthias smiled. The steps had been booby-trapped, which meant the resistance wasn't over yet. Matthias saw the soldiers regrouping in front of the cellar, most of them standing back, while two of them fired canisters through it. It only took him a second to realize what they were doing. He had heard about the front, how the New Empire had launched poison gas at the Deugans. Bad enough in open trenches, Matthias thought, but this was even crueller. Firing the canisters into an unventilated basement — anybody who wasn't killed would be forced to stumble out the front door, choking and gagging, right into the path of the empire's rifles.

Flash! Matthias's body went numb, then Nono appeared, his cowl over his head, the town stretched out before him. Matthias flung back a vision of the street below him, then crawled toward Jakim. "Nono's almost here. We have to keep them off the *acambro* for just a few more minutes."

"We have to keep them off us!" Jakim shouted back. They could hear pounding beneath them as the soldiers battered at the door to their building. "Search the dead soldiers, we need more ammo."

Matthias rushed to obey. He grabbed new rifles off the first two he searched. Then he came upon one man who had grenades strapped to his arm. "Jackpot," he said, passing one of them to Jakim. "One for you, one for me." With that he ran back to the edge of the roof, pulled out the pin on his grenade, and lobbed it into the street below.

He was just in time. The explosion went off, throwing the street into chaos, just as the first Steffians made their stumbling way out of the cellar. Matthias looked down to see a tangle of limbs and bodies littering the street. The men emerging from the cellar seized the opportunity, drawing guns and knives and hacking at the soldiers as Matthias fired round after round into the street.

Behind him, Matthias heard Jakim shout, "They're in the staircase!" Matthias wheeled around to see Jakim open the door to the staircase and toss his grenade into it. A glance back at the street told him that the surviving soldiers had regrouped, forcing the straggling Steffians to retreat into the alleys. The soldiers started toward the cellar again —

— and a squadron of Steffians stormed into their rear, pistols firing. The Imperial soldiers turned too late, scrambling, screaming, dying. Nono had made it! But where was he?

"Matthias!" Jakim shouted. "They're still in the stairs. I need you!" Matthias turned and kneeled, his rifle trained on the doorway.

The assault never came. Instead they heard gunfire on the stairs below, and when it fell silent, Jakim opened the door to receive the Master of Secrets. The street below had gone quiet too, and Steffian fighters were already venturing into the cellar to retrieve the *acambro*, urine-soaked rags around their faces to protect them from the noxious gas. Matthias shuddered. As close as he had come to dying on this rooftop, he was glad that wasn't his task.

Nono filled them in as they made their way down to the street. All of the *acambro* transfer points had cable links nearby, and four of the seven had sent coded cables to the facility almost simultaneously, warning of Imperial raids. A rider from the facility had conveyed the news to Nono. He and Matthias had just saved the fifth drop-off, but they had no word from the other two. The empire hadn't yet located the facility when the rider left, but anything could have happened since.

They reached the street, and Nono exchanged some words with Rusul, a tall Steffian who Matthias knew as one of Master Gamoy's favourites. Clearly, Gamoy wanted one of his own men watching over Nono. Matthias thought of all the times Nono had complained about the infighting and politics within the Steffian organization, about how easy it would be for their brothers to tear the entire movement apart.

"If four of our drop-off points have fallen, we won't have enough *acambro*," Nono was saying. "We need to go there and get as much out as possible."

"But what if they've reached the facility?" Rusul argued. "They must have by now. We have twenty-five men, what are we going to do?"

"Maybe they're not there yet, and we can help defend it," Nono said. "If not, Matt and I can blow the place. But we haven't heard from them, and we need to know."

Rusul hesitated, then sounded resigned. "Damn it, you're right. We can't let them capture the facility, and I don't want to blow it if our own men are still inside." He clenched his fist. "May Good Steif protect all of us."

The trek through the jungle was long and tiring. The air was so humid that Matthias's clothes were plastered to his body within minutes, and he was sweating so profusely that he feared he would drown in it. The mood was tense. They all knew they could not abandon the facility, but they were afraid of what they might find when they got there.

Still, Matthias could not deny the beauty of this place. The jungle was alive with the singing of birds and the howling of monkeys. Green leaves draped overhead and tangled with one another, brightly coloured mushrooms grew from the sides of tree trunks and red and yellow flowers burst from bushes. At another time, in another life, this might have been one of the most peaceful places Matthias had ever seen.

At one point in the afternoon, when they stopped for a rest and some water, Matthias drew Master Nono away from the others and recounted what had happened the night before while he was mapping. "How do we know that's the first time she's spied on us?" Matthias asked. "Could she be the one who tipped off the Orastans?"

"I doubt that," Nono replied. "Where did you say she was again?"

Matthias thought, trying to remember where in the map he had felt her presence. "Gateway," he said. "So she's a Deugan, or a Brea. But her name didn't sound like either of those."

Nono straightened. "She gave you her name?"

Matthias nodded. "It was hard to pick up. We were losing our connection, and I could feel her slipping away, but I'm pretty sure she called herself Jaya."

"Or Jayla?"

"Could have been."

Nono gave a deep sigh in what sounded like relief. "That's incredible. She's alive."

"You know her?"

"Knew her," Nono corrected. His voice had changed. Softened. "She was a friend from another life. Long before I joined the Steffians. You said she was at the Gateway Well?"

"Yes, Master."

"Good," Nono said. He lowered his eyes. "That's good. I've been trying to keep tabs on her, but I lost touch, and with Deugan at war, I feared —" He stopped and glared at Matthias. "You will speak of this to no one."

"Of course, Master," Matthias said. "How could I? You've barely told me anything about her."

"I barely know anything about her anymore," Nono said. Then he added, sadly, "I'm not certain I ever did. But there may yet be time." He took another breath. "Matt, you'll tell me if you hear from her again, won't you? I may try to map and reach her myself, I haven't thought it all through yet, but — you will tell me?"

"I will," Matthias replied. He didn't feel any less confused. "Master, there was something about her. Her relationship with the energy. She felt uncertain, like she didn't know quite what was happening, but at the same time, she was so — well, *powerful* is the wrong word, but she had such a connection. You could tell the energy would do anything for her. Things it would never do for us, things that you and I have never even dreamed of." He hesitated. "Master, are you entirely certain she's not — dangerous?"

Nono smiled. "Always remember this, my friend. Any man who wants his women easy and his fights exciting has it backwards. You *want* your women dangerous — and you want your operations safe and simple. But we've failed at that today, haven't we." He grimaced. "We'd better get moving."

It was late in the afternoon when they reached the outskirts of the facility. As their advance scouts returned, it quickly became apparent that they had arrived too late. The New Empire had surrounded the facility, hundreds of men blocking the entrances and exits. So far the facility's guns had kept the attackers at bay, but with the soldiers' sheer advantage in numbers, overrunning the facility was only a matter of time.

The Steffian scouts fanned out, searching the area while keeping out of sight of the Imperial cordon. Eventually one of their scouts found another team of Steffians nearby and led the twenty-five to them.

The others had been manning an *acambro* drop-off point buried deep in the jungle, a place that would be impossible to find unless you knew exactly what to look for. Evidently the Imperial soldiers had known what to look for, because they had stormed it efficiently and ruthlessly. The Steffians were hopelessly outgunned and had retreated back toward the facility early on, where they had linked up with the facility guards and helped them sneak out as much *acambro* as possible. "We got a lot out," their commander said, "but the noose just tightened and we were forced to run. We only have fifty men who survived. The empire will have the facility by nightfall."

Rusul shook his head. "We have to blow it."

"Why?" the other commander asked. "They already know we're hoarding *acambro*. They raided enough of the drop-off points."

"But they may not know what the *acambro* is or what it does," Nono said, "and even if they figure that out, they still won't know how we harvested it, how we infused it, how we plan to use it. If we let them find all of the tests we've done — the last thing we want is for the empire to develop this weapon themselves."

"There are a lot of conventional weapons stocked in the facility too," Rusul said. "I wish we could get them out, but since we can't, Master Gamoy would have a fit if they fell into Imperial hands."

"How are we going to blow the place if we can't get inside?" the other commander asked.

"Nono says he can do it," Rusul replied, not bothering to call him *Master*.

"I think we can," Nono said softly. "How far are we from the centre of the facility?"

"About a league. Maybe one and a half."

"Perfect. Have any of your men trained in Secrets?" A few hands went up among the gathering, the older-looking ones. Nono nodded. "We'll need your help. The rest of you, you'll need to protect us. The power is going to resist what I'm planning to do, so I don't know how long it will take, and we'll be very vulnerable. There will be coloured columns of light stretching from the jungle floor up to the sky. The empire will know exactly where we are."

"You never make things easy, do you, Nono?" Rusul said.

"I never make things one way or another," Nono replied calmly. "It is Good Steif's doing. Always."

As the other Steffians dug a makeshift trench and set up a couple of machine guns that they had salvaged from the facility, Nono took aside the men who were trained in Secrets and explained the plan. At once Matthias realized the Master was right: this was not going to be easy. First they would have to tap into their own *acambro* and drain all of the energy out of it, until the *acambro* withered and died. That would be the easy part, since the energy would be eager to escape. The hard part would be controlling all of that energy and funnelling it into other *acambro* in the heart of the facility, a league or more away, *acambro* that was already bursting at the seams with more energy than it was ever meant to hold. If they fed enough energy back into the *acambro*, Nono said, they would overload it, causing it to explode. Matthias had his doubts. Whether that type of explosion was even possible — and if so, whether it would be strong enough to take down the entire facility — was anybody's guess.

When their preparations were complete, Rusul led the group in a prayer, and while Matthias bowed his head with the others, the words he whispered to the one god were his own. "Good Steif, I beg of you, forgive me for what I have done today, and for what I am about to do. And if you do see fit to allow me to leave this place and reach Deugan, please let them forgive me as well." But the words were ashes in his mouth. How would the Deugans ever forgive him for all that he had done? How would he forgive himself?

Matthias thought back on his day. He had personally killed at least ten men between the fighting in the inn and the firefight on the rooftop. They were all soldiers, no civilian kills at least, but all Matthias could think of was how easy it had been. Despite all of his doubts and misgivings, when the time had come to fight he had turned into a killer again, unhesitating, ruthless — and good at it! Of everything he had ever accomplished in his life, the two things he was best at were still Secrets and killing. He wondered if that was all he was. If he was, at his core, nothing more than a Steffian terrorist.

Now he was about to set off another bomb. As Nono slipped all of them into the map and the columns of light emerged around them, Matthias oriented himself and then scanned the Gateway Well, searching for a sign of the woman who had called herself Jayla. He found nothing. Only the other Steffians were with him.

Nono highlighted a tiny, glimmering fleck of light that would become their bomb. It was barely visible, nearly consumed by the column that represented the Kalidi Well. Quickly they got to work, draining their *acambro*, feeding it into the *acambro* in the facility.

It was as difficult as Matthias had anticipated. The energy did not want to go, and it could not be forced. Matthias found himself whispering to it, coaxing it as he might a scared child. Slowly, bit by bit, the energy started to move, but struggling, hesitant. As though Matthias was betraying it. Maybe he was.

After about half an hour the first soldiers arrived and fell easily to the Steffian bullets. Matthias felt the power slipping away from him, and he struggled to calm his heart and open it to allow the energy back in. It screamed at him and resisted, but he remained calm, guided it toward the facility, and it went. The speck of light was starting to glow, to change colours. It was working.

A wave of Imperial soldiers crashed into their position. The Steffian machine guns blazed, firing their chain belts into the attackers, who screamed and collapsed. Some of their bullets took the defenders in the chests or shoulders or heads, and then there was a shout of "Grenade!" and the Steffians were clearing the ground, diving for cover. When the dust cleared, one end of the makeshift trench had collapsed entirely, burying several of their men and one of their machine guns beneath it. Two Steffians continued firing the other one, mowing the soldiers down, while other Steffians took to the trees to fire at them from above. Nono screamed at the other Secrets-users to leave and help the defence. Matthias and Nono would have to finish the job on their own.

Matthias was certain the Imperial soldiers would be flooding over the collapsed side of the trench now, but instead they hung back, retreating out of range of the remaining machine gun. The bulk of their force was still storming the facility, Matthias realized, and they hadn't spared enough troops for the Steffians. Matthias and Nono struggled, coaxing the energy, guiding it. Sweat was rolling down their faces in the hot jungle air, and Matthias felt the additional heat, the waves of power that rolled off the Kalidi Well so close to the facility. The *acambro* light was glowing dangerously, now red, now orange, blinking brighter than the others. Through the trees, in the fading light of the day, Matthias saw a line of Imperial soldiers marching toward their position. Rifles fired, the machine gun rattled through its chain, the shouts and screams of battle swept down on them. The soldiers had almost reached them. He turned to the power and through the map, he felt Nono doing the same, felt the power reacting...

A massive explosion thundered through the jungle, drowning out all other sound, all other thought. Mounds of debris hurled through the air, and Matthias flattened his body against the ground for protection. The blast roared as though it would never end. Trees shuddered and fell. A body was blown from the ground and landed with a thud at Matthias's feet, blood spraying. Then the gust of wind screamed over Matthias's head, chilling him to the bone.

When it was finally over, Matthias pushed himself to his knees and looked around to see that Nono had done the same. Most of the other Steffians had made it. They were far enough from the blast. But some of the Imperial soldiers just a few yards away were not so lucky.

Rusul crawled over to them, his face pale. "What happened?" he demanded. "Didn't you set that bomb a league and a half from here?"

Nono coughed and panted. Matthias looked at the other Steffians, taking in their shock, their fear. Matthias swallowed hard as he tried to meet their eyes. *Steif forgive us*, he thought as bile rose in his throat, *what did we just do?*

CHAPTER FOURTEEN

Today, having been flooded with newsreel footage of the atomic bomb that exploded over the Dolshoi Republic, the acambro *bombs that terrified our parents' generation seem almost quaint. True, the bombs did not come with radiation that plagued residents for years afterward, nor were they accompanied by the striking visual effect of a mushroom cloud. What they did bring with them was utter devastation of everything in a league-wide radius. Not enough to destroy an entire city, perhaps, but it would take only one or two well-placed bombs to ravage a downtown core.*

Consider this as well. Today's nuclear weapons are in the hands of major powers with intense rivalries: Qir Ni, Koltaja and the like. These countries have no incentive to engage in nuclear warfare, knowing the retaliation it would invite. The Great War's acambro *bombs, on the other hand, were produced by the Steffian Army of Dignity. Since* acambro *leaves could be sewn into belts and clothing, stuffed in knapsacks or purses, even hidden in plain sight among other plants, they were the perfect terrorist weapon, virtually undetectable. The question was not whether the bombs would be used, but where, and when.*

And nobody had the answers.

— Emilio Gallinari, "Explosive Secrets: *Acambro* Bombs and the Transformation of the Steffian Movement," *Continental History Magazine* (1738)

His frame was lean and fit, and the muscles in his arms bulged beneath his uniform, but what Caryn noticed most were his eyes.

They were dark and hard. They were eyes that had seen too much, that had faced the fire.

"So Bogg goes down," the soldier said, "and we ain't got a leader no more. We see where the shot came from, but we don't know how many they are. But we see the flames too, lickin' round the door, and we know they gotta leave sometime. So Gall comes up with the plan." His eyes darted over to Hans now, betraying a hint of fear. "Gall says we flush 'em out, right? Like an animal, y'know, scare 'em so they run into the real trap. So we set an ambush in another hallway, the way they gotta go if they take the back way out."

Caryn imagined the Brea soldiers, as young as their own, trapped in the food storage room during the battle. She pictured the smoke swirling thick and heavy around them, knowing the Deugans were coming through the front way, running from the grenades that Gall was hurling at them, never guessing he was perfectly alone.

"They run right into the trap. Right where we want 'em, only there's still too many. Ten of 'em or so, and only the four of us. We get most of 'em by surprise, but man, the guys are falling right in front o' me. Bleedin' like nobody's business, and all I can think is keep shootin', keep shootin'." He looked like he was going to be sick from the memory. "So I keep shootin' until Gall shows up and finishes 'em. An' then, after all the fun's over, that's when the six guys from upstairs finally show, so they help us get the fire out."

"So it's just you and Gall who survived out of the six who went down with me," Caryn said softly.

The soldier nodded. "And all six of us stuck together the whole time. I swear that on my life, and on the four who didn't make it."

"You didn't see anybody else down there?"

He shook his head. "'Course, I wasn't in the rear. That was Adel. He's the one who woulda seen anythin', only he didn't make it."

Hans locked eyes with the soldier. "Tell the foreign minister how you found her," he said. "About the revolver."

The soldier nodded, looking uncomfortable. "Well, m'lady, we're on our way back to the comm hub to report, and we see you just lyin' there, and you're hurt, and we're checkin' you out, and Gall says, look Bart, d'you know the Sorceress has a gun? Beggin' your pardon, m'lady," he added quickly, "but that *is* what Gall says."

Caryn wasn't sure whether she wanted to laugh or cry. She fought back the feeling. "Go on."

The soldier took a breath. "So we both look at the gun, an' it's a Deugan gun, sure, but it's military issue, not one a civvy would have. An' not jus' that, but it's older, y'know? Like, not by a lot, but it went out o' standard issue two, three years ago? So I say, that's damn strange, and Gall says, we better take it to the cap'n."

Caryn leaned forward. "So you did? You picked up the gun?"

"Gall did."

"With his bare hands?"

The soldier just looked at her, confused. "Sure."

"And what happened?"

"Nothin' happened. He just picks it up, an' we give it to the cap'n."

"Which one?"

"Malitz. An' that's the last I know of anythin'."

Caryn looked at Hans, who nodded. "Thank you, Private," she said. "Soon to be Private-First-Class, I'm sure. This was very helpful." The soldier stood and saluted. She returned the gesture awkwardly, and he left.

"I spoke to Gall too," Hans said when the other man had gone. "Separately. Their stories match up. I believe them."

"So do I," Caryn said. "Whoever attacked me wasn't one of those six. There must have been someone else down there, hiding. Have you spoken to Malitz yet?"

Hans shook his head. "I'm a private now, remember? I can chat with the other soldiers, but if I start asking questions to a captain, people will notice."

"They may have already noticed," Caryn muttered, remembering Captain Toppel's warning. Toppel had accused Major Danzig of watching Hans' movements, but Caryn doubted that Danzig did anything without General Freed's approval. And why had Toppel given her that warning in the first place? "I'll speak to Malitz, then. You should head to the medical bay. Find out if anybody else was treated for smoke inhalation."

"I'll do what I can," Hans promised. He turned to leave, then looked back at her, and asked, "I don't suppose you're willing to let me in on any more secrets?"

"Like what?"

"Like where you went last night?"

"I went to the Well," Caryn admitted. If she couldn't trust Hans, she couldn't trust anybody.

"Alone? Why?"

"I just wanted to clear my head," Caryn said, "and that's where I ended up. I wanted to see what it was like. I mean, I wasn't going to stay there more than a couple of hours. I'm not an idiot."

"How did you get there without anybody noticing? For that matter, how did you get back?"

That was a trickier question. Caryn had made her way through the tunnel until it ended at an earthen wall that formed a perfect circle, with a dash of green light in its centre. It was too perfect to be an accident, so Caryn had turned her mind to the power for guidance, and soon the wall was spinning and opening. When Caryn crawled through it, she felt the energy vanish, the heat and pressure cease. She had crossed the threshold of the Well, and even though she was still underground, everything had changed.

Caryn kept following the tunnel until it ended at a trapdoor, and when she crawled through it, she found herself, amazingly, right back in the fort, in a sub-basement deep beneath Eolanis, the central satellite. Instead of telling Hans all that, though, Caryn merely smiled and said, "I think those are enough secrets for one day, don't you?"

She said it teasingly, and Hans laughed. "A woman must have her secrets," he admitted.

"A man too," Caryn said. "Do you know what Lana said to me the night before she died? That everybody has something to hide. Here in this fort, I'm starting to feel like she's right."

"We'll figure them out," Hans promised. "One secret at a time. Good luck with Ravencliffe."

"Don't remind me," Caryn said, but she smiled. "I'm glad you're not angry with me, Hans."

"You aren't easy to stay angry with." He returned her smile and left.

Caryn considered going to see Captain Malitz right then but decided her time would be better spent planning for her meetings with Ravencliffe and Freed. Her strategy for Ravencliffe had come to her in the Well the night before, and it was simple: show him she could understand him, keep up with him, think like him. Do it quickly, simply, without letting him head off on one of his tangents.

He had already told her she might be able to win his trust, but she would focus on winning his respect.

Freed was more difficult. Caryn knew he respected bluntness, directness. He expected honesty and always appeared to be honest with her. But he was clever too, much smarter than Major Danzig, and Caryn could barely even think of him without picturing herself pinned down amid the glowing orange rocks of the Well, his fists raised above her, poised to strike.

Janusz and Marwin arrived around lunchtime, squabbling. "I don't believe that for a second," Janusz was saying.

"Don't believe what?" Caryn asked.

"They found a body in the Well," Marwin explained. "One of our soldiers, dead, no sign of trauma. Like his heart just stopped."

Caryn felt her own heart stop for a moment, just as Janusz said, "I don't know where he gets these rumours from."

"It's true," Marwin argued. "Severin was in the group that found him. He told me himself. He was on the last sweep."

"Sweep?" Caryn asked.

"We've been sweeping the Well in teams," Janusz explained. "Not Marwin and me, since we're still in training, but the others. Making sure there aren't any more Breas hiding out there. I've heard they did kill a few stragglers and found some more already dead, ones who got wounded in the killing field and stumbled back to the Well for shelter. I never heard of one of our own soldiers being found, though."

"Well, I did," Marwin said hotly, "and what I heard was, the guy they found never should have been there. He wasn't on a sweep."

"Nobody knows why he was there?" Caryn asked.

"Nobody knows *if* he was there," Janusz said, winking at her. After just a few days of training, Janusz's back was already straighter, his head held higher. The softness that Caryn had noticed in his eyes in the aftermath of Lana's death was not gone, but Caryn saw new strength etched in his face too. When he winked at her, she could feel his presence.

"What was the man's name?" Caryn asked Marwin, who was still standing in the doorway of her quarters.

"I don't know," Marwin said. "I know he was one of Captain Toppel's men, but —"

"My lady," Janusz interrupted him, "we're losing time here, and we're back on duty soon. Can we help you with Ravencliffe?"

"I know how I'll handle Ravencliffe today," Caryn said. "It's Freed I'm worried about."

"He's not trying to shut you down?" Janusz asked.

"No, it's not that," Caryn said, but how could she tell them what the problem really was? That she had seen a magical prophecy about him hitting her? "I'm going to need more active support from him. Ongoing, up-to-date news from the fronts, and some way for Ravencliffe to get the same and to trust that it's accurate."

Marwin shook his head gravely from his spot in the doorway. He was as stumped as she was, but not for lack of effort or intelligence. The battle and the brief spurt of training had changed him too, Caryn thought. He was more thoughtful, more mature somehow.

"My lady," Janusz said, "what if you simply asked the general to give Ravencliffe a permanent telegraph link back to Brealand, and yourself one to Tomasburg?"

Caryn laughed bitterly. "Why not ask him to invite the king and queen over for tea?"

"Why not that too?" Janusz asked. "We're talking about a bid for peace. What's more peaceful than tea?" He leaned closer to her and said, "The general respects you, my lady. I know it can be difficult to see, but that's what it looks like to me. He didn't have to give you Ravencliffe."

"He wanted me out of the way," Caryn started to say, but Janusz stopped her with a light touch on her arm.

"You stayed out of everyone's way for five days after Lana died," he said. "I don't blame you for it. The Gods know I miss her too. But you were already out of the way. The general is the one who drew you back into the rest of the fort when he invited you to that conference." He moved his hands back to his lap but kept his eyes locked on her. "You've seen what Freed does to people he really wants out of the way. The only other women in this fort are the nurses, and when have you last seen any of them outside of the medical bay? Meanwhile, you're meeting with the high officers. You're interviewing important prisoners." Janusz leaned back in his chair. "There's no harm in asking, my lady."

Caryn nodded. There was certainly no harm in asking, but Janusz hadn't been in the Well with her last night. She finally understood what it must have been like for Brenner so many years ago. She understood how prophecy could change a person.

When Janusz and Marwin bowed to her and returned to their training, Caryn's thoughts remained with Brenner. So many things were starting to come together. The way she felt when Janusz leaned close to her. The feeling in her stomach when he touched her arm. The way she heard his words and wanted to believe them. She'd always thought Janusz was handsome, but she hadn't felt these sensations before last night, when she'd returned to a Well and connected through the energy with Brenner or someone close to him. It couldn't be a coincidence.

It couldn't be safe, either. Never mind that both of them were still mourning Lana, and that they were colleagues, and that they were trapped in the Gateway and surrounded by enemies. There was something about Janusz that Caryn had never quite trusted, though she was finding it hard to remember what it was.

It was too complicated to consider right now, with so much work ahead of her. She found Captain Malitz in his quarters but learned little. He did remember Gall returning the outmoded revolver to him, but he'd given it only a cursory inspection before passing it on to Major Danzig.

Caryn knew that Danzig would not give her the time of day, so that was a dead end. She chose to meet the general next, since he scared her more than Ravencliffe did. Her fears did not play out today, at least. Freed was surprisingly receptive to her requests. After abusing the president for ordering this farce of a mission, Freed quickly consented to giving Caryn free use of their telegraph links back to Tomasburg, subject to interruption for military necessity. "If I don't, Willem Toppel will just give it to you behind my back again," he said bitterly. "You'd think I don't control my own damn fort." He rejected telegraph access for Ravencliffe, of course, but he left her some hope for an opening in the future: "If you can manage to win him over, really win him over, then maybe we can talk about setting one up as a reward. To firm up a final deal. But you can't say a word to him in advance, or else he'll just play you to get the link."

"I know that much," Caryn snapped. "This isn't the first time I've negotiated with anyone."

"I can tell," General Freed said, and he actually smiled. "You drive a hard bargain, Minister Hallom. Now here's what I want. Hans."

"You have Hans," Caryn replied immediately.

"No," the general said, "I don't. He's still working for you. He's running around asking my soldiers questions. He's looking for obsolete weapons. He's in the medical bay talking about smoke inhalation. Believe me, I would love to be interrogating Ravencliffe right now, but I've given him up, because that was the deal. You need to live up to your end."

Caryn opened her mouth to respond, then closed it again. She was trying to hang on to Hans's protection, and she could hardly be blamed for it after the attack, but there was nothing she could say that would sway Freed. A deal was a deal. "He's yours," Caryn said, not quite succeeding at keeping the bitterness out of her voice. "You have my word."

"Thank you." The general hesitated. "Minister, if Hans truly is my man, and I order him to tell me what he's been up to, he'll have to. I would rather hear it from you."

He looked old. Tired. For a moment, Caryn even wondered if the Well had gotten the prophecy wrong. But prophecies never failed to come true, not even Brenner's. "I'm led to believe you already know the answer," Caryn said carefully. It was what Toppel had warned her.

"Then why the hell would I be asking?" Freed shouted. "If something's happening in this fort, I need to know about it."

From defeated to furious in the space of seconds. Caryn felt more irritated than afraid. "Ask Hans, then. He has to take orders from you now. I don't." She turned on her heel and left.

She took a roundabout path to Ravencliffe's cell to let her anger fade. It wasn't very smart, she realized, snapping at the general. She was supposed to be a politician who could put on a winning smile and turn anybody into her friend. All things to all people, and especially Freed. She knew how much she needed him. But how could she stop her anger when she already knew that he was going to betray her?

She found Ravencliffe sitting at his desk, reading a dusty old book under the flickering glow of the electric light. He leapt to his feet when he heard Caryn approach. "Minister Hallom!" he exclaimed. "I feared you wouldn't come. Three days in a row of your delightful companionship seemed too much for a simple prisoner like me to hope for."

"Please sit down," Caryn said. After her meeting with the general, she was in no mood for Ravencliffe's games, but she had resigned herself to playing them for at least a short while longer. She gestured at the guard to close the cell door behind her. "You'll be pleased to know that I've been learning from you, Colonel Ravencliffe."

"I must admit I'm intrigued." Ravencliffe propped himself against one of the cell's stone walls.

"Logic," Caryn explained. "Rationality. The scientific approach. Of course, here in the Gateway, I'm not in a position to conduct any studies, so thought experiments have had to suffice."

"Naturally."

"I've been trying to imagine Brealand as a person," Caryn said. "You always describe the Realm as a single organism. Different aspects moving together. She is more than that, though, I think. She has hopes and dreams. Aspirations. Plans."

"This hardly sounds scientific," Ravencliffe said.

"Well, we have to set up the context," Caryn replied. "The histories all start with the two great empires. Wassia and Orastus. Their wars, their rivalries, their ups and downs setting a course for the entire Continent. Brealand has tough terrain, with mountains and deserts. She's marginal for farming. She's isolated. Outside the action. She wants more, but how can she compete? Where can she look?"

Ravencliffe laughed. "You're trying to explain Brealand, but you can't get outside your own head. You're telling me the typical Deugan folktale, of the poor farmhand who starts with nothing, who rises through the ranks using nothing but his wits. That's not the Brea dream."

"I'm not so sure," Caryn said. "I think it would grate on any Brea to open the histories and read about Wassia and Orastus, Orastus and Wassia, again and again and again." She flashed him a smile. "Humour me for a moment, anyway. Let's say Brealand did want to improve her stature in the world. What would her strategy be? Brealand does have certain assets, and naturally she'll try to maximize them. She has her mountains and deserts protecting her from the great empires. She knows they'll leave her alone, with so many richer lands easier to access. She has some resources to speak of, good for trading. And she has the sea.

"She starts with raids and plunder up and down the Deugan coast, across the islands to the north, beyond them to the northern continent. She's not united yet, but that's only a matter of time. A common culture crops up, distinct from the southerners across the mountains, different from the northerners beyond the sea, something entirely her own. The demands of survival push her people to cooperate. Over the centuries, informal arrangements are formalized. A Realm is born.

"She moves from plunder into trade. She sets up her networks, slowly, cautiously. Her fleets grow and their power expands. All the while the great empires are fighting each other, each holding the other in check. Now the Old Empire is dominant, now it collapses and Wassia seems to have won, now the New Empire returns with a vengeance. Their tug-of-war only strengthens the Realm. As long as they balance each other's power, neither can grow strong enough to threaten her, not with her mountains and deserts protecting her, not with her ships churning up the oceans. In fact, the great empires barely even notice the moves she is making.

"It's just as she wants it. She watches, and waits, because she is clever, and logical, and she knows.

"She knows that nations grow old and wither like men do. She knows that by controlling the waves, she controls not only her security, not only her trade routes, but her very future. She is strong, and young, and disciplined, and Wassia and Orastus will soon decline.

"But then something happens that our hero did not plan for: the emergence of a new rival, not a traditional empire, a rival even younger and more vibrant than she. One with the abundant natural resources she can only dream of, and a flair for industry, and overland trade routes which are just as lucrative as her sea routes. A rival located not in the distant south, but in the northwest of the Continent, right on her doorstep."

"Somehow," Ravencliffe interrupted, "I knew that Deugan would enter into your fanciful speculations. I thought you would at least make some effort at realism."

"Let me finish before we talk about realism," Caryn insisted. She was almost there. "What is really unexpected about the Realm's new rival is its ideology. It's driven by an idea, not fully formed even in its own mind, a jumble of individualism and populism and freedom, amorphous, contradictory, but dangerous. Dangerous above all, because this idea is diametrically opposed to the unique culture that has grown up behind the mountains, that has become key to our hero's success.

"What's more, the idea's spreading like wildfire. As the two great empires decline, it's the rival's culture that's filling the void, its radio programs, its literature. Pro-democracy movements erupt throughout the Fringes. There's a general strike in Orastus proper. The Wassian barony sees its power slipping to industrialists like Amaro Sullivan. There are even rumblings in Breland's own island colonies.

"Then the real hammer falls: Wassia turns its most important colony, Amim, over to home rule — and the Amimi people still want more!

"All of a sudden, the Realm is facing her worst nightmare. She had always relied on the two great empires holding each other at bay, but now she's staring a continental hegemony in the face, and she knows that no matter how many ships she builds, she will never be able to match it. Suddenly she feels squeezed and crowded in her little corner of the Continent, as though she's pressed against the edge of a cliff. Suddenly her greatest assets, the mountains and the desert that had served her as a fortress for generations, are starting to feel more like" — she gestured at their surroundings with her good hand to drive the point home — "a cell."

Ravencliffe was still feigning the same boredom as before, but Caryn thought she sensed a difference in him. Like she had struck a nerve. Like he was starting to pay attention.

"There seems to be only one thing to do," Caryn continued. "She has to destroy her rival before it grows too powerful to contain. She sends in her soldiers and she readies her fleets, never realizing how dearly she's miscalculated."

The look only lasted a moment, but in that instant Caryn knew she had him. She grabbed the wooden chair, placed it down in front of his bed and slowly sank onto it until she was looking him directly in the eyes. "The Realm can't achieve her goals through conquest," Caryn told him. "Breland went into this war to destroy Deugan, but in that brief moment, it forgot what it knew all along. That its true enemy isn't a nation, but an idea, and that you can't conquer an idea. If you win this war, Colonel Ravencliffe, then you will occupy Deugan for a time, but not forever. The Old Empire lost its Deugan colonies, so did the Wassians, and they were both land powers. Your strength is on the sea, and Tomasburg is leagues inland. When your occupation inevitably ends, our idea will still have survived."

She watched him, trying to tell what was hidden behind his dark eyes. He stared back at her, his face blank, but she felt that he was pondering, considering. She leaned toward him.

"Minister Hallom," Ravencliffe said at last, "listening to your so-called thought experiment was a passably entertaining way to spend an afternoon, and I'll grant you that you may have hit on a nugget of truth or two, as even a barbarian is bound to do. But don't even try to pretend you understand the Realm. Our goals, our aspirations, our culture, our psyche. They are so far beyond your imagining —"

"Then teach me," Caryn said. She tried to inject her voice with a desperate intensity, but it was all she could do not to grin. She had him! "I want to learn. Don't you see that?" He didn't reply, but Caryn didn't mind. She stood, dragged her chair back toward the desk and caught the eye of the guard to open the cell for her. "I'll be back tomorrow," she said before she left. "Teach me."

*

After the misery and depression of the last several days, Caryn felt almost giddy as she made her way back to her quarters. Her meeting with Ravencliffe had gone better than she had dared dream. There was hope, and hope was everything.

Caryn went straight to her bed when she reached her quarters, thinking that she would reward herself with a long rest, but that was not to be. No sooner had she lay down than she heard three loud raps at her door, which she opened to admit Hans. Her guard was businesslike today. "I'm sorry this will have to be brief," Hans said, "but the general's got me on a tight schedule. I don't think I'll be able to do much more investigating."

"You can't do any more investigating," Caryn told him. "General's orders, and he has the right."

"Even though he may be behind it all?" Hans asked darkly.

"Do you believe that?"

"Not really," Hans said, "but he was pretty quick to stop me from looking into it."

"I know," Caryn sighed. "I don't know what to think anymore."

"At least I made it to the medical bay before he shut me down."

"And?"

"Aside from you and the soldiers who put out the fire, there was only one other person treated for smoke inhalation the day of the battle," Hans said.

Caryn's heart skipped. "Who is he? Did you question him?"

"No use," Hans said. "He's dead."

"From the smoke?"

"No. That's the strange part. Apparently they found him dead in the Well a few days later. No idea what the cause of death was."

Another dead end. Marwin had already told her about the man they found in the Well. He had to have been her attacker, but how did he die? The Well's power, she thought, otherwise they would have figured out a cause of death by now. What did that mean, though? Was the man preparing a new weapon when some effect he was attempting backfired? Or — the thought came on her suddenly — was his master the one who knew how to use the Well's power, as she'd suspected all along, and killed the assassin to keep him from talking?

If that were the case, who was the master? An officer, surely, she'd been over that ground before. Which one, though? She knew Danzig hated her. She still didn't trust Freed. And the dead man, Caryn remembered, had been a member of Captain Toppel's platoon.

Caryn would not be resting tonight, she realized. She had one more person to talk to.

CHAPTER FIFTEEN

The earthen wall spun, its green light making dizzying patterns in the darkness of the tunnel. Caryn waited while it slowed to a stop, then crawled through the opening it had left, her knees complaining almost as much as her burned arm. As the secret doorway closed behind her, the warmth of the Gateway Well embraced her like a bath. The colours on the ground laid a path out before her. The power beckoned.

When she slipped into the place with the columns, he was already there, waiting for her. His was the only presence she felt. They were alone.

Across the distance his hand found hers. This time she did not startle or shy away. Instead she squeezed into him the same pattern he had made the night before: "Who are you?"

Caryn gazed around the Well as she waited for his answer. The columns of light were beautiful, but she also noticed the other lights, the small, flickering ones that she had never seen from the Wassian Well. She had first noticed them yesterday, but overnight their pattern had changed. She wondered what it meant.

Caryn felt the squeezing begin in her hand, and she focused on the letters they were forming. "Matt," she realized, her heart sinking. She hadn't actually believed that Brenner connected with her last night, but she had dared to hope.

She realized how foolish she was, running back to the Well a second night in a row in search of a stranger who might be worlds away, in any Well on the Continent. The man who called himself

Matt obviously knew his way around the energy. Caryn hadn't touched it in fourteen years. Who knew how dangerous he might be?

He was close to Brenner, though. He had to be. This place with the columns had been special to them. Caryn refused to believe that Brenner would teach it to just anybody. She grasped the distant hand and squeezed back another question. "Are you a Steffian?"

A pause. Then a short series of squeezes that confirmed what she suspected. "Yes." Another pause. "Looking for Nono?"

It was hard, coming up with dispassionate replies that could be coded this way, with the turmoil racing through her head. "Yes," seemed the simplest thing to say.

They were feeling each other out. She clearly couldn't trust him. He had admitted being a Steffian, after all. He was just as hesitant to connect with her, though, and she wondered why.

"Nono may come," Matt finally coded back to her. A pause. "In his time."

There were so many questions Caryn wanted to ask. Questions about the attack, about how it was possible for an energy weapon to function outside a Well. Questions about the place with the columns, what it meant, how they were using it to communicate. Questions about the dead assassin, the power that had silenced him, and why he'd gone to the Well the day he died. But she wanted Brenner's answers, not those of some Steffian. "Nono told you about me?" she asked instead.

"Said you are a friend."

"Anything more?"

"He kept tabs on you. From far away." Another pause. "Makes no sense." And then: "Must go. Others coming." His hand melted into ribbons and slipped away.

Caryn released the energy and watched as the cave brightened to orange. She stared down the length of the corridor as gratitude came over her. If Brenner really had been keeping tabs on her, it was obvious how he'd done it. Caryn had been under a spotlight almost from the moment she'd entered the Treasury Department. Photographs of her had been plastered across newspapers and magazines. Brenner would have recognized her instantly, would have known exactly who she was — but he clearly hadn't told Matt. In fact, the Steffians had never used her past in their propaganda. He must not have told any of them. He had kept her secret safe.

It wasn't much, but in these times, in this place, it was enough.

*

At first it was her desire to reconnect with Brenner that brought her back to the Gateway Well night after night, through the secret tunnel she had discovered beneath Eolanis satellite, but soon it became more about connecting with the energy itself. It was troubling. Caryn knew that the energy had stolen her childhood, poisoned her, left her on the brink of death. She knew that more recently it had attacked her, savaged her left arm, and shown her the prophecy that haunted her dreams. She also knew that quite apart from the energy, her journeys were fraught with danger. If somebody caught her sneaking to the Well, it could mean not only the end of her career, but the end of her peace initiative, the end of the president and the government that had put their trust in her, and possibly even the end of the national unity that had allowed Deugan to survive a war on three fronts for as long as it had.

Despite all of that, Caryn found herself drawn to the Well. She would resist the urge for days at a time, but inevitably it would become too strong. She tried to find justifications. Since she had already been attacked once, it only made sense for her to practice her skills with the power, for her own protection. She might stumble on a clue that would help her to identify her attacker. If she could earn Matt's trust or find Brenner, she might even learn what the Steffians were planning. Inside, though, she knew that she wasn't using the Well for any of those reasons. She was using it for comfort, to plug the hole that had grown inside her since Lana died, since she lost Hans to her deal with the general, since she was forced to accept the shelling and the siege as normalcy.

According to Janusz, most of the fort was feeling the same emptiness. Caryn might fill hers in the Well, but some men filled it with exercise, running in the safe areas to the south of the fort or drilling themselves with push-ups and sit-ups for hours, even after full days of training or physically demanding repair work. Some men excessively cleaned and primed their rifles. Some wrote endless letters to loved ones back home that might never be sent.

Those were the healthy types. Others filled their voids with alcohol and were more afraid of what would happen when their stashes ran out than they were of a Brea attack. Several gambled every night. For others it was pornography, or masturbation, even in the relatively public space of a barracks. Some men had developed nervous tics, while others broke down entirely and were taken to the medical bay to be sedated.

When Caryn asked Janusz what his coping method was, he answered without hesitation. "The chapel," he said. "The chaplain is brilliant, my lady, and we need the Gods more than ever. Armano's strength. Eolanis' wisdom. Lessandro's mercy."

Caryn nodded. What else could she do? "May they guard and protect us." It was half-hearted, and it wasn't enough to satisfy Janusz.

"Why haven't you been back there, my lady? If you don't mind me asking."

Because none of it is real, she thought. Because as much as she loved her adopted country, its obsession with its Gods might well have contributed to the war. Throughout her career, Caryn had been criticized for not being more passionate about faith, and she'd always found it ironic that she was being attacked for one of her better qualities. Janusz's question struck a bit too close for comfort.

Luckily, she had lived in Deugan long enough to know how to respond. "Because Lessandro said, 'There is one path to salvation, and it is through the Gods, but there are many paths to the Gods.' I take a different path than you, Janusz. In life, as well as in Gods. I take a different path than most people."

"That is what the greatest have always done," Janusz said, with a sad smile that touched Caryn more than he knew.

Janusz was a problem.

It was when she'd been flush with the idea of reconnecting with Brenner that something had awakened in Caryn, and she had started noticing the men around her, Janusz included. Now it had taken on a life of its own. She saw things she wouldn't have seen before. The way he walked. The way he cocked his head before he asked a question. The way his eyes moved when he laughed. She saw his confidence and swagger around the other soldiers, how he commanded their respect even though he was ten or fifteen years older than they were. She saw his tender side when he spoke about his home, or when he mentored Marwin. She saw a man who seemed to know his place in the world, who knew what he wanted and was fighting for it. She liked what she saw.

She didn't like her emotions, though, or her uncertainty. She didn't like how old it made her feel when she realized that most Deugans, the ones with ordinary childhoods, had gone through these sorts of feelings in schools or colleges. She hated her lack of control — and she hated conversations like this, when she realized just how different they really were from one another.

Somehow, despite all of the confusion, Caryn found her life settling into a routine. In the mornings she would sleep in if she'd been in the Well the night before, otherwise she'd head to the communications hub, where she would connect a telegraph line to Tomasburg and catch up on what had been happening on the fronts. The news was generally good, a welcome change from previous span. The new general they'd sent to the southern front was earning his keep, and their once-stalled offensive was picking up steam, pushing back the Wassian trenches and carving off chunks of territory. The New Empire was becoming more and more concerned with events in the Fringes, and its offensives in Deugan had mostly ceased. The Brea fleet, while growing in numbers, was still tied to its home ports by the Deugan subs. The Breas had tried overland attacks on three of their northwestern forts, and Deugan was able to throw all of them back, albeit with heavy casualties that the depleted ranks could hardly afford.

There was more than enough bad news to keep Caryn worried, however. The Wassians had intercepted a Deugan ship carrying arms intended for their Amimi allies. Their diplomatic efforts had stalled in the Fringes, and the pro-democracy movements were having trouble standing up to Imperial crackdowns. There were also rumours that the Steffians had developed a massively powerful new bomb, although Caryn had her doubts, since she figured the weapon would have been used by now if the rumours were true.

Worst of all, one fort actually did fall to the Breas in the Deugan northwest. It was the easternmost of their string of fortifications, on the edge of the desert, and the Breas had attacked unexpectedly through the desert itself. It was the same tactic the Breas had used in the Gateway when they'd sent men through the Well, yet the Deugans had fallen for it again. Forts weren't meant to stand alone, Caryn had learned from Marwin. They were only meant to hold off an assault long enough that an army could be brought into position. A flexible, mobile force was required to cover a fort's weak spots and respond to new tactics by the enemy. Deugan had an army in the northwest to do that job, but to cover the ground effectively they would really need three or four armies, and they just didn't have the men to spare.

Caryn finally understood how vulnerable she was here in the Gateway, where the fort's tiny garrison and the soldiers who had been sent off to guard the villages were the only Deugan forces for leagues around. At least the Gateway Fort had its satellites to cover some of the main fort's weaknesses, making the absence of a separate army less dire. Still, for all the general's planning, the real reason the fort hadn't fallen yet was that the Breas — whether to protect Ravencliffe, or simply because they didn't want to waste more lives on an enemy that would soon starve to death — had not yet chosen to reach out and take it.

After her dose of news, Caryn would return to her quarters to consult with Janusz and Marwin, and they would strategize for her afternoon meetings with Ravencliffe. She wondered why they bothered, since the meetings never stuck to any sort of plan. Instead, Ravencliffe would regale her with tales from Brealand's history or engage her in a debate on a political point, or challenge her with some aspect of Brea culture that he believed made his countrymen superior to hers. It didn't matter, though. Caryn could tell that her thought experiment had gotten through to him. He was taking her request seriously to teach her about Brealand. They were slowly circling each other around the ideas that the war was really about.

Caryn wasn't powerless, either. She was able to choose some of the topics for their debates, and she chose matters that might be relevant to the underlying interests that Deugan and Brealand were fighting over. They argued over economic patterns and whether Deugan was helping or harming the Fringes by buying their resources, and who won and lost from partnerships with the northern continent. They argued about political control and whether granting Amim home rule was a sign of strength or weakness by the Wassians, and whether a Givanno government propped up by Deugan funding could be considered a colony. They argued about religion, too. It was a difficult topic for Caryn, since she agreed more with the Brea position than the Deugan one, but if she couldn't argue both sides of an issue, she couldn't rightly call herself a politician.

Through it all, Caryn made time to give the general regular updates. He liked knowing what was happening in his fort, after all, and she wanted to stay in his good books in case she needed favours in the future. He seemed particularly concerned by the injury to Caryn's left arm, which was stubbornly refusing to heal. As the span went on she had regained some control over her upper arm and shoulder, but she still had no feeling from the elbow down, and the fort's nurses were losing hope that she would ever recover. It was maddening, and not a little embarassing. Caryn had re-learned how to dress herself, at least, but there were countless everyday tasks that now took several times as long as they should, if she could even do them unassisted at all.

The general, for his part, seemed so interested in the injury that Caryn finally broke down and told him how it had happened, now that the would-be assassin was dead. Freed seemed genuinely shocked, and he ran to Major Danzig to get the old revolver that had "exploded" in her hand. The general personally disassembled the gun in front of Caryn and Danzig, only to find its barrel stuffed with tiny green flakes that crumbled in Caryn's hand. "She's lying to us, Ern," Danzig said. "There's nothing here that could have exploded."

"The gun was found near her body," Freed said. "Her arm didn't burn itself. Do you have another idea?"

"One or two," Danzig said darkly. "Isn't that right? Sorceress?"

"Ralf!" Freed shouted. "The foreign minister's still our guest here."

"I want to get to the bottom of this," Danzig insisted.

"So do I," Caryn interjected. "I'm the one who was attacked. The hallway was filled with smoke, so thick it was hard to see. It happened fast. Could it have been magic, power, energy, whatever you want to call it? Outside the Well? I don't know, Major. All I know is that the man who has our answers is dead."

"How convenient," Danzig snarled.

"Ralf." Freed's voice was like ice. "Our guest was found unconscious. The nurses say she hit her head hard. Now she can't remember exactly what happened. That *is* convenient — for her attacker, not for her. Now stop embarrassing yourself. You're dismissed."

Danzig looked like he was about to argue. Then he thought better of it and walked away. Freed turned to Caryn. "I'm sorry, Minister. I don't know what's gotten into him lately."

"The siege," Caryn said. She too was trying to puzzle out what Danzig's reaction meant. Was he guilty and trying to deflect the blame? Or were his fear and suspicion genuine? "The siege has gotten to all of us."

Freed shook his head. "Major Danzig's a soldier, my lady. All his life. He's survived worse and fared better." He handed her the revolver. "If you can figure anything out, I trust you will tell me."

"You'll be the first to know," Caryn promised.

So her meetings with Ravencliffe and her updates to the general continued. Freed's interest seemed shallow, but he listened politely enough, and once even wished her luck.

Then one day, nearly two months after the battle, Caryn and Ravencliffe were discussing the shipping disputes around the Amimi Canal that had been the direct trigger for the war. Caryn was arguing that Deugan needed to protect its ships from the pirates known to prowl the Amimi coast, when Ravencliffe blurted out, "Come off it, Minister! You know that my Realm can never be secure if Deugan is churning out a fleet of warships. If you seriously think our needs can be met across a table, start there!"

Caryn was so shocked that at first she thought she had misheard him. Ravencliffe had said it in his needling, argumentative way, but it was, for the first time, an actual bargaining demand. An actual sign that all of the circling they had been doing was moving them closer to their goal.

When their meeting was finished, Caryn rushed to General Freed's office to tell him about the development. When she arrived, though, his door was closed, with Hans standing guard outside.

Caryn had known Hans long enough that one look at his face was all it took. "What's going on?"

"General's having a conference with the officers," Hans muttered. "Danzig, Malitz, Toppel, one or two more. Some of them looked angry, some of them scared. From what I heard, Joint Staff Headquarters has asked for his advice, like they always do."

"But what happened?"

Hans shrugged. "Only exactly what we knew would happen. What should have happened months ago," he said. "The Brea fleet has left the north harbours."

*

Caryn tossed and turned that night before finally drifting into a fitful sleep. Her dreams were dark. She was swimming in a sea, pursued by a fleet of Brea warships. She couldn't swim fast enough to outdistance them. One ship finally pulled alongside her, and Michael Ravencliffe leaned over the side to haul her onboard, but as soon as he grasped her hand, fire shot through it, the tendrils snaking up her arm and toward her heart.

The change in the air wrenched her from the dream. She sat bolt upright in her bed. Fear washed over her.

The door slammed.

She let out a gasp, not quite a scream. A harsh whisper answered her. "Minister, no. It's me."

She heard a heavy step, and the bang of metal on the floor. She heard the familiar hum as the electric light was switched on, but Caryn was focused on a different sound. A ringing, high in pitch, dancing at the edge of her hearing.

Captain Toppel stepped carefully toward her. His broken leg was no longer in a cast, but he wasn't putting weight on it. He held a single crutch, which he leaned on as though it were a cane.

"Get up," he said.

The way her ears were ringing, she almost didn't understand. "Get up," she heard again. She looked around for help, for Hans, for anybody. She thought of screaming, but then she saw the look in Toppel's dark eyes.

She got up. Her nightgown was thin cotton in the heat of the fort. Toppel was fully dressed, sharp black slacks, a buttoned green shirt. She felt naked in front of him.

"I tried to warn you," Toppel said. He was still whispering, but she could hear the anger behind his words. "You didn't listen. I need to know you're listening now." He took another step toward her, balancing on his crutch.

I should run, Caryn thought, *he can't use his leg, he can't catch me*, but the quarters were small, and Toppel was between her and the door. He took another step. The high-pitched ringing grew louder.

"You don't know how much danger you're in," Toppel said. "Some of the things you've talked to Ravencliffe about. All this sneaking off to wherever it is you go at night. It has to stop."

Caryn thought of the soldier, one of Toppel's own men, found in the Well, dead. He took another step toward her. Another. She heard the power with every tap of his crutch.

"Danzig is watching. Has been watching all along. Do you have any idea what he'll do?"

Caryn fought through her panic to reach out to it. The power was straining. It was trapped. It was furious.

Toppel had almost reached her bedside. More skilled with the energy than she, certainly. He knew she'd fought off the first attack, so he was being cautious, approaching her warily, but still approaching. What would he do when he reached her? Kill her, like the man in the Well? Use the energy to bind her, hold her down? And then what? Every instinct she had urged her to run, but she felt frozen to the ground. Her panic rose. The energy grew closer, screaming, throwing itself against its bonds.

It was scared, Caryn realized. Not just angry. The energy was as scared as she was. *I will let you out*, she promised it silently. *Do you understand? Help me. I will let you out.*

"I was walking past Janusz and Marwin's quarters," Toppel was saying. He was standing right in front of her now. His expression was at once stern and desperate. "Something strange —"

She kicked him in his broken leg, hard, the force of the energy pounding through her foot as she connected. He screamed in agony. His crutch flew out from under his arm and he crumpled to the ground, clutching his leg.

Caryn retrieved the fallen crutch, lifted off the foam piece that had been under Toppel's arm and ripped it open.

It was stuffed with the brittle green flakes of dying leaves.

CHAPTER SIXTEEN

I don't resent my childhood at the collective. Ours was a smaller farm that gave us a sense of bonding and community. We lived with about twelve families, though the number kept changing, so there were always other children to play with, and there was something visceral about physical labour, being close to the earth of the Realm.

But there was always tension lurking beneath the surface. We learned early on, for example, that certain things were always to be said in code, or communicated with looks and glances, in case one of our neighbours thought to report on us. We knew that the reason the collective's lone radio never picked up any Deugan channels had to do with censorship and not the strength of our antennas. The government shuffled families in and out over the years, both to keep us off-balance and to make sure we were seeded with spies they could trust. Mine wasn't an unhappy childhood, but we were far from naive.

Even so, it took four years at O'Keefe College, surrounded by students from the urban parts of Breland and from democracies elsewhere on the Continent, before I started to realize how strange my own childhood had been. The collectives were, in a way, a microcosm of the Realm: a myth of pride and unity that only concealed fear and suspicion, and a governance structure that claimed to be based on merit but assumed that only a few choice families could develop the necessary skills.

Of course, Breland would never admit to being a hereditary monarchy, even if it kept old titles like King and Queen. The Party selected the most qualified people from across the Realm to install as its royalty, or at least, that's how the national myth went. In reality, beneath this veneer of upward mobility lay an oligarchy dominated by eight or ten families, in much the same way that two or three farmers loyal to the government always seemed to control our collective. Loyalty was everything, and it was ensured through harsh labour, a domineering police force, and a populace cowed by the threat that even their own parents might report on them at any moment.

—Julia McDermott, *The Real Brealand* (1754), published from her exile in Koltaja

Jayla's muscles were taut and her fists were clenched. She couldn't remember being this angry in her life. "Brenner says you've been eating the magic," she said accusingly. "Right from the start, since day one."

"Reporting on me, is he?" Professor Terial smiled. "Besides, I thought we'd stopped calling it *magic*."

"*Energy*, then," Jayla said. "I don't care what we call it. You had no right."

The professor raised his eyebrows. From the side of the cavern, Brenner looked at them sullenly. "I tried to tell her she should just be grateful about it," Brenner said. "At least she's going to get out of here."

"Oh, shut up about that already," Jayla snapped at him. She'd tried to support Brenner, she really had, but he was becoming unbearable. She hadn't minded the first two span of comforting him, feeling his pain as her own. It made her feel closer to him than ever before. Like she was, for the first time in her short life, part of a team, Jayla and Brenner against the world. It had continued too long, though, and Jayla was exhausted. Maybe that was why her anger was so easy to set off.

She turned back to Terial. "Is it true? You've been eating it?"

The professor bowed his head. "Jayla, I wanted to give you and Brenner the best chance you could possibly have. I didn't want you to have to do it."

"But you knew what it would do to you," Jayla said. How could he have invited even more of the energy into his body, using it for sustenance even when Jayla and Brenner had real food to spare? Of course the power was going to affect him. Terial had already spent nearly sixty years in this life when they became trapped in the Well. Now his face was worn and wrinkled, his eyes pale and clouded. His beard was as white as the snow that must be blanketing Villasud. The sight of him had filled Jayla with pity, until she learned what he had done to reach this state.

"I did know," Terial admitted. "I knew that what you call *eating the magic* would speed up my aging and my illnesses. But you have to understand, Jayla, I've lived a long life. A life I'm satisfied with. You deserve to do the same."

Jayla wanted to cry. "It's not fair."

"And we've had to eat the energy for months now, anyway," Brenner added. "Our food ran out ages ago, and now our own aging's been sped up like crazy."

"True," Terial said, "but if I'd been sharing your food supply, you would have had to start that much sooner. I'd hoped that we might all get out within a month, and I could protect you from having to do it at all."

"Well, I for one am grateful," Brenner said, glaring at Jayla. "I know Jayla's going to get out of here because of it."

"You may get out too," Terial told him. Brenner scowled, but the professor was unfazed. "I see your anger, Brenner. I understand it. God, how I understand it. Listen to me now. One old man to another."

Amazingly, Brenner smiled at that, and suddenly came out with a bark of laughter. Jayla reacted, throwing her arms around him. She hadn't realized how desperate she had been to see him smile again.

"That," Professor Terial said, "speaks for itself. You can see how much Jayla cares about you. Stop pushing her away. If you're angry, be angry at the government. Not at the energy, and certainly not at her."

"I'm not really angry at Jayla," Brenner said. He looked at her. "I'm sorry. I've been acting like..."

"A complete idiot?" Jayla suggested.

Brenner laughed again. "Worse than that. You've been amazing, Jayla. Like you always are."

"The second point," Terial continued, "is that when you get out —"

"*If* I get out," Brenner muttered.

"*When* you get out," Terial insisted, "direct the anger you feel in a useful way. Wassia needs somebody who will fight to establish a government that protects its people instead of sending them wantonly to die. Somebody like your father, Brenner."

"That's not what my father was fighting for," Brenner said. "He didn't want a government at all. He just wanted his people to be left alone. Frankly, I don't blame him."

"He wanted to make Wassia a fairer place," Terial said. "That is the sort of man we need. What Wassia doesn't need is a man so consumed by anger that his only thought is revenge against those who've wronged him." He limped over to Brenner and put his hands on the younger man's shoulders. "Don't answer me now. Think on what I've said, and if you feel that you could use my aid, come to me."

Brenner only shook his head and twisted out of the professor's grasp, making for the room where he slept. Jayla turned to follow him, but the professor laid a hand on her shoulder. "Stay a moment, please, Jayla." He sounded as old as he looked.

They waited until Brenner was out of earshot. Then Professor Terial said, "You don't need to stay with him, you know."

It was the last thing Jayla expected to hear, and she had no idea how to react. She had spent so long comforting Brenner, growing closer to him, and he had done much for her, too. Ice gripped her heart, and she felt herself shaking. "What do you mean?"

"Jayla, you've only spent sixteen years in this life," Terial said. "There are many more years ahead of you. Do you really want to spend them pulling your best friend out of depression and rages? Or do you want to find a partner who can stand on his own? Who can share his strength with you?"

Jayla scowled. She knew the professor was old and sick, but now he wasn't making sense. "How can I even think about those sorts of things? I'll be a fugitive the rest of my life, if I even get out of here. The government can't let people know what they did to us. If they find out we escaped, they'll hunt us, and who else but Brenner will help me? My own family won't even recognize me. Besides, who else am I going to find, looking like this? I promised Brenner I would never leave him. I love him."

"Listen to yourself," Terial said. "Your first thought is of your own insecurity. Your second is of a promise. Love comes third."

Jayla blushed. "You're wrong."

"Am I? Your own parents were an arranged marriage, were they not? Industrialists like your father might have rebelled against the practice, but your mother was nobility. For them, love really did come third."

"That's just the order I talked in," Jayla insisted. "It doesn't mean —"

"I can help you," the professor said. There was urgency to his words now. "I have friends. Connections. The government *will* hunt you, but with a few letters, I can get you out of Wassia, beyond their reach. I can get you into a school to continue your studies. There are other ways."

"There's only one way," Jayla said fiercely. "I love him. He needs me, and I need him too. I'm not leaving him."

The professor bowed his head again. "If you change your mind, come to me. Just remember that I am old, and the Well continues to age me. I cannot say how much longer I will be able to help you."

Jayla knew it was not a thing to say to an old man, a dying man, but for reasons she had never understood, the words tumbled out, bitter and harsh. "Brenner and I can take care of ourselves. We love each other. We don't need your help."

*

Caryn remembered the rage she had felt that day, when she found out what the professor had done to protect her. It mirrored her anger now. She had expected that Captain Toppel's attack would leave fear and panic in its wake, but it hadn't. She felt only a resolve to end her helplessness. Only a fire blazing inside her.

Caryn wanted answers. She wanted to know what the leaves were and how the energy was being taken outside the Wells against its will. *Matt would know*, she thought. The Steffian had been meeting her more and more often in the place with the columns, slowly building trust, teaching her tricks with the energy. Surely he would know about Toppel's weapon, but Caryn couldn't reach out to Matt now. General Freed had refused to leave her alone after what had happened, and he would not relent until he was satisfied that Hans would be staying by her side. So there was nothing she could do but remain awake with Hans for the rest of the night, and when day finally broke, the fire inside her carried her not to the Well, but down the fort's stone steps to the sub-basement and the prison.

"I am sorry, Minister," Hans told her as they walked.

"You have nothing to be sorry for," Caryn replied. "You couldn't guard me all day and night even if you weren't working for the general. You did everything that could be expected."

"Still," Hans said. "The president never trusted the military; that's why he sent us here in the first place. Somehow we've forgotten that. General Freed has invited you to a conference in the afternoon. Are you going?"

Caryn sighed. "I think I have to."

"Weren't you just telling me how you hate being powerless, at someone's beck and call?"

"Yes," Caryn said, "but appearances matter. Besides, Toppel was behind the attack, not Freed. If Freed wants to help us, we'd better humour him."

She left Hans at the entrance to the prison and strode to Ravencliffe's cell. The Brea colonel looked as though he had just woken up. "Minister?" he asked, his voice groggy with sleep. "I must confess, I did not expect you at this early hour."

"I'm full of surprises," Caryn said sharply. "How did the war start?"

"Is this a quiz, Minister?"

"The Wassians closed the Amimi Canal," Caryn said. "An act of war."

"Parroting the government line?" Ravencliffe yawned. "I must say I'm disappointed."

"Life is full of disappointments," Caryn said. "We depend on trade as much as you do, even if we don't have the same shiny fleets."

"They are, indeed, rather shiny."

"The old empires were trying to tie a noose around us," Caryn continued. "Lock us into our borders and suffocate us. The New Empire was cutting off our overland routes and holding up shipments to and from the Fringes, in the name of fighting Steffians. When we tried to circle around them, Wassia closed the Amimi Canal. When we tried to bypass the canal by going around the cape, the ships we built were seen as a threat to Brealand."

"They *are* a threat to Brealand," Ravencliffe insisted. "I told you that yesterday. We need those assurances."

"I am going to do everything I can to get you what you need," Caryn promised. "Are you going to do the same for what I need?"

"Am I going to allow Deugan to flood Wassia and the Fringes with cheap products? Economic dominance over everything south of the mountains? I would have to be insane."

"It doesn't have to go that far," Caryn said. "A joint declaration recognizing Amimi independence. They can set their own canal policy."

"Amim's a Deugan outpost," Ravencliffe said dismissively. "I'll wager you already have a deal with them to get privileged access to the canal if you win. If we're talking about fairness, Minister, forget the allies that you bought and paid for. The Wassians keep the canal and guarantee everybody equal access, at an equal price. I'm certain my cousin and I can prevail on the Wassians..."

"Michael Ravencliffe! After a month and a half, you still think you can pull something like that over on me?"

Ravencliffe raised an eyebrow. "Are we on a first-name basis, Minister Hallom?"

Caryn laughed. She hadn't even realized that she'd shouted his full name, the way Jayla would have. "I suppose we are," she said. "Does that make you uncomfortable, Michael?"

"Not at all," he replied, though she could sense that it did. He hadn't said her own name yet. She wondered how she could use that.

"Well, Michael, here's the problem with your proposal. The Deugans will be the only non-Wassians using the canal, the only ones paying. Under your terms, Mike, they could effectively close the canal whenever they wanted just by jacking the price high enough. The Amimi already had home rule, and the canal's on their territory. Even if you don't support Amimi independence, Mikey, there's no justification for letting the Wassians control it."

"There's every justification," Ravencliffe replied. He pointedly ignored the nicknames. Fascinating, the little things that could faze a man normally so composed. "An asset like the Amimi Canal must be administered by the government for the common good. Amim is a colony. Its government, such as it is, doesn't have a shred of management experience. Wassia has the right to administer one of the most valuable assets in its territory."

"It's Amimi territory," Caryn insisted. "You're just worried about making any concessions in Amim because you think it will lead to demands from your island colonies."

"I'm worried about selling out Breland's allies," Ravencliffe rejoined, "especially in a manner that's doomed to failure. Think of Baron Halloway's land reform program."

"What about it?" This had suddenly become interesting.

"Why do you think it failed?"

Was it a coincidence that Ravencliffe had brought up Brenner's father? Or did he know somehow? Cautiously, Caryn probed him. "There are those who say Baron Halloway's program died when he lost his son. He was never the same after."

Ravencliffe swatted the notion away with a wave of his hand. "People have ridiculous ideas. Baron Halloway's program didn't fail because of some personal tragedy, it failed because it was idiotic. You can't just parcel off land to farmers and expect them to make a go of it, and you certainly can't expect the rest of the nobility to follow along. People need structure and direction."

He didn't know, then. Caryn breathed a little easier. "I imagine you would say your own land reform initiatives have been more successful? That whole collective system, or whatever you call it?"

"Since our reforms, we've seen marked advancements in innovation," Ravencliffe said. "Greater crop yields. Social cohesion too, I am told."

Caryn frowned. "I would have thought that innovation and yields would come from competition."

"A Deugan would have thought that," Ravencliffe agreed. "The secret is research. Each of our collectives benefits from what the others have learned. The National Department of Agriculture trains every collective and assists it in purchasing cutting edge technologies. Plus, the collectives foster a sense of teamwork, culture and identity, which are far more motivating to the workers than any profit could be."

"But you utterly control their lives," Caryn argued. "From what I understand, there are regimented schedules. Monitored production targets. Neighbours are urged to report on neighbours. And for all their work, the farmers barely get to keep any of the product or the profit. What can be less motivating?"

Ravencliffe looked at her quizzically. "You talk about the government's involvement as though it's a bad thing. It's the entire point. We develop expertise, and we apply it. A program like Halloway's, where you cut the government out and leave people to fend for themselves, it was doomed to failure from the start. That's exactly how you're proposing we deal with the Amimi Canal."

"You can't compare Halloway to your collectives," Caryn argued. "They're too different. Halloway wanted farmers to have freedom. The whole point of the collectives is to bring them under the government's control."

"The point of both programs was to make the populace better off by making better use of land. Government control or government abdication can only be means to an end."

"Perhaps," Caryn said, "but that's not how Baron Halloway saw it." Ravencliffe could not know how much time she and Brenner had spent talking through his father's ideas, so many years ago. "For Halloway, giving farmers land they could call their own, liberated from government control, actually was an end in itself. He believed that people should have the freedom to chart their own course. The freedom to fail."

"A freedom of which the good baron took ample advantage," Ravencliffe pointed out, "but be that as it may. If what you say is true, then Baron Halloway was consciously and deliberately acting against his own self-interest. Forget about giving away half his land. He was trying to weaken the very structures that kept him in power."

"You're right and you're wrong," Caryn said. "Personally, I think the reason Baron Halloway failed is that he *wasn't* willing to lay it all on the line. He wanted to make changes from within the Wassian establishment, and that limited him. He was still nobility. He had too much to lose." She paused. "You are right to an extent, though. Baron Halloway was far from selfish. In important ways, he did put his ideals ahead of his interests."

"Not unlike a certain Deugan foreign minister," Ravencliffe said with a smile.

"What do you mean?"

"Your Hallom Doctrine." Through all of their debates over the last month and a half, Caryn had steered the conversations away from her signature foreign policy. Now it seemed that the Doctrine would finally catch up with her. "A few minutes ago," Ravencliffe said, "you told me the New Empire cut off your trade routes on the pretence of fighting Steffians. But we both know there was a very real Steffian menace, and the trade the Steffians threatened was beneficial to Deugan and Orastus alike. So the natural Deugan response would have been to ally with the New Empire, root out the Steffians and protect your mutual interests. That's what anybody else would have done. But not Caryn Hallom."

This wasn't the first time Caryn had been called upon to defend her policy, and it was unlikely to be the last. "The threat to the New Empire wasn't just from the Steffians. There were independence movements cropping up everywhere. The situation was descending, fast."

"And the New Empire needed an ally," Ravencliffe insisted. "An ally with an interest in the existing relationships. Together, you could have preserved them, but you didn't. You supported independence."

"In an economic partnership," Caryn said. "Something akin to home rule. There was already precedent for it in Amim."

"It didn't matter," Ravencliffe said. "This is the New Bloody Empire we're talking about. They were never going to accept independence *or* home rule in the Fringes. You thought you could convince them, but deep down, you knew it. Yet still you put the Deugan ideal of liberty ahead of the Deugan self-interest in preserving the *status quo*. That was the essence of the Hallom Doctrine. That is why many of my countrymen can't take you seriously. They can't see you as anything other than a weak, soft politician who's unable to do what's necessary."

That word again. *Soft*. What he had mouthed to her during their very first meeting up in the chapel. "You don't see me that way."

"I don't," Ravencliffe admitted. "I see what the Hallom Doctrine was really all about. Perhaps even more than you do."

"More than I do?"

"You were — what's that Orastan expression? — going for the gold. Trying to get it all."

"I was," Caryn said. There was no denying that. "Home rule really was in the New Empire's best interest. They were about to lose the empire altogether, and the Steffians would be a terrible enemy. Home rule would have helped Orastus by allowing it to preserve a lot of the social and economic benefits of the empire. It would have helped us by keeping our trade routes open, with Fringes that would be grateful to us, and it would have helped everybody by completely undermining the Steffians."

"So you gambled that you would be able to persuade the New Empire to go along with it." Ravencliffe sat upright in his bed.

"That's not being soft, Minister. That's not avoiding the tough decisions. That is laying everything on the line. Sacrificing everything for a pragmatic solution."

Caryn was stunned. She couldn't remember Michael Ravencliffe ever paying her a compliment before. She suddenly felt unsure of herself. "T — thank you," she stammered.

"You are most welcome." Ravencliffe smiled. Then he leaned back against the stone wall and sighed. "Unfortunately, you lost your gamble. The New Empire did become your enemy. *That's* when they started making your overland trade in the east untenable. *That's* when you had no choice but to ship more and more goods through the Amimi Canal. But that could only anger the Wassians, since Amim alone was reaping all the benefits. So in a fit of pique, and knowing that the New Empire would support them, the Wassians closed the canal." Ravencliffe spread his arms before him. "Wassia and Orastus have been bitter rivals for centuries. Getting the two of them to team up against you? A remarkable accomplishment. Minister Hallom, have you ever considered that the reason you are so obsessed with seeking peace is that you feel guilty for starting the war in the first place?"

She slapped him hard across the face, glad that her stronger right arm remained uninjured. The fire was burning inside her. "How dare you," she shouted.

Ravencliffe gave no indication he'd even felt the blow, but he seemed to realize he had gone too far. "We can't have everything," he said apologetically. "I hear what you've said about Deugan's needs. Perhaps it is not my place to dictate how the canal is governed. As long as the Realm's interests are protected and our Wassian allies can be satisfied, I am certain an accommodation can be made with the Amimi. I will put some thought to it. I am happy to give your little southern outpost its 'freedom to fail.'"

"Thank you," Caryn said. She was still furious with him, but she couldn't deny that he had moved significantly over the last two days. Her fire had gotten results, though she still wasn't sure how. She stood to leave. "Colonel Ravencliffe. I realize we can't have everything. But I will have respect from you."

"You do have it," Ravencliffe said. "You are not nearly as soft as I'd been led to believe. I had thought that might be the case, and I'm pleased to discover I was right."

It was hardly the sort of apology Caryn had been hoping for. "Goodbye, Mikey," she said, and left.

*

General Freed's look was grave. He bowed to Caryn, deep, formal. Caryn returned it stiffly. The general simply looked away as he ushered Caryn and Hans into his office.

A number of chairs had been set up around his desk, and most of them were occupied. Marwin was there, and Janusz, Caryn's team. There was a woman there, too, the head of the fort's nursing staff. Her name was Hertha, and Caryn recognized her from repeated trips to the medical bay to have the bandages changed on her burned arm. The chaplain had been invited; Major Danzig had not. The general's conference had been carefully calculated, Caryn realized, to make her feel comfortable. That knowledge had the opposite effect.

The general stood behind his own chair and waited for Caryn to sit. She did, grudgingly. "Minister Hallom," he said, "I cannot begin to tell you how deeply sorry I am. Captain Toppel was one of my best men. In a hundred years I would never have imagined — but that is my failing, and you should not have had to suffer for it."

"Thank you," Caryn said. "As chance would have it, I was able to avoid suffering." Her anger had waned, but the ordinary panic had not returned to replace it. She felt weary, but her progress with Ravencliffe made her feel motivated, too.

"I have questioned Toppel myself. He denies everything. I showed him his crutch, stuffed with the leaves. He played stupid. I wish he hadn't. He could have made things a lot easier on himself."

"What will happen to him?" Caryn asked.

"Court martial," the general said. "As soon as we can convene one."

"Once the siege is lifted, you mean," Caryn said. To have a court martial, they would need to bring in an army lawyer and a hearing panel from Czemers, which was on the wrong side of the Hermann Gap.

"It will have to wait, yes."

Caryn looked around the table. Hans was leaning forward, an angry look in his eyes. Despite her reassurances, he still felt guilty about not being there last night. Marwin's eyes were fixed on the floor. Sorrow was etched on the chaplain's face. She could not read Janusz's expression. "In the interim," the general continued, "we will do what we can to improve your security. I trust you know Hertha, the head of our nursing staff."

Hertha was tall and slim, and older than Caryn. She had high cheekbones and a sharp nose. It was a hard face for a hard time. "My lady, I came to the general myself when I heard what happened to you," she said. "Dreadful. I wish I could say I've never seen anything like it, but I have. That is why my nurses have their own wing of the fort. There are guards, and there are other guards who watch the guards." So that had been necessary too, Caryn thought. "You won't be as comfortable as you are now in the officers' quarters, but you will be safer, my lady. There is a bed available."

Caryn nodded. She despised the idea of sequestering herself, but she did not see another option. She didn't have Hans and Reimund anymore, able to sleep in shifts so they could guard her all night. She was alone.

We can't have everything, Ravencliffe had told her. If you wanted to help the Fringes, you gave up friendship with the empire. If you wanted safety from attacks at night, you gave up the freedom to roam the fort. Would she be able to sneak out of the heavily guarded nurses' wing at night to make her way to the Well? Would she ever get a chance to question Matt about the Well's power? Not likely, but after last night, what choice did she have? "Thank you, my lady," Caryn said. "You are very kind."

Hertha shook her head. "I have seen more waking nightmares than you know. This is the least I can do."

Caryn could believe it. She was better known because of the years she'd spent in the public eye, but a woman of Hertha's age leading a military nursing contingent made her twice the trailblazer that Caryn was. Caryn shuddered to imagine the things she would have gone through.

"Minister," the general said, "I thought you would wish to know that I have already telephoned the president. I told him what happened and offered my sincere apologies."

"And berated him for sending me up here in the first place, I don't doubt," Caryn said.

"I couldn't help myself." Freed managed a smile. "My lady, if there is anything else I can do, anything at all, please let me know."

She looked around the table again. Captain Toppel had always been kind to her. Seemed to support her. Now the general was acting the same way, but Caryn knew from the prophecy that he would betray her, too. How could Freed help her with that?

Janusz leaned forward. He caught Caryn's eye and winked. Caryn was confused until she saw him mouth the word, "ships." *Of course*, Caryn thought. "Now that you mention it," she asked the general, "what would your position be, from a military standpoint, on discontinuing our ship-building program as part of a comprehensive peace treaty?"

"I'd think it was an invitation for the Breas to break the treaty in five years and land armies on our coasts," Freed said.

"That was my instinct too," Caryn replied. "I wonder if there might be some compromise. Work out how many ships we actually need to protect ourselves from an invasion, along with coastal installations on the land. Propose a plan that wouldn't make us an offensive threat."

"Is this something Ravencliffe has actually offered you?" Freed was surprised.

"We may have had something of a breakthrough," Caryn admitted.

Freed's entire deportment had changed. "I — well, it's not that I doubted you, but —"

"I doubted myself," she said. "Anybody would have. We're still nearer the beginning of a process than the end."

He was obviously impressed, and more than a little taken aback. "I — I will consult with Tomasburg. We'll get you a proposal to offer him." His eyes resolved into a glare. "You'd better get something Gods-damned good in exchange. What are you going to do about borders?"

Caryn had already thought that one through. "We'll end up with the pre-war borders, but I'll give him a song-and-dance about facts on the ground in Wassia, so he'll have to make some concessions to get them."

The general nodded. "Fine. If he gives you any attitude about facts on the ground in the Gateway, let him know, in no uncertain terms, that we're still here. We haven't fallen yet."

"Yet?" Caryn asked. A glance around the table told her that Janusz and Marwin had picked up on the word, too.

"Our food is running low," Freed admitted. "It takes a lot to feed 2,500 men, plus the nurses and the prisoners. We've been rationing tightly, but our supplies won't last another month. As you know, at the start of the siege I sent a number of our men to guard the villages and farms on this side of the Hermann Gap. I will ask them to ... persuade the locals to send some food our way. It will help, but it won't be enough. We'll need relief."

A grave silence followed. "Are we getting relief, General?" Hertha asked. Caryn found it interesting that the other woman would be bolder than any of the men in asking the obvious question. Hertha was outside the military hierarchy, less afraid of the general's rank, but perhaps it was also that she, like Caryn, had built a life out of standing up to authority.

"It's being hotly debated in Tomasburg," Freed said. "You've heard me say before that the war is a footrace. We need to knock Wassia out of the war before Breland breaks through in the northwest, so our offensive in the south and our defences near the coast are high priorities. It's uncertain how much of a priority we are. Some say we can afford to lose the fort altogether, because our trenches near Czemers can keep the Breas from getting any farther. Others argue that the Gateway is too strategic to simply abandon, and that we shouldn't let the Breas get within shelling range of Czemers."

"A million people live there," the chaplain said softly.

"I know that," Freed said, "but there's also the winter to consider. The Breas aren't the only ones we're racing against."

Caryn hadn't thought of that, but in hindsight it was obvious. She knew firsthand how harsh winters could be in Villasud. Once the seasons turned in the south of Wassia, their offensive would be stalled until the snow melted in the spring. In the desert heat of the Deugan northwest, Breland's attacks would face no similar problems.

They had launched the war in the winter, Caryn remembered. The Wassians had closed the canal to them in late autumn, when the shipping season was already winding down, so Caryn assumed that she would have all winter to negotiate its reopening. It was not to be. The Amimi leadership wanted to declare their move from home rule to full independence in winter, so they could consolidate their power before the Wassians had a real opportunity to invade. Deugan wanted to take Wassia by surprise in any event. So the plans were made, and it was on a frigid winter's day that the Deugan ships had surprised the Wassian fleet at anchor, and that the First Army had crossed the border into Estagan.

Now winter was coming upon them again. Almost a year, Caryn thought. How many more months could they let this continue? Was it really her fault for reaching too far?

"Now it is my turn to make an offer," Caryn told General Freed. "If there is anything I can do —"

"There isn't," he said sharply. "Just rest. Don't eat too much. Keep working on Ravencliffe. Pray." His eyes went to the chaplain, and then to the ceiling. "We need all the help we can get."

CHAPTER SEVENTEEN

Mila took a long puff on her cigar. She held her breath for a moment, savouring the taste, then sent the smoke wafting through the canvas tent. She was a stout woman, not tall but muscular, even though she was nearing fifty years in this life. Across from her, Matthias sat on the ground, waiting.

"We done you much already," Mila said finally in the broken Orastan she spoke. She hailed from the Range, the strip of land north of the Selliar Mountains that separated Orastus from the sea.

"And we for you," Matthias said simply.

Mila shook her head and folded her arms across the leather vest that she wore to cut the wind in the mountains. "Coins. No use in Range. What you give is promise."

She was right, Matthias reflected. The Rangers had given much to the Steffians, and guidance through the mountains was only the start of it. More valuable still were the donkeys bearing packs of dried fruit and salted meat to add to the provisions that Matthias's own team had brought up from Orastus proper. Heavily laden donkeys travelling from Orastan cities to the country's remote north would have raised suspicions. The same provisions in the hands of the nomadic Rangers was a fact of life.

Mila was right about another thing, too. The payment the Steffians had made for the Rangers' services had been limited to coins, guns and promises they were unlikely to keep.

"The Steffians want their own land," Matthias said. "They want control over those parts of the Fringes where Steifar are a majority.

Then they will spread the word of Good Steif throughout the remainder of the Fringes, and then across the Continent." He paused and locked eyes with the Ranger. "The Steffians will accept any ally, reward any friend who brings them closer to these goals."

Mila took another puff on her cigar, then slowly exhaled. "We know this," she said at last. "You fight empire. We like. But mountains between us and empire. No mountains between Brealand."

The nomads lived in tribes, worshipping gods they shared with the northern continent. Many lived by hunting game, still plentiful beyond the mountains, but many more were smugglers. They knew the passes through the Selliar Mountains intimately, knowledge that commanded handsome compensation from unscrupulous traders on the northern continent, and from crime rings and political dissidents in Orastus proper.

And now from the Steffians. It was unusual for the organization to engage a woman, but Mila's reputation had preceded her. She and her sons knew the mountain passes as well as any Ranger and had a knack for keeping out of sight of the New Empire. All the same, Matthias couldn't help feeling awkward. It was rare that he met any women in the course of his Steffian duties.

This conversation was not about his Steffian duties, however. Matthias made himself lean closer to Mila, breathing in the smoky air. "I understand the needs of the Range," he said. "It is significant that the Steffians choose the correct ally." He left it there. He had probably said too much already.

Matthias could see the wheels turning in Mila's head. She was clever, Matthias had realized that early on. She would have to be, to earn such respect as a smuggler. Mila knew full well that certain alliances could be as bad for business as they were for the Range as a whole. There was no love between the Range and nearby Brealand, and a fair bit of fear.

Mila chewed distractedly on her cigar. "None will know?"

"I ask only for a map," Matthias said, "if you can draw one. I will keep it hidden. You can be leagues away."

Mila considered for a time, then abruptly nodded. "I will draw," she said. "You will look. Remember. Then burn. Nobody find."

"Nobody will find it," Matthias repeated. "You have my word."

"You are brave man," Mila said.

"Not as brave as you, in your line of work."

Mila smiled. Although she was nearly two decades older than Matthias, she had a self-confidence that he found alluring. "This not brave. This just walking in mountains. Brave is having babies. That is how woman dies in Range, no fancy doctor like in empire."

Not the part of the empire I hail from, he thought, but there was no sense debating that. "Then you are brave indeed," he said instead. "I know of your sons. I'll bet you have daughters as well."

She didn't answer. Only took another puff on her cigar. "You are not like other Steffians," Mila said.

"That is a lovely compliment."

She laughed. "Good. We agree. So no one find map."

"No one," Matthias promised. He clasped the woman's hand, then withdrew from the tent into the cool mountain air.

So simple. A few words spoken in a tent in the hills, a life set on a dangerous new course. The day of decision was creeping ever closer. Soon Matthias would have to risk all to break with the Steffians, or give up his chance, possibly forever.

It had been a long journey to reach this point. The Steffians had made a headlong retreat from Kalid in the aftermath of the facility bombing, while the New Empire scoured the jungles, arresting hundreds. The Steffian Council convened at a remote spot in Accarro, where an intense debate broke out over whether to persist with a western operation or whether to use the limited *acambro* they'd salvaged in the Fringes. As always, only the presence of Pellor Amad, Master of Dignity, could calm the tensions. After an impassioned speech about rising above the challenges of present times, Amad declared that a contingent of four hundred men would go west with what *acambro* could be spared. If the western operation failed, little would be lost, but if it succeeded, it could change the shape of the Continent.

The warriors on the western operation were split into several teams, the better to travel unnoticed. Matthias' group crossed into Orastus proper from Accarro, easily climbing an unguarded section of the fence that divided the Imperial heartland from its colony. Still the journey was fraught with tension. The Steffians knew that one of their own had betrayed them to the New Empire in Kalid, and suspicions were everywhere.

At least the power was with him. Matthias had three *acambro* belts encircling his waist, and *acambro* was woven into several pieces of his clothing. The energy still objected, but he was able to soothe it, calm it. *I need you now*, he told it. *Just a little longer. Just until we reach Deugan. Then we'll be free.*

Matthias's companions, Master Gamoy's stooges all, were even angrier than the energy at being taken into Orastus proper. Two of them had never been before, and the differences from the Fringes were striking. Even the smallest, most backward villages had electricity and running water. In town after town they saw magnificent palaces or temples or arenas, beautifully preserved or restored from the days of the Old Empire, broadcasting the ancient Orastan glory. Several of the old buildings had been converted into courthouses or government offices, where they retained the opulence of their past. Seeing them, Matthias felt his own childhood anger returning. He went to sleep most nights seething at the thought of what that sort of wealth might have done for the Fringes.

But now, finally, Matthias had made it through Orastus and to the threshold of his new life. He was deep in the Selliar Mountains that divided the New Empire from Deugan. He had food. He had the *acambro*, still almost fully charged. He had the Steffian financial records he'd pilfered, safely tucked away where the others couldn't find them, a perfect gift for a government that might be persuaded to forgive Matthias's past. Soon he would also have Mila's map of the alternate routes into Deugan, the secret paths through the mountains that only the Rangers knew.

Only one piece was missing from his puzzle, and Matthias wasn't certain that he wanted to find it. Until he did, he could still turn back. Once he made contact, though...

Matthias had mapped as often as he dared during his month-long journey through Orastus, hoping to connect with her. He spoke with her, taught her, learned from her. He felt the power rush to her, saw her relax in it as though it were effortless. She was incredible.

Then, without a hint of a warning, she'd disappeared. Matthias had mapped nightly for the last two span without catching any sign of her. He had feared to move too quickly, knowing who she was, but now he worried that he'd lost her entirely. He knew the Gateway Fort was under siege. Anything could have happened.

He hadn't told Nono that he'd puzzled out Jayla's true identity. How many Deugan women would Nono be able to keep tabs on from the Fringes? A few, perhaps, but Caryn Hallom was the one who had disappeared from public view just when Nono claimed to have lost contact with "Jayla." Hallom's whereabouts had been subject to intense rumours, more than one of which placed her in the Gateway. And who but Caryn Hallom would show such a keen interest in the Steffians as to return to Matthias, night after night?

Now she had stopped coming, though, and the frustration was maddening. Matthias, through the grace of Good Steif, had made the acquaintance of the one person on the Continent who could guarantee him a welcome in Deugan, and now she was gone.

He knelt beneath a tree. The wind was growing stronger, colder. He clasped his hands to his heart and whispered a prayer to the one god. Below him on the hill, through the gathering dusk, he could see the tents his team and Nono's team had pitched. Many more Steffians would be arriving in the coming days, but Nono would move even before all of the others were here. He did not need an army for the first stage of his plan, and after what had happened in Ciorala, even the energy could sense the storm brewing.

The official news had not yet caught up with the teams in the hills, but Matthias had tipped himself into the map just in time to see a large batch of *acambro*, its colours shifting dangerously, suddenly flash and disappear. Even within the map Matthias recoiled, nearly losing the energy in the shock that touched his mind. He sought another Secrets user through the map and squeezed out a quick question in sailor's code. Master Gamoy, he was told, had finally managed to set off an *acambro* bomb, and he'd done it in the administrative heart of Ciorala. Gamoy and Amad would announce that they had struck a blow for the Fringes against the colonial ambitions of the empire — but would the Cioralae see it that way?

So Master Nono would move quickly. While the strength of the *acambro* bomb was fresh in his enemies' minds, but before the Imperial crackdown could grow too strong, before any backlash in the Fringes could overtake events in the west. Within days it would begin, and only Steif knew how it would end.

Sighing, Matthias made his way back to the tents, climbed into his own and closed the flap. He had lingered as long as he could. It was time to act.

Matthias grasped one of his *acambro* belts and spoke softly to the energy. It crept to him, hovering between trust and wariness.

Another soothing word, a closing of the eyes, a clearing of the mind. He conjured a vision of his mother, a fountain of love and warmth. He wondered what she would think if she saw her son now, in the borderland between Orastus and Deugan, so terribly far from home.

The columns emerged. The smaller lights flickered. And Caryn Hallom's hand closed around his.

Relief swept through him. "I missed you," he squeezed in sailor's code, so quickly that he wondered if she would understand.

If she did, she showed no sign of it. He sensed a coldness about her, even through the map, a feat he had never seen the energy perform for another. "Your people bombed Ciorala," Hallom said.

"Against my wishes," Matthias squeezed. "I learned afterward."

"Why believe you?" Harsh. It was far from promising.

Yet it carried the moment of truth with it all the same. If Matthias was going to break from the Steffians, he needed to act now. Matthias steadied himself, grasped her hand tighter, and started to squeeze in the code: "Because I can teach you." And then: "This is a map."

Slowly, painfully, he told her as much as he could through bursts of sailor's code. That the brightest column was always the Kalidi Well, and the two in a line nearby were Pascuay and Accarro. How to identify the others once those first three were in place. How the *acambro* showed up as flickering lights, carrying the power within it. How any *acambro* could become a bomb, but only with extraordinary difficulty, after hours of constant effort.

He sat back, the lump in his throat growing. Several seconds passed. Then, slowly, Hallom squeezed back to him: "You are close."

He looked around the map, impressed. A cluster of *acambro* was positioned not far outside the Gateway Well. Matthias's own was among it. More *acambro* was winding its way northwest through Orastus; others scattered the Fringes. Hallom had seized on the danger more quickly than Matthias expected. "Close," Matthias agreed. "With forty men. More coming."

"How many?"

If he answered that question, he had betrayed the Steffians in truth. There would be no turning back. But he had already betrayed them, Matthias reminded himself. He had betrayed them in thought, and that was enough.

He crossed the threshold. "More than three hundred. Less than four." He paused to let the numbers sink in. "Warn the government and the fort," he added.

A longer pause this time. Her presence in the map grew stronger, magnified by the power that clung to her in the Gateway Well. She was cold again. Colder than the wind sweeping through the mountains. "Nono told you who I am." It was not a question.

"No. I guessed."

"Why tell me this?" Hallom demanded.

"To prove my friendship," Matthias said. It was more direct than he would ever be in person, but it was difficult to express subtlety through sailor's code. He scanned the map again, just to be certain no Steffian was watching them.

"What do you want?"

A blunt question which needed a blunt answer. The threshold had been crossed. "Asylum," Matthias said.

He waited. The columns glowed around him, and the *acambro* lights shimmered. If Hallom refused him, only Good Steif knew what would Matthias would do. He was surrounded by Gamoy's men, who had no love for him or Nono. He would be found out, he was certain of it. He would avoid the Council's wrath only because he wouldn't live long enough to make it back to them. He raised his eyes to the top of the fluttering tent, illuminated in the light of the columns.

Hallom's response was stern, untrusting. "You are a Steffian," she coded to him.

"I am," Matthias admitted. Silently, he begged Good Steif for mercy. "That is why I need your help."

"How many men have you killed?"

At first he recoiled. Then, almost like magic, the answer leapt into his mind. After months of searching, after years of prayer, Good Steif was finally showing him the way.

"A fair question," Matthias coded back to her. "I admit I have killed many. But ask this question instead." He allowed his emotion to build inside him. He let himself feel scared, weak, desperate. When he could barely contain the depth of his feeling, he brought a picture of Mila's donkeys to his mind, laden with packs of food sufficient to feed the full Steffian expedition. His body went numb. Then his fingers and toes started to tingle, and the sensation worked up his arms and legs and through his chest.

When it was done, the vision planted in Hallom's mind, Matthias sat back, and with the strength of the one god coursing through him, said, "Ask how many men I might save."

CHAPTER EIGHTEEN

"Asylum," he had said.

The word was a magnet, drawing them close. After several span of circling, after training Caryn with the energy while dropping subtle hints about disagreements with his brothers, the Steffian had finally declared his allegiance. Now Caryn could only hope that Matt could be trusted.

Dawn was breaking over the Selliar Mountains, and Caryn's entire body was sore from the previous night's march. The mission had set out under cover of darkness to hide their movements from Brea and Steffian eyes, and they had covered the entire distance from the Gateway Fort to the Selliar foothills in only a few hours. It did not seem to pose much difficulty for the trained Deugan soldiers, but for Caryn, after spending most of the last two months seated at telegraph machines or in Ravencliffe's cell, the pace had been gruelling. In the end, it was only by leaning on Hans and cursing Major Danzig under her breath that she had made it at all.

Danzig simply didn't believe the tale she told: that the president had spoken to her on the telephone and passed along a tip that the Steffians had a lightly guarded food caravan hidden in the Selliar Mountains. Caryn herself realized how foolish it sounded, but she couldn't very well tell them she had seen the food through a vision sent to her by a Steffian turncoat using energy-powered leaves. Caryn had no idea whether the general actually bought her story, but he declared that if there was even a chance her tip was correct, they could not afford to ignore it.

Even so, Major Danzig and the other officers might have derailed the mission had events not begun unfolding exactly as Matt said they would. The communications hub received a cable from a source in the Fringes, asking that Deugan send a single representative to meet with Brenth Nono, Master of Secrets, in the foothills of the Selliar Mountains. The message mentioned the Steffians' powerful new weapon, their mutual enemy in the New Empire, and an offer Nono wished to present which could change the course, not only of the war, but of history.

It was a message, Caryn had no doubt, that Freed and Danzig would otherwise have ignored. But if the Steffians really were in the mountains — if Nono and his protectors would be at the meeting place instead of guarding their food stores — if Matt could be trusted...

In the end Danzig consented to the raid, but on strict conditions. If the foreign minister wanted this mission, she would have to bind her own life and her friends' lives to it. It was the only way to be certain Caryn wasn't lying to them, leading them into a Steffian trap or a Brea one. So Janusz and Marwin were assigned to the raid on the food stores, and Caryn and Hans would attend the wilderness meeting with the Master of Secrets. With Brenner.

Caryn stared around the camp as she rubbed feeling back into her legs with her good hand. The soldiers were stirring, packing up their tents and bedrolls and eating their sparse breakfast. She wondered whether they were scared of what lay ahead. She could sense Marwin's anxiety, though he was trying gamely to hide it.

If the soldiers were nervous, Caryn thought, it wasn't just because of the upcoming raid. The news from the northwest had shaken the Gateway Fort, and morale was only beginning to recover. Last span the Brea fleet had finally joined the war, barraging a Deugan border fort and barring reinforcements from reaching it. Within days the fort had fallen, and its inland neighbour was taken shortly afterward. The Deugan army had made a well-organized retreat and had anchored its new trench line only a few leagues further south, but psychologically the battles were devastating. Losing the Hermann Gap to a Brea sneak attack was one thing; Brealand muscling its way into two Deugan forts in frontal assaults was another. Worse still was the sheer magnitude of the casualties on both sides of the battle. Caryn told herself that Ravencliffe was wrong, that all of those deaths hadn't been her fault, that the generals and the politicians were on a warpath that had nothing to do with her foreign policies. But even if Caryn hadn't started the war, she had also singularly failed to end it, and now she was marching into battle herself.

Caryn, Hans, Captain Malitz and two other men set off for the meeting place around midday. The rest of the expedition had ascended into the mountains earlier, taking their positions for the raid against the Steffians' food stores. Caryn's group, meanwhile, was meant to distract Nono and his protectors for as long as possible, to give the raid its best chance of succeeding. Caryn cursed Major Danzig again. She and Hans were bait, and soon she would catch her first glimpse of Brenner in fourteen years. She didn't know what to expect, or even what to think. Her anxiety must have shown, because Hans looked at her, concerned, but she shook her head and stared pointedly at the ground. *He isn't Brenner anymore*, she told herself. *It's been fourteen years, he isn't Brenner*, and then she saw Brenner.

She was glad that she didn't have to speak, because her heart lodging in her throat would have made it impossible. He stood on a grassy hill a few yards above the Deugan team, as though on a raked stage. His cowl covered his head, but his body language radiated power, so unlike the moody, slouching Brenner she had known. Yet he was Brenner all the same, in his eyes, in his face, in his warmth. Unconsciously she sidled behind Hans, as though perhaps that way Brenner wouldn't notice her, wouldn't see how much she had changed over the years, how easily Jayla had been lost beneath the pressures of Caryn Hallom. Brenner himself appeared to be alone, but Caryn could hear the high-pitched ringing that told her the energy was with him, struggling against the leaves that Matt had called *acambro*.

Then he spoke, and he was Brenner no longer. Brenth Nono the Steffian towered over them on the hill. "Welcome, my friends!" His voice was unnaturally magnified, and Caryn faltered backward in surprise. She was impressed by his showmanship, but she saw her team exchanging uneasy glances. Like most of the Continent, they had not seen the Well's power before. "I'm surprised to see so many of you," Nono continued. "I'd asked for a single representative."

Malitz overcame his surprise. He stepped forward, climbing the hill a few feet. "I'm your representative," he shouted. His voice sounded shrill and weak compared to Nono's amplified tones. "Tell your snipers to come out into the open and drop their weapons, and my men will drop theirs."

Caryn looked up and saw the two ridges now. Of course. The Steffians would have a perfect view of the meeting place below. Nono was as well protected as if he were surrounded by machine gunners. Caryn felt suddenly afraid.

She saw Nono give a nonchalant shrug, so out of character that she nearly laughed. He had obviously been practicing; he looked almost as natural as Ravencliffe. "Your men can keep their weapons," Nono said. "I have weapons of my own." He snapped his fingers.

The energy erupted out of the *acambro* unlike anything Caryn had experienced before. In a matter of seconds the cloudless sky had darkened and the heavens had opened. The rain thundered down on them in sheets, soaking them to the bone, drowning the grass beneath them and churning it into mud. The wind howled around them, strong as Brea shells.

"The Steffians have come to offer you their friendship," Nono announced, the energy amplifying his voice above the pounding rain and the shrieking wind. "As we speak, Steffian operatives, armed with the same power you see around you, are sneaking into the Realm of Brealand through the Range. Our weapons can be turned against the Breas. Storms to ravage their fleets. Bombs to break their trenches and decimate their armies."

Caryn could see Malitz and the others, braced against the downpour. Malitz was struggling to move up the hill, closer to Nono, to prove he wasn't afraid. Hans and the other soldiers were following. Caryn, on the other hand, was searching for the energy Nono was drawing on. She cleared her mind and let the rain wash over her, feeling it warm her, move her.

"What do you want from us?" she heard Malitz shouting.

"An alliance," Nono repeated. "The most natural one in the world. You're already at war with the New Empire, as are we, but you've funded militia groups who fight against us. It makes no sense." He snapped his fingers again. Instantly the rain turned to hail, pelting them painfully. "If Deugan will recognize Steffian sovereignty over the Fringes and fight with us against those who would oppose our liberty, we will fight with you against Brealand."

It happened when Nono snapped his fingers that second time. Caryn, her mind and soul tuned to the power, felt the shift, and suddenly she realized where it had come from — Nono's own clothing! The *acambro* leaves were woven into it, hidden in plain sight. It was so delicate, so elegant. Captain Toppel's methods, stuffing the leaves into a gun barrel or a crutch, seemed childish in comparison.

"Hail doesn't win battles," Malitz shouted. He was braver than Caryn had imagined, facing down the power with nothing but a rifle in his hands. Caryn stretched her mind, reaching for the energy that Nono was drawing on. Might she be able to draw it out of the *acambro*, as she had that night against Toppel? Nono was the Master of Secrets, certainly stronger than Toppel, but Caryn knew the energy's hatred for the *acambro*. With Nono concentrating on his voice amplification and the rain effect at once, she might have a chance.

"Hail alone doesn't win battles," Nono agreed. He snapped his fingers, and the ice pellets melted back into a heavy rain. "But surely you've heard of the Steffians' bomb?"

Malitz spat. Hans and the others had come up beside him. "Tales and rumours," Malitz said. "What happened in Ciorala? Some 75-millimetre shells and a flamethrower could have done that."

Nono merely smiled, a smile that Caryn had seen hundreds of times before. Her stomach knotted at the memory. Nono did not seem to notice. With a gloved hand, he grasped a pouch that hung from his belt, reached into it and extracted a single tiny shred of an *acambro* leaf. Caryn could see it changing colours, now red, now orange, now yellow, and she heard the high-pitched screeching of the energy, even louder than the wind. "I believe it is time," Nono said, "for a demonstration."

He let the *acambro* go.

The wind shifted so that it carried the tiny leaf northward, away from the soldiers on the hill, and Caryn marvelled at Nono's control. Finally, when it had fluttered almost out of sight, Nono pointed at it, and the Selliar Mountains were rocked by an explosion so powerful that the soldiers were flung handily to the ground, the mud beneath them cushioning their fall.

Nono stood. The rain still pounded around him, but in the moment he'd set the bomb off, Caryn had tapped into the energy and drained as much of his *acambro* as she could. Keeping up three effects at once, he hadn't seemed to notice.

"The Steffians' bomb is real," Nono said to the soldiers, who were also struggling to their feet. "That was a mere shred of *acambro*. Imagine what could be done with a whole leaf, or with an entire vine."

Malitz finally looked cowed. He was shivering in the cold rain, and Hans looked more afraid than Caryn had ever seen him.

"Don't look like that," Nono said in a friendly tone. "We are friends here, after all. We want to use this power to help you. Although I must admit," he added, "that some among us would be willing to accept help from other sources."

He trailed off, but the threat was clear. Deugan might be the Steffians' more natural ally, but the same offer would be made to Brealand. Betray the New Empire, recognize Steffian independence, and enter a mutual defence pact that would dominate the Continent. Caryn's mind raced. If *acambro* could be woven into cloth, it could be hidden anywhere. In homes, in factories, in stadiums. She remembered the Steffian she had interviewed in the prison in Tomasburg, a member of a home-grown cell who had schemed to bomb Deugan government buildings. The operatives were already in place, Caryn realized. If the Steffians' bomb was nothing more than *acambro*, there might be one hidden in the heart of the capital already.

"Take your time to consider," Nono said. "I imagine you'll have to consult your superiors in the army, and your elected officials —"

Nono was still speaking, but Caryn couldn't hear him. Her entire body had gone suddenly numb, and then a vision flashed before her eyes. Two men, sniper rifles dropped and forgotten, one with a bullet in his skull, the other with two in his chest. The dead men were atop a ridge, looking down on a group of Deugan soldiers below.

Caryn struck out with her mind, draining the rest of Nono's *acambro* and in a fluid motion driving the energy into the ground beneath him. To Malitz and the others, it would look as though Nono had merely slipped in the mud, but as he fell, the rain abruptly ceased, and Caryn pointed and shouted, "Seize him!"

The seconds that followed were the ones that would feature most prominently in Caryn's nightmares about the war. Not, as she would have expected, the memory of being attacked herself in the basement of the Gateway Fort, nor the time Captain Toppel ordered her out of bed in the dead of night, nor the mangled bodies she'd seen during the battle. What would haunt Caryn's dreams was the order she gave, and its consequences.

For had she thought it through, instead of reacting to the vision in the moment, Caryn might have realized that she had been shown only one ridge, not two. She might have stayed her order, and the soldier who had rushed to obey it might have lived.

Blinding white light erupted over the second ridge. The surviving Deugans charged up the hill to the fallen Master. And Caryn collapsed in tears, overwhelmed by all that she and Deugan had lost.

*

The rain fell in sheets, and Matthias shivered. He was cold, wet and scared. Ranne huddled beneath a heavy cloak, clutching a rifle in his hands. "Useless," he muttered. "Can't see a damn thing."

Matthias shrugged, trying to make it look casual. "Means anyone out there can't see us either," he said. He needed to move. Now, when the visibility was bad, now was his time. But he hesitated. The Steffians had been his family these last several years. He had eaten with them, laughed with them, fought with them. They were the brothers he had never had.

Even after all the Steffians had done, it felt wrong somehow. It felt wrong to be betraying Master Nono, who had taught him so much. Wrong to leave Jakim and so many other friends. Most of all, it felt wrong to be abandoning the fight in the Fringes before their task was complete. The New Empire was teetering, but it still stood.

A flash of anger came back to Matthias at that. Thirteen years of his life dedicated to a single purpose; everything else faded into the background, family, old friendships; and he had failed. His home colony of Pascuay had issued a declaration, but that meant little unless the empire could be defeated, and it couldn't. Not by the Steffians. That was why they had come here, to the distant west, to beg protection from Deugan and Brealand. A shoddy sort of independence.

But there was nothing to be done. His anger was a childhood relic, and the time had come to let it go. To leave his past behind him, once and for all. Caryn Hallom had offered him a new life, and he intended to take it.

"You're sure this rain isn't real?" Ranne muttered.

"I'm sure the power's making it happen," Matthias replied. "It's still real enough."

There was a clap of thunder, a gust of wind. "If Nono can do that," Ranne asked, "why does he need his back guarded?"

Matthias needed to extract himself from Ranne. He had arranged matters so that the two of them would be alone, guarding this path between their camp and the meeting place. Getting away from one person shouldn't be difficult, but in the moment it was harder to do. Matthias didn't want to kill Ranne if he didn't have to. He wanted to be through with killing — and Good Steif would want that, too.

"Rain doesn't stop bullets," Matthias said shortly.

"Don't give me that."

"Truth is," Matthias said, "nobody ever fought wars in Wells. The Wells weren't on the front lines. Since you couldn't use Secrets anywhere else, the energy doesn't have much experience in fighting."

Ranne understood. "The Old Empire used it for prophecy, mostly. I remember learning that."

Matthias nodded. "Nono's creative enough that in a pinch, I'm sure he could come up with some way to defend himself. But it's not something we've practiced enough to leave to chance."

He'd buried his pack beneath some bushes near the start of the path he intended to take into Deugan. He had filled the pack this morning: a skin of water, a hunk of salt beef and a packet of dried fruit, a shirt and a change of pants woven with *acambro*. Knife, rope, matches. He had almost added the financial records before thinking better of it and stuffing them into the clothes he was wearing. They were too valuable and too damning if they were found.

When the pack was ready, Matthias had clasped his hands over his heart. One last prayer to Good Steif, who had led him this far. One last thank you to the power, one last promise. "You've been patient," Matthias whispered. "You've been kind. By day's end, I will be in Deugan, and there I will set you free. If Steif wills it."

Now the energy shifted. Around him it started to hail. He wouldn't have a better chance. Matthias closed his eyes briefly, feeling the ice pelting against him, then opened them again. Ranne was still huddled beneath his cloak and hadn't noticed anything, but when the ice touched Matthias's skin he felt a presence in it, as though another person were inside the energy, probing.

His heart fell. What was Hallom doing there, beneath the guns of Nono's snipers? She was his ticket into Deugan. If anything happened to her...

"Matt." Ranne snapped to attention. He was looking at Matthias strangely. "You're looking sick. You see something?"

"Feel something," Matthias said carefully. A half-truth was more powerful than a lie, Nono often said. "Someone's using Secrets who isn't Nono. Who isn't one of us."

Ranne swore. "Empire?"

"That's what I thought too. But I can't be sure." It was time to move. Matthias stood, screwing his face into a look of urgency. "It's coming from the ridges, where Nono is, and I don't think he's noticed. I've got to check it out."

"Alone?" Ranne frowned.

"Someone needs to guard the pass," Matthias said. "I'll be back soon." He clasped his hands to his heart. "May Steif protect both of us."

"Praise to Steif," Ranne said, and Matthias was off.

He made his way to the ridges. The hail turned back to rain as he was walking, and Matthias pushed through it, wishing he could be going in the other direction, toward the pass he had chosen to Deugan. Why had Hallom come? What if something had happened to her already? What would he do if Nono saw him trying to save her?

Matthias started to run. His shoes made footprints in the wet ground, but there was nothing to be done for it now. He would have to try to hide his tracks when he made his way back.

Matthias had just come across the first ridge when the *acambro* bomb exploded. The force of it was overwhelming, the noise terrifying. Matthias saw the soldiers below thrown to the ground. The snipers on the ridge before him covered their heads in their hands, trying to shield themselves from the strength of the blast.

It was not an opportunity to waste. Matthias drew his pistol and shot the first sniper in the back of the head, silently asking Steif for forgiveness as he did it. He missed the first shot he aimed at the second sniper, but as the man turned around, Matthias caught him with two quick bullets in the chest. Matthias looked over the ridge at Nono and the soldiers and hurled a vision down to Hallom.

As soon as he did it, he knew it was a mistake. He saw Hallom pointing, the snipers on the other ridge firing, the Deugan soldier falling. Matthias had been too quick to show her that one ridge was cleared, and she'd assumed that both were. He started to panic. The other snipers would make short work of the Deugans now, and Hallom was among them. Desperately, Matthias reached out to the *acambro* he had woven into his shirt, and it answered him. It erupted into a flare on the other ridge, bright as the sun that Steif made to patrol the skies of his Worlds.

Matthias saw the Deugans binding Nono's arms and dragging him off, his *acambro* drained to nothing. He saw the snipers on the other ridge rising, beginning to recover from their blindness, but too late. Hallom was saved, but they had taken Nono, and Matthias had helped them do it.

There was no time to think about it, to grieve on it, even to pray for Good Steif's guidance and mercy. Matthias was standing above two dead Steffians, and if the snipers on the other ridge didn't find him, others would. He had to move, and fast.

He ran back the way he'd come, then turned west and charged into the trees, making a wide circle around the place where he had left Ranne. He trudged southward for nearly an hour, struggling to picture Mila's map in his mind. At length the trees thinned out and small bushes arose to replace them. Matthias slowed and scanned the ground. He was close to the path he meant to take, which would lead him down into the Gateway, not far from the Well. There he could take cover, release the energy from his *acambro*, and finally meet Hallom face to face.

The entrance to the path was hidden in the bushes, but a curved rock marked its place. He found the path and started toward it.

Then he saw his pack.

It was lying in the centre of the path, sliced open. The ground where he had buried it was dug up. His waterskin lay on the ground, emptied, and his food and supplies had disappeared, with a single exception. His knife had been driven hard into a fallen log, marking the place where a word had been carved into the wood: "traitor."

The fist took him in the gut.

Matthias doubled over, clutching his stomach. He looked around wildly for his assailant and saw nothing but empty air. The next blow caught him in the side of the head, and he fell to the ground hard, the air knocked out of him. No sign of the other man. Nothing but the howling of the wind.

He turned his mind to his assailant, forcing himself to stay calm, though his breathing was shallow and his vision blurred. He loved his attacker, Matthias told himself, rising again to his feet. He wanted to be closer to him. Matthias bent his mind to reach for him, stretch for him, he and the power together.

When the next blow came Matthias blocked it. Then he grasped the invisible hands as tightly as his tired state would let him. Matthias felt the energy hands as though they were his own, an extension of his body. He used his real hands, clenched in fists, to direct them, guide them. He felt the other man's energy hands wrestling against his own, strong, and Matthias strained to hold them off.

Then Rusul stepped into view, crawling out from behind a bush, his pistol levelled at Matthias's heart.

Matthias took a deep breath, still waiting for the dizziness to clear. He heard footsteps behind him and turned to see three more Steffians, below him down the path he meant to take into Deugan. The barrels of their rifles gleamed in the sunlight. Behind Rusul stood the Secrets user who had attacked him, a broad-chested man named Hakal. His face was screwed up in concentration as his real hands struggled to control his energy ones.

"Start talking," Rusul said.

The dizziness was finally subsiding, though Matthias felt a trickle of blood running down the side of his face. He grunted with the effort of holding off Hakal's energy hands. Both men's real hands looked as though they were grappling the air as they wrestled with each other across the distance. "Talking about what?" Matthias forced himself to say.

Rusul strode toward him and struck him in the head with the butt of his pistol, right where Hakal had wounded him. Matthias's temple exploded into pain and he fought to keep his balance. "Your pack was full of supplies. Where were you going?"

"I keep a full pack hidden in case there's an emergency," Matthias said.

A flimsy excuse, and Rusul knew it. Rusul aimed the pistol at him. For a terrible moment Matthias thought he would shoot. Then he heard a snort of laughter behind him. "What's so funny?" Matthias asked.

"Your hidden pack was not especially hidden," Rusul said. "A flare exploded from it, not half an hour ago. Why?"

It would be easier to think of responses if he didn't have to wrestle Hakal and battle the pain in his head at the same time. "I don't know," he managed.

"This is not a game," Rusul replied, levelling the pistol at him again. "Why did you set off that flare?"

"I didn't," Matthias insisted. "Think about it, Rusul, if I was running away from you and trying to hide it, why would I plant my pack half a league from your camp and set off a flare over it?"

"What if you were leading someone else to our camp?" Rusul asked darkly.

"Then I'd set off the flare over the camp itself," Matthias said. "No need to take the *acambro* out here and bury it. Are you sure none of your men set it off?"

"I will ask the questions," Rusul shouted. He paused. "You couldn't have set off the flare," he said finally. "You were too surprised when you saw the pack dug up. But none of my men did either. Could it have been done from the fort?"

"That far away?" Matthias grunted. He thought, though it was difficult. His muscles were straining from the effort of battling Hakal, and if he turned his mind from the energy for too long, he risked losing the invisible hands altogether. "Someone really powerful. Nono could, maybe. I couldn't." Hallom could probably do it, but why would she? And how would Rusul know she was a Secrets-user? Or was he not talking about Hallom at all? "You've got a mole in the fort," Matthias realized. "Damn it, Rusul, you didn't tell Nono?"

Rusul swung at him again. Matthias turned his head and caught only a glancing blow, but it distracted him enough for Hakal to move past his defences and land a blow on his side. He doubled over. The rifleman laughed again. "Nono knows," Rusul said coldly. "You weren't told because you didn't need to know, and now it's clear you can't be trusted. So answer my questions. If we have an agent in the fort, but he can't do it from the fort, what does that mean?"

"It means he's not in the fort anymore. He's nearby." Matthias had started to figure out what was happening, even if the others hadn't. "I think this was all a coincidence. He was trying to tap into the nearest *acambro* he could find, and it happened to be mine. He only had a split second away from the others, and he was trying to warn you."

"Warn us of what?" Rusul demanded at the very moment that a man appeared on a crest behind Hakal. "Rusul!" the man panted, nearly out of breath. "Deugans! In force! At least a hundred of them, coming up the next pass!"

Rusul rounded on Matthias. "You knew about this!"

"I swear, Rusul —"

"Is that where you were going, to join them?"

"I'm trying to figure out where the flare would have come from," Matthias said. A half-truth was more powerful than a lie. "It's the only thing that makes sense."

He saw Rusul flip his pistol around again and move in to strike him with the butt. He saw Hakal, stretching and twisting his real hands to control the energy hands as they wrestled. Just as Matthias had done so far, just as any man caught off guard by a sneak attack would have done, or any amateur.

Matthias kept his grip on Hakal with his energy hands, while one of his real hands shot up to block Rusul's blow. The other formed a fist that cracked Rusul across the side of his face, sending him sprawling to the ground and the pistol skirting out of his hand. He saw Hakal's jaw drop and seized his opportunity. Matthias's energy hands closed around Hakal's leg and yanked it out from under him. Hakal lost command of his own energy hands when he hit the ground, and they dissolved into mist.

Matthias ran, the invisible hands forgotten. The riflemen were still between him and the path he intended to take to Deugan, so he ran south along the hilltop, toward the next pass where the Deugan soldiers would be coming. He flew across the grass as fast as his legs would take him, and he heard the Steffian riflemen pounding after him. A shot was fired and Matthias's shoulder erupted in pain, but he kept running, madly, blindly.

Finally, he heard Rusul call off the riflemen, shouting at them to make for the camp to defend against the Deugan attack. Matthias kept running, his feet churning up the still-wet earth. He didn't stop until he was well beyond the next pass, the one he'd instructed the Deugans to take. Then he sat and rested, struggling desperately to catch his breath.

The Deugans would have arrived by now, he guessed, and a pitched battle would be raging. Most of the Steffians hadn't arrived yet, and with Matthias, Nono, Ranne and the four snipers away from the camp, there would only be about forty Steffians guarding it. The Deugans should make short work of them.

It would barely affect the mission, though. The vast majority of the Steffians would arrive after the Deugan expedition was long gone. Nono's capture would throw a wrench into the plans, but Rusul cared little for Nono, and he would push forward regardless. The loss of their food supplies would make the Steffians want to move faster. Rusul would push for either the Deugans or the Breas to accept the Steffian offer, playing one off against the other.

Matthias wondered whether the Deugans would accept. They had to, he told himself. They couldn't afford to have the *acambro* fall into Brea hands. But if that did happen, Matthias could defend them. The bombs were surprisingly easy to defuse, if you knew how. Another gift Matthias could lend his new country, another proof of his loyalty.

If only he could get there.

When Matthias had caught his breath, he took account of his injuries. His head was still bleeding, but barely. He ripped a strip off his shirt and wrapped it tight around his wound, like a bandana. If he was lucky, the energy woven into it might even help him to heal.

Worse was his shoulder. Matthias turned another strip from his shirt into a bandage and wrapped it tight around the wound, but he had no way to extract the bullet. He had lost a lot of blood, and his shoulder was already swelling. Matthias sighed, gritted his teeth and rose to his feet.

He knew from Mila's map that there were no other passages into Deugan that he could reach from here. To the south, the gradual mountain slope ended and a sheer cliff took its place, and Matthias had no rope or tools with which to scale it. He would have to descend back into Orastus and make his way to the next path, several leagues further south. He would miss the rendezvous he'd scheduled with Hallom in the Well, but he might still make it into Deugan.

It took him three days to descend the mountain. Matthias was sore from the blows he'd taken, his muscles weak from the struggle with Hakal, his head spinning from the blood he'd lost. Without any food or water, he'd turned to the energy for sustenance, but it was a huge drain on his stores. Worse still was the wound on his shoulder. He had persuaded the power to patch him up and heal his skin, but with the bullet still lodged there, the wound kept re-opening. Eventually Matthias realized that he didn't have enough energy to keep healing himself. He'd exhausted the *acambro* woven into his shirt and had drained a fair amount from his pants too. The belt was still full, but the rest of his *acambro* had been lost with his pack. He would have to leave the wound alone for now, clean it and wrap it as best he could and hope it could be treated properly when he reached Deugan.

As the fourth and fifth days passed, Matthias began to doubt whether that would ever happen. He spent the days trudging southward through Orastus proper, Steif's hot sun beating down on him and draining what little strength he had left. On the sixth day, when he finally started back into the hills, he found himself unable to climb, and he could do little more than crawl into some brush to hide himself and sleep.

Matthias was woken by a boot in his ribs. When he blinked his eyes open, he was staring down the barrel of a rifle.

"Who are you?" a harsh voice called. Matthias looked up to see the uniform, the emerald green of the Imperial Army.

He had no papers, no identification. He tried to speak, but he could only cough. His shoulder ached terribly.

A second rifle appeared, a third, a fourth. Too many for Matthias to fight, even with Secrets. It was as he had told Ranne — the power had no experience in war. Hakal had been clever with his energy hands, but four hands would be of little use against four rifles.

"Strip him," the first man said. They did it, with crisp efficiency. Matthias felt the power slipping away from him as his pants and belt were torn from his body.

"Holy hell," he heard one of the men say, and Matthias knew they had found the financial records. "Sir, you better see —"

"You a Steffian?" the first soldier asked, the rifles moving closer.

"Not anymore," Matthias said, resigned. It was more powerful than a lie, but not powerful enough.

CHAPTER NINETEEN

Thus says Good Steif: "You shall spread out in the world and bring its peoples to My side; they must be turned to My favour. Those who diligently study My teachings, I shall guide to the higher Worlds; but those who turn from Me, those who worship false gods, they must be judged. They must know no rest, no mercy. They have denied My name, as the false god Rao did, and they must be struck down, as he was."

Yet thus also says Good Steif: "Lift not the sword against thy neighbours. Treat them with love and kindness, shower them with justice. For it is through your love that they shall find Mine."

These teachings, contradictory though they may seem, are easily reconciled. Man is to spread the light of Good Steif through love, not through war. It is the visible example of love, truth, justice and peace, shining in the heart of every Steifar, which will guide the non-believers to His light.

As for those who are so wicked that they cannot accept love, yes, they must be judged; but not by their fellow men, crafted for truth and kindness. The wicked must know no rest, no mercy; but it is not for men, spirits of hope and faith, to deny it to them. This is the teaching of the One God: that the burden of judgment shall rest on Him alone.

A terrible burden it is, for one who loves.

— Edict pronounced in 1487 by Tinok Maday, High Cleric of the Western Congregation of the Steifar, headquartered in Amim. The teachings of the Amimi clerics are normally disregarded by the Eastern Congregation, based in the Fringes.

"A leaf." General Freed leaned back in his chair and rubbed his temples. Nearby, Major Danzig paced nervously.

"Yes, sir," Captain Malitz replied. "He floated it away on the wind and set it off, and the explosion —" He shuddered, remembering. "I've never seen anything like it in my life."

For a long while the only sound was the thudding of Danzig's footsteps against the floor. Finally the general spoke again. "We've seen those leaves before."

Danzig's head snapped around. "Do you think —"

"That all of these weapons are connected? Yes, I do."

"But that means we could have a Steffian in the fort," Danzig said.

"Captain Toppel and I will be having a little chat," Freed replied. "Have no concerns on that front."

Danzig shook his head. "It doesn't make sense. If the Steffians have the leaves and an operative here, why haven't they blown us up already?"

"How should I know?" Freed asked. "Maybe they still want an alliance with us. Maybe Toppel was the only operative, and we intercepted him before he had a chance. Maybe their mission was just to target the foreign minister. There could be a hundred reasons."

"One of those bombs could be ticking in the fort as we speak," Danzig said. "And somebody had the bright idea of kidnapping their Gods-damned Minister for Magic."

Caryn rose. She felt herself shaking and tried to hide it. She glanced at Janusz, glad to have him by her side, but she still wished that her left arm was working. It wasn't that she needed it right at this moment, but it would make her feel less broken. "In my defence, our capture of Colonel Ravencliffe has kept the Breas off us for months. Taking Brenth Nono could have the same effect with the Steffians."

The general rubbed his temples again. "But they offered us an alliance. It was a parley."

"It was a diversion," Caryn reminded him. "We were raiding their food stores. We never intended to respect a parley."

"Which is why we need to move fast," Danzig said. "They must be furious with us, but they did call us their natural allies, and they're right. There may still be time to make amends before they hand their super-weapon to the Breas."

"What do you suggest?" Freed asked.

"Contact the Steffians immediately," Danzig responded. "Send a cable on the same line they used to reach us, or send a rider back to the meeting place. Offer to release Nono, return the food we stole, apologize, do whatever it takes to make sure that they keep their offer open. Then get on the phone to Tomasburg."

"Would you agree, Captain?" Freed asked Malitz.

Malitz nodded. "In my respectful opinion, sir, we need that weapon."

"We may," Freed allowed. "Minister Hallom?"

Caryn chose her words carefully. "From a military standpoint, I cannot say whether we need any particular weapon or not." She hesitated and glanced at Janusz, who nodded encouragement. "I do believe that even if the weapon could remove Brealand from the Continent at the turn of a crank, an alliance with the Steffians would be a high price to pay."

"What price would we pay if the Breas get the weapon?" Danzig demanded. "Have you thought about that? How many millions of Deugans might die?"

"I'm sure we've all thought long and hard about that," the general said before Caryn had a chance to answer. "There aren't any idiots at this table." He turned to Caryn. "Do you know how to clear an enemy trench? Gas has worked wonders at times, but the Wassians have learned to defend against it. The only other ways we've found have been flamethrowers and hand grenades."

"Not artillery?" Caryn was surprised.

The general shook his head. "Not without some very lucky shots. The main thing artillery's good for is covering fire. If it's focused and intense, it'll let your men get close enough to use their flamethrowers and hand grenades. Even so, they're running into machine guns that can fire 600 rounds a minute. Trenches can be taken, and in Wassia we've taken plenty of them, almost all the way down to the Amimi border in some places. But it has come at enormous cost. Tens of thousands dead or wounded."

Caryn took a deep breath. "So it's not just about keeping it away from the Breas," she said. "Even in our hands, this weapon could save Deugan lives."

"Not only that," Danzig said. "With a weapon this powerful, we could win the war itself in a matter of span. Just imagine how many lives that would save."

"The entire war was only supposed to last a matter of span to begin with," Caryn reminded him. "It's been nearly a year."

"All the more reason to seize this chance," Danzig insisted. "General, we have been offered the means to break open Brea positions effortlessly, and it's practically free. We only need to fight the New Empire, which we're doing already."

It's not the general's decision to make, Caryn thought. Still, she knew that whatever Freed recommended to Joint Staff Headquarters would be taken seriously in Tomasburg. Caryn may well be able to sway the president, who mistrusted the military, but the Assembly would follow Headquarters' advice.

"We'll need to do more than fight the empire if we accept this deal," Caryn argued. "We've been asked to enter into a formal alliance and a mutual defence pact with a terrorist organization that we've refused to even negotiate with."

"Which has never made any sense, and makes even less sense now," Danzig shouted. "We can win the war, secure Deugan's borders and liberate the Fringes in a single act."

"Do you really think turning the Fringes over to the Steffians counts as 'liberating' anybody?"

"Enough." General Freed stood and laid his hands on his desk. "I will not have you two squabbling like children. Minister, Major Danzig is right. That weapon could turn the tide of the entire war. In our hands, it could finish off the Wassians and convince the Breas to sue for peace. In Brealand's hands, it could be an unmitigated catastrophe. And we *are* fighting the New Empire already. I hate the idea of allying with the Steffians, but —"

"Hear me out, then," Caryn said. "Please, General." Freed nodded. "First, let's take a close look at what's actually been offered. Master Nono was extremely careful never to say that the Steffians would give us the bomb. All he offered us was an alliance."

Freed understood. "So we're being blackmailed. I think we already knew that. Give them what they want, or they take the bomb to Brealand."

"But they won't give the bomb to Brealand either," Caryn argued. "The bomb is their leverage. The Steffians will keep it for themselves." She looked around desperately. Her breathing was getting shallow. "Say we do ally with them, and we help them take over the Fringes. Now they not only have the bomb, they've also got half the resources of the New Empire. How strong will their blackmail be then? How long will Deugan have to go along with everything the terrorists ask for?"

Freed frowned, and even Major Danzig was taken aback, but Captain Malitz said, "With respect, Minister, how do you know they're not actually looking for friendship? Maybe this will be an alliance that lasts."

"No alliance lasts forever," Freed muttered.

"Much less with the Steffians," Caryn added. "You know they won't be satisfied with the Fringes. Their goal is to unite all the Steifar under one banner — and to make the entire Continent Steifar."

"That's speculation," Danzig piped up. "Nobody in Deugan really knows what they want. They say they want the Fringes."

"For now," Caryn insisted. "The Western Congregation of the Steifar is based in Amim. Uniting the two camps, which basically means taking over the Westerners, has been a goal of the Eastern Congregation for centuries. The Amimi have been our allies from the start. What will we do when the Steffians ask us to sell them out, if we have a military alliance, a mutual defence pact, and the bomb hanging over our heads? And then there's Villasud," she said, bulling past Danzig, who looked ready to interrupt her again. "The holiest site in the entire Steifar religion. The Steffians are never going to rest until they control it."

Danzig shrugged. "Villasud? The light of Wassia, or whatever they call it? If it's so damn important, let them have it."

"And cut off any chance for reconciliation with Wassia?" Caryn asked. "We share a 300-league border with Wassia. Aside from Givanno, we don't border the Fringes at all."

"Are you certain the Steffians will want Villasud?" General Freed asked.

"Yes," Caryn said. As tightly as the Wassian government tried to control it, you couldn't grow up in Villasud and not learn about the Raolin Temple ruin. "The Steifar believe that their god created thousands of worlds and set a spirit to guard each of them, but our world is the only one where he struck down the spirit and took command himself. It's one of the most important tenets of their faith, that our world is unique, special, for exactly that reason. Villasud is where they say it all happened. What's more, for centuries

Wassia denied Steifar the right to visit the site. Would you trust a Wassian with the shrine, or even a Deugan, if you were them?"

"I think we've gotten away from the main issue," Danzig said. "Even if we don't want an alliance with the Steffians, there's still that little problem that if we say no, they'll take their bomb and head straight on over to the Breas. Maybe it's blackmail, but what choice do we have? We can't fight a weapon like that."

Matt might be able to, Caryn thought, but she couldn't say that out loud. Besides, he had missed the rendezvous they'd planned in the Well. She had no idea what might have happened to him. "We can't be sure the Breas will say yes," she said instead. "I think it'll be a tough decision for them. Yes, they'll want the bomb, and they'll want to keep us from getting it, but it would mean selling out the New Empire, their most important ally. It would mean ruining their reputation on the Continent for decades. Would they do it?"

"Can we take the chance?" the general asked. "I don't disagree with you, Minister, but at the end of the day, there seem to be only two options. Either we get the weapon, or they do."

"Then let's create a third option," Caryn said. The idea would have come to her earlier, if only her mind had been in the right state for it. It was difficult to focus after what had happened in the hills. "You all know that Colonel Ravencliffe and I have been negotiating toward a comprehensive peace. We're still quite far apart, but I believe there's enough common ground that we can reconcile."

Danzig looked skeptical, but Freed motioned for her to continue. "This Steffian offer might be a blessing in disguise," Caryn said. "We don't want to be blackmailed and have the threat of the bomb hanging over our heads for decades, but the Breas will hate that as much as we do. We don't want to sell out Amim or the Fringes, but they won't want to sell out the New Empire. And even with their bomb, the Steffians aren't strong enough to take on Deugan and Brealand together. That's why they're here playing us off against one another. So what if we agree that we'll both reject the Steffians' offer, expedite this peace treaty, and show a united front to the real enemy?"

Janusz, Danzig and Malitz all started speaking at once. It was Danzig's voice that carried over the din. "Ravencliffe's only negotiating with you because he's stuck underground without anything better to do," he declared. "Brealand isn't like Deugan.

They're not going to negotiate a peace because they think it's the right thing to do, they'll only negotiate if they don't think they can win. The minute they get their hands on this weapon —"

"Enough," the general demanded, slamming his fist on his desk. "Having all of you shouting over each other doesn't help anybody. The foreign minister has raised some interesting points. Let's all take some time to think about them before we figure out what in Lessandro's name to do about the Steffians."

Danzig charged toward the general, stopping when he was only a foot away. "How much time do you think we have?" he shouted. "The Steffians may be chatting with the Breas as we speak, and like you said before, we've seen those leaves inside the fort. Who knows if there are more of them here? The Steffians could blow the entire place any second."

"I don't think so," General Freed replied. "I don't believe they would willingly kill their Master of Secrets. Not without giving negotiations another chance. For better or for worse" — he glanced at Caryn — "Brenth Nono is a prisoner here."

"General?" Captain Malitz said timidly. He had not moved from his spot in front of Freed's desk. "With all respect, sir, I'm not sure that's true."

All eyes turned to Malitz, and the general gave him a withering look. "Are you telling me, Captain, that Master Nono is not in fact in our custody?"

Malitz swallowed. "No, sir. We have him all right. It's just, back in the hills, it was too easy, as it were. He's got snipers on the ridges but they only take one shot. He's blowing up bombs and making hail, but he doesn't do anything when we move in to take him. The whole thing just seems off." He took a deep breath before concluding, "Sir, I think Nono wanted to be captured."

Silence fell as they pondered the implications. If the Steffians had an operative in the fort, perhaps Nono wanted to meet with him. Toppel was in prison, of course, but Nono would have no way of knowing that. Or maybe, Caryn thought uneasily, she was the one Nono wanted to see.

The general must have had the same thought; his gaze was settled firmly on her. He no doubt remembered Caryn's reaction when she had recognized Nono's photograph in this very office. "Minister

Hallom?" Freed asked in a mild tone that barely concealed the suspicion underneath. "Might you have any insights?"

Janusz looked at her, puzzled. She felt a lump rising in her throat, but she forced herself to say, "I knew Brenth Nono, years ago. We went to college together. He used a different name then, and as far as I know, he had no connection with the Steffians. We were close friends for a while."

There was a brief silence. Danzig broke it. "How close were you, then?" he snarled.

"Ralf!" Freed snapped.

"It was a long time ago," was all Caryn said.

"You have one secret too many," Freed said dangerously. Caryn could feel his temper rising, and she recoiled. "You should have told me this months ago. Certainly before I sent you on the team to meet him. You weren't objective."

"I hadn't seen or heard from him for half my life," Caryn retorted. "My order to capture him may well be keeping all of us alive."

"So he means nothing to you?" Freed asked in disbelief. Caryn struggled to keep her face a mask. "Well, if Nono wanted to be captured, you may still mean something to him. Do you think he trusts you?"

Caryn kept her eyes on the floor. "I haven't seen him in years. I have no idea. But he might."

"Then you'd better learn what you can from him," Freed said. "You're dismissed."

"General —" Danzig started.

"I know, Ralf," Freed snapped. "I'm not happy. I'm going to pray to any God who will listen that I'm not wrong to trust her. But we're in crisis mode here, and if she can find out anything that will help us, I'm willing to take that chance."

"There's one more thing, General," Caryn said. She knew she was risking his wrath by raising this now, when he was already upset with her about Nono, but it needed to happen, and soon. "If we are to seriously consider moving forward with a proposal to the Breas, we need Michael Ravencliffe looped in. There's only so much he can agree to without any communication with his government, and without any news of the fronts that comes from a source he can trust. Two months ago, you and I talked about getting him cable access if he cooperated. I think the time has come."

She turned away from the general then, not wanting to see his reaction. She could not read Janusz's expression, but Malitz and Danzig looked horrified. Finally, the general said, "I think, Minister, that you may be right."

Danzig's face flushed. He opened his mouth, but Freed held up a hand to cut him off. "Ralf, let's discuss this privately. The rest of you are dismissed." When they didn't move, he added, "Now."

They shuffled out of the office. Malitz took off quickly in the direction of the officers' quarters, while Janusz lingered with Caryn. She was taking deep breaths, trying to process all that had happened. "I've made an enemy," she whispered.

Caryn had thought that these meetings would get easier. It was exhausting, constantly trying to prove herself against people who were not inclined to listen. What if she was wrong, and the Breas did join with the Steffians? What if the *acambro* bombs started exploding over the Gateway and the northwest and Carrak-on-Sea, or even Tomasburg?

Janusz took her arm, supporting her as she walked, as Hans often had. Through the closed door of the general's office, she could hear Danzig shouting. She made out the word "traitor." Then Freed's voice: "saved us ... the food ..." And Danzig again: "... soft spot for her." Their voices faded as Janusz led Caryn away.

They stopped in the middle of a corridor. Janusz put his hands on her shoulders. "You agree with me," she said plaintively. She didn't like the weakness in her voice, but she was too overwhelmed to control it. "Don't you?"

Janusz hesitated. He looked her in the eyes. "I respect you," he said. "You've said things that are bound to be controversial. Giving Ravencliffe cable access. Counting on the Breas to say no to the bomb. But you're never afraid of doing it, of pushing the envelope. You're very brave."

"So you agree with Danzig."

Janusz looked away, then back at her. "It doesn't matter if I agree with you. I respect what you're doing. I respect how much you've given me to think about. These are tough questions, and the right to debate them is what makes us Deugan."

Caryn nodded again. She heard him, and in a way she understood, but it was a blow all the same. "It does matter," she said, staring at the ground. "Not having any support..."

She looked back up at him. His hands were still on her shoulders, and he drew her closer. "It must have been terrible," he said softly. "Losing Hans."

Caryn felt the tears welling up in her eyes. "I gave the order" was all she had time to say before the sobs started racking her body and she collapsed into Janusz's arms. He held her and stroked her back as she thought of Hans and Lana and all of the other friends she had lost, or left behind.

CHAPTER TWENTY

Brenner had that look on his face again. Jayla skipped up to him, poked him in the stomach and darted away as he swiped at her wrist. "Okay," he said. "What now?"

"You look like you swallowed a porcupine."

Brenner laughed. "You coughed enough this morning, I thought you were trying to spit one out."

"So you're okay?"

"Yeah," Brenner said. He opened his arms, and Jayla found herself inside them again. "I'm okay."

Jayla wasn't certain that she was. The coughing had gotten worse, especially in the mornings. Her muscles were feeling weighted, her joints stiffer. Then there was the one time with her breathing, not that she couldn't do it, just that she couldn't do it deeply enough. The panic that raced through her made her breathing even shallower. It had only happened once, and that was two span ago, but it was all the reminder Jayla needed that the Well was poison.

Brenner had suffered too. He'd become prone to frighteningly high fevers that would break after a day or two, and he complained of headaches afterward. He often had difficulty sleeping, too. There were plenty of nights that Jayla fell asleep in his arms while he lay with his eyes open, staring at the ceiling of the cavern.

She couldn't help it. The things they did tended to tire her out.

It had grown more intense after her conversation with the professor. Jayla had marched up to Brenner right in the central cavern, as though she had something to prove. Brenner barely had the chance to register the look in her eyes before she was on him, kissing his lips, his neck, then his chest. He stopped her long enough to give her a curious look; she just raised her eyebrows and kissed him again as she pushed him toward the relative privacy of the room where he slept.

That was the first time she had seen him fully naked, and as much as the Well had aged his body, she found herself aroused. In that moment she wanted him more than she had ever wanted anything in her short life. Brenner's eyes were hungry; her new attitude was exciting him, and she could tell. They wrestled each other to the ground, and Jayla snarled at him when she realized he was letting her win. She tried to retaliate by tickling him in the ribs; he pinned her arms behind her back and started kissing her neck, moving downward inch by inch until his lips and tongue were tracing the shape of her breast. It was exciting, but she forced herself to say, "If you give me my hands back I'll make it worth your while," and she did.

She didn't understand why she cut him off from touching her that first time. She was still scared, or shy, or something. But it did not last long. On the third day, Brenner started stroking her legs and thighs in such an awful tease that she nearly begged him to bring his fingers inside her.

It was Jayla who first discovered the hands. It was during one of their playful wrestling matches, the ones that Brenner always won unless he let her. This time Brenner had pinned her arms and was teasing her by nibbling at her neck while she struggled. As she strained her mind to reach her real hands toward him, the power suddenly erupted inside her, and she felt as though Brenner's weight on her hands had lifted, although his grip was as firm as ever. She reached around and squeezed his behind, and Brenner jumped three feet in the air. Jayla had never laughed so hard in her life.

For a while afterward, Brenner insisted that their relationship be "natural," meaning energy-free. He talked about nostalgia and personal connection and intimacy, while Jayla teased him for being afraid of a little grabbing. Eventually, he agreed to let her try the energy hands again. She managed, if she could say so herself, a rather convincing demonstration of the potential advantages extra hands might have, and soon they were working with the energy to expand the effect even more. After a month, Brenner could manage six separate hands without breaking a sweat. Jayla actually reached eight once, but she left Brenner with a nasty bruise when her concentration broke, and from then on, Jayla was the one insisting on the "natural" approach whenever he used his fingers inside her.

They were fully clothed now, Jayla wrapped inside Brenner's arms. She felt his body shift, and she looked up at him. He shook his head. Then he let her go. He looked nervous.

"What is it?" Jayla asked.

"I said I'm okay." He shook his head again. "Jayla, there's something I wanted to ask you."

She took a deep breath. There were butterflies in the pit of her stomach. She waited.

"I — next time — I think we should go all the way."

As close as they had become, it was difficult to talk about. Actually, it had been difficult to talk about anything lately. Trapped together so long, there was little they could tell one another that they didn't already know. Words were used mainly for complaints about aging or sickness or prophecy. Often it was better without them. "I don't know," Jayla said in a quiet voice. "We're only sixteen. I'm not sure we should push it."

Brenner looked stung. He swallowed hard. "It's okay. Forget I said it."

"Brenner, I love you. You know that, right?"

He nodded. "I do. And I love you. But something's been not quite right."

Jayla's reaction surprised her. It was relief. "I've been thinking that too. All the stuff we've been doing. I wonder if we should be scaling it back a bit. Not a lot," she added quickly, seeing the hurt look on his face. "Just a bit. Like, to regroup."

Brenner stared at the floor. "Here I am asking you to go further, and you're asking me to pull back. I feel like such an idiot."

"Don't," Jayla said. She wanted to hug him again, but she decided it would just confuse him. She stood her ground. "It's not about you. It's just that before we started doing all of this, we were mad at each other, remember? With the prophecy and whether we were going to get out? We just let that slide away."

"I thought that was a good thing," Brenner replied. "I thought we got over it."

Jayla wondered if that was true. To her, it felt more like they'd ignored it. Her muscles were aching terribly. "I'm not sure either of us is going to make it anymore," she said.

"Hey," Brenner said. "Don't say that."

"Why not? It's true. Part of me is saying, well then, we should just sleep together. Because who knows when we'll be dead."

"That's not why I want to do it," Brenner replied.

"Me neither," Jayla said. "I like being with you. A lot. I just want to make sure that we're both doing this for the right reasons."

Brenner nodded. He turned away in thought. Then he turned back to her. "Let's do it right, then," he said. There was a fierceness to his gaze that she hadn't seen in several span. "Not at a time when we're bored. Not when we're stressed, or depressed. We have to be happy. We have to make it romantic. Make it about us, you and me. Brenner and Jayla. Everything it's supposed to be about." He looked her in the eyes. "What do you say?"

She could have said no. Brenner had never pushed at her barriers, never questioned them. It was one of the things she loved him for. If she maintained that they should scale back, she was sure he would understand.

Instead, Jayla shoved her doubts aside and squeezed Brenner's hands. "I say let's do it."

*

Jayla's hands were over her eyes. Brenner guided her, his hand solid on her back. "Can I look yet?"

Brenner laughed. "Jayla Sullivan! That's the third time you've asked!"

"I want to see all this romantic stuff you planned."

"You will."

"I expect to be swept off my feet," she declared.

Brenner responded by placing an arm under her knees and lifting her into the air. Jayla shrieked, and her eyes opened in spite of herself.

They were in the room where Brenner slept, but it was different. Shadows masked the walls, leaving tiny shifting gaps where their natural orange could shine through. It gave the impression that the room was lit by thousands of tiny, flickering candles. It was breathtaking. "How did you —"

"Shh." Brenner spun her around, then laid her gently onto the ground. The air was charged with the energy surrounding them. "If we had food, I would have cooked you a gourmet dinner. If we had flowers, I would have strewn the ground with the petals. But at least I have candlelight. And I have you. That's all that matters."

Jayla smiled. "Brenner, you're amazing," she said. He was kneeling close to her; she reached to place her arms around his neck and draw him down beside her. She was about to tell him she loved him — but somehow that seemed wrong. Disconcerting. She shrugged it off.

Brenner was quick to catch her reaction. "Are you okay?"

"Yeah," she said, and kissed him lightly on the lips.

"Still want to do this?"

She nodded. She felt a buzzing in her head — a warning? No, she was just feeling nervous because it was her first time. "Yes."

Brenner smiled. "Me too."

It started slow. Doing it right meant not rushing it, they'd both agreed on that. It meant long kisses, eyes meeting, fingers intertwining. It meant undressing each other slowly, letting hands run across chests as shirts were lifted. It meant touching, little by little, and slowly growing firmer, stronger, more urgent. It meant losing themselves in each other. The warning tones were still a hum at the back of her mind, but then Brenner was distracting her, touching her legs, now moving between them, and the sound dulled.

Jayla reflected on how little she knew. It wasn't the sort of thing her noblewoman mother would ever have spoken with her about, and she didn't have any sisters. There were all sorts of wild rumours she'd heard at the university, of what it was supposed to feel like, how much it was supposed to hurt —

"Jayla," Brenner whispered. "You're so tense."

"I'm scared," Jayla admitted. It wasn't a very sexy thing to say, she realized, but Brenner took it in stride.

"Don't be," he said. "I'm here." But he pulled away slightly and raised his eyebrows, a question.

"Here is where I want you." Jayla drew him close again.

It did hurt at first, but not as much as she'd feared. She tried to relax her muscles, and when she did, she started to feel better. To feel pretty good, actually, although she found herself missing the extra control he had when he used his fingers. *This is new for him too*, Jayla reminded herself. Maybe not his first time, but close.

Then she realized that she was just lying there and wondered if she should be doing something more. She started to shift, and Brenner shifted awkwardly in response. They both started to laugh, and then they were kissing and Brenner was thrusting and the movements were growing sharper, and faster —

Jayla tossed and turned that night. It was a startling reversal of roles, Brenner asleep and snoring, Jayla wide awake, staring at the cavern. The walls had brightened to their normal orange. The thousand flickering candles now seemed a blazing fire, ready to consume her.

Brenner had done everything right. Setting the mood, taking it slowly, calming her when she was scared and then laughing with her as they connected. And he had asked her. More than once. She had every chance to stop, and she didn't.

The thoughts circled each other through her mind, and each moment brought a new jolt, a louder panic. She tried to take deep breaths. She wished she knew why she was feeling this way.

It was one of the longest nights of Jayla's life, and by the time she felt Brenner starting to stir, she was no closer to an answer. She slipped away from him, gathered her clothes in silence and moved back to her own room to dress. She spent some more time there, alone and exhausted. The energy was silent.

Jayla found Professor Terial writing in his room. She stopped at the edge of the room and watched him. At length he noticed her, laid down his pen, and beckoned her forward.

Jayla stepped toward him gingerly. She struggled to control her breathing. "Professor, we talked a month ago about — about what I'll do when I get out of here."

The professor stared at her, waiting. Jayla's mouth tasted like ash. She pressed forward. "Say I was thinking of maybe trying to get into Deugan." She took a deep breath and forced herself to say the next word. "Alone."

Terial bowed his head. "Oh, Jayla."

"I haven't decided anything yet," Jayla said, her voice starting to waver. "But please tell me. If I wanted to go to Deugan, how would I do it?"

*

They brought Brenth Nono to her old room in the officers' quarters of the fort. Caryn waited for him with a growing unease. She hadn't set foot in the room since the night after Toppel attacked her, when Hans and Marwin had helped her move her things into the nurses' wing. That was just over a span ago, but already it felt eerie to be back here among the ghosts. Lana, who used to sleep here. Hans, who but for her order would still be by her side.

Now she stood across from another ghost, another memory from her past. The guards withdrew just outside the door, and yet Caryn and Nono stood, staring at each other, taking in the years.

Nono looked to be in his sixties, though Caryn knew that like her he had spent only thirty years in this life. He looked healthy, at least. He still had the lean frame she remembered from their days in the cavern, but he had added muscle to his legs and chest. His hair was grey and his face was clean-shaven, which was jarring after the beard he had once sported, but his smile was the same. Only the gaunt look in his eyes spoke of his experience in the Wassian Well so long ago.

Caryn could see him sizing her up, just as she did him. What did you say to an old friend, an old lover, fourteen years later? How did you reconnect, pretend the time had never passed? How could she ever have predicted that Brenner would be standing across from her, a Steffian terrorist taken prisoner at her order, at a military fort where Caryn felt half a prisoner herself? The absurdity suddenly became too much, and she started to laugh, and seeing her, Nono started to laugh too. He extended his arms, and Caryn stepped forward and hugged him, grinning. "It's really good to see you again, Brenner," she said.

"You too, Jayla," Nono replied. "You too."

They stepped backward and looked at each other again. "I can't remember the last time anybody's called me Jayla," Caryn mused. Now that they had broken the ice, she almost felt like Jayla again, young and excited, a life ahead of her. But she was wary, too. The years she had spent in politics weighed on her. "It's probably safer that you call me Caryn, though."

"I'll try. It's hard for me to think of you as anyone other than Jayla Sullivan." Nono smiled. "Maybe not that hard. I've seen you quoted in the newspapers. Heard your speeches on the radio. Saw you taking command on that ridge. You really have grown into Caryn Hallom." He said it slowly, lingering on her last name.

Caryn felt herself blushing. She did feel like a teenager again around him. "It would have been Halloway," she admitted.

"But?"

"Professor Terial said it sounded too Wassian. Plus, everybody knew Amaro Sullivan's daughter and Baron Halloway's son had disappeared around the same time. If I showed up at the Deugan border with a passport that said Halloway, it would have been suspicious. So I shortened it."

Nono stood, one hand on his hip, his face pensive. It was a look Caryn remembered so well that it was all she could do not to laugh. "What did Terial say about that?" he asked finally.

Caryn smiled. "He asked if I really wanted to marry you that badly. I said I wanted to be sure I remembered you."

"I could never forget you."

They stared at each other awhile longer. Caryn had so many questions for him, and that was just personally. The general wanted her to find out about the Steffians' plans, and now that she'd angered Major Danzig, she felt she had to bring them something solid. Where could she possibly begin?

Uncharacteristically, it was Nono who broke the silence. He had still been ruminating on their previous words. "I'd always wondered how much help Terial gave you," he said.

"A few letters," Caryn said. "He knew someone who could get me a fake Deugan passport and birth certificate, and other documents, showing the age that I actually looked. There was a banker who gave me access to some of his money to start me off. And he knew the Dean of Helsengraf University in Carrak and gave me a letter to take to him. A recommendation to let me in."

"That must have made it easier," Nono said bitterly.

"He would have helped you too," Caryn said. "I was there when he offered, but you never went to him. Besides, it was still hard." The words started flowing out. In fourteen years, she had nobody to confide in. "I was a sixteen-year-old girl in the body of a forty-year-old woman. I remember saying to the professor, 'How am I supposed to act like I'm forty? They'll know my secret as soon as I open my mouth!' So he told me not to open my mouth when I could avoid it. Just watch adults, listen and learn. For the first two years I spoke less than you did. No friends. No community. I buried myself in schoolwork just to stop myself from thinking, but for most of those years I was so lonely I wanted to die. I thought about trying to find you a million times."

"You should have."

"You were in Amim!" Caryn exclaimed. "It wasn't independent yet, it was still under home rule. I'd have to go back through Wassia to get there; there's no way I would have made it. Look, it doesn't matter anymore. We've both gone through some terrible things and come out stronger. I'm the foreign minister of Deugan, and you..." She couldn't hold the question in any longer. "How in Lessandro's name did Brenner Halloway get to be Master of Secrets of the Steffians?"

Nono didn't respond. He turned from her and went to sit on the bed that had been hers. Finally, he said softly, "There was a time I told you everything."

Caryn moved to sit beside him. "I know."

"Damn it," Nono said suddenly. "I don't know what I was thinking. I thought this would be easy, like old times, I thought — but I've gotten used to hiding everything from everybody for so long — and now, I want — but — do you have any idea what I mean?"

"More than you can possibly know," Caryn assured him. General Freed's voice echoed in her head: *You have one secret too many.* "I don't expect it to all be the way it was before. I think it will take a long time before we can truly trust each other again. But let's start, okay? Let's at least catch up?"

He thought. Nodded. Then he took a deep breath. "I joined the Steffians for the energy."

"The energy?" That surprised her. The Brenner she knew had hated the energy. Had blamed it, and not without reason. "Didn't you have enough of it after six months?"

"You'd think so, wouldn't you? Life is funny that way." Nono had a far-off look in his eyes. "I was living in the south of Amim. The greatest place on the Continent. In the summers, at least. It was so cold that first winter, I didn't think I'd make it." He flashed her a smile. "I did, though. Through the summer I helped on the farms. I was a terrible labourer. They had to find me the simplest tasks because I'd mess things up otherwise, but they seemed to appreciate any help they could get. Then in the winter I joined the hunt. There are all sorts of huge animals that can actually live on the ice, eating fish in the lakes that don't freeze. Anyway, hunting was something I was actually good at. The only useful thing a noble's son in Wassia learns. Somehow, by the end of that winter I was one of them. As though I'd lived there all my life."

"Very different from life on the manor," Caryn observed.

"It was exactly what I needed," Nono said. "Physical work. Sweat. Something to distract me for hours out of a day. Being surrounded by the kindest, friendliest people on the Continent. I never thought I would want to leave.

"But the past has a way of catching up with you, no matter how far south you go. My village was traditional Amimi, through and through, but we had a neighbouring village that we traded with during the summers, and that joined us for the hunt in the winters. They were mostly Steifar, and with the way Wassia was repressing the independence movement, well, the Steffians smelled blood."

"The Western Congregation..."

"Has always been less radical than the Eastern, that's true," Nono said. "But the Steffians weren't trying to sell people on blowing things up. They were offering food. Money. Tools. Things people needed." He sighed. "I'd been in Amim for two years when they announced they were funding a pilgrimage down to the Amimi Well, at the southern tip of the Continent. The energy and the Wells are sacred to the Steifar, but poor Amimi couldn't afford the trip on their own. This was the opportunity of a lifetime for them."

"So you went? Not two years after escaping the Wassian Well?"

"No," Nono said, grimacing. "A six-month trek through the snow to the coldest place on the Continent? I wasn't a Steifar, I never even considered it. But as our neighbours geared up for the journey, I found myself starting to panic. I couldn't function. I lost my appetite. I got back the insomnia I had in the Well, and the headaches. I was a complete wreck. It made me realize that the energy and I had unfinished business."

Caryn felt a chill pass through her, as though she were trekking through the bitter southern winds herself. "What do you mean, unfinished business?"

"I needed to understand what had happened," Nono said. His anger came through as clearly now as it had all those years ago. "One day the energy suddenly let us out of the cavern, after months of keeping us trapped. Just as random as everything else it did, or didn't do. Then you left for Deugan, and it seemed like the energy was behind it. I never figured anything out. It stole twenty-five years off my life, and I never knew why."

Caryn shifted away from him on the bed. He was starting to make her nervous. Nono pressed on, oblivious. "I realized I needed closure. I needed to understand if I was ever going to move on. So one rest day, I travelled to the nearest city. The Wassians had set up one of their library projects there, books to civilize the savages and all that." He rolled his eyes. "I searched the library up and down for books on Wells. You want to guess what I found?"

He locked eyes with her. Caryn could still read him, just as Jayla had. "Nothing. You didn't find anything."

"The Wassian government had purged it," Nono said. "Completely censored. I started looking around out of curiosity. There was nothing related to religion in the entire library. No books about the Steifar, the traditional Amimi faiths, not even the ancient Raolin. Since the Wells are sacred to the Steifar, they got purged too.

"But I knew they hadn't hidden the knowledge from everybody. I knew one organization was still studying Wells, surreptitiously. So the power led me to the Steffians.

"It started with wanting to control it. Command it. Over the years I learned — well, I learned what you tried to tell me for months back in Wassia. Maybe I was too young and immature back then to listen to you, but now I know. The energy can't be commanded. Can't even really be understood. But you can build a relationship with it. It still has a mind of its own, but if you build that trust, you can — train it. Set up patterns for it, and it will follow. Once you've done that, powers that used to seem random can be repeated, over and over, until they become second nature."

Training the energy, Caryn thought. She remembered a conversation they'd once had about dogs. She was starting to feel sick.

"By the time I learned all that, I'd been with the Steffians several years," Nono continued. "I paid lip service to their god, but my real goal was always the energy, and I was relentless. I had the head start from the Wassian Well, and I was good at it. It wasn't long before I'd surpassed all of them, and when Dawud died, I was the natural choice for Master of Secrets.

"I took it. By then I already was looking forward to the next steps. To the things Terial used to talk about, battling injustice, fighting for governments that stand behind their people. Don't get me wrong, I had no illusions about the Steffians, but they were fighting the New Empire, and doing it well. I started to realize just how useful they could be."

"Useful for what?"

"A lot of things," Nono said cryptically. "It always came back to the energy, though. They supported the research, the training, and finally the *acambro* project. Years after I'd resigned myself to the fact that the energy can't be commanded, along comes a leaf that can carry it anywhere on the Continent. The Steffians achieved the breakthrough that scientific powerhouses like Deugan and Brealand never could, being so far from Kalid where the *acambro* grows. So now the roles are reversed. It's not the energy holding us prisoner any longer."

Caryn saw the satisfaction on his face as he said it. She was still disturbed, but part of her disgust had turned to pity. She suddenly felt like she was back in the Wassian Well, trying to comfort her best friend, her heart breaking for him.

Since their escape, Caryn Hallom had earned a university degree, worked her way up to chief of the Treasury Department and then foreign minister, and set herself up as a role model for young women across the Republic of Deugan. She might not have had lovers, but she had friends and confidantes. She had made a life for herself.

But it hadn't been that way for Brenth Nono. He hadn't misinterpreted his prophecy after all. It had come true in the most horrifying of ways. "You never got out," Caryn said softly. "Fourteen years later, and you're still in the Well. Oh, Brenner."

Suddenly he was shaking, and Caryn wrapped her right arm around him and held him the way Janusz had held her just hours ago. "Brenner," she said. "Brenner, Brenner. I'm so sorry."

"What for?"

"Everything," Caryn said, and she kissed him.

CHAPTER TWENTY-ONE

When Caryn awoke the next morning, her lips were tingling as though Brenner was still there. *The Well is poison*, she told herself, but she had never listened.

Caryn had fled her old quarters soon after the kiss and went straight back to the nurses' wing. She avoided the nurses and told Hertha they would talk in the morning. When morning came, though, Caryn slipped out of the wing before the others woke and made her way down to the prison.

She had her heart in her throat as she approached Nono's cell. He looked up at her in surprise and came to the bars. "Caryn. About yesterday —"

"It's okay," she said. "I may not have liked everything I heard, but I'm glad you told me."

"Good." Nono breathed a sigh of relief. "I know that chasing the energy over the years may not have been so healthy, but I was trying to move on with my life the best way that I knew how. I was looking for peace, and eventually I think I found it. For all the terrible things they've done, the Steffians really did help me."

"You were saying there's more that they can help with?"

"I think so," Nono replied. "For now they'll be going along with the plan. I won't bore you with the internal politics, but I don't think your arresting me is going to change much. The change will have to come later."

"What are you talking about?"

"Not here," Nono said. "It's too public. Just remember I've kept my eye on the target."

"The Wassian government?"

"Oppressive governments everywhere," Nono clarified. "Frankly, the way you Deugans are going on your southern front, I think Wassia's suffered enough. What matters is how we rebuild it."

He was right, Caryn realized. Something to bring into her discussions with Ravencliffe, perhaps. "Sounds promising. I'll make sure we get another chance to talk."

"Thanks," Nono replied. "We're friends again?"

She extended her good arm and hugged him through the bars. The prison guards looked on suspiciously. "Yes," she said. "Friends."

She was on her way out when she heard a prisoner in a nearby cell hissing her name. She turned around and blanched. Captain Toppel was staring at her through the bars.

"I have nothing to say to you," Caryn spat.

"Minister. Please. You have to listen to me."

"I don't have to do anything," she said. "You attacked me."

"I was trying to warn you," Toppel said. "Danzig's men were watching. I had to come at night. I had no choice."

"You always have a choice. What would you have done if some huge man who's stronger than you had come into your room at night and ordered you out of bed?"

"Maybe I'd have kicked in his broken leg, too," Toppel shot back. "Only I don't think I could have done it that hard." He leaned in as close as he could get to the bars. "In fact, I don't know anybody who can kick that hard. Do you, Minister?"

Caryn's breathing turned shallow. "Expose me, then," she whispered. "Why haven't you?"

"Because I'm still trying to protect you, though only the Gods know why," Toppel hissed.

"Or maybe it's because you can't do it without exposing yourself," Caryn snapped. "That must be why you never went to Danzig after you attacked me during the battle. You couldn't tell him without admitting that you were using the energy yourself."

"I don't know what you're talking about," Toppel said. "I never had any desire to go to Danzig. I was trying to tell you —"

"That Danzig doesn't think very highly of me? I was able to figure out that much on my own," Caryn said. "You know what you did.

You know what was in that crutch, and so does the general. So which of us do you think he's going to believe?" She turned on her heel and walked away.

As she climbed the stairs out of the sub-basement, she ran into Michael Ravencliffe. He was with two other Brea prisoners, surrounded by an escort of guards. "Minister!" he said when he noticed her. The procession stopped. "I've just come from your communications hub. It was delightfully quaint. Were you seeking the pleasure of my company?"

"It is always a pleasure, Colonel, but no."

"You were visiting the Steffian, then?"

"Who I may have been visiting is none of your business."

Ravencliffe sighed. "Are we not yet close enough friends that we are able to share these personal anecdotes? That's a shame." He looked at her meaningfully. "The news I have for you is potentially ... explosive."

The Steffians. Caryn kept her face carefully blank. This was what she'd wanted, wasn't it? Ravencliffe brought up to speed? She turned to the guards. "Take them back to the prison for now, but bring Ravencliffe to my chambers in the officers' quarters in an hour."

Ravencliffe gave her a deep bow in an elaborate mockery of the Deugan style. Caryn shook her head and went back to her quarters, her kiss with Brenth Nono pounding in her heart.

*

Caryn used her hour to catch up on news from the fronts. In the northwest, Brealand had been pushing back their trenches, but slowly and at great cost to the attackers. There was a naval battle, too, in which a Deugan fleet was routed, and the Brea navy was pursuing it relentlessly. Soon the Breas would be in a position to blockade most of the Deugan coast, though Joint Staff Headquarters believed they would at least be able to keep open a narrow corridor around Carrak to ship supplies and launch subs.

The news from the east was scarcely better. The New Empire had masterfully played on the Steffian bombing of Ciorala, using the tragedy to unite its people under its banner. The colonies of Kalid and Accarro, usually tepid supporters of the empire, held spontaneous rallies in solidarity with the government. In Merguisio and Pascuay, the Steffian strongholds, opinion was becoming polarized between the terrorists and the Orastans, the pro-democracy movements being squeezed out. Only in Cioro itself — the colony of which Ciorala was the principal city — was it unclear where the fallout would land. The Deugan diplomatic effort there was nearly as strong as the Orastan one; Deugan was pushing to portray the pro-democracy movement as a viable alternative to empire and *acambro* bombs alike.

Then there was the south, and Wassia. In many ways the situation was no different than it had been for several span. The Wassians still held the coast, while Deugan commanded much of the country's north and centre and continued to push south. But buried in one report was the news that Caryn had been dreading since the war began. The Deugan army had just reached the outskirts of her hometown.

Villasud was built on a hill, making it, as the Old Empire had repeatedly learned, a maddening target for any army. Two smaller hills stood sentry to the east, hosting guard towers that had survived from the ancient wars. Just a few leagues to the south was another natural boundary, the River Sella, which marked the Amimi border. West of the city lay a narrow but strategic valley called the Maxalo Pass. A highway ran through it, connecting Villasud with the capital, Garameche, out on the coast.

The northern approach was the easiest route into the city, but also the most populated. The slopes of the hill there were gentle, and well water was plentiful, making it the natural place for Villasud's wealthiest suburbs to grow. It was where Caryn had grown up, where her parents, as far as she knew, still lived. Right in the path of the Deugan army.

Caryn had learned enough about military tactics over the last two months to realize that hundreds of thousands would die if they tried to storm the city. It would be easy for the Wassians to mow down Deugan soldiers with machine guns as they scrambled uphill, but at the same time, Villasud was so densely populated that Deugan shells would wreak havoc on the population. She thought about telling that to the general, but he would already know, and in any event, he had no power to overrule Southern Command. The president could intervene, but would he? And how would Caryn explain why she cared so much about saving those particular lives?

She had not yet made a decision by the time the hour was up. She made her way back to her old quarters, dark thoughts running through her mind.

Michael Ravencliffe cut a striking figure. He had been permitted to wear his Brea officer's uniform for his visit to the communications hub, and its pins and medals were resplendent even in the paltry electric lighting of the fort. "You've transformed me, Minister Hallom," he said as he caught her staring at him. "I take it I have you to thank for this morning's unexpected treat?"

Caryn nodded. "It's important that you be able to communicate with your government," she said. "There's a lot of work to do, and time is running out."

Ravencliffe laughed. "You have one thing right, Minister. For this conglomeration of tribes that you Deugans call a 'Republic,' time is indeed running out. My dear cousin and her royal husband have informed me of an intriguing development, of which I can only imagine the Foreign Minister of Deugan would also be aware."

"I am certainly familiar," Caryn agreed, her voice cutting. She did not like Ravencliffe's newfound confidence, and he hadn't exactly been lacking in self-esteem until now. "You have my word, Deugan is committed to consulting with Brealand to determine our joint response."

Ravencliffe raised his eyebrows. "Joint response? It seems to me that the Realm needs only give one response, and your Republic will cease to exist."

"And the Continent will be poorer for it," Caryn said lightly. "I wonder what you would do, Colonel, if you did conquer Deugan. In Carrak-on-Sea there are rows and rows of pagoda houses in the Wassian style. They meet in a central square surrounded by Orastan pillars. The rounded arches were smashed and destroyed, but otherwise the city hall and the provincial court building still evoke the Old Empire. Then, overlooking the ocean, just south of the modern industrial parks and the shipyards, there are ruins from an indigenous Deugan culture. Stepped pyramids, pointed arches, statues of onyx and clay. I wonder if Brealand would add its own styles to the mix, enriching the city's diversity still more. Or if instead it would tear down Carrak's history brick by brick, until only a poor replica of Hastingvale is left." She gave him a sad smile. "I hope I never find out."

Ravencliffe smiled back. "Carrak-on-Sea would make an exceedingly poor replica," he assured her. "In Brealand we would never have left standing the structures of two peoples who had conquered us. Do Deugans have no pride? Are your people actually nostalgic for the days when foreign leaders made the tough decisions for you?"

"Decisions like how to respond to a terrorist threat? We know how, and so do you. By dropping our petty differences and banding together against them. Honestly, Colonel, why is atheist Brealand even thinking about allying with religious fundamentalists? With people who won't even give you their weapon, so they can hold it over your heads for the next century? With people who've demanded your help in destroying your closest ally? You think you have no choice, that either you have to destroy us or we'll destroy you, but there is another way. We're so close to a comprehensive deal. What did the queen have to say about our ship-building proposal?"

Ravencliffe drew himself up to his full height. "I thought that might be why you gave me communications access."

"Of course it is," Caryn said, confused. "If we're going to make a deal —"

"This is the first contact I've had with the outside world in two months," Ravencliffe said, "and you expected me to use it to carry out a Deugan agenda."

His practiced calm had burst like a dam. For the first time since Caryn had met him, there was fury behind Ravencliffe's eyes. "Did you really think that's what I would do?" he shouted. "Even murderers in Deugan get to send their one cable to a lawyer. Twenty-four hours to charge or release, isn't it? But that doesn't apply to prisoners of war. I have been sitting beneath your fort for span after span, isolated, starving, hearing my countrymen down the hall moaning as they're crammed into packed cells, wondering if any of them will survive, and you thought I would reward you for the right to exchange a couple of cables?" Ravencliffe clenched his fists, and Caryn backed toward the door. Her guards were waiting outside, and she almost called to them. Ravencliffe wasn't moving, but he was shaking in anger. "I don't want your peace! I don't want a joint response to the Steffians, and I don't want some pale-faced barbarian woman telling me what Brealand should do. I want to destroy you,

Minister, and I don't care if the weapon I use comes from the Steffians or the Orastans or the bloody Rangers!"

Ravencliffe took a deep breath to calm himself. He stared past Caryn at the door. He genuinely seemed to struggle to say what he did next. "But it's not about what I want. It's not about the fact that I've been kidnapped, deprived of news and companionship, underfed, and suffered terrible wounds to my admittedly exaggerated sense of pride. It is, and always will be, about what's best for the Realm. If Brealand's needs can be met through negotiation, then a peace treaty with Deugan may well be better for the Realm than a deal to embroil ourselves in the politics of the Fringes for the rest of time. Especially with the overseas powers looming, Qir Ni and Koltaja, sniffing the air for a whiff of weakness."

A long silence followed. "I'm sorry," Caryn finally said.

"Why? You have a dangerous prisoner on your hands. He'll always do what's right for his country. You have to do what's right for yours, and keep him locked up." He sighed and cast his eyes down toward the floor. Another show of emotion. It was so unusual. "Tell me this truthfully," Ravencliffe said at last, leaning against the frame of the bed she'd once slept in. "Is it actually possible for you and I to make a deal that's better than what the Steffians are offering? Because they're certainly offering a lot."

"I believe it is," Caryn said.

"But how? For the last two months we've done nothing but argue about our differences. It was the same in the cable I received from His Majesty today. How are we supposed to make a peace, he asked me, when at the most basic, fundamental level, we disagree? About everything?"

"Not everything," Caryn said softly. "Neither of us wants to reset the clock on this Continent."

He stared at her. "How do you mean?"

"Wassia and Orastus have been fighting each other for more than 1,500 years," Caryn said. "Now they're allied. What do they have in common? There's a world they both want to preserve — a world of empires, surrounded by colonies to keep them prosperous. A world with more land to explore, frontiers to press against. A world where the centre spreads the light of knowledge to the periphery."

"So what my Realm and your Republic have in common is that we want their world to vanish?"

"Exactly," Caryn said. "We are young, both of us. Vibrant. We have visions for the future. We don't want the power centres remaining in the south of the Continent. We both want social organizations that are based on merit, not hierarchy and birth. We don't see modern manufacturing, urbanization, telephones and automobiles and electricity as the corruption eating away at civilization. We see it as an opportunity to transform the Continent for the better." She realized she was still hovering near the doorway and forced herself to step toward him. "All we disagree about is what a better Continent would look like, and who in Lessandro's name cares? You can build one world in Brealand, and we can build a different one in Deugan. But let's not let the new worlds die."

"That's all well and good in theory, Minister, but in practice —"

"In practice," Caryn cut him off forcefully, "you and I, a Brea and a Deugan, could sign a peace treaty this afternoon, and Orastus and Wassia would have to live by its terms. That has never happened before. We're standing at a crossroads, Colonel, with the power to shape the course of history, and you want to cede that power to the Steffians?"

"Is it about power, then?"

"It's about independence," Caryn replied. "You Breas may believe your government should control its own people, but you sure don't want anyone else controlling you. You may want your island colonies, but you don't want the colonial projects of the past, where officials of the great empires sit in their palaces and mark off boundaries on a map, where entire economies are based around bringing materials in from the colonies on the cheap. Brealand is as fiercely protective of sovereignty, not just its own, but the very idea, as any nation on the planet. That's what it's about, the freedom to break from expectations and chart your own path."

Ravencliffe gave her a small smile; whether it was genuine, or merely sardonic, she could not tell. "Few people are as fiercely protective of *that* freedom," he said, lowering himself in another overwrought bow, "as Caryn Hallom."

*

Those were the words that propelled Caryn to the general's office, and she arrived just in time. Freed and Danzig were at the tail end of

241

an argument, poring over maps of southern Wassia.

Caryn quickly learned that the president himself had ordered the conquest of Villasud, to make a statement to their enemies while finally linking up the Deugan army with the Amimi. Joint Staff Headquarters had dutifully drawn up a plan, but Southern Command had balked. They argued that Villasud was a death trap if attacked directly. They would need to besiege the city and starve it out, and there wasn't enough time before winter hit. Even for a siege, they would need to take the sentry hills in the east and the Maxalo Pass in the west, and the loss of life would be staggering in those battles alone.

So Southern Command had drawn up a different plan, one that would circumvent Villasud and bring Deugan's forces within a stone's throw of Garameche, the Wassian capital. Southern Command was looking for Freed's support to help persuade Tomasburg.

Freed was hesitant to give it. "The Garameche plan is too risky," he explained, and Caryn could see from the look in Major Danzig's eyes that they had trodden this ground before. "The terrain may well be easier, but there's so much more of it to cover, and even gentle slopes with trenches on them can be hell to take. Garameche is further north, so there's no way to combine arms with the Amimi. Once we get there, our troops will be raw and tired and hungry, the Wassians will be able to reinforce their positions from the sea, Brea crack troops will already have landed, and we'll have the most strategic city in Wassia sitting untaken in our rear."

Danzig had the opposite view. His argument was that both plans were risky, but since the Deugan movements so far had been entirely directed to an attack on Villasud, the Garameche plan might take their enemies by surprise. Not only that, it would help them in their negotiations with the Steffians in the north. They would avoid the risk of damaging the Steifar holy site in Villasud, and they would have little difficulty capturing the Wassian Well, which lay between their army and Garameche. "I pray to the Gods that we get this Steffian alliance," Danzig said, "but if we don't, and we have to defend ourselves against those bombs, we may need to learn about the Wells' power in a hurry. Access to one more Well could save Deugan." Caryn understood the words he had left unsaid: their hold on their existing Well, in the Gateway, was tenuous at best.

General Freed nearly fell off his chair when Caryn announced that she agreed with Danzig. She spoke about Wassian culture and the rivalry between the two cities. She explained that since Villasud was the commercial centre of the country, it was resented, especially along the coast where the Wassian army was stubbornly holding out. She explained the Wassian mythos around the capital, a city even more ancient than Villasud, which had never been taken by an enemy force, even though it had fewer natural defences than its rival. Caryn concluded by reminding the general that the war was a footrace. "If Villasud were taken, the rest of the country would still fight on. But if they lose Garameche — if they even see a credible threat of losing Garameche — I honestly believe that will be the end of the southern front."

They all went together to the communications hub. Caryn hashed it out on the phone with the president while Freed and Danzig dictated cables to Joint Staff Headquarters and Southern Command. Caryn's route back to the nurses' wing afterwards took her past the chapel, and she entered on a whim. She thought about Lana as she approached Seppina's wall, the river surrounded by green woods, teeming with life, and for the first time since she arrived in Deugan nearly fifteen years ago, Caryn Hallom wondered if the Gods might really exist after all.

CHAPTER TWENTY-TWO

Nearly a span passed before Caryn and Nono were able to meet privately again, and in the meantime the fort was far from idle. General Freed had been corresponding with a Steffian leader named Rusul, sending riders into the Selliar Mountains with letters written in the general's own hand. Freed assured the Steffians that the Deugans were carefully considering their offer, and he promised financial compensation for the food that was stolen and the Steffian lives lost in the Deugan raid. Nono, on the other hand, was a bargaining chip the general had decided to hold. His release would be offered only if a deal was consummated.

Freed had also dictated a cable to Joint Staff Headquarters, and another to the Office of the President, setting out Caryn's and Danzig's arguments about the Steffians' offer. The Foreign Ministry, the Defence Ministry and the entire Cabinet were now debating the matter. Meanwhile, Caryn was working the telephone with the president and anyone else in Tomasburg who cared to listen, assuring them that Michael Ravencliffe was still willing to talk and that the Steffians' Master of Secrets had hinted he might be prepared to break from the organization.

Caryn ran into Marwin one day as she was headed toward the prison to meet with Ravencliffe. The boy was emerging from the sub-basement, a rifle slung over his shoulder. "They had me on guard duty," he explained. "Subbing in for Otto, who got sick with diarrhea. They're keeping him in the medical bay in case it's a flu. It could run through the fort like wildfire."

"What do you think about the whole Steffian situation?" Caryn asked. She hadn't seen much of Marwin since the raid on the Steffians' food stores. She remembered how scared he'd looked marching out to his first battle, but he had returned in high spirits. He was proud that he had made it through the ordeal, and Caryn was proud of him.

Marwin frowned. "I'm not sure I know enough to be able to say. It's not like before, my lady, when you used to send me to wait by the comm hub and run you the news. As a soldier, I just get rumours."

"This is what you wanted," Caryn reminded him.

"I know," Marwin said. "It's just hard. So many of us are getting sick now because of the food stores going down. The prisoners are worse. At least three or four have already died, and the others are starving. It was tough being down there, guarding them."

He'd matured quickly, Caryn thought. When they'd travelled up on the train together, war was still a game, and a glorious one. But he was learning. "I am doing everything in my power to end this war," she assured him.

"I know, my lady. I just wonder — if we do join the Steffians, maybe that would end it sooner."

"Maybe." There was little more to be said. She had always liked Marwin, but the siege and the deal she'd struck with the general had taken him away from her and stuck him on the front lines. He was growing up, but Caryn wondered if that was a good thing, or if it was happening too fast.

When she wasn't on the phone with Tomasburg, Caryn tried to advance her negotiations with Ravencliffe. The outline of a potential deal was coming into focus, but all the old sticking points — the status of Amim and the Fringes, the Deugans' right to a navy, the final borders in the north, the protection of trade routes — still remained. Caryn also visited Nono in prison when she could, but he refused to talk about his plans in front of the guards, and he was pulled away for interrogation too frequently for Caryn's comfort.

Finally, Caryn managed to schedule a time when Nono could be brought to her old quarters again. He arrived looking haggard and exhausted, but his eyes lit up when he saw her. "Caryn. I'm glad you were able to arrange this. We have so much to talk about."

The guards withdrew, and Caryn closed the door. She looked at Nono seriously. "Have they been treating you all right?"

He nodded. "The questions have been pretty intense, but they're not beating me, if that's what you're asking. Still, it's not as though they welcomed me with a spread and a bottle of wine."

Caryn laughed. "What would a Steffian do with a bottle of wine? Isn't the whole point of your organization that the religious ban on alcohol is more important than the religious ban on murder?"

"You listen to some of them, it's as though the only reason Rao had to be struck down is that he was drinking on the job." Nono smiled. He sat on her bed and motioned for her to join him. "You know those people who practice the Steifar religion but want to distance themselves from us, so they use that line, 'A Steifar is not a Steffian'? Well, not every Steffian is a Steifar, either."

"How did you get away with that?"

"By saying the right things in public and thinking the wrong things in private." Nono shrugged. "The truth is, when you spend enough time immersed in it, it does start to rub off on you. It's comforting to feel like there's someone up there, someone watching over us. Like after you die, there are thousands of other worlds, and you at least have a chance to make it to one that's better than ours. But I'm still not really sure I believe all of that. I think we've got to assume this is all we have and work to make this world better."

"The Steffians aren't making the world better."

"No," Nono agreed. "The Amimi are." He took a deep breath. "The years I spent in Amim were the best ones of my life. I've already told you why I left, but I'm still not convinced it wasn't a huge mistake. It's hard to describe it. There's the natural beauty, everybody knows that. The glaciers rolling out as far as the eye can see. The old forests that axes have never touched. The mineral lakes, turquoise and crystal blue, so large that you can sit on a boat in the middle of one and never see a shore. You need to go there, Caryn. You need to see it for yourself."

Caryn smiled. "You just said a whole bunch of words, all in a row."

"I'll say a few more," he promised, "because the real beauty is the people. They were so warm and welcoming. They had so little and shared so much. I've never seen anything like it, and I think it happened *because* they had so little. It's a tough life there, rushing to harvest before the short summer ends, taking to the frigid wilderness to hunt through the winters. You bond over it. It's a community, in a way that a Villasud or a Carrak-on-Sea could never be."

"You've spent the last ten years in the Fringes," Caryn said, confused. "It can't just be that poverty makes people bond. Pascuay is as poor as Amim, and Merguisio is poorer."

"But Pascuay and Merguisio are oppressed," Nono said. "Amim is a community, where the Fringes aren't, and the New Empire has a lot to do with that. They deliberately set people off against one another, to divide and conquer. Steal Merguisian grain to feed Cioro. Raise taxes in Givanno to build a railway in Orastino. Put an Accarro-born governor in charge of Pascuay and appoint Pascuayan judges to try cases in Accarro.

"It's not just Orastus, either. The Brea government encourages all of its people to inform on one another. The Wassian government stands up for the barony against the industrialists, the atheists against the Steifar. Even here in Deugan, you see Tomasburg doling out cash to the central regions that support it and denying infrastructure funding to the Gateway. Every government does it, except Amim's, because Amim is basically governed by the communities themselves. Sure, there's a central government with some oversight, and under home rule the Wassians would check in from time to time, but for the most part, each village goes its own way. Sets its own policies based on its own culture and history, and the needs of its own community. There's respect. There's kindness. And most importantly, there isn't anybody stealing what you have to give it to their political allies, or killing and starving their own people, or sending innocent kids like us off to die in a Well because of a feud with their fathers."

"Not every government is like that," Caryn argued. "I'll never forget what Wassia did to us, and Brealand is downright terrifying, but we do have Deugan. We are different."

"Are you?" Nono said it softly to take the sting off his words, but Caryn felt it all the same. "Isn't this the country that invaded its neighbour over a shipping dispute?"

"We have a long way to go," Caryn admitted, "but we're heading in the right direction. I do believe in this country. I know it can be hard for you to see, but the government means well, and slowly..." She paused, troubled. She was remembering what had happened to Janusz's wife from the northern continent. How much would

Deugan really change in accepting differences? How much could the government do about that, and how badly did it want to? Tomasburg would never stop playing the regions off against one another, and if the majority always ruled...

"In Amim," Nono said, "if you were in the community, you were part of the community. There was no other way. You needed to stick together to survive, and you learned to respect each other. There was no government to tell you not to."

"That's not what the Steffians stand for at all," Caryn argued. Attacking the terrorists was easier than justifying Deugan's own flaws. "They want a single government dominating the Continent and converting everybody to their religion. They're not about respect for outsiders or allowing local villages to do what they choose. They want to rule the Continent with an iron fist that would make a Brea tremble."

Surprisingly, that brought a smile to Nono's face. "The Steffians might not be around forever."

"What do you mean?"

"I mean that my brothers could start tearing each other's throats out at a moment's notice," Nono said. "It's Pellor Amad who keeps them in line. Without him — let's just say that I understand them, and I can make certain that they collapse. The problem is that if I do it today, governments like Brealand's will fill the void, and we'll be no further ahead. If, on the other hand, the Steffians destroy the existing powers, rule the Continent for a few years, and *then* collapse, well, 'power vacuum' would be an understatement. The locals will have to fend for themselves for a time, building their own communities to replace the government power that's disappeared — and we'll be in the perfect position to guide them in the right direction. In Amim's image."

Caryn pushed herself off the bed, which was difficult to do with only one good hand. "Brenner, you're scaring me. A lot. Are you actually suggesting —"

"I'm suggesting that we start over. The last two thousand years, the battles of the empires, it hasn't worked. We need another way. If we can't have governments that will protect their own people, we at least need governments that will leave them the hell alone. It's already started. Orastus is on the verge of collapse. Thanks to your armies, so is Wassia. The Brea people will welcome liberation."

"But Deugan is different," Caryn said again, helplessly. She was starting to wonder whether he was right. Aside from Amim's, there was no other government on the Continent that Caryn would want to live under, and even Deugan's was far from perfect. If death threats and the sorceress libel were really the best a government could offer...

Nono's thoughts were along the same lines. "I know Deugan's been good to you in a lot of ways, but open your eyes and be honest with yourself. Your life here has been tough. You've been attacked and ridiculed in a way that no person should ever have to endure. Yes, in theory Deugan has a lot of promise, but you and I both know that in practice, once the shells stop flying and the guns fall silent, another ninety years could pass and Deugan still won't have a woman president. Do you know the one place I've lived where women have actually been respected as leaders? In Amimi villages where they're the community elders. They talk, and Steif help you, you listen."

"What about the *acambro* bombs?" Caryn asked. "How are you ever going to bring down the Steffians if they have that weapon?" She said it instinctively before she realized what it implied. That part of her was accepting Nono's premise. That she had moved on to practicalities.

"The Steffians' supply of *acambro* is limited," Nono said. "We sent most of our *acambro* on this western operation. Enough to protect ourselves in a hostile country and to plant bombs in Deugan and Brea cities. But once the great powers fall, they'll have very little *acambro* left. Not enough to survive the infighting that's to come."

Caryn shuddered. So the bombs had already been planted. If the Breas agreed to the Steffian alliance, the bombs in the Deugan cities would be set off, and Nono wanted to blow both sets of bombs at once. Caryn tried to calculate the number of people who would die in the simultaneous explosions. Then she had to stop, because the number was so staggering that she felt sick. It wouldn't necessarily end there, either. The Steffians might be short on *acambro* now, but if they controlled the entire Continent — "Couldn't they just produce more?" she asked.

"Not for a long time," Nono said. He had an amused look that Caryn found not at all reassuring. "There's only one place on the Continent where the *acambro* grows. There was only one facility to extract and infuse it. The facility was expensive and difficult to build. It will take years to replace. And I blew it up."

"You *what*? But you said you're still a Steffian. How did they not find out?"

Nono laughed. "They ordered me to do it! It was about to fall into the empire's hands." He leaned forward conspiratorially. "The facility was very well hidden, and so were the storage sites the empire raided. Someone must have tipped them off. I wonder who..."

It was too much for Caryn to take in. She wasn't sure what was more disturbing, that her old friend and lover was proposing such a thing or that part of her actually wanted to go along with it. "Brenner," she said, trying and failing to keep her voice steady, "why are you telling me all of this? What is it you want from me?"

Nono paused for a long time before he answered. "I need you," he finally admitted. "At first I didn't understand why. I just kept reaching for you. Bending my mind to you, trying to bring you closer."

Subtle, Caryn thought. Nono was describing how to produce the energy hands, and he knew exactly what memories Caryn would associate with them. "This can't just be about —"

"No. That's what I thought at first, but soon I realized it wasn't anything that mundane. It was you. Your spirit." He looked at her. "I know how crazy I must sound, but I just don't see any other way to build the type of society that both of us want to see. Yes, the first step is destruction, but the second step is rebuilding. When that happens, I need you by my side. You have the heart, the humanity, the courage to make real change. To make sure we're not setting something up that's just as bad as what we've replaced."

"I'm not going to be able to do that," Caryn replied. She was surprised at how hard it was to say. "I'm sorry. I can't get behind the bombings. I can't murder the very people I'm trying to protect."

"I understand," Nono said sadly. "I just hope they're as willing to protect you." A chill passed over Caryn. "I know how you live in fear here. Not just of the Breas, but of your own officers, your own soldiers. I know why you don't sleep in these quarters anymore. Rumour gets around." He sighed. "I remember what it's like to live in fear. It's awful. I know you don't support violence, and part of me doesn't blame you, but — but you don't have to live like this, Jayla, and you don't have to protect the people who make you."

He paused again, leaned closer to her, and added, "I may be able to get you out of the Gateway. To get you away from everything, somewhere safe. Ask yourself whether your president and your general would be willing to do the same."

CHAPTER TWENTY-THREE

I hate the re-enactment. Sure, it's good for business, thousands of drunk tourists who are all too eager to part with their cash, and that's why I come back year after year with my books. But I hate the way they've taken the Battle of the Maxalo Pass and turned it into an attraction.

You want to re-enact the Maxalo Pass? You want to know what it was really like? I'll tell you. I remember retreating across the valley at the end of the first day, when the Breas countered and drove us out of their trenches. We were stumbling over corpses that were already starting to bloat, covering the ground so thickly you couldn't avoid stepping on them. If you ever hit a patch of grass, it was trampled and squishy and oozing purple blood. That's what everybody's celebrating. That's what they want to re-enact.

Yeah, I know. I'm Amimi, so I'm supposed to be proud. "Maxalo is where Amim became a nation," they say. That may be true, but it's not because we came together and fought so valiantly against the Breas and the Wassians. It's because at Maxalo, we learned how alone we were. How expendable we were even in the eyes of Deugan, our so-called ally. We had no choice but to band together as Amimi, because in their eyes we weren't even soldiers. We were bait.

— Interview with Baka Intit (1732), author of The Spirits were Silent: Memoir of an Amimi Soldier

The submarines launched past the watchful eyes of the Deugan coastal batteries. They took a well-worn path. A wide circle around the Brea naval blockade, then northward. Too far out to sea for the Breas to attack without support, not worth the cost of pursuit.

The blockade had closed firmly around the Deugan coast. Coastal batteries and roving army units kept Brea soldiers from landing on the shoreline, but the Brea naval cordon was tight, and few ships could slip in or out. What remained of Deugan's fleet huddled around the batteries in the south. They were dedicated to keeping open Carrak-on-Sea, Deugan's lifeline to the outside world. There the shipyards still built submarines and battleships and destroyers, and the ports buzzed with merchant vessels carrying goods under heavy escort.

It was strange, Caryn thought, reading about Carrak in snippets. Brief, dry cables failed to capture the frenzied ports. "0910 Sub gps 3 4 5 launch. 1137 bear N spotted but no pursuit." North to Brea waters, to harry the food ships. This was the Deugans' remaining weapon on the sea.

Caryn exchanged a glance with General Freed across the communications hub. "Nothing more today," he said kindly. "Tomorrow, and the day after. There will be a place here for you."

When she returned the next morning, the communications hub was bustling with activity. "0730 intensify shell WA posn N of VS." Deugan was not the New Empire, shelling trenches for days on end, telegraphing its attacks. The Deugans' signature tactic was to engage in casual shelling across nearly the entire length of the front, then suddenly ramp up to an overpowering volley in a tiny, focused area. Their attack would follow mere hours later, catching the Wassians off guard.

"0742 WA aircraft over VS." Their enemies' response times were getting quicker. The Deugans had their own aircraft over Villasud, spotting for their artillery, focusing it on the Wassian trenches. The Wassian fighter planes tried to take them down, to blind them.

General Freed had showed Caryn how Southern Command intended to deploy its troops for the attack on Villasud. The Deugan army was entrenched north of the city, thousands of soldiers backed by rows upon rows of tanks, the improved models that Deugan had designed after studying the failure of Brealand's tanks in the Gateway. The cream of the Wassian army stood between them and their objective, dug in partway up Villasud's hill.

The key to the city's defence, though, was not the northern approach, but the Maxalo Pass in the west. Freed insisted that without the pass, the city would never be taken, and the Wassians knew it. So they had swallowed their pride and invited a Brea Expeditionary Force to defend Maxalo, a battalion that was better armed and trained than any Wassian unit. Against the Breas stood the largest Amimi army that had ever been assembled, reinforced with Deugan artillery. It was an impressive force but inexperienced, up against the most elite units of the Armed Power of the Realm.

"0853 AM engage BR." *So simple*, Caryn thought. *So bland. So removed.*

The Maxalo Pass became a nightmare. The Amimi surged into the valley, the Breas stood firm against them, and the pass descended into chaos, shells whistling and bursting, dirt churning into mud, guns blazing, men screaming and dying. The Amimi were crawling across no man's land, flattening themselves to the grass and diving into the craters left by the shells, desperately shielding themselves from the Brea machine guns as their artillery pounded the Brea positions. Men crawled over their dead fellows to reach the enemy, and then they were there, hurling grenades into the Brea trenches, falling to the death rattle of the machine guns, catching on barbed wire and briefly breaking through before the Breas counterattacked, driving them backwards.

It was evening before the attackers were finally beaten back. The Amimi losses were staggering, but so too were the Breas', nearly half their number dead or wounded, their ammunition running low. North of the city, nothing had changed. The Deugan shelling had intensified, the men and tanks were readied, but no man's land was still, balanced on the point of a knife.

Wassian divisions from the coast arrived during the night to reinforce the Maxalo Pass. They spent the night restless, huddling in the southern valley, listening to the artillery pounding their positions, following the reports from Villasud of shelling growing stronger and closer.

The Amimi attack came right at dawn this time, a fresh wave of men crashing into the Brea positions, hurling their grenades as the machine guns blazed, mowing them down. "0625 AM engage BR." As the sun rose over Villasud, the Deugan shelling grew more intense still, and then, Caryn read with a lump in her throat, "0710 DE 3d army engage WA N of VS." A wave of Deugan soldiers leaping over the top, scrambling uphill toward the Wassian trenches.

The Wassians scrambled their aircraft again, but the Deugans were already in the sky, finding the Wassian fighters as they launched, bringing them down. The Deugan air force was relentless, blinding the Wassians as the Amimi surged into the Maxalo Pass and the Deugans charged toward Villasud. It was as though the world had narrowed to the valley and the hill.

Just as the Deugans wanted.

Five leagues north of Villasud, the tanks sat, readied, waiting. In the intensity of the battle, the Wassians hadn't noticed them disappear.

In the Gateway Fort, Caryn and the others stood anxiously, watching the telegraph machines, waiting for the word that was sure to come. Thirty minutes passed. An hour.

Then the cable. "0820 Incr WA radio traffic think they know." Caryn saw General Freed's face turn grim. It would start now.

Near a town called Caban, which had seen only light shelling over the last span, the Deugan artillery suddenly let loose a furious volley. The tanks turned westward, gunning for the Wassian positions.

"0841 Engage WA at Caban."

The Deugans hurled themselves at the Wassian lines again and again. Many of their tanks broke down before ever reaching their enemies, but others pushed through, pounding the Wassians and pinning them to their trenches as the Deugan infantry surged across no man's land. The machine guns still tore into the attackers, and the barbed wire raked and clawed at them as the defenders fired their rifles and stabbed with their bayonets. For hours the battle raged, the Wassians desperately holding off the Deugan onslaught, until —

"1312 Caban taken. WA in retreat. Pursuit ordered."

The Wassians fled, and the Deugans followed hard on their heels. Wassia mobilized its reserve units as quickly as it could and charged out to meet the retreating men. As the afternoon grew later, and the Brea Expeditionary Force finally beat back the Amimi again, they too turned on their heels and rushed to meet their fleeing allies.

The Deugans were faster. They caught the stragglers that evening southwest of the Wassian Well, before they had a chance to dig in. The pursuers surrounded their prey and destroyed them.

It wasn't until the next morning that the Wassian reserves arrived to find an entrenched Deugan position, reinforced by hundreds of troops shipped in by overnight train. The Wassians were weary from their march, and the battle was over almost before it began. The

Expeditionary Force changed course yet again and made for Garameche, the Wassian capital, where it could link up with Brea reinforcements that were arriving by sea from the north.

But the reinforcements never came.

At first it didn't seem to make any sense. The Brea navy had made short work of the Deugan fleet that tried to block its path, sinking three Deugan ships and sending the rest skulking back to Carrak-on-Sea. The Deugan navy, as a force to be reckoned with, had all but disappeared.

But three wolf packs of submarines had also disappeared, turning west after the Breas had seen them going north, refuelling at an island base, then striking southeast to Wassia as fast as their crews could take them. The Brea ships, having run over the token Deugan resistance, were just a touch too reckless. The ambush surrounded them and destroyed them.

The King of Wassia, his reinforcements lost, his army broken and the road to his capital laid bare, personally wrote a cable to the president of the Republic of Deugan offering, in exchange for a ceasefire, an immediate and unconditional surrender. No sooner had the president accepted than he had the news relayed to his foreign minister.

As Caryn Hallom read the Wassian surrender aloud, the communications hub erupted. Applause, shouting and cheering, clasped hands and hugs, as days of pent-up nerves were released at once. Caryn threw herself at Janusz and they hugged for a long time, neither wanting to let the other go.

Their hands lingered together as the embrace ended. Caryn was feeling nervous, in a good way. She leaned in toward him and saw him lean forward too, his lips slightly parted. She grasped his arm. Their lips almost touched. For a brief moment, Caryn believed he wanted to kiss her, too.

Then the moment passed. Caryn heard the voice in her head, the one that reminded her who she was and what she was. That she looked like she could be Janusz's mother. That she was the Sorceress from the South, and that she was trapped in the north, surrounded by enemies.

She pulled away from him, embarrassed. The celebration in the communications hub was suddenly unbearable. She put on her politician's smile and bowed to General Freed, Captain Malitz and even Major Danzig before retreating to the nurses' wing to rest.

*

It was early in the evening when Caryn went to sleep; it was mid-afternoon the next day by the time she woke. As she sat up in her bed she felt a brief rush of panic, as though she had forgotten where she was. Then she remembered the cable from the president and the euphoria that had run through the communications hub. Caryn allowed herself a moment of satisfaction. The war in the south was over, and Villasud was saved.

In the north, however, the conflict still raged. Brealand held a swath of the Deugan northwest and was pushing the trenches eastward. The Breas were moving ever closer to Deugan's oil country, which fed the factories around Tomasburg that turned out their arms and ammunition, the ships and submarines that resisted the Brea fleets, and the tanks that would now become essential to their offensives. If the Breas captured the territory, it could wreak havoc on the entire Deugan war effort.

Worse, the Breas might not even need to conquer the north at all. All it would take to disrupt Deugan oil production, Caryn thought ruefully, would be one or two well-placed *acambro* bombs. Yet neither Deugan nor Brealand had yet accepted the Steffians' offer. The Breas, unwilling to lightly betray the New Empire, still wanted the Steffians to turn over the secret of the bomb itself, which the terrorists were unwilling to do. General Freed, meanwhile, was using every stall tactic he could think of to buy time for Deugan's politicians to debate the matter, and for Caryn to advance her negotiations with Ravencliffe.

Amid all of these tensions, Caryn found her thoughts drifting back to Janusz, to their almost-kiss in the communications hub. They had been surrounded by other soldiers then, so Caryn's instinct to abort had probably been for the best, but inside she knew that wasn't why she had stopped. She had stopped because she couldn't believe that a man of Janusz's age might actually be interested in her. What if she were wrong, and he did want her? What did she want?

Then there was Nono. Caryn hadn't told a soul about his plan to destroy Deugan and Brealand together. She still wanted to protect him, her oldest friend, but by keeping it a secret, she was placing all of Deugan in grave danger. Nono was still their prisoner, but Caryn couldn't help wondering whether, by covering for him, she might allow him to escape and follow through on his scheme. On the other hand, though, even if she went to the general this instant, how would she explain why she'd waited an entire span, Cabinet debating the offer and Freed bargaining with Rusul all the while? How could Caryn Hallom ever be trusted again?

The peace would save her, Caryn thought. If Deugan and Brealand agreed to present a united front against the Steffians, it would be obvious that the terrorists might try to attack either or both of the western powers. Nono's plan would no longer be a secret, and the entire west would be working together to counter it. All Caryn needed was her peace treaty, and the victory over Wassia might be her chance. Already the veterans of the Wassian campaign were travelling northward, and the substantial Wassian fleets were being confiscated for Deugan use. The Breas would want to make a deal now, before Deugan's war machine arrived on the northern front.

Caryn waited until evening before visiting Ravencliffe in his cell. She wanted to be certain that he had the opportunity to visit the communications hub first. She wanted him to hear about the Wassian surrender from his own sources, and be ready to deal.

Two Deugan soldiers were on guard duty when Caryn reached the prison corridor. They were used to seeing her and paid her little mind. She arrived at Ravencliffe's cell to find him standing expectantly at the bars, as though he had been waiting for her. His face showed his usual practiced calm, no sign that he was affected by the news from Wassia. Once Caryn was inside the cell, Ravencliffe bowed to her, and said, "I believe congratulations are in order."

"Thank you," Caryn replied. "I regret the Brea losses. I'm told the Maxalo Pass was devastating." She shook her head. "It's such an incredible relief to see quiet on the southern front. It's time we end the war in the north as well. I was thinking we could start with the Amimi question. I actually had a couple of creative ideas —"

"I'm sorry," Ravencliffe interrupted her. His face remained blank, but there was a note of sadness in his voice. "I'm afraid there's been some sort of miscommunication. When I said that congratulations were in order, I meant that you ought to be congratulating me."

"For what?" Caryn was taken aback.

Ravencliffe actually seemed uneasy. He hesitated and said quietly, "For the conclusion of a military alliance between the Realm of Brealand and the Steffian Army of Dignity."

It was as though a weight had dropped into Caryn's stomach. She felt like she was back in the Wassian Well. Trapped. "Why?"

Ravencliffe shrugged. "It was thought," he said, "that the Wassian surrender might shift the balance of power in the war. The abject failure of the Brea Expeditionary Force to prevent it, and the manner in which we were outsmarted by savage cunning, were seen as highly disturbing. The decision taken at the highest levels was that desperate measures were required to protect the interests of the Realm."

"*We* were going to protect the interests of the Realm! You and I. This alliance, you know what it means for Brealand in the long term."

"Of course I know," Ravencliffe said calmly. "You and I have been over this ground many times. The Steffian alliance is certainly contrary to the Realm's interest in extricating itself from the politics of the east, but it accords perfectly with an even more important interest: to end the threat your Republic poses to our civilization, as quickly and efficiently as possible."

"What about the New Empire?" Caryn was finding it hard to breathe.

"Since the third span of the war, the New Empire's been bloody useless to us," Ravencliffe spat. "They're sitting in a tiny corner of Deugan, wasting their ammunition and occasionally their lives. They haven't managed a competent offensive in months. All they've done is to lose three of their colonies, and soon they'll lose Cioro, too. You said it yourself. Not only is the New Empire dying, so is the very world it inhabits. The Steffians, on the other hand, are younger than any of us. Vibrant. Powerful. They are the world to come."

"I don't believe that," Caryn declared. "I thought —" She stopped and took a breath. She couldn't cry. Not in front of Ravencliffe. "We were so close," she said, sounding as defeated as she felt. "Weren't we?"

There was a long silence. Ravencliffe's face was still a mask, but his discomfort came through in the way he stood, the way he crossed his arms. "This was not my decision," he said finally. "Nor does it make me entirely comfortable. That being said, I can't say that I truly disagree. It is time for this war to end, and now it will, on acceptable terms." He sighed. "I will miss our discussions, Minister. They were entertaining, and dare I say it, at times even enlightening."

"The whole point of our discussions was to change both our countries, and the entire Continent, for the better," Caryn reminded him. "Maybe we still can. It's not too late."

"It is too late." Ravencliffe's voice was firm. "That is why I am about to presume upon your patience once again, and offer you some advice. I've managed to persuade His Majesty that it is not in the Realm's interest to utterly destroy the collection of ruins on an anthill that you call your capital. I argued that an angered enemy will continue fighting back, whereas a neutered one will pose no threat. I argued that the destruction of millions of lives through the bombing of urban centres will rid the Realm of its goodwill and reputation, which will jeopardize our relations with our trading partners overseas. And of course, any excuses upon which Qir Ni or Koltaja might seize to justify an intervention on the Continent are to be assiduously avoided. My arguments were accepted."

"I suppose I ought to thank you, then?" Caryn asked bitterly.

"Accepting my advice will be thanks enough," Ravencliffe said. "In the next span, you will receive an ultimatum from my dear cousin and her royal husband. It will not look anything like the terms you and I have been discussing. I imagine they will demand that you cede some territory in the Deugan north, recognize Wassian sovereignty over the whole of Amim, pay substantial war reparations, and other conditions that you will find equally unpalatable. When you receive this offer, your instinct will be to embody the Deugan ideals of independence and individual heroism, and reject it out of hand.

"My advice, Minister, is that you instead consider the Brea values of logic, reason and putting the needs of your country above all. The Steffians' bombs have already been planted in five of Deugan's largest cities, including Tomasburg and Carrak. To my cousin, these lives are barbarian ones which she would not hesitate to destroy. When she offers to spare them, my advice is to put aside your pride, and accept."

*

Think, Caryn told herself. *You can't break down. You can salvage this. Think, now.*

She withdrew from Ravencliffe's cell and retreated down the corridor with only a cursory nod to the guards. *Think.* She needed to go to General Freed immediately. The Steffians had promised him an opportunity to match any Brea offer. Freed needed to call in that promise.

But that was exactly what Ravencliffe would expect her to do, Caryn realized. He wouldn't have told her about the Brea-Steffian alliance unless he was absolutely certain that it was too late for Caryn to stop it. The general had just stayed awake for thirty-six consecutive hours, and Caryn would be waking him for nothing.

She still had to tell him. She *had* to. But she was frightened. Why? For herself? For what Danzig might do to her? It was time to put Brea values first. She could take punishment if she had to. The general needed to know. It was the right thing to do.

Yet still she hesitated. Was there a chance Ravencliffe was wrong, and the alliance wasn't as firm as he claimed? She found it hard to believe that the Steffians would so cavalierly abandon their Master of Secrets. Brenth Nono was still a Deugan prisoner. Surely they wouldn't agree to a Brea alliance without even giving Deugan a chance to respond.

Unless, Caryn realized, they believed they could rescue him. Captain Malitz certainly thought that Nono had wanted to be captured; what if Nono knew, somehow, that his imprisonment would be temporary? Then there were Nono's own words to Caryn: "I may be able to get you out of the Gateway. To get you away from everything, somewhere safe." Caryn's heart sank. Nono did have an escape plan. He had played them for fools, all along.

Caryn wondered if she should go with Nono anyway. He had offered to protect her. He also wanted to destroy Deugan, but surely he could be persuaded to abandon that plan. What Nono really wanted was a better world, and Deugan had the promise. Caryn thought she could convince him — but she'd also thought that she could convince the New Empire to accept the Hallom Doctrine, and that she could convince Ravencliffe to strike a deal to end the war. Caryn was obviously less persuasive than she liked to believe.

So she could only go to the general and tell him everything. But every time she thought of doing so, warning bells sounded in her head, and she had long since learned to trust her instincts. If Danzig found out that Caryn had been hiding Nono's plan for an entire span, that she and Nono had more history than she'd let on, that Nono intended to escape the fort and take her with him — Caryn just knew that something terrible would happen, and she had no idea what.

She knew only one person who might. She felt the familiar anxiety and willed herself to drown it out. Caryn had to see the general. She just needed to be prepared first, to know what she was stepping into. That was all she would ask for. He couldn't hurt her.

She rattled the bars of the cell against their hinges, and then she waited, her heart in her throat. The evening was growing late, and the prison corridor was dark. It felt to Caryn like hours were passing. Her heart was beating furiously.

At last Captain Toppel stepped into the light. He stared at her in disbelief. "Minister Hallom?"

"Don't think I trust you." Her voice was wavering. "I haven't forgotten what you did. But events are moving fast, and we might all be swept away. If you still have a warning for me, I need to hear it. Now."

"Minister, I swear by all the Gods, I had nothing to do with the leaves," Toppel said. "I know coming at night was stupid, but —"

"Captain. I don't have time." Caryn tried to make her voice curt, but she couldn't get the shaking to stop. "You know something about Major Danzig?"

She saw Toppel freeze, then swallow hard. "The only thing I *know* is what I've already told you. Danzig's planning something. I don't know what, but I think it involves you."

Caryn shook her head vigorously, hoping that would clear it. She had to think. "Anything between me and the major doesn't matter right now," she said. "Tomasburg itself might be bombed into oblivion." She saw Toppel startle at that. "I need to get the word out. I need to know if Danzig is going to try to stop me, and how. I need to know which side he's on."

Toppel was taking deep breaths. "I wish I knew more," he said. "I think that this is more than some petty spat, at any rate. Yes, the major hates you, and he's trying to take you down, but that's not all. You're a means to an end. But what's the end?" He leaned against a wall of his cell and rubbed a hand over his face nervously. "That's what I could never figure out. That's why I went to your room that night. Until I knew Danzig's endgame, I needed you to be on your guard. I also needed your help."

"How could I have helped you?"

Toppel hesitated. Then he said, "You're close to Janusz."

Caryn felt her breath quicken. "What does Janusz have to do with this?"

"I was about to tell you that, just before you kicked me," Toppel said. "I was passing by Janusz and Marwin's quarters one night. The door was closed, but I saw these strange flashes of light through the crack, and I heard a noise that I still can't describe. So I started to keep an eye out for them. At first I was watching Marwin pretty closely. Something seemed a bit off, but nothing I could put my finger on. So I moved on to Janusz, and I started to notice that he and Major Danzig were spending a fair bit of time together. Not excessively, but it's unusual for any officer to be socializing like that with a private. Danzig's traditional, like Freed. He's usually pretty strict about the hierarchy."

"So you think Danzig was pumping Janusz for information about me?"

"I'm not sure," Toppel replied, "but I saw them talking a few times, and Janusz never looked uncomfortable. He looked like he wanted to be there."

It was all so overwhelming. Caryn felt frozen, uncertain what to do. Confront Janusz? Avoid him? Or ignore all of this, and go straight to the general about the Brea-Steffian alliance?

"Whatever Danzig's planning," Toppel said, "he and his supporters are going to move soon. Maybe even tonight. The rumour down here is that he's a hero now for the part he played in the Wassian attack. He's going to act while his star is still high, while he can afford to take risks. You need to find out what he's going to try, and Janusz probably knows."

Caryn gripped a bar of his cell with her good hand and held onto it as though it was keeping her from drowning. Could Janusz really be part of Danzig's scheme? Since Hans died, Janusz had developed into her best friend at the fort. Did he really respect and care for her, or was he only spying on her for Danzig? Did the kiss they had almost shared mean anything at all?

"Is there anything else I should know?"

"Only one other thing I heard Danzig say," Toppel said. "He was talking to Freed about where you were going at night. I couldn't hear them too well, but at one point I definitely heard Danzig say that every rumour has a basis in reality."

Caryn's mind went to the same place Toppel's had. "He thought I was going to the Well. That the Sorceress rumour had some basis in me being able to use the Well's power."

Toppel nodded. "That's all I know. I don't have any other advice for what you should do. All I can say is, for the love of Carmel and Seppina, do it fast."

He was right; she had to act quickly. If Danzig was planning to make his move tonight — but how could Caryn know that? All she had against Danzig and Janusz was Toppel's word, and why should she believe him? Janusz had been a friend, had supported her and comforted her. Toppel had ordered her out of bed at night, had brought *acambro* into her quarters, and was almost certainly behind the other *acambro* attack, the one with the revolver in the basement of the fort. Yet for some reason, Caryn did not think Toppel was lying.

What if he wasn't? If Toppel wasn't behind the revolver attack, it meant the real assassin was still roaming the fort. Could the assassination attempt have been Danzig's doing, too? Or could the mastermind have been Freed himself, who had sent her into the fort's basement that fateful day with a specially chosen escort, who had been all too quick to let Toppel take the fall?

The questions were becoming too complicated. The simple answer was to put Danzig's scheme aside, focus on the Brea-Steffian alliance, and go to the general. The thought still terrified her, for reasons she could barely explain, but she forced herself to put one foot in front of the other. She could warn Freed about Toppel's speculations and ask him not to get Danzig involved. She could protect herself. One foot in front of the other. Through the sub-basement, past the generator room, to the stairs leading up to Freed's quarters.

Caryn had just started to climb the stairs when she heard footsteps. A figure was moving down the steps toward her.

"Caryn," Janusz said with a smile. "I thought I might find you here."

CHAPTER TWENTY-FOUR

Caryn wanted to bolt and run, but there was nowhere to go. Janusz was blocking the staircase leading out of the sub-basement. The generator room was a dead end. The prison guards knew her, but there were only two of them tonight, and she had no idea whose side they were on. Toppel had implied that Major Danzig had a whole league of supporters he could mobilize. It was too risky.

Janusz stood before her, tall, muscular. His hands could as easily caress her as tear her apart. The attraction she had always felt mingled with fear as she mapped escape routes in her mind. Janusz had been her best friend in the fort these past span, she reminded herself. He had comforted her and supported her. She only mistrusted him based on Toppel's word, and she had no reason to believe Toppel. She took a deep breath.

Janusz's face was puzzled. "Caryn, what's wrong? Are you okay?"

"Ravencliffe says that the Breas have made a treaty with the Steffians," she told him. "I have to tell the general, now. But I'm afraid."

Janusz's face turned a shade paler as he placed his hands on Caryn's shoulders. She noticed his strength again, at once comforting and terrifying. She wished she knew what to think. "The general went to sleep three hours ago," Janusz said softly. "He was awake for nearly two days. Maybe it's best if we give him a bit more time to rest while we figure out what to do."

Caryn's heart dropped through her chest. The Janusz she knew would have insisted that they wake the general up immediately. It was the right thing to do, the only thing to do. For Janusz to be putting it off — "What do you mean?"

"I just mean that we have an hour to talk about this," Janusz said innocently. "To calm down and make a plan for approaching the general together." When Caryn didn't react, Janusz added, "Caryn, I'm trying to help. It's just an hour."

"Just an hour," Caryn repeated. It did sound reasonable when Janusz put it that way. Or was that just what she wanted to think, because she didn't like the implications of Toppel's warning? She'd been attracted to Janusz since the day she met him, and she'd given herself away last night. She'd tried to kiss him. He knew.

He squeezed her shoulders and stepped closer to her. He was still between her and the staircase. "Just an hour," Janusz said again, "and just to talk. Somewhere private, where Freed and Danzig and their men can't hear us. We get ourselves ready. Then we take Ravencliffe's news to the general."

Caryn nodded. "Okay."

Janusz's hand closed around hers, gently. Butterflies filled her stomach, but whether from attraction or fear, she could not say.

She went with him. Together they climbed the stairs out of the sub-basement and walked through the underground corridors of the fort. Major Danzig would act soon, Toppel had said, maybe even tonight. Caryn had to figure out his plan, but how? She would never be able to force information from Janusz, but he was so strong, there was no telling what he might do to her.

Caryn looked around again for places to escape, but part of her didn't even want to. She wanted Janusz's support. She wanted him to hold her, to kiss her as he should have done last night. She didn't want to believe that he was the enemy.

Even if he was, thoughts of escape were pointless. Her left arm was still useless from the elbow down, and with her bad knee, Caryn would never outrun him. Inwardly, she cursed the Well for aging her.

The Well.

If she could get Janusz there, she could defend herself. In all of Caryn's panic and uncertainty, that thought burned into her mind. The energy would fight for her, even if no one else would. And if Toppel was right about the direction of Danzig's plan, she thought darkly, then Janusz would want to go. He would want to see whether she could really use the Well's power.

That was when Caryn noticed that they were in the tunnel connecting the main fort to Seppina satellite. When she glanced at Janusz, he smiled and said, "Marwin's in my quarters. If we want privacy, we'll have to head outside."

"Just for an hour," Caryn repeated. "Then we tell the general together."

"Together," Janusz assured her. He gave her hand a squeeze.

They reached the satellite fort. There was some activity here, but the soldiers they passed paid them no mind. They made their way toward the eastern exit and found two soldiers guarding it. Janusz brought himself up to his full height and in an authoritative voice said, "The foreign minister needs some fresh air, and she's asked me to accompany her. We'll be back within the hour. You can count it if you like."

The soldiers straightened. "Understood," one of them said. He stood aside.

They walked until they were far enough from the fort to be invisible to its watchers in the darkness. They were halfway to the Well when Janusz stopped her. "Yesterday," he began. He sounded almost shy. "When the announcement came in. I saw you —"

"There were too many people," Caryn blurted.

"We're alone now." Janusz leaned in toward her.

Caryn thought about resisting, but only for an instant. Then his lips were on hers, and she gave herself over. A short kiss, and then a longer one. Her good hand found his neck and held him close to her. She kissed him again and lingered in his arms.

The warnings in her mind grew fainter at first. Then they rose again. Janusz hadn't agreed to go the general immediately, as he ought to have done. He had taken her out of the fort, in the direction of the Well. Janusz knew Caryn was interested in him, but why would he be attracted to her? It was suspicious, but she wanted it to be real.

Get to the Well, she told herself again. Suspicious as it was, in the Well she could defend herself. There she could afford to take chances.

Caryn broke away from Janusz. "Not here. We're too out in the open."

Janusz nodded. "Let's go, then." Caryn took off in the direction of the Well. Janusz was only a half-step behind.

She paused when they reached the threshold, and Janusz did too.

Then he took her hand, took a deep breath, and guided her into the Gateway Well. Caryn watched him react to the sudden heat, the pressure and the other nameless feelings that jolted him as the Well's power pounded at his body, demanding entry. His face was alarmed. He shuddered, but then he stood tall, forcing himself to be brave.

It took a moment before Caryn realized that she ought to have acted that way herself. Would he guess how familiar she was with the Wells and their power? Belatedly Caryn tried to act nervous, hesitant. She put her good hand on Janusz's arm as though asking for support, and he covered it with his own hand and gave her a reassuring smile. He didn't seem like an enemy.

They wandered through the Well, hand in hand. Janusz had turned the conversation to their lives back home, their hopes for when the war ended. Casual. All the while they pressed onward, deeper into the Well. The ground was soft. Rock formations surrounded them, illuminated by dashes of orange light. Caryn started to feel more at ease.

They came to the entrance to Caryn's tunnel, the one she always used to enter and exit the Well through the sub-basement below Eolanis satellite, but they didn't walk toward it. Instead, Janusz looked around, thought for a few seconds, then continued on the path they had been taking. Just a few yards away was the entrance to another cave, a yawning gap in a wall of stone. Janusz made for it.

The entrance opened into a large cavern. Its walls let off a furious orange light and the ground beneath their feet glowed yellow and blue, in alternating circles. Caryn startled as she recognized it, and her stomach started to turn. Fear welled up inside her.

Then Janusz's arms were around her, and he was holding her, stroking her, kissing her. She gave herself to him once more. Their kisses grew more passionate, more intense. Caryn began fiddling with the buttons on his shirt, a distraction. It was actually a benefit to having only one useful hand: buttons took her a long time to deal with, and just now, time was what Caryn needed. She had to think.

They broke apart, just for a moment. Caryn took a deep breath and saw Janusz do the same. "We spend so much time together," he said sadly, "without ever really getting to know each other. Not just you and me. So many of us."

So you want to get to know me? Caryn thought. Toppel's warning played in her mind. Her suspicions were growing stronger, but she still had no idea what to do about them. *Might as well play this out.* "It seems we are getting to know each other," she said, raising an eyebrow. Caryn finally finished with his buttons and slipped his shirt off of his shoulders. He wore a thin white undershirt. The muscles in his arms and chest bulged beneath it. "Did you really bring me here to talk about why I'm afraid of the general?"

"No," Janusz admitted. "I did want to get to know you, though. In more ways than one."

"Why?"

"Because I've never met anybody like you," Janusz said. "So strong, so creative, so willing to take risks. Yet sometimes you seem scared, too. Human."

"I should hope so," Caryn said lightly.

Janusz seemed flustered. "Caryn, you are an inspiration. And I want to know how you do it. Who you are." He took a few steps back from her. Took another deep breath. Sighed. "I have something to confess."

Caryn's ears perked up. Her heart started to beat a little faster. "What is it?"

Janusz hesitated. He looked around the cavern, as though searching for signs of movement, to make sure that they were really alone. Then he said, "This isn't my first time in this Well."

Play along. "Sweeps?" she asked. Caryn knew that the fort's garrison had searched the Well for straggling Breas after the battle.

"No," Janusz said. "I was still in training when the general did that. It was years ago. After my wife left for the northern continent. I needed to get away from it all, so I hopped a train to the Gateway. The government was controlling access to the Well, only allowing in some small tours, mostly for Steifar wanting to pray there. I got in on one, and somehow I managed to slip away from the tour group."

"For how long?"

Janusz looked at the ground, sheepish. "Twenty-two hours," he said. "I was going to make it twenty-four. I felt like I had so little to live for then, maybe the Well could save me, or maybe I'd just stay in there forever. Let it age me, so I'd be done with this world sooner."

Caryn shuddered. Her heart and mind reached for him. "Oh, Janusz. I'm so glad you didn't."

"I am, too," he said. He looked up again. "There's an instinct, I guess. A will to live. On my way back I ran into a search party that had already been looking for me. They took me to a hospital in Czemers and brought in a priest to talk to me. The Gods saved my life."

Caryn shook her head. "You were the one who found the searchers. You saved your own life." *One*, she thought. *A start.*

"I still think about it sometimes," Janusz said. "How close I came. But I'm stronger now. I got past it. I'm so glad I have someone who I trust enough to tell about it."

Caryn went to him, reached for him. She wanted him closer. He took her in his arms. "It's okay," she told him. "We're here now."

"And I intend to make the most of it," Janusz grinned. He lifted her up in the air, placed her back down, and kissed her again. Caryn's heart was in her throat, but she kissed him back. *Two.* He came on stronger, kissing her as he touched her neck, her shoulders, then worked his hands down toward her breasts.

She put her good hand on his chest, pushed him back slightly and wrenched her lips away from his. He didn't stop. He pressed in closer to her, keeping his hands on her breasts. "Janusz," she whispered. She was breathless. "Wait. There's a better way."

That stopped him short, as she hoped it would. As she feared it would. She forced her mind to reach toward him again. The power stirred. *Three.*

"I have a confession to make, too," she said.

Her good hand was still on his chest. She slowly removed it and stepped away from him.

Janusz's eyes widened, and his mouth dropped open. He could see her hand, a foot away, but it felt like it had never left him. An invisible hand had taken its place.

"Don't be scared," Caryn said. "You wanted to know more about me. This is who I am." She ran the energy hand down along his chest, across his stomach, to his leg. She took a step toward him, just out of arm's reach. Her energy hand passed over Janusz's thigh, the way it had Brenner's so many times before. Back and forth, now one leg, now the other, then working between them.

Caryn stepped toward him again. She erased his fear with a kiss. "Now you know," she whispered, as she stroked him, up and down. She ran the energy hand along the shaft, down to its base. He was hard for her. "You know my secret." She felt tears in her eyes.

She wrapped the invisible hand around Janusz's scrotum and squeezed. "What's yours?" she demanded.

Janusz's howl was like nothing human. His hands shot toward his crotch but never reached it. The second and third energy hands grabbed Janusz's wrists and yanked his arms behind him. He tripped and stumbled to the ground, swearing. "Damn it, Caryn, what's wrong with —"

He screamed as she squeezed him again. "Did you really think I was that gullible?" Caryn shouted. "That you could make up a story and I'd tell you some deep, dark secret in return?" Janusz was grunting, moaning, taking short, difficult breaths. "You've never been in a Gods-damned Well before," she snarled. "I saw that plain on your face when you stepped across the threshold."

"It was years ago! You're crazy. Let me go."

"You've never been in a Well before," she repeated, "and there's only one reason for you to lie about that. So I would be tricked into telling you something similar. Drop the charade and tell me why you're here."

At first he still refused to answer. His real arms struggled against the invisible ones holding them. Her other energy hand squeezed him again between the legs until he roared. "Danzig," he gasped. "Carmel and Seppina, save me. Danzig sent me."

She loosened her grip and saw the relief on his face. "Why?" she insisted.

"Thought you used the Well's power," Janusz panted. "Lied to the people. Thought it would prove you were a traitor, connected to Steffians, or it would prove you had some kind of secret past. With an eyewitness to you doing sorcery, you'd be out of office."

Caryn's mind raced. It was exactly as Toppel had suspected, but Toppel thought that getting rid of Caryn was only a stepping stone for Danzig, a means to an unknown end. "Why does he want me out of office?"

She saw the terror on Janusz's face. "Thinks you're a traitor," he repeated. "He doesn't trust you. Thinks you're selling Deugan to the Breas or the Steffians."

"That's not all," Caryn said dangerously. "What are you trying to hide?" She made sure that the energy hand was still hovering around his crotch, where he could feel its outlines. "You will tell me what Danzig's plan was, or your next hours will be a nightmare."

She didn't have to ask him again. "He thinks the general's fallen for you. Giving you exclusive access to Ravencliffe, then letting Ravencliffe into the communications hub, then letting the Steffian alliance slip away, all these things he did because you asked him. All these disasters for our war, is how Danzig feels."

"It's how you feel, too," Caryn snapped. "Why else would you agree to help him?"

"Fine," Janusz said. "I did agree. The general's judgment has been compromised. He's relied too much on your advice. Major Danzig thinks that he's no longer fit for command."

"So Danzig's going to take over. Expose my past with the Wells. Destroy my credibility. Take the general down with me, since he's been on my side." She had been so afraid of the general. The entire reason that she had come here with Janusz was that she hadn't felt safe talking to Freed alone. She couldn't believe she had been so stupid. "Danzig's going to move tonight, isn't he?" She remembered Toppel's warning. "With his coup?"

"Not a coup," Janusz insisted. "Military regulations say that if the commanding officer becomes unfit to lead, the second-in-command has a duty to take over."

"Tonight?" Caryn asked again.

Janusz looked at his crotch fearfully, and nodded. "It's too late for you to stop him."

"No, it's not," Caryn snapped. "His plan needs you. An eyewitness to me using the energy. Do you think I'm going to let you crawl back to him?"

"Do you think you have a choice? How stupid do you think I am? Do you really believe I'd take a sorceress into a Gods-damned Well without any back-up?"

Caryn blanched. She actually hadn't thought of that. She'd come to the Well so she could defend herself, but only against one man. Even with the energy, she could never fight off a whole army. "You're bluffing," she said shakily. "You've been screaming your head off. If you had back-up, they'd have heard you, and they'd be here by now."

Janusz looked scared again. "I *do* have back-up," he insisted, but his face told Caryn everything she needed to know. The back-up hadn't come when it should have. Janusz was scared it wasn't going to. "It doesn't matter," he said. "You're out of options and you're out of time. If you let me go, I tell them what I've seen and felt. If you don't let me go, you have to kill me. Major Danzig's plan works just as well if the general's been taking direction from a murderer."

He was right, Caryn realized. A third option might be to keep Janusz in the Well, alive, and guard him — but forever? At some point she'd need to sleep. His back-up might arrive. And her disappearance itself might give Danzig all the ammunition he needed to depose General Freed.

She had to warn the general, but how? She couldn't run back to the fort. The moment she stepped outside the Well she'd be powerless, and Janusz would seize her. Could the energy do it? Matt had taught her how to send visions. She let her fear and desperation build up inside her, let her emotions overwhelm her. She felt the tingling sensation as numbness worked through her body, starting at her toes and working up her legs and into her chest and arms. When it was ready, she tried to direct it to General Freed, but she couldn't. Freed had never used the Well's power, and even if he had, he was far outside the Well and lacking *acambro*. He had none of the energy to draw upon.

The numbness vanished. The effect withered and died, and Caryn felt the energy hands dying with it. Janusz's arms were released, and he moved them to his crotch gratefully, holding himself. He made no sign of coming after her, but she panicked nonetheless. She had to warn the general. The thought of Danzig taking over was unbearable. She had to find a way.

But she couldn't think. She racked her brain desperately and found it empty. The fear was overpowering. Blindly, she threw herself to the Well, praying that it would find her a solution. *Please,* she begged it, *please, send him a message, warn him.* She pictured herself in the general's quarters, waking him, telling him. She yearned for it as she had never yearned for anything before.

Caryn felt the energy stir inside her. For a brief moment she dared to hope.

Then she noticed the vision lingering at the edge of her consciousness, and her joy turned to ashes. "No," she groaned. "No, no, no."

It was too late. The nausea overcame her and she fell to the ground, banging her knee painfully on the floor of the cavern. Caryn clutched her head with her right hand and struggled to keep her eyes open, but the energy was forcing them shut, stronger than her power to resist.

The visions came. Caryn saw an old woman, ancient and wrinkled, riding a horse-drawn carriage into the darkness.

She saw a man she did not recognize but who seemed strangely familiar. He threw open a window and stared into a square below. It was filled with men, and horses, and guns.

She saw the generator room of the Gateway Fort. Her gaze was drawn to a pile of materials scattered on the ground. A piece of piping lay there, evidently discarded. It was glowing, now red, now orange, now yellow, its colours shifting furiously.

Finally Caryn saw herself, collapsed on the floor of a cavern in the Gateway Well. She saw her eyes squeezed shut, her head clutched in her hand. A few feet away, she saw Janusz sitting in his undershirt, his hands on his crotch. Behind her were several Deugan soldiers, their faces at once wary and menacing.

Caryn opened her eyes and slowly turned around. She was staring down the barrels of their rifles.

CHAPTER TWENTY-FIVE

The orange glow off the walls shrouded the soldiers' faces in shadow. Their leader stared at Caryn through the sight of his rifle. "Minister Hallom," he said. "You'll come with us."

Three of them had pulled Janusz to his feet. The others kept their guns trained on Caryn. Her knee complained as she rose unsteadily. "No sudden movements," the soldier warned her. "First sign of sorcery, we shoot."

Caryn barely heard him. Her mind was focused on the prophecy. Glowing pipes, colours shifting. Only once before had Caryn seen anything like it. "There's a bomb," she said. "In the fort."

"Walk," the soldier ordered. "Hands over your head, where I can see them."

"Didn't you hear me? There's a Steffian bomb in the fort. It's going to go off, we have to —"

The lead soldier cracked her across the face with the back of his hand. Caryn's head erupted in pain. She went sprawling to the ground, where she lay until another soldier roughly yanked her back to her feet. She could barely see, the pain was so blinding. "No talking," the leader said calmly. "Move."

She obeyed, making for the entrance of the cavern. Janusz was ahead of her, walking bowlegged. The prophecy replayed in her mind, again and again. Discarded piping, glowing dangerously. She had to stop it. Otherwise they would all die, every single one of them.

They exited the cavern. It was still dark outside, the moon a sliver in a cloudy sky. The rifles nudged Caryn's back as she walked. She needed to map. It was the only way to see whether the bomb was dormant or whether the Steffians were already trying to detonate it, but the soldiers would shoot her the instant a column of light burst from the ground. She couldn't take the risk.

They trudged through the Well, Caryn's anxiety growing. Janusz's back-up, Danzig's men come to ferret her out. To march her to her death, with all the rest. "Please," she dared to say. "We could all be in danger. The entire fort —"

The soldier slung his rifle over his shoulder and grabbed Caryn with strong arms. She struggled feebly. "The Steffians have a bomb," she started to say before he fastened a strap over her mouth, and she couldn't speak at all.

She marched in silence, the rifles at her back, Janusz ahead. He had slowed down, and one of the soldiers shoved him forward, gesturing with his rifle. They were as rough with him as with her, Caryn realized. Were they not his back-up after all? If they weren't Danzig's men, who were they?

Then they crossed the threshold of the Well, and her last chance vanished. The energy seemed to evaporate, and the night grew suddenly chilled. She was powerless against the bomb now. They all were.

Hours seemed to pass before they finally reached the fort. They were admitted through Seppina satellite; the guards there were not the same men who had let them out. The lead soldier removed her gag as they entered the fort. "Where are we going?" Caryn asked.

"To see the general."

"What for?" she asked. "What does he think we've done?" She received no response.

Caryn expected soldiers to stand and gape at them as they were paraded through the fort, but all the men she saw rushed past them purposefully with barely a backward glance. She didn't understand, but it felt ominous. Had Danzig's coup succeeded? Were the other soldiers dead, or under arrest? Was the major now the one calling himself a general?

It was hard to keep her thoughts straight with the prophecy burning in her heart. She stretched her mind, searching for a hint of the energy, an indication that the bomb was already at work. At one point she thought she felt it, and she drew in a breath of fear. Then the feeling faded. Was she imagining it? Or was there *acambro* in the fort, waiting to be detonated?

She strained to catch another sense of it, but they reached the general's office before she could. Her captors knocked, then threw open the door, shoving her and Janusz inside. Caryn managed to keep her feet, but Janusz ended up headfirst on the ground, pawing it helplessly as the soldiers filed in.

General Freed stood behind his desk, with Major Danzig at his right-hand side. Four soldiers waited with them. Two of them were armed, and they were strangers to her, but she recognized the unarmed ones as the guards who had let them out of Seppina not so long ago.

A feeling suddenly flooded over her, powerful. The energy, grasping. Caryn reeled and nearly fell; one of the soldiers caught her by the arm to steady her. The energy receded, but it left behind its telltale sign, a high-pitched ring, dancing at the edge of Caryn's hearing. Her eyes darted around the room, searching for it, fearful.

General Freed leaned across his desk menacingly. "Where are they?"

"Who?" Caryn asked. She still didn't know what was happening. Another wave of energy crashed over her. Again it withdrew. It was close. "General, you have to listen to me," she pleaded. "There's an *acambro* bomb in the fort. We have to evacuate everybody. At least a league away, as far as the Well."

"Is that why you were hiding there?" the general asked darkly. He slammed his fist on his desk. "I don't have time for this. You will answer my questions truthfully, for the first time in your Gods-damned life, or, Armano help me, you'll wish you had. Now where is your lover?"

At first the question confused her. Janusz was sprawled on the floor right in front of him. It took her a moment to realize that Freed wasn't talking about Janusz at all. "Brenth Nono? Isn't he in his cell?"

The soldiers looked at each other incredulously. Danzig rolled his eyes. Freed stepped out from behind his desk, his fists clenched. "I am giving you one last chance."

"General, please," she begged. "I don't know what you're talking about, but we could all be in danger. Please at least let me look." The energy washed over her again. The ringing sound spiked, then softened. The power was here, in the fort, a mass of it, rolling off the bomb in waves. It was growing stronger, and stronger.

The general grabbed Caryn's good arm and twisted it behind her back until she screamed. "Where are they?"

"I don't know," she gasped. "Lessandro have mercy, I don't know!" He twisted her arm even further, and she choked back the pain. Yet through its haze a question came to her. "Where are *they*?" she asked, repeating the general's words. "Not just Nono? Not — no. Oh, no."

The general did not loosen his grip. "Yes. It's time to stop playing stupid, Hallom. Your lover Nono, your friend Ravencliffe and all of the Breas, gone. The exact same night you and your entire team disappear. You're found hiding in the Well. And you expect me to believe you had nothing to do with it?"

The pain in her arm was overwhelming. Tears welled up in her eyes. She fought through it to catch another hint of the bomb. The energy was roiling. How could they not feel it? How could none of them feel it? "I had no idea," Caryn gasped. "You have to believe —" She stopped. Shuddered. "My entire team?"

She glanced at Janusz on the ground. His eyes were wide. He'd had the same thought. "Where's Marwin?" he breathed.

The general let Caryn go, and she shook her arm out gratefully. Freed went over to Janusz instead. "I was hoping you'd tell me where Marwin was," the general hissed. "Not hiding in the Well with you two? Taking off in opposite directions? I will have answers —"

The office plunged into darkness.

Shouts went up all around her, but to Caryn's immense relief, nobody shot. She'd guessed right, the room was too crowded; they wouldn't risk firing a gun into the blackness. Frantically Caryn turned her mind to the *acambro* in the sub-basement, feeling it from its distance, pushing at its boundaries, exploring.

Major Danzig shouted and jumped backward as the first column emerged at his feet. It was a deep green, majestic. The purple column rose on the other side of the general's desk. The bronze one came next, mingling with the far wall, brighter than the others. *Kalid,* she thought, *and Accarro, and Pascuay.* Caryn could feel the rifles trained on her, but still nobody dared shoot. The Orastino Well turned up in pale blue, bursting out of the ground right where Janusz was lying. It immediately set to sparking, bathing the general's face in its changing patterns. Then there was Amim, and Wassia, and finally, at the corner of the office, the Gateway. The local Well's column was crimson, and a tiny light flickered beside it, its colours shifting.

The room collectively drew in its breath. "Armano guard me," she heard Janusz whisper, "Lessandro have mercy."

The soldiers were nervous, and Danzig gave voice to what they felt. "It's the boy."

His presence was unmistakeable. Though none of them knew the Well's power, his aura flooded them, surrounded them. Marwin was in the map. His attention was focused on the flickering light just west of the Gateway Well. Caryn could feel the energy shifting as it hopped from one strand of *acambro* to another, from the Steffian stores into the fort. As the bomb was loaded. Filled to the bursting point.

She had no choice. She was about to plunge in when she felt a hand on her shoulder.

General Freed had recovered from his shock. He whipped her around. "What in Lessandro's name are you doing?" he demanded. His pistol was pressed against her temple. He could shoot her now, without risking the others.

"I'm trying to save all of our lives," Caryn panted. "There's a bomb —"

She started to gag. Her good hand went to her throat, clawing at it. The general threw his arms in the air, as if to tell the others that he wasn't the one choking her. Janusz still prayed on the ground. Danzig looked shaken. Caryn forced away her panic, reached into the map, searched for the Steffian. It wasn't Marwin; there was more than one. She found him, grabbed the fingers. It was like talking with Matt through sailor's code, only he had always squeezed her arm, never her throat.

Caryn yanked the man's fingers backward. Through the map she could feel his anger. She felt the blood rush from her head as she strained to breathe. The Steffian struggled against her as she bent his fingers backward, felt his pain, felt his scream roll off her. Suddenly the grip loosened and Caryn sucked in the air. He came after her again, but now Caryn could sense him, evade him. "The Hermann Gap," she said, through ragged breaths. The map let her trace them. "They ran south, to the Brea trenches."

"How do you know that?" Danzig asked.

Caryn ignored him. She looked plaintively at the general. "Please, General. You can feel Marwin, I know you can. He's trying to set the bomb off." Caryn dove into the map again, seizing on the energy in the bomb. It was unstable. She had to act, now. "Look at all the men you have here," she said. "You and the major are armed. Janusz and I aren't. You may not believe me, but you can't take the risk. You can spare two soldiers to see if I'm telling you the truth."

She had never seen the general look this scared. It was how Hans and Captain Malitz had looked in the Selliar Mountains when Nono snapped his fingers to make it rain. "What would you have the men do?" Freed asked.

"Go to the generator room," Caryn said quickly. "You'll see a piece of piping that's glowing different colours. That's the bomb. Take it and sprint toward the Well, like Lessandro running from the mob. Don't stop until you're a good two leagues away." She shuddered. "Then pray to Seppina you can get back in time."

Major Danzig stepped forward, but Freed held up his hand. "She's right. We can spare the men." He pointed at two of them. Even in the dim light of the columns, Caryn could see them go pale, but they accepted their burden without question. They were soldiers.

She remembered just in time, as they were heading out the door. "For Lessandro's sake, wear gloves!" Then they were gone, and it was down to her, and the Steffians, and the power.

She counted five Steffians in the map. Nono wasn't among them; Marwin was the only one she recognized. The Steffians were ignoring her, focusing on the bomb. Caryn's own source of energy was unsteady, growing stronger and weaker. It was difficult to fight them. She reached her mind toward the bomb, trying to empty it. Some of the energy leapt to her, grateful to escape the *acambro*, but other energy was untrusting, and there were five of them, catching it, funnelling it in, too many, too many, too many.

Caryn felt the sweat rolling down her face, the muscles in her neck and shoulders clenching. Vaguely she made out Freed watching her in fascination, and Danzig in fear. A wave of energy rolled in and retreated, the high-pitched sound screaming and softening, the columns dimming and brightening. The Steffians struggled with the power. She could feel them, each of them separately, their personalities, their essences. Marwin was the strongest. He had been in the Gateway, at the Well. He had been practising.

The door of the office burst open. Caryn nearly lost her concentration and tumbled out of the map, which might have doomed them all, but she caught herself before the power could slip away. "We found it," the soldier in the doorway was saying, his voice shaking. "Oskar's running it up to the Well. I was going to, but he insisted, said he was faster."

There were murmurs in the office. Words about Oskar's bravery and sacrifice. Caryn could barely hear them; her task was all-consuming. The minutes dragged and still she held on, siphoning energy from the bomb, struggling against Marwin and the Steffians as they tried to force it back. It was growing harder. Caryn felt the bomb moving, more distant. She was slipping, her connection weakening.

Marwin felt it too. One instant he was focused on the bomb. The next he turned on her and blinding pain erupted in Caryn's skull. She screamed and grabbed her head and struggled to stay in the map. The power was drifting from her. Caryn grasped at Marwin desperately. She felt as though her head were splitting apart as she squeezed letters into Marwin's arm, spelling in sailor's code, "Why?"

She never got an answer. The next burst of pain in her skull drove her from the map. Electric light flooded General Freed's office, the columns vanishing into the air. Caryn shouted "No!" just as Freed yelled, "Get down!" Caryn flattened herself against the ground. Her head was throbbing. She heard the high-pitched ring in her ears, screaming at her in fury.

Then it stopped.

The explosion began as a rumble, as though the earth were creaking and groaning. Soon it was a roar, a thousand tigers calling to them, sound to end all sound, furious, terrifying. Caryn felt the ground beneath her shudder, saw the walls shaking. Books toppled from shelves as pens and papers flew from the desk. Then the noise changed into the shrill howl of a heavy wind, screaming through a makeshift shelter.

Calm returned. The sudden silence was more jarring than any sound. The fort was eerie in its stillness.

Caryn lifted her head. All around her, slowly, the soldiers did the same. Then came the shouts and cheers, the clasped hands and the hugs. They were uninjured. They had survived.

Caryn stood. She was unsteady, though the room had stopped

shaking. She looked at the general with a smile, panting in relief. She'd done it. She'd held the Steffians off long enough for Oskar to get the bomb away. She'd done it.

General Freed did not return her gaze. He stared at his desk instead. "Damage report," he said quietly.

The celebration silenced at Freed's voice. Tension returned to the air. He pointed at one of the soldiers. "You. Get me a Gods-damned damage report. You," he added, raising his voice and pointing at the soldier nearest the door, "The gunnery. Make sure it's staffed and ready. Now that Ravencliffe's escaped, the Breas may follow up the bombing with a full-on attack." The men saluted and left to carry out his orders.

General Freed followed them to the door and slammed it shut. He motioned at the remaining soldiers and they remembered themselves, raising their rifles toward Caryn and Janusz. "Now," he said, looking straight at Caryn, "I need answers."

Caryn took a deep breath. The entire room was staring at her. She had just used the energy with abandon, in front of all of them. Barely thinking, acting on instinct in the heat of the bomb threat. Now that the danger had passed, she was horrified, and alone.

Major Danzig drummed his fingers impatiently on the general's desk. Caryn swallowed. "I wish I had the answers," she said. "It seems that Marwin was a Steffian all along. I can only assume he's the one who let the prisoners out, because his Master of Secrets was among them, but I don't know. I had nothing to do with it."

"I felt Marwin," Danzig said, shivering. "As though he were in this room, invisible. It was the strangest thing I've felt in my life. But how do we know he was a Steffian?"

Caryn stared at him, incredulous. "He set off an *acambro* bomb. I tried to stop him, I held him off as long as I could, but —"

"The major's right," Freed said. There was no softness to his voice. "All we know, Minister Hallom, is that you cast a spell and then we felt Marwin's presence in this room. You saved our lives by warning us about the bomb and telling us where to find it, I recognize that, but what proof do I have that Marwin set the bomb off? Or that he's a Steffian?" He glared at her pointedly. "Or that he acted alone?"

Caryn wavered, uncertain how to answer, when she heard Janusz's voice from the floor. "The wine," he croaked.

"What wine?" the general demanded, wheeling around to face Janusz.

"Sir," Janusz said faintly, "in our first span here, you gave us a bottle of wine. Marwin refused to drink any of it."

"What does that prove?" Danzig scowled.

"A sixteen-year-old kid, away from his parents, refusing free alcohol?" Janusz asked. "Stranger things have happened, I suppose."

"So he may be a Steifar," Freed allowed. "A Steifar is not a Steffian."

"Why hide it then?" Janusz asked. "Why trumpet so loudly that he believes in the Five? Besides, didn't you find him looking older? More mature?" Caryn startled. She had noticed that too, but she had put it down to the stresses of the war. Freed and Danzig were among many soldiers who looked older than they had two months ago. But now that she thought on it, she realized it was more than that. Marwin was actually, literally aging.

"Carmel and Seppina," Caryn swore softly. There was something else she had just remembered. "Marwin's the one who told me about the soldier who died in the Well."

"Gustav Tanker," Freed said at once. "Dead at age nineteen, with no sign of trauma and no cause of death that any of the doctors or nurses could figure out." He glared at Caryn. "I'm asking you for answers and you're raising more questions. Is there any mystery in this fort that you're not at the centre of?"

Caryn ignored the barb. "Hans believed that Gustav was the one who attacked me during the battle," she said. "He was obviously killed using the Well's power, but how did Marwin know about that as soon as it happened? And why did he tell me that Gustav was one of Captain Toppel's men? Marwin must have killed Gustav so that he wouldn't talk about the assassination attempt, and then he tried to frame Toppel for it." She stopped as another thought hit her. There had been a jailbreak. "Where is Toppel now?"

"In his cell," General Freed replied. "The others broke him out, and he went along with them for a time. Then he lost them and returned to the prison. He wasn't able to learn where they were planning to go, but —"

"He didn't see Marwin among them?" Caryn asked.

"He saw someone masked who was more or less Marwin's size," Freed said. "Of course I assumed it was Marwin when we couldn't find him afterward, but Marwin is your man, Minister, and you disappeared as well."

"You saw me being choked," Caryn argued. "You saw him attacking my head."

"I did," the general agreed. "You're no actor, so I believe you were in a fight. I believe you wanted to keep the bomb from exploding. That still leaves a lot of questions unanswered." He grew stern again. "Like what the hell I just saw you do, a league away from the Well."

Danzig nodded his approval. The rifles were levelled at her heart. "Sorcery," Danzig said with a smile.

"Not sorcery," Caryn insisted. She felt strangely calm. She expected herself to panic, but now that the bomb had spared them, her anxiety had vanished. "There's no such thing as sorcery. There was *acambro* in the bomb for me to tap into. I was using the Well's power. Any of you could have done it."

It was the reaction she expected. Fear and anger from the gathered soldiers. Mutters of "sorceress" and "Steffian." But before either Freed or Danzig could react, the door to the office was flung open. It was the soldier Freed had sent, returning with the damage report.

The two easternmost satellite forts, Seppina and Armano, had been utterly demolished. The eastern wall of the main fort had collapsed in places, and fires were smouldering alongside it, which the soldiers were rushing to put out. There was significant damage to the mess hall and the kitchen, which were toward the eastern end of the fort, and only minor damage to the barrack areas. Ninety men had died in the explosion. At least three hundred more were wounded.

Generally, though, the fort remained in good condition. The communications hub, the main gunnery, and virtually all of the storage rooms were untouched. The same was true of the medical bay and the nurses' wing at the western end. The Lessandro and Carmel satellite forts were pristine, and Eolanis was damaged but not beyond repair. Caryn had held off the Steffians just long enough. Had the bomb exploded in the generator room where it had been planted, the entire fort would have been reduced to rubble, and none of them would have survived.

The general barked orders for repairs. The soldier at the doorway ran to obey, and the attention of the remaining soldiers quickly settled on Caryn again.

She didn't need to be asked another question. She had used the Well's power in front of all of them. Her secret had been revealed, and she had saved Freed's life with it. He deserved the truth. "When I was sixteen years old," Caryn told them, "I was trapped inside a Well for six months."

"The Gateway Well?" Danzig asked, incredulous. "The government would have known. Deugan never would have allowed it."

"It wasn't Deugan," Caryn explained. "It was the Wassian Well. If you look at Wassian newspapers for the autumn of 1678, you'll see a reference to an avalanche. They said there were no survivors. They were wrong."

Finding those newspapers years later, in the archives at Helsengraf University in Carrak, was a surreal experience. At first Caryn was surprised the avalanche had been reported at all. Jayla, Brenner and Terial had all assumed the Wassian government would cover it up. Eventually, though, Caryn started to recognize the logic. The base camps at the east and west ends of the Wassian Well would know about the avalanche, so the news was bound to get out. Better for the government to control the message. By declaring that anybody trapped in the Well must have been asphyxiated within minutes, and that experts had deemed it unsafe to attempt a rescue, the government put an end to the public interest in the incident while deterring any private rescuers from poking around. Not only that, the government also gave itself a credible excuse to refuse Steifar pilgrimages to the Well for the foreseeable future.

"The Wassian government had declared me dead," Caryn continued. "If they knew I'd survived, I would be in grave danger, because I could expose what they'd done. Meanwhile, the Well had aged me twenty-five years, so I couldn't return to my family or friends. They wouldn't even recognize me. The only thing to do was to start a new life. So I came to Deugan."

General Freed shook his head. "That's quite a lot you're asking us to believe."

"The newspapers will confirm —"

"The avalanche, we know," Danzig spoke up. "General, we've heard all we need to hear. By her own admission, she's a Wassian who came into this country illegally and has been lying to the Deugan people ever since. About her identity, her birth, and her sorcery. Deugan is at war with her country, and she's had access to all manner of confidential military intelligence. She's spent the last year trying to persuade the government to spare Wassia from war. Even if she hadn't released all of our prisoners, it would still be a travesty." He looked around and took a deep breath. "I want her arrested, immediately, for treason."

The soldiers closed in around her. She saw the look of satisfaction on Danzig's face, and the glee on Janusz's, sweet revenge. Caryn watched them coming. She was not afraid.

Nor was she resigned. She took a deep breath, made her face impassive, and said in a mild tone, "I've never committed treason." She paused, looked Danzig in the eyes, and added, "Unlike some people in this room."

Everything seemed to happen at once. Soldiers grasped for her, Janusz recoiled in horror, the two men from Seppina glanced at Danzig and quickly away, Danzig charged toward Caryn with fury in his eyes, and General Freed pushed through the crowd to reach her first. Freed's face held an anger that Caryn had never seen before. He held up a hand to freeze the other soldiers in place. "I am running out of patience. You had better explain yourself, and fast."

"I've never committed treason," Caryn repeated. "I love this country more than life itself. Yes, I was born in Wassia. I came here after the most traumatic experience of my entire life. After the country that raised me left me in a Well to die. I came to Deugan alone and penniless, my body aged, my mind devastated. I was accepted here, and nurtured. This is where I got my second chance.

"I love Deugan. I love everything it stands for. I love that the government has to be accountable to the people. I love that politicians can be criticized without fear, even when I'm on the receiving end. I love that a woman here can rise through the ranks and make something of herself. People always assume that immigrants are loyal to their old countries, but if they were, they never would have left. I came to Deugan fourteen years ago, and I feel like I've lived here all my life.

"After all of that, do you think I would sell secrets to Wassia? After what that government did to me, after those people stole twenty-five years off my life? I hate them. I want to tear the royal palace down brick by brick. I didn't oppose this war for the sake of Wassia. I opposed it for the sake of my country. For Deugan."

She stopped to catch her breath. The others were staring at her. Freed looked troubled, as though he wasn't sure what to think. Danzig's face was a mask. Caryn took another deep breath and continued. "I admit I've committed crimes that are contrary to Deugan law," she said. "Possession of forged documents. Knowingly presenting false information to government officials. I committed those crimes fourteen years ago, when I was young and scared and running for my life, but I committed them. I take responsibility. But not treason. Never treason."

The room was silent. Freed grimaced and rubbed his temples. "This is Gods-damned incredible. What in Lessandro's name am I supposed to believe now?"

"General," Danzig said in a respectful tone, "in spite of the foreign minister's sudden show of patriotism, all this talk about fourteen-year-old crimes is misleading. She's been relying on those forged documents and her fake Deugan citizenship for her entire career, including her appointment to foreign minister just two years ago. She's shown us that she uses the Well's power, after publicly denying it for years. How can we believe anything she tells us?"

"General," Caryn cut in, "I know this is difficult for you. I know that my disappearance with Janusz during the prison break is still at the front of your mind, and you won't be able to trust me until you've heard the truth about why we went to the Well."

"We've heard enough," Danzig insisted. "I say we arrest her now, and leave these explanations for her trial. The Well's power is enough to impeach her."

"I agree," Freed said, "but there's a difference between impeaching a cabinet minister and arresting her for treason, especially when she's saved all of us from an *acambro* bomb. Besides, we need the truth about this prison break. I don't have any Gods-damned clue if the truth is what she's giving us, but unless we hear everybody's story, we'll never figure it out."

It was no ringing endorsement, but it was the opportunity she was waiting for. She told General Freed about Toppel's warning and why she'd followed Janusz to the Well. "Eventually," Caryn said, "I got him to admit his true purpose in leading me there. He wanted to trick me into using the energy, so that he could force me from office."

Freed glanced at Janusz, lying on the floor looking ill. "Dare I ask how you persuaded him to tell you that?"

Janusz had been listening to Caryn's story with a look of growing outrage. Now, it seemed, he couldn't hold himself back any longer. "She did it with fucking sorcery!" he shouted. "You grabbed my balls and squeezed them, you crazy bitch. She's fucking dangerous and she needs to be behind bars!"

"Is this true?" Freed demanded. Caryn nodded. Freed backed away from her. He was starting to look sick himself. "You — I can't believe —" He turned on Janusz suddenly. "And you! Luring her so you could impeach her? How stupid do you have to be to go into a Well with a sorceress, alone?"

For the first time since Ravencliffe told her about the Brea-Steffian alliance, Caryn allowed herself a smile. "Janusz wasn't alone," she said. "He arranged back-up. A couple of soldiers who'd been guarding Seppina satellite. Only your men arrested his back-up, General. Didn't they?"

They all looked at the two soldiers from Seppina, the only ones in the room, save Janusz and Caryn, who were still unarmed. General Freed looked at one of the armed men questioningly. The leader of the expedition, the one who had spoken to Caryn in the Well and gagged her. "Sir," the man said, "I thought it was strange how they seemed to know exactly where Janusz and Hallom had gone, but never tried to follow them or stop them. I didn't arrest these men, sir, but I had them taken to you, in case you wanted to question them."

"The foreign minister was exactly where these two told you she would be?" Freed asked.

"Yes, sir."

"And these two were alone at Seppina's north entrance?"

"Yes, sir," the soldier said, "and that was also strange. I thought you'd ordered ten-man rotations, with respect."

"I had," Freed said evenly. "In fixed teams. Janusz would not have been able to ensure that two specific men were alone at that entrance. Not without help. From someone with influence." He looked at Caryn. Then at Danzig. "You say Janusz wanted to see you use the energy so he could force you from office." Freed was talking to Caryn, but he stared at Danzig as though seeing him for the first time. "It strikes me that Ralf has a similar aim. 'The Well's power is enough to impeach her,' he said moments ago."

It was strange how sad she felt. There was no joy in this victory. It was a time for delicacy. The peacemaking that had come naturally to Jayla had to meld with Caryn's stubbornness. "Major Danzig," she said, "you and the general have been friends and colleagues for decades. Today I let out a dark secret that has eaten at me for half my life. It was difficult, but I gave the general the truth. Please. It's time he heard the same from you."

Caryn expected Danzig to balk, to deny everything. She barely had any evidence. Unless Janusz confirmed her story, she could prove nothing, and Janusz had no reason to help her.

But she'd underestimated Danzig. He was braver than she'd ever imagined. He was a soldier through and through. "General," he said, "I did arrange Janusz's back-up. We hoped to catch Minister Hallom using the Well's power, in order to discredit her and impeach her. We've talked about this many times, Ern. She can't be trusted, and there's been an over-reliance on her advice that's harming the war effort. I thought that once you saw our proof, you would agree."

"And if I disagreed?" Freed asked. "What then, Ralf?" There was sadness in his voice.

Danzig lowered his eyes to the floor. "I would have formed the opinion that your judgment had been compromised, because of her."

Freed understood. "Unfit to lead. Following military regulations. Not treason, then. Only betrayal."

"Ern," Danzig said, "you have to believe me. It would have killed me to do it. I prayed to the Gods it would never come to it."

"But it has," Freed said sadly. Caryn was struck by how weak he looked. "Major, your weapons, please."

"Ern," Danzig objected, "I never acted against you. I never betrayed anybody. This doesn't change what we all saw and felt, with the columns —"

Freed cut him off with a glare. "Your weapons," he demanded.

Danzig looked around the room. The two men from Seppina were unarmed. So was Janusz on the floor. His allies. He offered his pistol to the general, followed by a revolver and two knives. Freed accepted them bitterly. "You three," he said, nodding to three armed soldiers near the desk. "Escort Major Danzig and his friends to his quarters. Keep them there under guard until further notice."

The men saluted. One of them helped Janusz to his feet, and the conspirators and their guards shuffled out of the office in silence.

When the door closed behind them, the room felt eerily empty. Only four soldiers remained, along with Caryn and Freed.

Freed looked as though he might cry. Caryn started toward him. "General —"

"Shut up," he snapped with a venom that shocked her. "Just because Ralf betrayed me doesn't mean you didn't."

"I saved your life," Caryn said, taken aback.

"After we dragged you back here, into the bomb's range," Freed shouted. "If we'd let you hide out in the Well where you couldn't be hit, would you still have stopped the bomb?"

"Of course I would —"

"How do I know that?" Freed demanded. "How did you even know about the bomb if you're not one of them? Gods! Ralf was right. I have a soft spot for you. It makes me want to believe you, even though you've told me nothing but lies since the day we met, and that *is* a betrayal, Minister. It may not be a treason against Deugan, but it's a betrayal against me." He shook his head and started to pace. "Let me get this straight. You save all of us from an *acambro* bomb. Ralf admits that he sent you and Janusz to the Well while the prison break was happening, which means you couldn't have been behind it. You can use the Well's power, we would have known if you'd learned in the Gateway, so maybe you did learn in Wassia."

Suddenly his pacing stopped and he erupted, slamming his fist on the desk. "Damn it!" Freed shouted. "It's all plausible, but where's the proof? Brenth Nono would know who planted the bomb and whether Marwin was behind the prison break, and he's the only person on the Continent who could confirm your insane story about being trapped in a Well. But he's gone." The general looked defeated again. Helpless.

But Caryn wasn't helpless. A chill passed through her. It would be horrible, but she knew exactly what she had to do to win back the general's trust. The energy had shown her the way, all those span ago.

"Then let's get Nono back," she said.

CHAPTER TWENTY-SIX

They trudged over scorched and dying grass, passing heaps of rubble that had once been their satellite forts. Armano and Seppina, the god of war and the goddess of life, lay shattered, side by side. Eolanis, the central satellite, had been bruised but not broken. Deugan soldiers already swarmed it, making their hasty repairs. Only a couple of them glanced over to watch their general's procession.

Freed led the group, with Caryn walking by his side. Hertha, the fort's head nurse, followed a few paces behind them, seething. The four remaining soldiers from the confrontation in Freed's office took up the rear, their rifles readied. Ahead of them, to the east, the sun's first light peered over the horizon. Though the grass crunched sickly beneath their feet, and though clouds were gathering overhead, Caryn could see that dawn was breaking.

She could also see how heavily Major Danzig's betrayal weighed on the general. It was painted in his gait, his posture, his face. She felt sorry for him, despite everything.

"This all could have gone very differently," Freed muttered, as though he had read her thoughts. Caryn often forgot how perceptive he could be. "When I got the news of the prison break, I knew there was a traitor inside the fort. I handpicked a team of soldiers, the ones I trusted most. If it had been a different group of men in my office, when I asked Ralf to hand me his weapons..."

"I'm so sorry," Caryn said. "Ralf was never a friend to me, but I know how much he meant to you."

"I appreciate that," the general said, "but I can't be a friend to you either." She heard regret in his tone. "I'm sorry, Minister. It doesn't matter what today proves. I'll have to arrest you, when all is said and done. Not for treason," he assured her, seeing the look on her face, "but there are other crimes you've confessed. As an officer who sends boys off to die so that Deugan can keep the rule of law — I have my duties."

Caryn understood. She was saddened, but not surprised. In his place, she would probably do the same. "It was fourteen years ago," she reminded him.

"No, it wasn't," Freed said. "Ralf was right about that. Whatever forged documents you used to enter the country back then, you've been using the same ones ever since. Those, or documents you got based on the forged ones." He sighed. "Then there's the crime you admitted to committing just a few hours ago. Aggravated assault."

Caryn was confused, then stunned when she realized what he meant. "Janusz?" She felt Hertha coming up beside her, saw similar outrage on the nurse's face. "He was out to get me. He took me to the Well himself! I had Toppel's tip, I found out what Danzig was planning —"

She stopped short. For all the times that Freed had yelled at her that night, his quiet disappointment now cut her most deeply.

"Do you support torture as an investigative technique?" Freed asked. "I thought you, of all people, would remember what we're fighting for. Why it even matters whether the Steffians blow up this fort or not."

"That isn't fair," Hertha snapped. "The foreign minister was acting in self-defence." Hertha had been angry from the moment Caryn filled her in on the plan, and Caryn had feared that she might refuse to participate outright. Ultimately, though, Hertha had gritted her teeth and followed Caryn and the general silently out of the fort.

Hertha was right, too; Freed wasn't being entirely fair. Not only had Caryn been trying to defend herself against Janusz, but Freed himself had twisted her arm behind her back as part of his own investigation into the prison break. Still, Caryn understood the general's mood now that Danzig had betrayed him, and she felt compelled to defuse the situation. To mediate, as Jayla might have done. Besides, Caryn had to admit feeling some shame. She remembered Janusz lying on the floor, still sick and pained hours later. There were no easy answers. She still did not know what else she could have done. "It's all right, Hertha," Caryn said. "I won't hide from what I did. The general can do his duty, if he must."

That seemed to satisfy Freed, and Hertha evidently thought better of responding. As they walked toward the rising sun, Caryn filled in some of the colour of her past in Wassia, and Freed explained what had happened earlier that night. There had been two soldiers guarding the prison, and Marwin overcame both of them through a combination of surprise and *acambro*. According to Toppel, Marwin freed Nono first, then Ravencliffe and the other Breas. Some of the Breas were too weak and malnourished to escape; Ravencliffe ordered them killed before he vanished with the rest. There was no attempt to steal weapons or do further mischief within the fort, likely because the Breas were so weak that the attempt would have been suicidal. "They probably figured they'd let the *acambro* bomb finish us off," Caryn said.

"That was my thought, initially," Freed agreed, "but Toppel told me that many of the Breas were urging Ravencliffe to stay behind and wreak havoc, and at one point Ravencliffe almost agreed. It doesn't sound as though the Breas knew about the bomb. The Steffians may have kept it secret from them."

Freed had sent a rider into the hills to contact Rusul, the Steffian leader. It was obvious by then that the Steffians had aligned with Brealand, given the jailbreak, but Rusul's confirmation still stung. "The Breas made us an offer," Rusul said. "The Steffians are angry, thanks to Orastus, and hungry, thanks to you. We are tired of waiting."

At least, Caryn thought, they would wait a while longer before bombing the Deugan cities. True, the Steffians had attacked the fort, but that was a military target. Ravencliffe had promised her that there would be an ultimatum before any civilians were bombed. Caryn had no reason to believe him after his escape, but she did.

The general stopped the procession as it reached the edge of the Gateway Well. He looked troubled. "Are you certain you want to go through with this?"

Caryn felt suddenly weak. She steeled herself. "I have to."

"No, you don't," Hertha insisted. "General, I protest. This entire scheme is a travesty."

"Don't protest to me," Freed snapped. "I've never liked this plan.

It's Minister Hallom's idea." He turned to Caryn and said, more calmly, "There must be another way."

"There probably is," Caryn allowed. "I don't know. What I know is that we're running out of time, and that my way will work."

"How do you know that?" Freed asked.

Caryn gazed bitterly into the Well. "I've seen it."

"That also concerns me," Freed admitted. "Especially now that I've told you of my intention to arrest you. How do I know that if I take you into the Well, you won't —"

"Treat you as I did Janusz?" Caryn asked. Hertha rolled her eyes. "I don't have any reason to. The whole point of this is to regain your trust. Besides, you have four armed men with you. I could never fight them all at once, even if I wanted to." She sighed. "I don't suppose there's anything I can say that would give you certainty. You'll have to trust me."

They locked eyes then, as the others looked on warily, some of the men sneaking nervous glances downward. Finally the general gave her an abrupt nod. He stepped across the threshold. Hesitantly, the others followed.

The Well, the epicentre of the bomb, was a scene of utter devastation. The ground, normally soft, was hard as stone beneath their feet. The flat land had been pitched, forming ridges and valleys laden with rubble. Rock formations had shattered and collapsed, strewing the landscape with barriers that had to be climbed or circumvented. The Well had become an obstacle course, chaotic and desolate.

"Here, sir?" one of the soldiers asked when they finally came upon a flat stretch of ground.

General Freed shook his head. "This could take time, and we don't know when the Breas or the Steffians might attack. We need a spot that's defensible."

"General, sir," another soldier piped up. "The cave where we found her would work. It's only got one entrance, easy to guard."

"If it's still standing," Freed said, looking around. "Well, we may as well try."

The going was slow and the destruction sobering. Caryn looked around, taking it in. She was trying to prepare herself for what was to come.

At last they came upon the tunnel leading to Eolanis satellite. The mouth of the tunnel had caved in from the force of the bomb, barring access to the gentle ramp that led underground. A few feet away, though, the explosion had opened a hole in the ground large enough to fit a person. Caryn stole away from the group to examine it. The drop was four or five feet, but she could see the ramp through it, blue and yellow lights marking its path.

Their destination lay just a few yards beyond the tunnel, but it was a different world from the rest of the Well. The cavern was fully intact, an oasis amid the surrounding destruction. The scattered debris ceased abruptly as they reached its entryway. The soldiers looked more scared than ever, and General Freed asked Caryn, "Do you have any idea what this means?"

"It means the Well chose to spare it," Caryn said.

"The Well *chose?*"

"The energy has a mind of its own." Without thinking, Caryn found herself using Nono's analogy. "It's like an animal. We can't control it. All we can do is try to train it."

The general looked as scared as the rest. He was in beyond his depth. "So you've trained it?"

"Normally I feel like it's trained me," Caryn grunted. Hertha scowled at that, but when Freed glanced at her, she bit her tongue.

"You have no idea why it spared this cave?" Freed asked.

"No," Caryn said. "But the energy seems to like me, better than others." Both Matt and Nono had told her that. She wondered how they knew. "I can only imagine it thought this cavern would be useful to us."

Freed stared at the gaping entrance to the cavern. From outside, they could make out the blue and yellow circles on the ground and the orange glow from the inner walls. "Are you certain this is the only way?" he asked her again.

"There may be hundreds of ways," Caryn replied. "This is the way I'm choosing."

"Why? To prove something to me? About your willingness to sacrifice? I don't need you being a martyr."

"The energy does," Caryn said softly. His question had reminded her what was about to happen. She suddenly felt scared.

Freed looked scared as well. "It really has trained you, then. If this is what the energy wants, it's not your friend."

It was striking how much he sounded like Brenner when he said that. It only reinforced in Caryn's mind that this was the way to bring Nono back. "I don't need it to be my friend," she replied. "I need it to be my ally. You and I are about to be fighting *acambro* bombs."

"Some allies are not worth their price," Hertha broke in. "Haven't you spent the last span urging Deugan to reject an alliance with the Steffians?"

"This isn't the same," Caryn said. "The energy may not be my friend, but it's not my enemy either, as the Steffians are. The energy just is. Most people avoid it. The Steifar praise it as a mystery, a higher power. The Wassians study it for a scientific explanation that doesn't exist. The Steffians try to turn it to their own purposes, and so have some Deugans and Orastans. But nobody tries to understand it. To dig deeper, without trying to change."

"Except you?" Freed asked.

"Nono, to an extent," Caryn admitted. "Mostly me. It's responded to that. In its own thoughtless, painful way, it's offered me something unique. We always see prophecy as inevitable. A straight reading of the future that controls us, no matter what we do. Which makes it useless. There's no point getting a warning about something you can't change."

"If I understand what you told me back in my office," Freed said, "you did change something based on a prophecy. You said you saw the bomb about to go off, and you stopped it from destroying the fort."

"Exactly," Caryn said. "I never actually saw the bomb explode. The prophecy showed me the bomb being detonated, but the energy let me influence the time and the place. It gave me an incredible power." She surprised the general by resting her good hand on his shoulder. "This is exactly the same."

Freed's eyes went wide. "You actually believe I would do it anyway. You're just choosing to have it done with now!"

In that instant, the calm she had felt so far vanished. She was hit with the enormity of her decision, of the Well's decision. They really did need to do it now, before she lost her nerve. "The energy has given me the opportunity to influence a prophecy. To control when it happens. It may never have given this chance to anybody before. If I show it that I understand, if it appreciates how I've followed it, I believe that not only will the energy bring Nono back, but that in the coming span, it might save all of our lives."

"That does not reassure me," Hertha said. "General, I renew my protest. I do not want to have anything to do with this."

"You can wait outside, then," Freed said. "You will go to her afterwards, though. Remember your oath." Hertha scowled again, then nodded briskly. The general turned back to Caryn. "Hertha is not alone. This idea makes me very nervous."

"Why?" Caryn asked. It made her nervous too. Her fear and panic were rising.

"You want me to blindly follow a power we can't control, can't understand, and that doesn't seem to have our best interests in mind." He sighed. "You're a woman, too. Maybe there's another —"

It was too much to bear. "In Lessandro's name, get over yourself," Caryn snapped. "This is going to hurt me a hell of a lot more than it'll hurt you, and every second we wait makes it worse." The soldiers were shocked. They had probably never heard anybody speak to their commanding officer that way.

The general only shook his head, resigned. "Let's make this fast."

It was strange to think that she and Janusz had come here together only a few hours ago. Caryn stood in the centre of the cavern with Freed, the four soldiers surrounding them. The soldiers had their rifles trained on her, still afraid she might use the Well's power against them. "Are you ready?" Freed asked.

Caryn felt her fear rising. She used it, embellished it, trained it. She felt the tingling begin at her toes, and she kept it there, waiting. "Yes," she said. She could only hope Nono had some *acambro* nearby, to see her message.

"I'll go as easy as I can," Freed promised.

"No," Caryn snapped. "You can't pull your punches. This is Brenth Nono we're talking about, the Master of Secrets. If it's not a hundred percent real, he will know, and he won't come."

"He may not come anyway," Freed warned.

"He will," Caryn said. "He'll rescue me." She was absolutely certain of it. The prophecy had shown her Nono on horseback, riding hard northward through the Gateway, juxtaposed against the general hitting her in this very cavern. She knew what the energy wanted her to do.

"Fine," Freed said. "I've been at this a long time. I know where to hit you that won't cause any lasting damage. But you'll have to stand very, very still."

Caryn shuddered. "I don't know if I can." She thought back to the prophecy. "Better have your men hold me."

Freed nodded. Three of the soldiers pinned her legs and her good arm. The fourth knelt by her useless arm, his rifle readied. Caryn looked up at Freed, the orange glow from the walls illuminating the lines on his face. "Do it now," Caryn pleaded. "Please, General, the waiting is the worst part. Do it now."

Still the general hesitated. Then he threw his fist into her stomach.

Caryn had thought that after having her face struck in the Well, after the general twisted her arm behind her back in the fort, after the Steffian nearly choked her to death and Marwin sent blinding pain into her skull, that the prophesied beating would be painless by comparison. She was wrong. The first blow was so strong that she screamed. Thought fled her, and only pain and shock remained. Then the Well took over and the tingling spread up her legs, turning to numbness. The second and third blows came in quick succession, and Caryn screamed again. By the time the fourth blow came, the Well's power had numbed her stomach and she barely felt it. Still she was frenzied, desperate, her mind searching for Brenth Nono. Then she found him and the vision passed to him. She could feel it playing for him, the general's fists attacking her, her agony from the earlier blows, her screams.

The attack stopped. The energy faded. "Is it done?" the general asked.

"It's done," Caryn said. "Let's get out of here."

"No," Freed said. He sounded as shaken as she was. "Let Hertha check you first. We'll wait outside."

Freed and the soldiers withdrew to give them privacy. Caryn's whole body ached terribly. After a moment Hertha returned, working briskly. She removed Caryn's shirt, measured her heart rate and breathing, examined her wounds. When Hertha was finished, Caryn could sense her relief. "You'll have some painful bruises," Hertha said, "but that's the worst of it. I'll give you a salve that will help. There won't be any other damage." She helped Caryn to her feet, but her face remained cold. "I hope you're satisfied."

"This was harder for me than for you," Caryn said. She was too sore for tact. It was difficult even to move.

"Caryn, what I am about to say is in the spirit of friendship. You and I have shared quarters, and I've enjoyed our conversations. My nurses clearly look up to you, as so many Deugan women do. You must not allow any of them to find out how you undermined them."

Caryn's adrenaline rush was passing. She was too exhausted to feel hurt at Hertha's accusation. "I did what needed to be done."

"You sent a message to Ernst Freed and four other soldiers, which will no doubt spread across the fort. That a man in a position of power can hit a woman when it seems like it might help the war effort. Or for any other reason."

Caryn froze. That was exactly what Caryn would have thought of her decision, had it been made by another woman instead of her. Despite the stands Caryn had tried to take throughout her public life, when her own pain was at stake, everything felt different. She had been so caught up in placating the general and the energy alike that she hadn't even considered it. Caryn looked at Hertha, studying the older woman. "Were you ever —"

"Never," Hertha said with venom. "But if even Caryn Hallom thinks that's the only reason I would object to this beating, then Deugan has farther to go than I believed."

That cut close to the bone. Caryn took a difficult, ragged breath. "I'm sorry," she said. "But I was faced with a prophecy. The energy decreed it was going to happen, but once I saw it, I took charge of it. The time, the place, the circumstances, everything. I even made the energy numb me. I barely felt it."

"You never should have been put in that situation in the first place," Hertha declared.

Caryn bowed her head. It was difficult to bring words like *should* into the equation where the energy was concerned. "You're probably right," she admitted.

"So when will you stop coming to the Well?" Hertha asked. "My gods, Minister, when Willem Toppel came into your room, you fought back. If you wouldn't let him hurt you, why are you letting the energy do it?"

"We have to stop the Steffians," Caryn replied, "and that means we need the energy onside. No matter the cost. There's no other way to fight an *acambro* bomb."

"So once the Steffians are defeated, you'll be done with the Wells?" Hertha asked. "Leave the energy behind?"

Caryn hesitated. The question ought to have been simpler, but Caryn had never blamed the energy the way Brenner had. Was he actually right? Was Caryn the one who was blind? Before Captain Toppel came into her room that night, Caryn had snuck out to the Well whenever she had the chance, drawn to the power that had imposed all of this on her. What did that say about her?

Hertha shook her head. "This is Deugan. We can agree to disagree about whether the right thing was done today. I know that this was not an easy choice for you. I just hope it troubles you as much as it does me."

"Have no fear on that front, my lady," Caryn replied. "I've been troubled by every aspect of this war for a very long time. It creates impossible decisions and forces flawed people to muddle through them." She started to move toward the entrance of the cavern. Hertha came up beside her, allowing Caryn to lean on her. "It was incredibly brave of you to choose this nursing career that put you constantly at war, among armed men. Why did you do it?"

"My family was poor," Hertha replied. "The Coastlands Rebellion was launched during my teenage years, and when the Wassian Intervention started, Deugan put the call out for nurses and aides. Enrolling in the volunteer nursing corps meant three square meals a day and one less mouth for my parents to feed. When the Intervention was over, a salaried position opened up, and I never left." She paused. "As for being surrounded by armed men, well, I made sure I could be armed as well."

"You did?" Caryn asked, surprised.

Hertha smiled. "I demanded that they train me in their most common weapons. Pistols and rifles, bayonet work, even some martial arts. I was good enough at stitching their boys up that they didn't want to lose me, so they agreed. I'm a good shot, I'm told."

"You won't defeat a trained soldier in a fight, though," Caryn said. "If anything happened, and you escalated it, wouldn't that just wind up worse for you?"

"Perhaps," Hertha said, "but there's power in it all the same, in knowing that you can. You, Minister, have to know that you can stand up to the energy, even to the point of leaving it behind. You can stand up to the Ernst Freeds of the world as well."

"She already has no difficulty standing up to me," General Freed said as the women passed through the entrance to the cavern. There was pride in his voice. "How is she?"

"Fine," Hertha responded shortly. "Let's go."

They walked back to the fort in silence. The sun was high in the sky, and the clouds were starting to clear. Hertha and one of the soldiers supported Caryn as she struggled through the Well and then the charred field beyond it. Caryn felt the bruises forming as they walked. She would be in pain for days. She hoped it was worth it.

It felt like hours before they finally reached the dry moat at the edge of the emplacement. The soldiers helped Caryn across. It was easier to walk by then, but her muscles were stiffening. She realized that she hadn't slept the entire night. It was difficult to keep her eyes open.

The general released the others when they reached the main fort, and Hertha bowed and left for the medical bay without looking back. For a time Caryn and Freed stood alone in the fort's entranceway. "Nono will come?" he asked again.

Caryn nodded. "On horseback."

"We'll be ready," Freed said. "I'll give the orders now. Along with the order to release Captain Toppel."

A pause. A strained silence. Then Caryn said, "I told you before. If you need to arrest me, I won't try to stop you."

The general looked surprised. "Are you serious? Minister Hallom, you are as strong and courageous as any soldier I have ever worked with in my forty years in the armed forces. Your willingness to sacrifice yourself is the ideal we ask of all our men. You deserve a rest."

"You said it was your duty."

"It is," the general replied. "I will have to turn you over to the civilian authorities, eventually, but I also have other duties to my country. With the Breas and the Steffians allied against us, the war is about to enter its most difficult phase. It strikes me that my duty to Deugan requires me to maintain unity behind the elected government. Not to throw a cabinet minister into a circus trial that would divide the nation, not until the war is over, at least. In light of your exceptional bravery and loyalty, I am convinced that there's no risk of you running off before then."

"So I'm out on bail?" Caryn asked wearily.

Freed smiled. "Please, Caryn. Go to sleep."

"Thank you," Caryn said. She started to go. Then she came back and bowed to him. "I'm truly sorry about Ralf."

Freed turned away. "So am I." He left without looking back.

Caryn stumbled through the fort in a daze, down steps and along corridors. It wasn't until she reached the door that she realized she hadn't gone back to the place where she'd slept the last several span. In her exhaustion second nature had taken over, carrying her to her old room in the officers' quarters of the fort. It was for the better, she decided, since Hertha was still upset with her. She could sleep here today.

She pushed the door open and froze, stunned. Michael Ravencliffe was there, lounging casually on the bed where Lana had slept all those span ago.

Ravencliffe stood when Caryn entered. He bowed to her in the Deugan style, not in mimicry but formally. Caryn fought through her shock to find words. "What are you doing here?" she finally asked. "Why didn't you escape?"

Ravencliffe answered with one of the nonchalant shrugs he had been rehearsing his entire life. "We have a deal to finish."

CHAPTER TWENTY-SEVEN

Jayla snuggled up against Brenner and placed her head on his chest. His fingers intertwined with hers, and she tilted her head to kiss him. Her body might be old and breaking down, but it fit with his. She felt comfortable. Peaceful.

It had taken them time to reach this place, but Jayla was glad they'd done it. It was different than before, when they'd thrown themselves at each other to escape their fear. It was more organic now. Their renewed intimacy could have spoiled it, but it hadn't. It had only focused them on what was really important.

Or maybe the professor had done that.

Jayla and Brenner had laid him to rest a few span ago, when he finally succumbed to age and the Well's poison. His end had come quietly, while he was sleeping, and that at least gave them some solace. Still, it affected Jayla more than she'd expected. They'd known that he was nearing the end of his time in this life, but even so, there was emptiness without him. There was a loneliness that the living could not fill.

Through their tears Jayla and Brenner had bonded again, picked up the threads they had left to dangle. They tackled the pain together, cried together and rose together. They were still hesitant at first, the past close at hand, but slowly they learned to remember each other, the quirks and habits, the small things. Hugs and smiles, whispered words, jokes, laughter. It was not a starry sky or a sparking fountain, but there was magic in it all the same.

Brenner had flushed and balked the first time she suggested sex again. "Is this some kind of trap?" he asked. "We both know what happened last time."

"There was so much bound up in it last time," Jayla said. "There isn't anymore."

"Maybe there is for me," Brenner replied.

"Then forget I said it," Jayla said. "I just thought it would be nice."

Brenner stared at the floor. "It would be," he admitted, "but I don't want to lose you."

It was Jayla's turn to look downward. "I wish I could promise that. I just don't know what's going to happen."

"You used to say you loved me," Brenner said softly.

"I do," Jayla replied. It was automatic, but that didn't make it any less true. He was her best friend in the world. She felt closer to him than ever before. "I wanted to do it last time. I had no idea I'd react that way. I — I thought — I mean, you keep saying you want to understand me better, but I don't even understand myself. So what can I say?"

Brenner thought for awhile. "That's fair," he said at last. "Doesn't make it any easier."

"I know." Jayla hugged him. "At least we can be confused together."

"Yeah." Brenner smiled. "We've got that."

She didn't understand much more about herself now than she did then. She learned that she liked sex when it wasn't bound up in the other stuff, when she gave herself the chance to enjoy it. She liked doing it with Brenner, with someone who cared about her, whom she trusted. With someone who had shared the same ups and downs, the same fears, the same heartbreaks. It was special.

She didn't even mind his moods after a while. Brenner was who he was, her friend, her partner. He was part of her world, as much as the air she breathed, the rocks that glowed as her sun, and the ever-present energy. It was comfortable.

Too comfortable.

Jayla had never stopped practicing her Orastan, the way she had with Terial when he was still alive. She tried to write a journal in the language, to translate her thoughts, to tell herself stories. She tried to remember everything Terial had taught her about the coastal culture, about its history, about the great Deugan city of Carrak-on-Sea. When Brenner turned sullen, Jayla kept herself occupied.

Then Brenner would return, like today, and all would be well. She kissed him, and they wrestled, laughing. He darkened the cavern and brought the columns out around them, and Jayla pulled them along until they melded into shimmering rainbows. She made up a story for him about an apple that struggled to break loose from a tree, and he told her one in return, about a bear that followed a river down to a waterfall and tried to fish among the rapids. Jayla interrupted by poking him in the chest and started finishing his story for him, dancing away from him as he chased her amid the rainbow lights. She wasn't done the story yet when he caught her, and he stopped her from going further with a kiss. "I only know one way to make you stop talking," he said teasingly.

"It's a good way," she said, and kissed him back.

Jayla did feel safe with him. That was the problem. They had been here six months and lost twenty-five years. Her cough was worsening, her shortness of breath coming too quickly. Jayla still saw the professor in her mind's eye, how small and frail he looked in death. Life was short, Jayla was realizing, and hers shorter than most. She would not feel fulfilled until she had pressed against the boundaries of her comfort. Safety was a luxury from another world, the world of wealth and connection that she had left behind.

Brenner leaned in to kiss her again. Their lips came together. Then Jayla leapt back in surprise.

She had reached into the energy on instinct, and something new was happening. The rainbow lights flew past her, dizzyingly quickly, and the columns streaked by like comets. The cavern went dark, then bright, then dark again.

Jayla felt the Well's power growing in her heart, pumping heat and energy through her body. It was like being in a bath, but only for a moment. Then the warmth drained from her, and Jayla felt a chill, and terror, and then a glimmer of hope.

She felt Brenner's arms close around her in the darkness. She kissed him on the cheek, but he only squeezed her tighter, as though he knew.

The cavern brightened to a dull red glow. Jayla felt the power of the Well, hovering at her fingertips, waiting for her to grasp it.

She turned toward the green rocks that blocked the entrance to the cavern. She noticed Brenner's face out of the corner of her eye. He looked as scared as Jayla felt.

Jayla took a deep breath and gathered her courage. She was ready. And the energy knew it.

*

It was late in the evening when they brought in Brenth Nono. Caryn caught a glimpse of him in the hallway leading to the prison corridor while she was returning to her quarters from a meeting with Ravencliffe. A team of soldiers paraded past her, ushering Nono along at gunpoint, and he stopped just long enough to flash her a look that spoke of hurt and betrayal.

They brought him to Caryn's quarters the next day. It was midday, and Caryn had just finished waving away the lunch she had been offered, thin soup that was mostly water. The food they had stolen from the Steffians was mostly gone, and their stores were running perilously low. The farms on the fort's side of the Hermann Gap would not see another harvest for months, and the soldiers Freed had stationed there were quickly eating through the farmers' own larders. Caryn could eat the energy, at least, but the rest of the garrison was only a span or two away from debilitating hunger.

If General Freed was concerned about starvation among his men, he showed no sign of it. His demeanour was crisp, businesslike. "Nono has confirmed your story," he told her. "It seems you had an interesting childhood."

"You could say that."

"There was more he didn't say," Freed said. "I need to know about the Steffians' bombs. How we can fight them."

"I can try," Caryn said. "I won't press him too hard, though. He's still my friend, strange as it sounds."

Caryn waited for Freed to get angry at that, to remind her of her professed loyalty to Deugan, but the general only nodded. "Be careful. Brenth Nono the Steffian may not be the same person you knew. Fourteen years is a long time."

"I know," Caryn said sadly, thinking of Jayla.

They dragged Nono in, looking dishevelled, thin and hungry. Caryn rushed to him as the soldiers withdrew, as fast as her bad knee allowed. "Brenner! What happened? Are you okay?"

One look at him froze Caryn in her tracks. There was something in his eyes that she had never seen there before. Something dangerous.

"Stop," Nono said. He was standing in front of her, his arms crossed across his chest. "Okay, Jayla? Just stop."

"Stop what?"

"I don't want to talk to you." Nono's breathing was shallow. He was glancing around, looking anywhere but at Caryn.

Caryn was lost. She stepped toward Nono again. "What did they do to you?"

"*They* didn't do anything." He took a step away from her, and then another. He pointed a finger at her. "You're the one who lured me back here. Into a cell."

"I didn't —"

"Don't lie to me," Nono said through gritted teeth. "I'm sick and tired of it. It was your vision, Jayla. *Your* bait. I was dumb enough to take it, and here I am, back where you want me. Trapped."

Jayla would never have snapped at him, but after all of her years in Deugan, fighting the personal attacks and the screeching of the media, his aggression made Caryn bristle. "Do you have any idea what kind of trap you left me in when you escaped? You promised to take me with you, but you didn't. You just ran off with Marwin, who everyone knew was my aide. Of course they thought I was the one who'd let you out. Didn't you think about what would happen to me?"

It was a mistake. The rage Nono was carrying burst. "*Nothing* happened to you!" he shouted. "I thought that the bomb had gone off and destroyed the fort. That you and Freed had escaped and taken refuge in the Well, but he was blaming you for it and — and torturing you for information or something. But he wasn't! You faked it all to trick me into coming back here. How did you think I'd react when I found out you'd duped me? Did you think I'd shrug and go on with my life? I don't have a life anymore, thanks to you. I can't go back to the Steffians. Not after stealing a horse from their Brea allies and facing down their rifles to save you."

"You were planning to betray the Steffians anyway," Caryn said. "You told me so yourself. I'm the one who almost died. I'm lucky I wasn't hanged for treason. If I hadn't figured out a way to bring you back —"

"So you did it to save your own neck," Nono spat. "You don't get it, do you? It's not all about you, Jayla."

"I never said it was," she told him, surprised.

"I almost died, too," Nono said. "What if I really had to attack the Well, solo, my Secrets against all the Deugan survivors of the bombing? I was prepared to risk everything for you, and you were using me." He grunted, turning away from her. "I don't know why I keep doing this. Steif almighty, why can't I let go? You hurt me, again and again, and I keep following you. It's pathetic, and I'm sick of it. I'm sick of myself."

Caryn had nothing to say to that. She looked away as well. Fourteen years later, nearly fifteen. Could he really still be in love with her? Had she known that all along, and played on it?

"I worked for years to get into that position," Nono continued. "I had a plan to make the Continent a better place."

"Your plan was to kill millions of people," Caryn reacted, a bit too strongly. She took a deep breath to calm herself. "Brenner, you are my oldest friend. My best friend. I've never stopped caring about you, and your dreams don't have to die. Deugan has a government that's accountable, and I'm high up in it. This is our chance for change, and your Steffian friends want to destroy it. We need your help."

"Why should I help you?" Nono demanded, rounding on her. "What have you ever done for me, except betray me, pull me away from the only support I have on the Continent, and drag me into prison in a fort that's about to starve?"

"Brenner, I — for fourteen years — I didn't know who you were, where you were. What was I supposed to do? But I have done things for you." Nono raised his eyebrows skeptically. "I protected your secret. Your plan to blow up all the major cities in the entire west. That really would have been treason, if one of those bombs had gone off and I'd never warned them. I protected you."

"Some protection," Nono snorted. "I'm not talking about secrets. I'm talking about saving your Steif-forsaken life!"

"Saving my life? What in Lessandro's name are you talking about?"

He paused and looked at the floor. It was bizarre, until it became uncomfortable. The seconds passed, the quiet stretching. "Brenner?" Caryn asked.

Still he was silent. He turned away from her again. Finally he muttered, "Never mind."

"Tell me." Her voice had started to shake.

"Jayla. Leave it."

There was no energy nearby, but still Caryn felt the sensation of a shift in the air, as though the world around her had changed, irretrievably. She stepped toward him. "Please."

He nodded at the bed behind her. She went to it and sat. "You've got to remember where I was," Nono said softly. "In the Fringes. Surrounded by Steffians day and night. It's not like Villasud or Tomasburg, with telegraph stations on every corner. There might be one in a town, if you're lucky, and they'd have it infiltrated. You couldn't send a message without Gamoy's men seeing it."

Caryn had no idea what this had to do with Bashar Gamoy, the Steffians' Master of War, but she bit her tongue. She felt her heart rate rising as she waited for Nono to continue.

"Ever since the Hallom Doctrine, the Steffians have been targeting you," Nono told her. "I sat in meetings where Gamoy and his lackeys were drawing up plans to kill you. The one person I was never able to stop loving, or protecting, pathetic as it was." He sighed. "I needed to warn you, but how could I? I was half the Continent away, and even if I did sneak a cable out to you, you'd probably have a secretary glance at it and discard it."

He stopped again and took a deep breath. "Jayla, please, you have to understand. There was no other option. Gamoy is ruthless, and he's meticulous. If he'd arranged a bombing, a knife attack, poison, you wouldn't have stood a chance. So I — made a different suggestion.

"I gave them a batch of *acambro*, filled to the bursting point, like a prototype of the bomb. I left the energy packed in there, stewing in anger, knowing it would be several span or even months before it reached you. I told them the energy would be so furious by then, and so desperate to escape, that it would attack the next person it touched.

"I was right — but I knew how strong you were, how intimate you were with the Well's power. You could defend yourself easily, there was no way it would hurt you. Not only would you survive their attack, but it would warn you about the *acambro*. Give you a reason to go to the Well, to remember the power you used to know. It would get you ready for whatever other attacks would come — like Marwin's bomb. I not only saved your life, I saved the lives of every man and woman in this fort."

Caryn struggled to process everything he had said. It was overwhelming. Her mind was running blank, fury building inside her. "Get out," she said.

"What choice did I have?"

"How about not sending an assassin after me! How could any choice possibly be worse?" Her breathing was shallow. "I could have died, don't you see that? I almost did. The energy was stretching through my ribcage. If I'd been half a second later — and my arm!" She used her right hand to lift up her useless left one, then let it flop down by her side. "That's permanent."

"Better your arm than your heart," Nono replied. "Didn't you ever wonder why Marwin only attacked you the once? Never tried to finish the job?"

"I suppose that after sending an assassin to trail me, you somehow convinced him to back down?" Caryn asked sarcastically. "What lie did you feed the Steffians this time? Wait, let me guess. We both know your buddy Marwin eventually tried to blow up the fort. You must have planned that all along, so he couldn't do anything that would blow his cover. He couldn't kill me with a knife because he needed to kill me with a bomb."

Nono at least had the grace to look sheepish. "I didn't want him killing you at all, but I had to sell Gamoy on the idea. So I told him the *acambro* was the only way to make sure the attempt on you wouldn't be traced back to our agent. So our agent could plan more attacks in the future. It worked. I kept Marwin off you for months, and you did stop the bomb."

"What if I hadn't?" Caryn argued. "What if Marwin hadn't followed your directions? You planted a Steffian terrorist next to me. What if he took matters into his own hand and stabbed me?"

"He didn't, and he wouldn't."

"How do you know?" Caryn screamed. "Why are all your plans like this? First an assassination attempt, then you want to let the Steffians dominate the Continent and manipulate them into collapsing. You don't have that power. Gods damn it, Brenner, they're sophisticated, dangerous terrorists. They're not just animals you can train, any more than the energy is!"

Nono took a deep breath. "Jayla, look. I know you hate me right now, and I'm not too pleased with you either, but fighting isn't going to help anyone. I'd like you to listen to me for a moment."

Caryn's anger hadn't faded, but she had to admit she was tired of shouting. "Fine," she said, scowling.

"A kid like Marwin is more a victim than a terrorist," Nono said calmly. "He's a teenager in Deugan, from an immigrant family. They're working hard to establish themselves and not paying much mind to their children. They're devout, so they have eight or nine kids, and Marwin's the sixth or seventh, more or less forgotten. He's bright, but it doesn't matter, because his prospects are limited as soon as people hear about his religion. A couple of meetups with the wrong crowd, a way to make something of himself, to apply all the brains and talent he's got — for a Bashar Gamoy, he's ripe for the picking."

Caryn took a deep breath. She knew Nono was right, but it was difficult to have sympathy for someone who'd tried to murder her. "If you feel so bad for him, why'd you use him?"

Nono snorted. "Like Gamoy was going to let me criticize his choice of agents. Besides, why bother fighting it? If not Marwin, it would have been someone else, and I figured a teenager was more likely to blow his cover and bungle the whole operation."

Caryn shook her head and sat on the bed again. "He was so passionate," she said softly. "So excited about life. It's hard to believe he would join the Steffians."

"That's *why* he joined them," Nono explained. "I got one of Gamoy's students to tell me how they found the kid. He joined up three years ago, after he'd spent only thirteen years in this life. Seems Marwin was bursting at the seams with enthusiasm and ideas, with nowhere to put them, like so many others. Not the greatest family life. He got drawn toward religion, found meaning in it and met an older kid at his temple who became a mentor. He drifted away from his parents and siblings. Eventually, when he was fifteen, he signed up for a training camp out in Pascuay. Told his parents it was a trip sponsored by the temple, and they were probably thrilled. An opportunity they'd never be able to give him, to see some of the Continent. At the camp, the Steffians build him up, make him important, surround him with peers from across the Steifar world who share his most fundamental beliefs."

"They brainwash him."

"Exactly," Nono said. "At the end, they tell him he's been singled out because he has more promise than most. They offer to introduce him to the Master of War, a man who's been built up in his mind as a real live hero. When Gamoy himself asks Marwin to take on a special mission, the kid is going to jump at it.

"As for Gamoy, when he looks at Marwin, he sees an asset that's hard for the Steffians to find in the east, where their power base is. Someone who's intelligent and eager, who was born and raised in Deugan, who has a Deugan citizenship card and passport, knows the culture, knows the politics, knows the dialects. What's more, someone who's not in it for himself. Someone who's not fighting because the New Empire went after his family, but who chose to give up on comfort because he believes in the cause. That kind of kid, who's doing it out of passion for his heroes, he's going to follow every single word that comes out of the Council members' mouths. He's not going for a lark on his own, and he's not going to stab you if I tell him not to."

"You didn't stop the bomb, though," Caryn pointed out.

"The others interfered. Gamoy's men, who hate me."

"You let them try to kill me," Caryn said. "Again."

"Damn it, Jayla, I can't be perfect," Nono said. "I did save your life more than once. I would have done it again after you sent me that vision, but it was all a ruse." He grimaced. "Now? I may as well just help you."

"What?" Caryn asked, surprised. "Why?"

He shrugged. "I can't go back to the Steffians after what you've done. What else am I going to do?"

His tone irritated her. "That's not an answer," she snapped.

"Fine," Nono said. "The Steffians are not going to rest until Caryn Hallom is dead. There are going to be more attempts and more attacks, and it's going to start right here at this fort. And even though you've rejected me and manipulated me, I don't seem to be able to let go of you. Of how I've always felt about you." His tone softened, and his eyes did, too. "I can't abandon you. Part of me wishes I could. Wishes I were stronger. But I'm not."

"It's not about strength," Caryn said. "Don't you think I want to run away too? After I find out you sent a Gods-damned assassin after me? But I can't do it either. I know you were trying to help me in your reckless, crazy way, but it's more than that. We spent six months together. We were each other's only supports and companions. We fell in love. You're the only person on the Continent who understands what I went through back then. Nothing is ever going to change that, even if it should." She gave a sad sigh. "That's still not a good enough reason, though."

Nono turned away again, wandering in the direction of the door. "I've screwed up most of my life," he muttered. "I've wanted to do something worthwhile, but I've spent the last fourteen years just picking up the pieces from what happened to us in the Well. I've worked toward a plan, and now it's gone, but I don't want to stop trying." He leaned against the closed door of Caryn's quarters. "I don't trust the Deugan establishment, but short of Amim's, it's the best one we've got. If nothing else, it's a system that's not as rigid as the others. Change may happen here, over time. Besides, I have a person who I trust in Cabinet. I don't know that Deugan and democracy will actually work, but the Great Experiment's not over yet. I want to give you that chance."

Caryn stood and crossed the room, offering her arm to him. Nono hesitated, a flash of his stubbornness showing, before he gave in, extended his own arms and hugged her.

"We'll do this together," Caryn promised. "Jayla and Brenner."

"No," Nono said sadly. "They're gone. It's just Caryn and Brenth now."

CHAPTER TWENTY-EIGHT

Givanno lies at the crossroads of the Continent, bordering Deugan, Orastus Proper, Wassia and Orastino — Orastino, of course, being the present-day colony which was once the heart of the Old Empire. In a better world, Givanno's location might have been an asset to it, allowing it to grow wealthy as a centre of trade and commerce. As it is, policymakers and military analysts deem Givanno "strategic," and its lush valleys and rolling hills have nearly always been under the occupation of the Orastan Empire.

A quick glance at its geography tells us why. When the Old Empire was powerful enough to take to the offensive, Givanno was the perfect staging ground for incursions north into what is now Orastus Proper, or west into what is now Deugan. More crucial, though, is the defensive risks to the Empire should Givanno fall into Deugan or Wassian hands. Givanno extends like a wedge between Orastus Proper and Orastino, reaching all the way to the banks of the River So. If Deugan or Wassia ever controlled the territory, the northern and southern halves of the Empire would be in grave danger of being severed.

In light of these risks, will Givanno ever achieve independence? That will likely be possible only with the backing of a strong external sponsor, one with an interest in extending its influence on the Continent, and with a death wish for the New Empire.

Fortunately for the Givannans, there have always been plenty of those.

— Maser Ralinay, "At the Crossroads: Geography and the Givannan Independence Movement," Wassian Journal of Political Science (1684)

It was the most unusual gathering that Caryn had ever been part of. Behind the desk sat Ernst Freed, the Deugan general. Brenth Nono the Steffian stood across from him. To Nono's left, leaning back in his chair as though he hadn't a care in the world, was Michael Ravencliffe of Brealand. It was strange, Caryn reflected, how quickly war and politics could make bitter enemies into tentative allies.

Captain Malitz, Captain Toppel and three other officers rounded out the gathering. Malitz looked wary at the prospect of conferring with a Brea and a Steffian, but Toppel's look was bland. He stared from Nono to Caryn and back again, but his mind seemed elsewhere.

"There are three key factors when you're trying to use the Well's power," Nono was explaining. "Task. Distance. Source. The energy's not like a rifle, where you pull a trigger and it fires, every time. The energy has to want to help you, and it's more willing with some jobs than others. Detonating an *acambro* bomb is one of the most difficult tasks imaginable. It's like pushing an elephant into a cubby hole with your bare hands."

"How did Marwin do it?" Freed asked, absently crumpling the cable he had clutched in his fist. The Brea ultimatum.

"He had help," Nono replied, "and he had time, and practice. Most of all, though, there's the distance factor. Marwin brought the bomb almost to the bursting point while he was sitting right on top of it, here in the fort. He finished the job from the Hermann Gap, ten or twelve leagues away. Some of you," he added, nodding to Captain Malitz, "saw me do a similar trick in the mountains. I prepped a bomb in the morning while it was practically in my hand. During my demonstration, I was able to quickly finish it off. The other *acambro* bomb I've used, out in Kalid, took about two hours to detonate, a league or so from my target, with five men helping.

"Which brings us to source. All of those short-distance examples used *acambro*. You transfer the energy from one leaf to another. But that just makes it tougher, because the *acambro* can't hold much energy, and it's struggling to escape the whole time. At a longer distance? Attacking Tomasburg or Carrak-on-Sea from the Hermann Gap? Nearly impossible. I might be able to do it, but not the men I left behind."

Nono looked around to make sure the gathering was still following him. They were, except for Ravencliffe, who looked as though he couldn't be bothered. "What the Steffians need," Nono said, "is a better source. If they want to bridge the distance to their targets, they need an unlimited supply of energy. They need to be surrounded by it, immersed in it."

"They need a Well," Caryn said.

"Exactly," Nono replied. "The Steffians have *de facto* control of the Pascuay and Accarro Wells, but distance is still a factor, and they're on the other side of the Continent. The Wells in Orastino and Orastus proper are closer, but they're in the hands of the New Empire. The Breas and Steffians won't reach them anytime soon."

Ravencliffe nodded agreement. "Our erstwhile Orastan allies do seem rather disenchanted with us, I regret to say."

"I can scarcely imagine why," Freed said dryly. "I see where you're going with this, Nono." Caryn saw the distrust in his eyes. It must be difficult for him, taking instructions from a Steffian. He was used to having Ralf Danzig by his side. "Deugan's secured the Amimi and Wassian Wells, which are farther away in any event. The Steffians need the Gateway. They'll be coming here."

"They'll be coming for the fort," Nono added. "It's so close to the Well that they'll need to neutralize it. I expect that the Brea army will be on us within days, with Steffian back-up. Sound right?" he asked, looking at Ravencliffe, who merely shrugged. Nono turned back to the general. "That ultimatum you're holding, it's given you a span, hasn't it? They'll want the Well before that time is up. Not after. Czemers is the closest of the targeted cities. They'll want to blow it the instant your ultimatum expires."

"They're not going to wait for the fort to starve?" Caryn asked.

"We can't," Ravencliffe said bitterly. "The Wassian travesty has forced the Realm's hand. An entire Deugan army that should now be lying dead on the slopes of Villasud is instead massing near Czemers, preparing to take back Hermannsburg." Ravencliffe glanced at General Freed. "Don't look surprised, General. You've known for some time that the Realm's military intelligence outstrips your own. I could draw an analogy to other forms of intelligence, but I would hate to be seen as unduly provocative."

"You?" Caryn smiled. "Never."

"Fine," Freed said. "The Third Army is preparing an attack on the Hermann Gap from the south. It wasn't done until now because the Wassian offensive was the priority. Now that that's over, it's time to break the siege. But if the Breas take the fort first, from the north —"

"Then you lose Czemers," Nono said. It was that stark. "You lose Tomasburg the next day, Stamburg the next, Carrak-on-Sea the day after that. Can you hold them off?"

"I have two thousand Gods-damned men," Freed complained. "Three thousand if I recall the ones I sent to the villages, but that barely changes anything. Sure, I can hold the Breas off for a time, but who knows how long it'll take for the Third Army to relieve us? It could be days, even several span."

"Who is to say whether you'll be relieved at all?" Ravencliffe asked. "I have to commend you, General, the Hermann Gap is a brilliant defensive position. A trench line anchored in the foothills of two separate mountain ranges. I wish we Breas had thought of it first. Fortunately, we've conquered it, using guns we placed in the mountains. Those guns are still there, overlooking the position. Our defenders number in the thousands, and we will be aided by Steffian Secrets-users, as they so quaintly call themselves."

"I am very close to asking Captain Malitz to remove you," Freed warned him.

Ravencliffe was unimpressed. "You never had any obligation to invite me to your strategy session. I've made it clear that I'm not an ally of Deugan. I've remained in your fort as an ambassador of the Realm. We have ongoing peace negotiations, and they will never succeed if your republic is pinning its hopes on relief from the Third Army. The Armed Power of the Realm will crush you and *impose* a peace, on Brea terms. No, don't trouble Captain Malitz, I'll escort myself out."

Ravencliffe stood and sauntered toward the door of the office, but Nono spoke before he reached it. "Colonel, wait," Nono said. "I don't think General Freed needs to hold off your ridiculously-named army until relief comes. It may be enough if he can hold them off for a short while. Just long enough for our own Secrets users to complete a special mission." He smiled at Caryn. "What do you say?"

"What are you talking about?" Caryn asked. It might be only a childhood habit, but she still felt drawn to him, wanting to trust him. *He's dangerous*, she tried to remind herself, *more dangerous than Janusz ever was. He plotted to destroy Deugan and Brealand alike, betray the Steffians and drag the Continent into anarchy. He arranged my assassination and claimed it was to save my life. What more might he be capable of?*

"*Acambro* bombs can be defused," Nono said. "It's much easier than detonating them. You just pull the energy out. Normally, it's happy to go."

"That won't be enough," Caryn said at once. "The *acambro* will still be in our cities. We can drain the bombs all we want. If the Steffians take the Well from us, the ultimate 'source,' they can just funnel more energy back in."

"Is there a way to seal the *acambro* after it's been drained?" Captain Toppel asked. "So they can't put more energy into it?"

"I don't know," Nono said thoughtfully, "but I wouldn't be surprised if there was. The energy is creative and powerful, and it despises the *acambro*."

"Then why hasn't it sealed off the *acambro* on its own?" General Freed asked.

"Because the energy's a parasite," Nono explained. "It seems powerful, but on its own, it's impotent. It has to act through one of us. It doesn't trust easily, but it knows me well, and if I go in offering to help it escape the *acambro*, it may well reveal the secret. I'll just need some time to work with it, to coax it."

"To train it," Freed said. Nono looked at him, surprised. "I don't like handing a Steffian a Well, but I don't think I have a choice. You'll get your chance, Master Nono."

"I am confident, General," Nono assured him. "It may take me a few days to learn how, but I'm certain the energy can do this."

"How's that, Ravencliffe?" Freed asked.

"I am suitably impressed," Ravencliffe said with a bow. "I will advise His Majesty that the republic believes it can fight *acambro* bombs, and that the Steffians' Master of Secrets has defected to assist. I anticipate receiving a broad mandate to negotiate an end to a conflict that has, if nothing else, grown substantially more engaging."

"Can we avoid the attack altogether, then?" Caryn asked. "If we conclude a treaty before it comes?"

Ravencliffe shook his head. "There, Minister, I will have to disappoint you," he said. "Master Nono is wrong about a fundamental premise, which I suspect is not an uncommon phenomenon. Defusing and then sealing the *acambro* bombs will not be sufficient. The Realm still holds the upper hand in this conflict.

Our armies in the west are mere leagues from your sources of oil, without which the Deugan war effort will collapse. Our fleets still rule the waves. We need only conquer the Gateway and defeat your precious Third Army, and we can cut off your oil country from reinforcements. We will attack it from both sides, while a separate army marches on Tomasburg. Deugan's position will be rendered completely untenable, *acambro* bomb or no." He took a deep breath. "His Majesty will no doubt take that chance, and if he succeeds, he will not settle for anything less than full Deugan capitulation."

If Freed was intimidated, he did not show it. "What if you fail?" the general asked. "What if the fort holds until the Third Army drives you out of the Gateway?"

"Then the situation changes," Ravencliffe admitted. "Nothing would stop us from attacking your oil sources from the west, but without a two-pronged attack, victory would be less certain. The probability of success will only decline as more Deugan units return from Wassia to reinforce your position. Our advantage on the sea would remain, but now that you have Wassia's resources in addition to Deugan's industrial base, you may well build enough ships to cost us dearly over time. We would still win the war, I believe, but if a treaty were to appear that could achieve the Realm's interests at a fraction of the cost..."

"You would jump at the opportunity," Freed said.

"I intend to create that opportunity," Ravencliffe said. "Your foreign minister has quite inspired me."

Caryn was starting to blush. She forced herself to remain calm. "You're saying that whatever you and I may negotiate, in order to make it stick, there will have to be a Second Battle of the Gateway."

Ravencliffe nodded gravely. "One that will make the first resemble a schoolyard scuffle."

"And one," General Freed said, staring at the crumpled ultimatum, "that we can't afford to lose."

*

Caryn's next days were spent in the communications hub, locked in intense negotiations with Ravencliffe. She had briefed the president by telephone, and a diplomatic war room had been created in Tomasburg, placing the Foreign Affairs and Defence departments at her disposal. Ravencliffe had a telegraph link back to Hastingvale, the Brea capital. Between furious consultations with their governments back home, Caryn and Ravencliffe hashed it out, debating the future of a Continent.

Borders in the north proved easy to resolve. There was no sense in the Breas keeping the Deugan northwest, where there were no natural boundaries to defend. Ravencliffe wanted the Gateway, but the Realm was about to invade the Gateway anyway. Since the Breas would only accept the peace treaty if they lost, it didn't make sense to treat them as though they'd won. The energy's newfound power made Ravencliffe uneasy, since there were no Wells in Brealand, but that problem could be resolved by giving Brea researchers access to Deugan's Well. Pre-war borders were the order of the day.

The south proved more difficult. Facts on the ground supported Amimi independence, and even the dissection of Wassia itself. On the other hand, all it would take was a Brea victory in the north and the Deugan position would collapse. The Breas were wary about supporting Amimi independence when they relied so heavily on their own island colonies for food. They were also concerned, as Caryn had suspected all along, about the spread of Deugan influence across the Continent. They wanted a strong Wassia as a counterbalance.

The breakthrough came when Caryn recalled Brenth Nono's musings about how a post-war Wassia might be rebuilt. Over several hours of back-and-forth negotiations, they finally arrived at the structure for the Wassian Reconstruction Commission, a board with equal Wassian, Brea and Deugan representation. It meant that Deugan would get international acclaim for providing very real funding, but it could be outvoted by the Brea-Wassian alliance on how those funds were spent. It may be difficult for some Deugans to swallow after so many of their boys died there, but to Caryn, a strengthened Wassia and a reasonable limit on Deugan influence seemed a small price to pay for official recognition of the State of Amim and a fair policy on the Amimi Canal.

Most difficult of all was the east, where the Breas had an awkward position. They had betrayed the New Empire and promised the Fringes to the Steffians, but that was in exchange for the *acambro* bombs. Now Nono thought that he would be able to seal off the bombs. "If the bombs do not detonate," Ravencliffe said, "that gives me the pretext I need to call off the alliance. We can tell the

Continent that the Steffians sold us a false bill of goods. But we have no interest in doing so unless we can repair relations with the New Empire. We need official recognition of Orastan sovereignty throughout the Fringes."

"That's impossible," Caryn said evenly.

"Would you prefer Steffian sovereignty?"

"No," Caryn said. "We need to have our own relations with the Fringes. Without our trade there, Deugan collapses. Or have you forgotten how the war started in the first place?"

"I thought we'd agreed that your Hallom Doctrine started the war in the first place," Ravencliffe replied, pretending to be confused. "Perhaps we should write that into the treaty. Deugan admits guilt for starting the war by adopting stupid foreign policies."

"Yeah, that's the way to a long-term friendship," Caryn said sarcastically. "We'll be back at war within twenty years."

"The point is," Ravencliffe said, "the Realm entered the war to prevent Deugan's culture from poisoning the entire Continent. I'm already giving you Amim. I can't give you Cioro."

"We're limiting our warships so that you can feel safe trading overseas," Caryn argued. "We need our trade overland."

"How do you know the Fringes would agree to trade with you?" Ravencliffe asked. "We've already seen what Pascuay and Merguisio have done with independence. They've chosen the Steffians." Ravencliffe saw her discomfort and laughed. "I knew it. Deugan's not such a big supporter of independence if people are going to choose the wrong governments."

Caryn had a thousand angry retorts, but at that moment there was a commotion at the doorway, and one of the officers burst into the communications hub. "Minister Hallom," he said. "General's asked for you, and it seems urgent. You'd better come."

Caryn glanced at Ravencliffe, whose face remained carefully blank. "Go ahead, Minister," he said. "We were only negotiating an end to a war that's killed several million people. Nothing that can't wait." Caryn scowled at him and left.

The general's office was mere steps from the communications hub. Freed saluted the officer and quickly dismissed him. Then he closed the door behind Caryn. They were alone, save for Captain Toppel.

Freed had a manner about him that Caryn had seen only once

before. His sternness had melted, and he reminded her of a grandfather, kind and serene. "We have a need for your expertise," Freed said mildly. He nodded at Toppel. "Please, Captain."

Caryn and Toppel stared at each other. They had not spoken since that night in Toppel's cell, when he had warned her about Danzig's scheme. Caryn had never properly thanked him for that. She wondered if he would forgive her for all the span he spent underground, locked up for a crime he had not committed.

The young captain swallowed and spoke with difficulty. "The officers have been meeting about the battle," Toppel explained. "The Hermann Gap is a strong position, especially with those Brea guns in the mountains overlooking it. Unless we can take them out, the Third Army doesn't stand a chance, and neither does your peace." Caryn nodded, waiting. Freed leaned closer. "We were throwing out all sorts of crazy ideas," Toppel continued. "None of them would work. You can't just scale a mountain with cannons on it. It's too close quarters for our planes to manoeuvre. At one point I asked whether there might be a way to do it with the energy. General Freed said that even if there was, we couldn't send you or Master Nono into the mountains. We need you defusing bombs."

Toppel locked eyes with Caryn, and when he spoke again, he could not keep the resentment from his voice. "I told him that it wasn't you and Nono I was talking about."

Caryn's jaw dropped. "You?"

"Gods damn bloody Marwin, may Seppina take him," Toppel said. "The energy is evil, and he just planted — he knew what it was like, he must have. If it's close to you, it will attack you, probe at you, until it gets in. We all know that in a Well, when it's surrounding you, you last about twenty-four hours. When you're carrying it under your arm without even knowing it — feeling like something's off, but never guessing what, all the while having it nestled up next to your chest — Gods, it might take longer than a day, but within a month, it'll get to you. Inside you." He shook his head violently, as though to clear it. "I was listening to Nono talk about how the energy is a parasite. How it needs someone to act through. So it'll just use you."

Caryn walked over to him and laid her good hand on his. She remembered the moment in the Wassian Well when she first realized she was trapped. She remembered thinking of all of the things she might never be able to do. "I am so sorry."

"It's not your fault," Toppel replied. He gave a sharp bark of laughter. "I probably ought to thank you. You're the one who took the crutch away from me and drained the energy out of it. If only you hadn't sent it into my leg."

"I'm sorry," Caryn said again, but she saw Toppel starting to smile, and Freed looked relieved.

"I've mostly recovered," Toppel said. "I can get into the foothills, if I have some help."

"Captain Toppel is one of my best men," General Freed added. "After what he has gone through, I would not have imposed this burden on him, but he volunteered. There's a chance he can save Deugan, if you'll teach him what he needs to know."

Caryn shook her head. "I'm no teacher," she said. "Nono's the one you want. Master of Secrets. He's trained the best."

"I don't trust Nono as far as I can throw him," Freed said. "Besides, I thought you were the best. Did he need to train you?"

That actually brought a smile to Caryn's face. "I trained him, in a lot of ways," she said. She turned to Toppel. "The Well itself was my teacher, and it needs to be yours, too. I know you hate it now, but turn your hate to Marwin. Open yourself up to the energy. Explore it. You have to earn its trust."

"Do I have time?" Toppel asked.

"Yes," Caryn replied. "For what you need to do." It was instinctive; six months in a Well, and you never forgot. She wasn't a fighter like Brenth Nono or his student Matt, but Caryn knew what she would do if she were headed into battle. "It's the simplest effect there is. The one I turn to when I'm desperate and panicking and don't have the presence of mind to do anything more. Like when a strange man bursts into my room at night."

"I'm going to kick the mountain's foot?" Toppel asked.

"In a manner of speaking," Caryn said. "You're going to take the energy from the *acambro* and drive it into the hill, as hard as you can. An avalanche is what you'll be hoping for, but even if you just shake the ground a bit at the right spot, that might be enough to dislodge their guns."

"He'll need *acambro*, then?" General Freed asked.

"Yes," Caryn said. "This isn't something I can do from the Well, because it doesn't go through the map — the columns. You'll have to take the energy where it's needed. It's a blunt instrument, hurling the energy at a target." She smiled at Toppel, who still looked unsure. "Go to the Well," she told him. "Practice. Build your strength, and your patience. I have faith in you."

"Thank you, my lady," Toppel said.

"Somebody else should lead the expedition," Caryn said, striding over to Freed. "Captain Toppel will have too much on his mind. But it should be someone he trusts."

"Leave that with me," Freed said. "Thank you, Minister. Deugan owes you a great debt."

"I'm sorry," Caryn told Toppel again. "Just know that I'm here for you."

Toppel looked at her strangely. "I know."

*

It was late by the time Caryn made her way back to the communications hub. Ravencliffe was still awake, waiting for her. "Minister Hallom! I feared you would never return. I was growing so desperately lonely."

"Not as lonely as Captain Toppel must feel," Caryn said sadly. She filled Ravencliffe in on what Marwin had done to him, though she didn't mention the plan to take out the Brea guns. Ravencliffe might have become a friend, but he would always put his Realm first.

Ravencliffe listened without interrupting, for once. He seemed genuinely dismayed at the news. "It's a shame," he said finally. "Captain Toppel was a fine soldier. He had to be, to capture me."

"That's the Michael Ravencliffe I know," Caryn smiled. "Any new thoughts on the Eastern Front?"

He shrugged. "You've given us the ship-building guarantees. You need something big in return if your Assembly is going to accept this deal, and what you really want is trade in the southeast. Not to mention the need to set the right precedent for the future. The powers across the ocean will be watching." He leaned back in his chair, placing his hands behind his head. "Let's do the right thing, Minister. Confirm that all of this is internal Orastan politics, commit to non-interference, and I'll throw in Givanno for free."

"What do you mean, throw in Givanno?" Caryn asked. "We already have Givanno, and we can't abandon the rest of the Fringes. Non-interference means the New Empire wins. They're still stronger than all of the Fringes put together."

"Indeed," Ravencliffe said. "Make no mistake. Formally, you and I will be confirming Orastan dominance. But ask yourself, what are we giving the New Empire in substance? A decade. Maybe two. You said yourself that the old worlds are ending. The New Empire cannot survive as it is, not for long. Colonies will be lost, inevitably."

"So we wait?" Caryn asked bitterly. "Wash our hands of it in the meantime? Injustice and repression continue, and Deugan does nothing?"

Ravencliffe leaned toward her. "Deugan needs do nothing," he said in a voice barely above a whisper. "Deugan has already won. The world has changed, and if the Orastans can't see it yet, they soon will. So let Brealand be seen to be supporting its old ally. Grant Orastus the opportunity to learn the lessons of this war, when three of its colonies declared independence and a fourth reached the verge of doing the same. Let the dissolution of the empire come through negotiations rather than fiat from the western powers. Can you debase yourself to that?"

It was late, and before long the tide would be upon them. She thought of Captain Toppel and the sacrifice he had volunteered to make, after Marwin had taken everything from him. What Deugan was fighting for was important, but just as important was finding an ending, for all of them.

Caryn frowned and considered. "You'll give us Givanno?"

"We'll forget to mention Givanno," Ravencliffe said. "When we declare our mutual pact of non-interference with the other six Fringes, that silence will be deafening. Givanno's the overland pathway between Deugan and the rest of the Fringes. To the extent your position is based on crass self-interest rather than these higher ideals you profess, you'll have your eastern trade and the gratitude of your ally."

"Crass?" Caryn said. "Since when have you opposed nations going after their self-interest? Admit it, Mikey, you've been learning lessons from a barbarian." His face was impassive, but she knew him well enough by now to guess that he was hiding a smile. "I'll have to talk to my government," she added. "If we get Givanno, we can probably wait a few years for the other Fringes. Beyond that, I'm just trying to figure out how we would spin it for the press."

Ravencliffe did give her a smile at that. "Long live democracy."

CHAPTER TWENTY-NINE

By the time they went to bed that night, they had reached an agreement in principle. They spent much of the next day haggling over semantics. Finally, by late afternoon, it was done. Caryn dictated the draft treaty to a staffer in Tomasburg to place before Cabinet and then the Assembly. Ravencliffe cabled the text directly to his king and queen, with his recommendation that it be adopted.

Just like that, the treaty was out of their hands. It was strange, after so many months pushing for it. Now there was nothing to do but hope that the two governments would agree, and wait for the battle to come.

A battle that Deugan had to win. Caryn remembered Ravencliffe's words in the meeting a few days ago, telling them that the Deugan position was hopeless, that their Third Army would never break through the Hermann Gap before the fort fell. If that was true, the agreement they had negotiated would never see the light of day, and Deugan might be evicted from the Gateway entirely. It seemed to Caryn the most likely outcome of the battle that lay ahead. Thousands of fresh Brea troops were about to descend upon a fort that was battered, sick and starving.

At least their garrison was growing. At General Freed's orders, the thousand or so troops that had been guarding villages on this side of the Hermann Gap had trickled back into the fort, bringing some able-bodied villagers with them. The fort today could count just under three thousand soldiers, and another eight hundred warm bodies. Some of that number would have to guard Captain Toppel as he made his way to the mountains to wield the energy against the Brea guns stationed there, and more would be sent to the Gateway Well, to protect Caryn and Nono as they attempted to defuse and seal the *acambro* bombs. The remainder would stay in the fort, a few thousand against the fury of the Realm.

It was nearly evening when Brenth Nono returned to the fort. He came to Caryn's quarters with Toppel in tow. "I've done it," Nono said. "I've sealed some of the *acambro* I brought with me. I haven't been able to try it on the bombs yet, but I know it can be done."

Caryn hugged him. "I knew you could do it," she said. "It's easy enough to learn?"

"He taught me," Toppel said proudly. "If I can do it, so can you. And now I have my very own *acambro* belt." He gestured at it, taking care not to touch it with his bare hand.

Nono smiled at that. "It's only dangerous when it's overloaded," he said. "See?" He placed his own bare hand on the belt; nothing happened. Caryn recoiled nonetheless. She remembered the tendrils of flame reaching through her ribcage.

"I'm to set off tonight," Toppel said.

"Good luck," Caryn said gravely, forcing Nono's assassination attempt from her mind. "May the Gods protect you."

"And you, my lady." Toppel's look was grim. "Thank you for your help. Both of you." He gave each of them a bow before he left.

Caryn and Nono made their way to Freed's office, stopping at the communications hub to collect Ravencliffe on the way. Freed was sitting with the other officers when they arrived, going over plans for the upcoming battle. "Do you have good news for me?" he asked when he saw them.

"I've learned how to seal the bombs," Nono announced.

The relief in the room was palpable. "We have a chance, then," Freed said. "A small one, perhaps, but a chance."

"Why only a small one?" Caryn asked.

"Because the Hermann Gap needs to be a quick victory if the Third Army is to relieve the fort in time," General Freed explained. "We need to hit the Breas from behind, or from above, but we can't. So we'll just have to attack, and pray to Armano that the Fort can hold out long enough."

"We should get started right away, then," Caryn said. "Defusing the bombs."

"I wish you could," Freed replied. "Your defensive position in the Well isn't complete yet, and the Well is treacherous in the dark even without Breas and Steffians around. I'm not prepared to take any chances with you. If you two die before the bombs are defused, there's no hope for any of us."

"Is there time to wait?" Caryn asked.

"I expect the Breas and Steffians to attack tomorrow morning."

"I neither confirm nor deny that," Ravencliffe added pleasantly. Freed ignored him.

"You should rest tonight," Freed told Caryn and Nono. "We'll escort you to the Well early in the morning, when it's safe. Master Nono tells me that your task depends on mental focus and concentration. I want you at your best." He turned to the officers. "The same goes for the rest of you. Tomorrow will be the crowning moment not only of this war, not only of your lives, but of the entire history of the Republic of Deugan. May Armano protect you, may Seppina preserve you, and whatever happens, I thank you all for your service." The officers saluted and filed out.

Ravencliffe waited until they were gone before he spoke. "It seems your plans are in place," he said softly.

"The general neither confirms nor denies that," Nono said with a smirk.

General Freed glared at both of them. "Colonel, I can't tell you what our plans are. You represent Brealand, you've made that perfectly clear. But I don't mind telling you that our strategies have been finalized. We're as prepared as we're ever likely to be."

Caryn watched Ravencliffe carefully, but he didn't react the way she expected. Not with a raised eyebrow or a witty retort. Instead he stared at the floor and then rose, slowly, as though a great weight were on his shoulders. When he spoke again, his casual tone, normally so practiced, was strained and unconvincing.

"That's fantastic, General," Ravencliffe said. "Between your no doubt excellent battle planning, Master Nono discovering how to seal the *acambro* and Minister Hallom and I concluding a tentative agreement, it would appear that there is only one matter as yet unresolved. I regret to advise that the time has come to arrange my untimely and rather unfortunate demise."

Caryn was certain she had heard him wrong. From the looks on their faces, Freed and Nono were just as startled. "Excuse me?" Freed asked.

"General, if you would hand the foreign minister your pistol," Ravencliffe continued, "I believe it would be most appropriate if she were to do the honours."

It was as though Ravencliffe had punched her in the gut. Caryn looked up sharply, feeling winded. "What are you talking about?" Her voice rang shrill in her ears. "You want me to — why?"

"Minister Hallom, I'm disappointed. Do you not remember the very first day we met? In your chapel?"

"What about it?" Why were her ears buzzing? Why was her breathing so shallow?

"You told me I was not only a prisoner, but a hostage," Ravencliffe said. He stared into Caryn's eyes. "You warned His Majesty that you would execute me at the first sign of any Brea attack on the fort. Don't imagine for a second that he has forgotten." He broke eye contact and glared at the others. "The first signs of attack are here. Shelling has intensified. Troops are massing on your border. Your general anticipates a battle tomorrow morning." He turned back to Caryn. "Do you remember what else you told me that day, about your threat to murder me?"

It suddenly hit her like a brick wall. She realized what was happening to her, too late to stop it. It had come from nowhere, and she had forgotten what it was like. How thoughts were driven from her mind. How difficult it was to breathe. Her voice was small when she responded. "I said that Deugan needs to prove we're willing to follow through on our threats."

"That is truer now than it ever was," Ravencliffe said. "Our treaty is only a sheaf of paper. I can make recommendations, and Deugan can win tomorrow's battle in a rout. It won't matter. If our enemy is too soft and weak to follow through on a simple hostage threat, the Realm is not going to hand you back all the land it's conquered, throwing in Amim and Givanno besides. His Majesty will invade you and crush you."

"If we win tomorrow's battle, he won't be able to," Freed snapped.

"Perhaps not," Ravencliffe agreed, whipping his head toward the general. "If you lose tomorrow, your position will collapse. If you win? It could spell not the end of a war, but the beginning. A struggle that could last years and kill millions, leaving the Continent devastated. I personally believe the Realm would prevail, but your Republic would also have reason to be confident. Faced with such uncertainty and bloodshed, the Realm's clear interest lies in accepting our treaty, but His Majesty won't see it that way. Not if he sees Deugan as too weak to do what is necessary. Not unless he knows that if he does not sign, you will pursue him to the bitter end." He turned back to Caryn. "If I've taught you anything about Brealand in these last three months, Minister, you'll know I'm right."

Caryn could barely focus on his words, so loud was the buzzing in her mind. She imagined holding a gun to Ravencliffe's head and squeezing the trigger. She couldn't. Her panic was rising. She couldn't. She couldn't. "You —" she stammered helplessly. "You could have escaped — and you knew?"

"It made no difference," Ravencliffe said. "The treaty was in the interests of the Realm, and the Realm comes first. But don't moralize, Minister, you knew it too. From the very first time you and your remarkably handsome bodyguard barged into my cell, you knew that you would never be able to back down from the threat you'd made just days earlier."

Did she? The room was spinning and Caryn felt sick. *Did she?* There was always a chance the Breas might attack. If nothing else, Caryn had known that. She felt unsteady on her feet. She put her good arm out for balance as General Freed stepped in front of her protectively.

"Leave her out of this," he said as Brenth Nono nodded agreement. "Ravencliffe, this is insane."

"Why?" Ravencliffe demanded. "We could have taken this fort any time we pleased in the last three months. The only reason it's still standing is because my cousin believed your threat. What would you do in her place if after all this time, you found out the threat meant nothing?"

The general stepped backward, his face heavy. "I would take advantage," he admitted.

"Then the Realm and the Republic are not so different after all," Ravencliffe said. "Give Minister Hallom your gun."

"Wait," Nono said, stepping forward himself. "If Brealand believed the threat, why are they attacking now?"

"No doubt because I stayed behind when I could have fled,"

Ravencliffe replied. "I inconvenienced them. They no longer find it worthwhile to protect me."

"Then why would they care whether the Deugans kill you?"

Ravencliffe sighed. "Master Nono, you really should allow the foreign minister and the general to conduct the fort's intellectual activity. I'm afraid it is not your strong suit." Nono bristled, but before he could say anything, Ravencliffe continued. "It's already suspicious that I chose to remain behind after the prison break. Now I am recommending a treaty that provides Deugan substantial concessions. If I didn't know better, I might even start to doubt my own loyalty." *Loyalty*, Caryn thought through the haze, through the dizziness and the panic. *Loyalty, to the Realm above all.* Was that it? Was there something more? "If His Majesty is not convinced that I remain Deugan's enemy, then our peace is over. Before it has begun."

"Which is why you want Caryn to do it, you sick bastard," Nono realized. "She's the one pushing for the peace, so you're trying to teach her a lesson. Well, I'm leaving. I don't want to be part of this."

"Do you think I want to be part of it?" Ravencliffe asked softly. They all froze. Watched him. He moved deliberately toward the general. "I have not reached this conclusion lightly. I am rather attached to this life. The least you can do is allow me to choose the manner in which I leave it. I'm afraid I must insist on the foreign minister."

"Why?" Brenth Nono demanded. "Look at her. She's shaking." Caryn was losing control. Her mind was going blank as the panic consumed her, terrifying. She heard Ravencliffe's answer as though through a fog.

"A lesson, you said." Ravencliffe looked at Nono thoughtfully before turning to Caryn. "Before I die, I want to see that you've learned what I'm trying to teach you. That peace has a cost. That ideals must give way to the harshness of reality. That your hands need to be dirtied."

"Ask Captain Toppel about his leg," Freed argued. "Ask our soldier Janusz about his time in the Well. Minister Hallom is one of the most refreshingly moral people I have had the privilege to meet, and she has already dirtied her hands more than she ever should have had to."

Ravencliffe said something back, but Caryn could barely hear him.

The room was swaying, making her nauseous. She managed to get out the words "excuse me" before she fled.

She burst from General Freed's office and stumbled down the corridor, holding the wall for support. The fort would not stop spinning. She was hyperventilating and couldn't find the words to calm herself. She pressed onward, one foot in front of the other. Vaguely she was aware of Nono coming after her, and then she saw Ravencliffe's hand on his shoulder, whispering to him, and he stopped.

Caryn reached the fort's south entrance before she had to stop and rest. Her head felt like it was about to explode, and her stomach roiled. The soldiers guarding the entrance swayed before her, and the only words she made out were "medical bay," but she shook her head vigorously. She didn't want Hertha and the nurses seeing her this way. "Fr — fresh air," she stammered instead. "Please." The leader barked an order, and they escorted her outside.

No sooner did her feet touch the grass than she keeled over. She was trying to retch, but she had been eating the energy for so long that there was nothing to throw up. Her throat burned and her mouth tasted of acid. She kneeled there, panting, struggling to catch her breath.

The evening was cool. The sun was setting, its stunning red light shining through the peaks of the Williston Mountains, but she could barely see it. The panic was overwhelming. One of the soldiers brought her a cup of water; she drank it gratefully. "Leave me," she managed to say. "Please. I'll be fine." He looked wary, but he whispered to the others, and they withdrew.

Caryn retched again once they were gone, then crawled a few paces away and lay in the grass, staring at the sky. Slowly the world stopped spinning, the panic faded and her stomach started to settle. Too slowly. Each time she tried to stand, the dizziness would threaten to overwhelm her, and eventually she gave it up. She stayed on the ground, waiting for the pain to pass.

Caryn couldn't say how long she was alone with the world, watching the sun as it dropped lower and lower behind the mountains. The same mountains Captain Toppel was limping toward at this very moment. Her heart went out to him.

Her thoughts turned to her own panic as it finally drifted from her. She had not had an attack this severe in years. Strange, she thought, how fear for herself over the last months had not triggered any attacks, yet the prospect of killing an enemy officer had. She was not cut out for war, for any of this. The president should never have sent her up here.

She wanted to cry. She wondered if Ravencliffe was right, if this really was the cost of peace. Loneliness, misery, hands so unclean she would never be able to wash them. *No*, Caryn told herself. That was the cost of war, but war was insidious. It took peace and maimed it, distorted it, until it was difficult to see the difference between the two.

The soldier had returned. "Minister Hallom?" he said hesitantly. "I'm sorry to interrupt, but the fort is searching for you. The president's on the line from Tomasburg, and says it's urgent."

Caryn took a deep breath and let it out. She desperately wanted to stay in the cool evening air, in the shadow of the mountains, away from the hideous concrete of the fort. Her thoughts turned to the Amim that Brenth Nono had described, the forests and the glaciers, the thrilling landscapes far from concrete, glass and steel. One day, perhaps, she would visit Amim, if she survived tomorrow's battle. If any of them survived.

Resigned, Caryn offered her good hand to the soldier, and he helped her rise. She was still the foreign minister of Deugan, and Deugan was at war. Serenity might yet come, but for now, panic attacks or no, she would do her duty.

She made her way back to the communications hub, where she was ushered through the trapdoor down to the telephone room. The soldier holding the receiver exchanged some words with an operator on the other end and handed it to Caryn. "The president has asked me to transfer a call to you," the operator told her. "Please stand by."

Caryn waited. Then a voice came through on the line, speaking Orastan. "Good evening, Minister," the man said. "My name is Dante Legatti, and I have the honour of serving as foreign secretary of the Orastan Empire."

"What happened to Alessan?" Caryn blurted out before she could catch herself. She ought to have known better. If not for the panic attack, she would never have been so stupid as to ask after Legatti's predecessor.

The Orastan took it in stride, though, and responded with grace and a euphemism. "Foreign Secretary Peragimo has chosen to lay down his burdens after years of loyal service to the empire, and accept retirement in Domani." *Exile,* Caryn thought, *to the eastern coast of the Continent, well beyond the Fringes and the impassable Kalidi Well.* It was not so bad. Others who failed the empire had suffered worse fates. "Secretary Peragimo announced his decision shortly after we received confirmation that Brealand had betrayed the empire."

"I understand," Caryn said. So Legatti had been in his role only a matter of days. This could not be easy for him, either. "The Brea-Steffian alliance threatens the empire as much as it threatens us."

"Perhaps more," Legatti admitted. "In the circumstances, I've been instructed to offer you an immediate armistice, including the withdrawal of all Imperial troops to our pre-war borders."

"And in exchange?"

"Confirmation of Orastan sovereignty over the Fringes."

Caryn had no need to go that far. Now that the Breas had betrayed them, now that the Steffians had the *acambro* bomb and three Fringes had declared independence, the New Empire was desperate. Caryn saw no reason to offer anything more than she'd already promised to Ravencliffe. "We can guarantee you non-interference in affairs between Orastus and the Fringes, with the exception of Givanno, whose independence you will recognize."

"Absolutely not," Legatti responded. "It's all the Fringes or none."

"None, then," Caryn said. "You can't fight Deugan and Brealand separately, let alone together. You should be thanking me for not insisting on Cioro's independence, too."

"We are prepared to remove our armies from Deugan territory in order to hold onto the Fringes," Legatti replied. "If you're telling me we're going to lose the Fringes anyway, we may as well take our chances against Tomasburg. Our armies are not far from your capital, and if we capture it, its wealth will power our war against the Steffians."

"You'll hold Tomasburg for less than a year against Brealand," Caryn said.

"So will you," Legatti snapped. "I have an informer, very well placed in the Steffian hierarchy. I know about the Brea-Steffian plan to attack the Gateway, and I know about your plan to attack the Hermann Gap. It strikes me that the Deugan position is hopeless." He paused to let his words sink in. "You may recall that even though

Brealand occupied the Gap, we helped them take it. We had guns in the Selliar Mountains overlooking the trenches, and our own soldiers descended the passes to hit your defenders from both sides at once. We can't spare the soldiers any longer, but the guns are still there."

Afterward, Caryn dragged herself up the steps to find Freed, Nono and Ravencliffe waiting for her in the communications hub. Nono rushed to her, asking if she was okay, but Caryn didn't answer. She only motioned for them to follow her and led them through the south entrance of the fort to the place that had calmed her during her panic. She needed to be calm again.

The sun had fully set by then, but they could still see by the electric light that flooded from the open entranceway of the fort. Nono hovered over her, concerned. Caryn shrugged him off and approached General Freed. "Give me your gun," she said.

Behind her she heard Nono suck in a breath. Freed hesitated before holding it out to her. "Are you certain?"

"I've just betrayed three million people," Caryn said. "I can handle one more. My hands are dirty enough."

Freed pulled the pistol back from her. "What have you done?"

"I've sold out Givanno," she told him. "I've turned them over to the whims of the New Empire."

In the dim light she could see Ravencliffe's jaw drop. "I couldn't get Givanno out of you!"

"No," Caryn agreed, rounding on him. "A savage Orastan made out better than you did. How does that feel, Mikey?"

"What did you get in return?" Freed asked.

She was too angry to be truly pleased, but it still felt good to say it. "A chance to win tomorrow's battle." She quickly told them about the armistice agreement and the troop withdrawals before moving on to the guns in the Selliar Mountains. The fort couldn't spare the soldiers, so she'd arranged for the Orastans to man the guns and take orders from a Deugan officer. The New Empire had a forward operating base near the gun battery, which housed a radio receiver, so the Deugans could relay orders from the communications hub in the fort. As part of the armistice deal, Deugan would also get reparation payments, money for blood.

"Lessandro's mercy," the general mouthed when she was finished. "We could actually win this thing."

"Don't thank Lessandro," Caryn snapped. "I'm the one who bargained it. Thank me."

"You did the right thing," Nono said. "If we can actually end the war —"

"I know," Caryn sighed. "It doesn't make it any easier." She turned to Freed. "Give me your gun, General."

He thought. Looked from Caryn to Ravencliffe. Then he flicked off the safety and handed it to her.

The metal was cool in her hand. Caryn hadn't held a gun since the First Battle of the Gateway, when Marwin's weapon — Nono's weapon — had shot tendrils of fire toward her heart. She felt the shape of the general's pistol, flipped it around, and slowly let her finger slide onto the trigger.

She walked toward Michael Ravencliffe. He watched her coming, his face a mask. They locked eyes while Freed and the soldiers looked on. "I'm so sorry," Caryn whispered. She fought down the panic that was seeping back to her. She could do this. "Are you ready?"

She would never forget the look in his eyes. He was frightened. Terrified. But resolved.

She took a deep breath. She felt as scared as he was, the panic rising again. He caught the look in her eyes, turned away, and then —

"Wait a moment, Minister," Ravencliffe said.

Caryn stopped. Lowered the pistol. "I can do it."

"But you shouldn't have to." For the first time Caryn could remember, Ravencliffe's voice was shaking. There were tears forming in his eyes. "I have been insisting that you learn lessons from me and neglecting all that I might have learned from you," he told her. "The Realm has a certain strictness to it, a code of behaviour that separates us from those beyond the mountains. Not to dilute our civilization, we say, but you, Minister, have taught me — no. You *would* have taught me, had I been inclined to listen. But as I watched you suffer earlier tonight with the task I had placed upon you, I realized that at least one of your lessons has failed to entirely escape me."

Caryn didn't know what to say. The gun felt heavy in her hand, and in her soul. "I get panic attacks," she said. "You saw that the first time I visited your cell. It doesn't mean —"

"That you're weak?" Ravencliffe asked. "Soft? No. It does not. Such a foreign concept to the harsh realities of the Realm, that sometimes sympathy and caring are not weaknesses. That sometimes doing a kindness to a friend takes more strength than the greatest soldier can muster." He took a deep breath. She could see him gathering his courage. "Your pistol, Minister."

Caryn froze and looked to the general. He had aimed a revolver at Ravencliffe, and two of his soldiers had their rifles ready. "Your precautions are unnecessary, General," Ravencliffe told him, "but I can hardly fault you. I wouldn't trust myself with a pistol, either." He held out his hand for it.

Caryn couldn't let go. "You can't do this."

"It must be done," he responded simply. "My pain is the same either way, but I can spare some of yours by doing it myself."

Nono came up behind her. "Let me do it."

"Or me," Freed added, stepping closer, his revolver ready.

"This is remarkably flattering," Ravencliffe told them. "To see so many struggle for the glorious opportunity to assassinate me. It makes me feel all warm inside." He turned back to Caryn. "Will you respect my decision, Minister?"

Caryn nodded. She stepped forward with difficulty and held the pistol out to him.

"You have an incredible strength," Ravencliffe told her. "You have a way of inspiring those around you to be better than they are, better than they thought possible. You have given Deugan a hero."

His praise was unexpected, and all the more tragic for what she knew would follow. She struggled to hold back her tears. "I'll miss you," Caryn told him. "You're a good friend. A good man."

Ravencliffe sighed. "And I try so hard not to be. Farewell, Caryn. And good luck."

He had never used her first name before. She took a step toward him, but he shook his head, and she stopped. Nono was the shadow beside her, putting an arm around her. Caryn leaned on him for support, but her eyes were on Ravencliffe. "Farewell, my friend," she said.

For a time nothing stirred. The northern air was silent, the mountains loomed above them, and the only motion was the flickering of the electric light, and of the stars overhead.

Then Michael Ravencliffe raised the pistol to his temple and squeezed the trigger.

CHAPTER THIRTY

A gunshot rang out. There were screams and shouts, wordless, and the sounds of a struggle. It grew louder, more violent. Then he heard a second shot, and all was quiet again.

For a few minutes silence reigned. Matthias tried to stir but could not find the strength to do anything more than watch the bundle on the floor as it stared back at him, shuddering in anger. Then he heard the footsteps, hard against the stone floor, and the scraping of a weight dragged across the ground. With enormous effort Matthias turned his head toward the bars of his cell. There were the guards, resplendent in Orastan emerald green, and there was the dead man, trailing along behind them. He hadn't even reached the river. The only wetness was his blood.

Matthias laid his head back onto the stones and closed his eyes. The footsteps faded as the guards turned a corner and disappeared with their prey. Matthias started to whisper a prayer, mostly on instinct, but then the pain returned and his words became a groan. His wrists and ankles were scraped raw, and his cheek burned like a thousand flames. The questioning wasn't intense anymore, now that Matthias had a history of cooperating, but that was scarcely a relief. There was little more the ropes could do to him. There was not enough of him left.

They'd taken him from the mountains by horse-drawn carriage, barely feeding him, allowing the wound in his shoulder to fester. They forced him onto a train, then into an open horse-cart. There was no sense hiding where they were taking him. They wanted him to know. To fear.

The Penitentiary Avali was notorious for breaking men's spirits as well as their bodies. A squat, grim building, it stood on the edge of an industrial park on the outskirts of Avali Nova, the capital of the Orastan Empire. The river flowed past it, carrying industrial waste southward toward the Fringes. The man this evening wasn't the first fool to try to escape that way, nor was he the first to end up worse for it.

Matthias was a fool himself. He had tried to resist, and that had been a dreadful mistake.

In another life he might have succeeded, back when he had something to fight for. Then he might have sustained himself in the darkness when they brought the brand onto his cheek, hissing as he screamed. He might have had a hope of rescue, a friend to give him strength, a hope that his suffering would guide him to greater faith and leave him a better man.

Matthias had nothing left, though. He had betrayed the Steffians, and they had tried to kill him. He had no loyalty to any cause, no fellow prisoners for kinship, no reason to deny Orastus the details that it so brutally demanded. It was only his unadulterated loathing for the New Empire that drove him, at first, to keep the Steffians' secrets, but pain defeated hatred. Torture defeated principle. Matthias knew that now.

Across from him, the bundle sizzled like the brand, dug like the ropes. It rocked like the ocean and rattled like death. A glimmer of hope it might have been, but that was when Matthias still had the strength to wield it. When he still had the will to care.

Rope tortures were a favourite of the Orastan Empire. Matthias had his arms pulled behind his back, tied together at the wrists and elbows, too tight yet chafing. From there a rope looped over his shoulders and back down again to his ankles; pulled tight, it forced his head into his knees, wrenching his back and shoulders in agony. They sat him on a stool for hours, rolled into his terrible ball of pain, hitting him whenever he threatened to fall.

And Matthias thought he could resist.

He lasted nearly two full days on the ropes. Gritting his teeth against the pain at first, then screaming, then reduced to a quiet agony. No sleep, no food, only horror. He steeled himself and prayed silently to Good Steif. Each hour of pain strengthened his resolve not to tell them anything, to die before giving one iota of advice to the evil empire.

Then they brought the brand out, and he was broken. It was only a small piece, answering a question about the *acambro* bomb that had exploded in Ciorala. Nothing the empire's own scientists wouldn't discover in time, nothing that betrayed a true Steffian secret, but the shame and the horror mingled with the pain. They only needed to break him once. His words would flow more easily the second time.

It was the kid who walked Matthias back to his cell that night. The ones tying the ropes and barking the questions were grizzled men, veterans of this kind of work. The kid's main jobs, it seemed, were to watch and learn, and to get Matthias back onto the stool when he fell. He remembered the kid's face, watching in fascination and horror as Matthias writhed on the ropes. Now that the pain had stopped, the kid was washing him and feeding him a thin soup and a heel of bread. Finally he said, "They're not all bad. You keep cooperating and they'll help you."

Matthias only shrugged.

"Come on," the kid said. "There must be something that'll make this all easier on you, and you'll get it if you make it easy on them."

He wanted to stay silent, but he saw an opportunity in the kid's pity. Part of him wasn't broken yet. He shrugged again, trying to be nonchalant. "Clothes I had on when they caught me," he said. "Sentimental value."

That was two span ago.

He was back on the ropes the next day, screaming even without the brand, and then breaking. They were asking him about the Steffian leadership, and he couldn't take it any longer. It was the Steffian leadership who had gotten Matthias caught. Gamoy's agent in the fort had set off that thrice-damned flare, and Rusul had tried to kill him. What loyalty did Matthias have to them? He told the torturers that Bashar Gamoy was a Steif-forsaken ass with a superiority complex, and they smiled and loosened the ropes and asked for more. In time Matthias was blathering about Harar and Amad, painting portraits of them with his words, talking about their inclinations and schemes and plans. He still bit his tongue when they asked him about Master Nono, but that was only a matter of time.

Matthias sobbed that night, praying to Good Steif that the

clothing would come, never guessing that when it finally arrived, it would be too late. That he would be too weak and defeated to use it.

They gave him the next day off, alone in his cell. Matthias's body was stiffening, his shoulder aching, the cheek where they'd burned him in agony. Still he forced himself to run on the spot and do push-ups to keep up his strength. It was no use. Back to the ropes the next day, and he had to make it stop. He had to give them something.

There was always more to give. When he thought he'd told them all he knew, the pain would drive back another memory, something, anything to satisfy them. He remembered meetings years ago that he'd thought he'd forgotten, operations that were contemplated but never reached the planning stage, quiet conversations around campfires. He told them about the first time he pulled off Master Nono's rain effect, about a kid who cornered him in an alley while he was living in Ciorala, about the hopes he and Jakim would share when they spoke of the end of the war. Then the pain would end, and he would be back in his cell, huddled against the darkness. He would feel dirty then, and weak, and most of all alone.

But he wasn't alone; the energy was with him now. The bundle on the floor, the clothing, surging with fury.

It was Matthias's energy, he remembered. He had taken that *acambro* from the stores they'd saved in Kalid. He had carried it with him across the Continent, from the most distant of the Fringes to the very edge of Deugan. For months this energy had a prisoner in the leaves, straining against its bindings even as Matthias made vain promises to let it out. "Once I reach Deugan," he had told it three span ago, "by day's end." Another promise broken.

Still, Matthias felt a rush of pride. Through the pain and torture, he had the presence of mind not to tell them of the energy, not to hint that he had *acambro* with him when he was captured. It was the one secret he had kept from them, amid the ropes and the brand, the starvation and the beatings. He had the power, and he had survived.

Too late, though. Too late.

He ought to let the energy out now. Two span ago he might have used it to escape, but there was no sense storing it any longer. The empire had taken everything from him, his friends, his dreams, his hopes. There was no sense living. There was no sense trying.

He thought of his home village in Pascuay, when the empire burned it. He could almost see his father, hair as orange as the flames, racing for the sea. Matthias was only paces behind him, and they made it to the water together. They dove into the nearest boat, its owners shouting at them from a nearby dock but not reaching them. They pushed off frantically and had barely gotten away before the pier itself caught fire. Matthias remembered, and felt nothing. The empire had broken him.

Matthias had hated Orastus then. His anger had kept him awake at night, even more than his hunger. He'd stayed with his father for a time as they travelled the Pascuayan countryside, searching for work and scrounging food. His father finally signed on with a mine in a company town leagues from the sea. Matthias had worked alongside him for only a span before he took off to find the Steffians, and justice. He had not seen or heard from his father since.

Now his hatred had passed. So had his anger, and even pain itself. Matthias would never reach Deugan. That was as plain to him as the charring on his face, as the scars around his wrists and ankles, the telltale signs where the brand and the ropes had burned him. The most he could hope for was release from this world.

Not that a purer world awaited him. Matthias had earned the scorn of the one god; he knew that now. He would be relegated to a lower world, but at least it would be a new one. A chance to start again.

The energy was all that was left. He could drain most of it, finally setting it free after months of imprisonment, and perhaps earning a measure of Steif's forgiveness with his final act. Then he could use the rest of the energy to make his end a painless one. *Yes*, Matthias thought, huddled on the floor in the darkness. That was the path Good Steif had laid out for him.

He turned his mind to the *acambro* and felt the fury within it. Strange, Matthias thought, how the energy was more alive than he was. Where had his anger gone? What had the New Empire done to him?

He felt a spark then, a new determination, a grim one. Matthias's anger had been with him since his childhood. It had driven him to greater heights than he or his father could ever have imagined, rising through the Steffian ranks, earning the notice of the Master of Secrets, corresponding with and even training the Deugan foreign minister. Anger was the one thing the New Empire could never take from him.

He felt the rage starting to return. The energy's fury and his own, breathing the life back into him. Not pleasant, but powerful. This, Matthias suddenly realized, was what the one god truly wanted.

Not abandoning the Steffians and skulking off to Deugan. Not succumbing to the Orastan torture. Good Steif had betrayed Matthias to the New Empire for a reason. To remind him there was no escape from his duty. To remind him, to have his own body play out, the pain that had been inflicted on the Fringes since the empire's birth. To rekindle the flame inside him. Good Steif had kept him from Deugan but delivered him to his true calling.

Matthias would curl on the floor no longer. He pushed himself to his feet, wavered there for a moment, then grinned in satisfaction as he found his footing. The Steffians were right after all. Theirs was not a god of patience and mercy. Theirs was a challenging god, a demanding god, a god who commanded loyalty and exacted vengeance, and expected his followers to do the same. Good Steif wanted the New Empire to topple, and he had given Matthias the tools to do it.

The clothing should never have been returned to him. The Orastans had their Secrets-users; surely someone could have detected the energy surging through it. That the kid had dumped a bundle of energy, of Matthias's energy, directly into Matthias's lap, it had to be Good Steif's work. How could it not be? The Well's power was a weapon from the one god. It was not a tool to bring Matthias into Deugan. It was a missile to aim at the heart of the Orastan Empire.

How to escape? Matthias knew that the man who'd died today was one of several prisoners who had tried jumping the walls of the Penitentiary Avali, only to be caught and hauled back within hours. Most escapees took to the river. It flowed north to south, its waters rushing down through Orastus proper into Orastino and Cioro, and finally out to the sea. Too long a journey, and too dangerous in the dark, with rapids and rocks and waterfalls. Imperial police manned the piers of the towns where escaping prisoners inevitably took to land, catching them every time. Swimming upstream against the current, in water heavy with waste from the Orastan factories, was even more suicidal than the normal route. Some prisoners ran westward on foot, away from the city, but the empire guarded the bridges over the river and had checkpoints and roadblocks on the highway. Matthias would never be able to flee that way.

But how many prisoners dared go the opposite way? How many took the road east, into the centre of Avali Nova itself? Who would guess that Matthias would journey toward the marble pillars, would pass beneath the rounded arches, would bury himself in the very heart of the capital city of the New Empire?

Matthias felt a moment of pity for the Orastans. The bastards should have let him escape into Deugan. They should have left him alone.

Then his pity was replaced with an anger that surged back through him, animating him, empowering him. He felt like a child again, a force of nature, the future bright before him. He would never make it to Deugan. Good Steif had stopped him once and would no doubt see to it again. But at least he would make it to a higher world, once he left this one behind him.

Matthias picked up the bundle. The clothes were warm in his arms, the energy straining against it. Its fury matched his own, but he held it, embraced it like it was an infant, kicking and squalling. Even through his burning rage, his mind was adept, subtle. He could control the power, release it slowly as though through an eye-dropper, one wisp at a time. He felt it entering the lock, careful, precise, no shred of the *acambro* wasted. He felt the power as though it were an extension of his finger, as though Matthias's skin were filling the grooves, pressing the pins.

He flicked his wrist, pulling the power with him. A click. A rattling chain.

Matthias stepped out of his cell and into the darkness beyond.

CHAPTER THIRTY-ONE

Do I believe she survived the Great War? No, I don't. I know you Deugans love all the speculation, but my father actually spoke to Caryn Hallom by telephone the night before the Second Battle of the Gateway, and she was at the Gateway Fort. By the end of the battle, the vast majority of the fort's garrison were dead, and there were so many casualties that most were shovelled into mass graves. If Hallom had been one of the few to survive the carnage, then surely we would have a reliable report of somebody, anybody, seeing or hearing from her again.

Still, it is humbling to think that my father might have been the last non-Deugan who ever spoke to Hallom. His journal describes her as obstinate, irritating, passionate and fiercely intelligent — the claims of her greatest detractors and her die-hard supporters, all rolled into one. She would have been fascinating to meet, and I envy my father the opportunity.

At least I might play some small part in helping Hallom's legacy to live on. My country may have rejected her ideas during her lifetime, but when future generations of Orastans wake up in the Commonwealth we are building for them, they will be in Hallom's debt. Few today may remember her short-lived foreign policy, but I can confidently say that I would never have been able to develop the framework for an Orastan Commonwealth had I not read her persuasive arguments in support of the Hallom Doctrine. I still find it difficult to believe that she was writing those arguments before the turn of the century, back in the 1690s. She truly was ahead of her time.

— Interview on Deugan television (1729) with Francesca Legatti-Ricci, Orastan Secretary of Internal Affairs. She is often credited as the architect of the Orastan Commonwealth.

Rest, the general had said, but rest was impossible. Caryn had been only a few feet away from Ravencliffe when he pulled the trigger. She saw him collapsing as though in slow motion, and then the blood, all of the blood...

It was too difficult. First Lana, then Hans, now another friend lost. How could she rest? How could she take it any longer? How many more would have to die before the horror finally ended?

Caryn eventually drifted into a fitful sleep. She woke twice during the night, and each time the shells crashing against the fort sounded louder, more frequent. It was almost a mercy when morning came with an escort of soldiers banging on her door. She roused herself and dressed in the darkness, wondering if it would be her last time.

Brenth Nono was already in the mess hall when Caryn arrived, eating a few scraps of salted beef. General Freed was there too, looking as though he had not slept either. When he saw Caryn enter, he pushed himself to his feet and beckoned her over. "I've made you as safe as I can," he said when she was close enough that he could whisper to her without Nono hearing. "There's a trench, barbed wire, machine guns, a couple of field guns too, but it may not be enough. You need to get in, defuse the bombs, seal them and get the hell out."

"I know," Caryn told him. She remembered the cavern that had survived Marwin's bomb, untouched. Clearly the energy wanted them there, and that gave her some comfort, but not much. The cavern had only one entrance. It would be all too easy to get bottled inside.

"It was already difficult to manoeuvre artillery in the Well," Freed explained. "After Marwin's bomb, there are only more obstacles. That means you're not going to be hit with heavy weapons. If they want to take you out, they'll have to storm it with sheer numbers. The machine guns will cut them up." He coughed. "What worries me is that they'll bring *acambro*."

"They won't need to," Caryn replied. "Inside the Well, they'll have the energy all around them. We'll be able to use the Well's power too, though. We have Brenth Nono."

"Can we trust him?" Freed asked.

Caryn glanced at Nono. He was finishing his breakfast, ignoring the Deugan soldiers around him, immersed in thought. He looked like an older version of the Brenner she used to know, but he was different, too. He had sent an assassin after her. He had planned to send the entire Continent into anarchy. But then he had come back to her and promised his support. Caryn shook her head. "We don't have a choice. We have to try."

"Now you're sounding like a soldier."

"I can keep an eye on him," Caryn assured Freed. "I know the energy in and out. Don't worry."

"I always worry," Freed admitted. He put his arm around her, and Caryn flinched until she realized it was a pretext. He was slipping a pistol into a pocket in her shirt. "I pray to Lessandro you will never need it," Freed whispered, "but if something goes wrong, you can't hesitate."

Caryn froze, a lump rising in her throat. She tried desperately not to look at Nono. "I won't," she promised in a small voice.

"Good luck, Caryn."

"You too, Ern."

Caryn had just finished her own breakfast when they heard a roar above the fort. "Airplanes," Freed said. "For artillery spotting. The Breas will be concentrating their fire, some on the moat, some on the satellites, the rest on the main gunnery."

"It's begun, then?" Caryn asked.

"Yes," Freed said. "You'd better move."

The trip to the Well was uneventful. Escorted by a team of twenty soldiers, they took Caryn's tunnel from the sub-basement beneath Eolanis satellite. Nono opened the circular door at the other end, the green light spinning maddeningly, and they crawled through one by one. From there the lights on the ground guided them. The exit from the tunnel had been caved in by Marwin's bomb, but as Caryn had discovered a few days earlier, there was now a hole in the ceiling above the ramp. A couple of soldiers scaled the walls of the cave, then tied ropes to help the others up. Caryn, who could not have climbed even if she had use of a second hand, had to be dragged to the surface.

The morning was growing brighter, the sun still hanging low in the sky. The Third Army's assault on the Hermann Gap was imminent, and the Brea attack on the fort had likely begun in earnest. The fighting hadn't reached the Well yet, though, and the team took off for the cavern where they would be stationed. The cave loomed over the destruction of the Well, an oasis in the storm. Caryn felt the energy there with every breath.

A trench line had been dug across the mouth of the cavern, and their escort joined a much larger force already stationed there. The soldiers lifted the barbed wire to let the newcomers in. The ground inside was still soft and spongy, not hard like the rest of the Well had become. "How long have you been in here?" Nono demanded.

"A couple hours," their leader said. "The guys who dug the position rotated out, and we relieved them. We're good for another twenty-two, but the general wants us out within twelve."

"Good," Nono replied. He turned to Caryn. "Let's do this."

Nono took the Deugan commanders aside and explained what was about to happen, so as not to panic the soldiers. Then he joined Caryn at the back of the cavern and drew them into the map. Caryn had been here many times, but it was strange to be back with Brenner in the place with the columns. Nono caught her look. "Just like old times," he muttered. He was staring intently at the map, puzzling over the pattern of flickering white lights. Caryn tried to orient herself. She found the column that represented the Gateway Well, then traced the lights surrounding it. The Selliar Mountains had emptied out, she realized, replaced by a cluster of lights southeast of the Well. The Steffians were all in the Hermann Gap, with the Breas.

Caryn saw other lights, though, and shuddered as she realized how real their threat was. The lights were arranged in groups of three, making a map of Deugan's and Brealand's largest cities. Three bombs in each city, well scattered to do maximum damage.

"Hermann Gap first," Nono said. They had agreed on that in advance: the priority was to smooth the road for the Third Army to break through the Hermann Gap and relieve the fort. That in itself would protect Deugan from the bombs and buy Caryn more time to defuse them, since the Steffians would not be able to set off any bombs without winning the battle and seizing the Well. On the other hand, if the Third Army were defeated by Steffian Secrets, it would scarcely matter whether the bombs were defused or not. As Ravencliffe had explained, with the Third Army out of the way Brealand could run roughshod over Deugan, *acambro* bombs or no. "You drain," Nono told Caryn, "and I'll seal. After you've seen me do it a couple of times, you'll be able to do it yourself. Focus on the Gap," he added, pointing at the main cluster southeast of them.

When she nodded, Nono moved his finger to a smaller group of lights further east. "One of those will be Toppel, but I can't tell which," he said. "We'll have to leave them."

They attacked the main cluster one *acambro* vine at a time. Caryn tapped into the map, explored the energy, then zeroed in on one of the white lights. She set it sparking until she could feel it, make it part of her. When the energy was in her grasp, she slowly let it out. It flowed eagerly, leaving the *acambro* behind. The white light flickered and died.

Caryn felt Nono sealing it as she found another vine to drain. She felt how he concentrated, cajoled and persuaded. He carried the energy between his fingers and wove it among the *acambro*, stitching it up like a wound.

Caryn suddenly understood how difficult the task must be, even at a short distance. If he was using the energy as his thread, sewing the *acambro* together, it meant that thread would be trapped in the *acambro* until the end of time. He was persuading a small part of the power to sacrifice itself to close the prison that bound the remainder. She marvelled at how effortless he made it look. The power must be struggling, she thought, but then again, maybe not. Sadness came over Caryn as she gazed around their cavern. It was the same sacrifice these soldiers were making, guarding them against the coming onslaught. It was the same sacrifice that Michael Ravencliffe had made, not easily, but willingly. It was what the war demanded of all of them. Life, and lives.

She sighed and returned to her task.

Caryn had drained a few more *acambro* vines when they heard shouts from the mouth of the cavern. An instant later the world around them had changed. The cavern burst into a cacophony of gunshots and explosions and screams, while orders were barked above the din. The rocks outside were being churned into a dust that blinded Caryn from seeing much of the battle, but she caught flashes of muzzle fire that competed with the lights of the *acambro* shining through the map. She took a deep breath and redoubled her efforts. They had to move fast.

Nono seemed unperturbed. He was stitching the *acambro* calmly, and Caryn admired his concentration. She focused on a new sprig of *acambro*, held it, drained it, moved on to the next. Efficient, methodical, siphoning the power away.

Nono finished a couple of stitches with a flourish. The sounds of battle grew heated, then died down. Their men had fought off the first wave. Nono panted and turned to Caryn. "There is another way, you know."

"What do you mean?" she asked. Tapping in, holding, draining. The energy was used to the pattern now. It was trained.

Nono stepped over to a column and grasped it, sliding the map along until Breland was directly overhead. The Gateway Well's column stood behind them, and in the darkness that followed, Caryn could see the smaller lights banded in groups of three. The nearest group represented Myerston, the largest city this side of the vast interior. She could place Sutton in the centre of the country, the railway hub that processed raw materials from the interior and sent them to the manufacturing centres on the coast. She made out Hastingvale, the Brea capital, just down the coast from the north harbours. Continuing along the coastline were Arlington and Portsmouth, illuminated in the darkness of the cavern, three by three. The bombs were waiting to be detonated, and the most powerful Secrets-users on the Continent were in perfect position, behind a strong trench line in the nearest Well.

"No," Caryn said.

"If the Breas lose Hastingvale, they'll sue for peace," Nono said. "They'll have to assume the Steffians betrayed them. It'll break up the alliance, and turn their ultimatum on its head. We have the source now, we're the ones with the power."

"No," Caryn repeated.

"How long do you think we can hold out here?" Nono asked. "Our plan is to defuse all the bombs, but how much are you willing to sacrifice? You may risk your life to save Deugan, but would you do it to save your enemy's cities as well?"

Caryn was forced to admit that he had a point. She looked around. The guns at the mouth of the cavern had fallen silent, for now. In the battle at the Hermann Gap, the odds were still against them. If they failed they would lose the Well, and with it they would lose this chance forever. Even if they won the battle, there was no guarantee that Breland would accept the peace treaty Ravencliffe had negotiated. The war could drag on for years, and the Breas might even win. If they could knock Breland out of the war entirely...

Caryn knew what Major Danzig would say if he were here. Even

General Freed would probably seize the opportunity. Caryn's mind raced, but at last it settled on Ravencliffe. How he had asked for her pistol for the sake of their peace. For the good of the Realm, and his trust in her.

"I'm sorry, Brenner," she said softly. "I still don't think you understand. Hastingvale and Myerston aren't my enemy's cities. My enemy is the war, and this is the only way to end it without millions more dying. We stick to the plan."

Nono was about to argue further, but just then the energy shifted dangerously. Nono froze. He had felt it too. "Someone else is here," he had time to say before Caryn's temples exploded into pain and she screamed. Nono's head whipped toward her, then back toward the columns as his mind reached for their attackers. There were two, now five, now eleven...

Caryn fought through the pain to keep herself inside the map. She could feel Nono fighting them, draining their *acambro* one by one, faster than Caryn possibly could have done. The *acambro* lights flickered and died, but a few were still glowing stubbornly. At the mouth of the cavern, the guns suddenly roared back to life, the field guns bursting with their shells, the rifles firing, the machine guns rattling. Shells exploded among their own lines too, and soldiers were being shot, and dying. Caryn finally fought down the pain and dove deeper into the map, searching for the Steffians. She saw Nono grasp his chest with both hands, and she screamed and crawled toward him. He fought back angrily, firing energy into a Steffian throat, watching the man choke on his own blood. Another *acambro* light flickered out. There were only two left in the Hermann Gap. "I can hold them," Caryn shouted. "You seal the ones we've already drained, and start on the bombs!"

She felt the energy bypassing her, attacking Nono again. He seized it disdainfully and redirected it into the drained *acambro*, his mind working nimbly as his finger traced the stitches he was making with the energy. Caryn fought back against the Steffian, seizing power from the man's own *acambro* and driving it into his chest. He was so occupied keeping his heart beating that he could not keep Caryn away from his *acambro*. Caryn's own source of energy was infinite. Another light went out. One left, and the most powerful of their enemies behind it.

Marwin fortified his *acambro* as he hurled effects at Caryn. The pain mounted in her head, a hand closed across her throat, she was punched in the gut. Still Caryn held on. She grasped at Marwin's hands with the energy, struggling with them, but he was strong and young and practiced. She targeted his *acambro* instead, trying to drain it, and he guarded it jealously as he sent a piercing pain toward her chest.

Only for an instant. Caryn seized the Well's power and formed a barrier, feeling Marwin's anger as he tried and failed to pierce it. Caryn grabbed him around the ankle and hauled him to the ground, and he fought back viciously, wending the energy around her barrier, then seizing the barrier itself and transforming it into a wall of fire that flew at her. Desperately Caryn threw her good hand out and harnessed the power as it came, the fire vanishing into smoke as electric air danced around her fingertips. She dug deeper into the map and hurled the energy through it. Marwin dodged easily, but Caryn had slipped her hand through the map as well, and as Marwin moved to avoid her attack she slipped beneath his defences and placed her hand on his chest. Marwin reached for his *acambro* to attack her again, and Caryn knew where it was, could sense it as part of him.

Caryn ignored the wave of pain in her skull as she ran her hand down to his belt. She focused the Well's power as though through a funnel and surged it into her hand at the other end. The belt ripped off Marwin's waist and he tumbled out of the map, screaming. Caryn could feel him clawing at the energy, trying to hoist himself back in, but it was too late. Marwin stared on helplessly as Caryn emptied his *acambro* and stitched it shut.

Caryn looked up, panting from the exertion. A pitched battle was being fought at the mouth of the cavern, the Breas charging the Deugan lines. Brenth Nono was still by her side, draining and sealing, dimming the white lights and extinguishing them, but something was wrong. The bombs were still there, three by three by three.

Caryn finally caught her breath. "What are you doing?" she shouted over the din of the shells.

"Taking out the Fringes," Nono replied. That was where the lights were going out, the Steffians' leftover stores back in the east. Caryn guessed that half of them were already sealed.

"Why the Fringes?" Caryn shouted. "The bombs are in Deugan!" She tried to stand, but she wobbled and fell, and that scared her even more.

"Distance," Nono shouted back. "If the plan is to end the *acambro* threat for the Continent, those ones are the hardest to hit. I'm stronger, I need to do them."

"You can do them later!" Caryn screamed. She tried to stand again. This time she made it, but she felt as though the ground was swaying beneath her. "Get the bombs!"

Nono looked up from his work. He was unsteady on his feet, too, as both of them stared at the entrance to the cavern. There were bursts of explosives closer to their lines, and Caryn could see the Brea uniforms on the other end, black as night, but some men were not in uniform at all.

It wasn't her imagination. The ground really was shaking as the Steffians drove the Well's power into it. The Deugan soldiers braced against it, their lines holding steady as the Breas charged. "Get the bombs!" Caryn shouted again. She turned her mind to the *acambro* near Czemers, locked onto the first one, drained it. Nono still stood there, staring at the cavern entrance, immersed in thought, then kneeling, patting the ground. She stitched up the bomb, then turned to the second one. She connected with the energy, let it flow to her, guided the tiniest piece to remain behind as her thread.

The battle grew louder, more frenzied. The second light in Czemers blinked and faded just as the columns did. The cavern plunged into deepest darkness, then brightened. Not orange. A dull red.

Caryn shouted in panic. She took a breath to calm herself, tried to bring back the map, but she couldn't. It was as though a switch had been shut off. She couldn't direct the energy. She couldn't feel the energy at all.

Nono was kneeling, his hands extended in front of him. White light burned in his chest, then passed through it and down his arms. As the light emerged from him it started to spin, dizzyingly quickly, a vortex of swirling energy.

Caryn started toward him. "The bombs," she panted. "You have to —"

"I can't," Nono said.

The energy burst into the floor of the cavern, still spinning madly, tearing up the ground. It was a drill, burrowing beneath them. Caryn gasped. After fourteen years —

She raised her good hand to her head. The power was gone,

blocked out, yet the effect remained, digging its way underground. Caryn looked at Nono in disbelief. "You?"

He nodded. "The Breas will break through any moment," he said. "I won't let us die."

Caryn remembered discovering the effect he was using. She remembered the warmth of the energy in her chest, the sudden chill, the power swirling between her fingertips. She remembered Brenner's arms squeezing her so tightly she could barely breathe, not wanting to let her go. She remembered carrying the energy to the entrance to the Wassian cavern, pounding at the green rocks, clearing a path. Brenner had looked on in fascination, and then the power leapt to him, so quickly that he faltered, startled, and then joined her, the two of them drilling through the barricade together.

"If they're coming, we need to stop the bombs," Caryn insisted. She didn't understand. "Brenner, come on!"

"I can't," Nono repeated. He didn't look at her. His focus was on the drill and on the other effect he was maintaining, the block on her head.

"Then let me," Caryn said. How could he lock her out of the energy? How was it even possible?

"No," Nono shouted. "I thought I could. I promised to help you, but I can't, okay? I can't sit here and let you undo the last fourteen years of my life. I'll drain *acambro* in the Hermann Gap. I'll drain *acambro* in the Fringes. That's all."

Caryn stared at him in disbelief. "Those bombs are going to kill millions of people!"

"They'll kill the systems that oppress millions of people," Nono snorted. "Systems that you're part of, Jayla, and don't deny it. What did you said yesterday about selling out three million in Givanno?"

"You're crazy," Caryn declared. She couldn't believe him. She was staring at her childhood friend and seeing a stranger. "You can't do this." She turned her mind to the energy, searching for it, but it was gone. Vanished. The drill was burrowing deeper and deeper. She needed to do something, anything, but what?

The gun. It was terrible, but she had no choice. The general had given her the pistol for just this reason. Caryn drew it from her pocket, but she didn't even have time to aim before it was snatched out of her hand and tossed handily to the ground. "You would kill me, Jayla?" Nono growled. The energy hand closed around her good wrist, holding her tight. She couldn't reach the power. She couldn't fight it. "Don't you get it? I'm saving your life. Again."

Caryn screamed, but the soldiers at the entranceway couldn't hear her over the pounding of the shells and the blasts of the grenades. The ground was swaying wildly, yet their line was holding. "You call this saving my life?"

"That tunnel from your fort isn't the only one crossing this Well," Nono shouted back. "I scoped it out over the last few days. There's a tunnel just a few yards from here that'll take us to a cave in the Selliar Mountains. From there it's a quick jaunt to the Range, where we'll be safe. I just have to dig us a path to it."

Caryn was still twisting futilely against the energy hand that held her. How could he do this, lock her out of the power and run the drill and seize her with energy hands, three effects at once? Caryn often had trouble with single tasks. She'd thought she would be able to manage him, but she had desperately underestimated the Master of Secrets. She had no idea how powerful Brenth Nono really was.

"I can't bring myself to abandon you," Nono continued, "so I won't. I'll take you with me as far as the Range. I hope you'll choose to stay afterward, but I won't try to force you. You can disappear in the Range, or you can catch a boat to the northern continent, or even waltz into Brealand. Just as long as I know that I've done what I can to keep you safe."

"I don't want to be kept safe," Caryn shouted. "I want to stop the bombing."

"Jayla Sullivan. Listen to me," Nono demanded. "The Breas are almost here, and every single person in this cavern is going to die. I will not be here when they come, and neither should you." He turned back to his drill. The path was almost complete. In the swirling white light, Caryn could see the larger tunnel in the distance that Nono was connecting to, the one that drove north into the mountains. "Come on," Nono said.

Caryn screamed again, but the sounds of battle still drowned her out, and the soldiers paid her no mind. The Breas and the Steffians were about to break through, and save for Czemers, the bombs were untouched. Nono took off toward his tunnel, the energy hand dragging Caryn behind him. She struggled against him, but she was powerless, and he was strong, so horribly strong. He descended into the tunnel, and he had almost managed to pull Caryn in too, the ground shaking beneath them —

— there was a cracking sound, barely audible over the guns, then a bursting above them. The energy hand loosened its grip, and Caryn shook away from it and scrambled out of the tunnel. Nono realized what was happening a split second later. He raced back toward the cavern, diving toward the mouth of the tunnel as it collapsed around him. He was almost fast enough.

The rocks came crashing down, burying Nono's legs in a mound of dirt and stone. Nono screamed and pawed the ground with his hands, but his feet were trapped. Caryn saw the terror on his face as the pathway closed behind him. Then an errant rock slammed into the back of his neck, and Nono's head snapped forward against the ground.

There was no time to think. Caryn ran to the pistol she had dropped, grabbed it and ran back to the collapsed tunnel. The block in her head was gone, and the energy was flowing to her, rushing about her furiously. Caryn cocked the pistol and aimed it at Nono's head.

Nono was stretched out before her, groaning in pain. He was dazed but still conscious. His eyes were unfocused, and he seemed to be struggling to keep them open.

Do it now, Caryn told herself, *do it now*. He wasn't knocked out, only woozy, and that could pass any moment. The instant Nono regained his strength she would be locked out of the energy again, powerless. She had to do it. She had only seconds to spare.

She couldn't. She remembered the general telling her not to hesitate. Brenth Nono was a madman who wanted to blow up ten major cities and plunge the Continent into mayhem. He had promised to give up that dream, and he hadn't. She couldn't let him walk away from this place or the entire Continent would be in danger. Yet she couldn't bring herself to pull the trigger.

She looked at him as he squeezed his eyes closed and open again, moaning. She tried to remember what Nono had become, but all she could see was Brenner Halloway. In him she saw the columns, not as a map but as a paradise of fireworks and fountains. She saw the comforting arms, the gentle hands, the whispered words. She saw the laughter, the way he could sweep her cares away, like nobody else she had ever known. She saw in Brenner a night sky filled with stars, endless, a place where hope for the future could not only live, but flourish.

Slowly Nono's eyes came back into focus. They settled on the gun in Caryn's hand. She knew what she had to do. She aimed again, her arm wavering.

It was no good. Caryn lowered the pistol and let it tumble to the floor. Her head was lowered too, and she choked back tears. Nono exhaled in relief and craned his neck to look at his legs, buried beneath the rubble. "I tried," he whispered. "I thought I could give it up. I really thought I could."

Caryn started gathering energy to her. If he tried to put the lock on her again — but he didn't. He was lying helplessly, staring past her to the entrance of the cavern. A machine gun had been dislodged and trampled. Breas were arriving, some of them in the trench itself, fighting with bayonets and grenades. Two more lines of their own soldiers, who had been waiting behind the trench, were fighting their way forward to help the others.

She looked at the gun and back to Nono. "I'll defuse the bombs," she said. "You drill us a tunnel and dig out your legs. We'll go as soon as we're both ready."

Nono took a ragged, difficult breath. "You'll come with me?"

Caryn stared at the ground again. She knew how he felt now, why he loathed himself. The six months they had spent together had locked them in for a lifetime, no matter what horrible things either of them did afterward. He couldn't find a way to leave her, and she was just as powerless around him. She had abandoned him in Wassia, driven him to the Steffians, then lured him away and smashed his dreams. He had betrayed her, sent an assassin after her, nearly kidnapped her. None of it mattered. They were connected, Caryn and Brenth, Jayla and Brenner. They were trapped.

Caryn drew herself into the map, the cavern darkening, the columns emerging around them. It was not difficult to find the bombs, the white lights arranged in teams of three. She nodded at Nono, her heart heavy. "I'll come with you."

CHAPTER THIRTY-TWO

The train jerked and shuddered as it pulled into the station. The horn blew, the doors slid open, and a throng of people exited, spilling onto the platform. Matthias allowed himself a moment to watch the train disappear into the tunnel, around a bend and out of sight. It was ridiculous and maddening. These people could run trains underground on electricity alone when most of the Fringes had no power for industry or cooking or even light. One more injustice to chalk up to the New Empire.

Matthias pulled the hood of his coat over his head and followed the crowd up the steps. He had to hurry. Even the hood did not entirely cover the wound on his face where the brand had burned him, marking him as a fugitive from the Penitentiary Avali. By now the empire must be hunting him, distributing his photograph around the capital. He could have sworn that the men at Obaldi station had noticed him, and they could tell the authorities exactly which way Matthias had gone.

Matthias shivered and pulled the coat tighter. He had stolen it from a shop near Obaldi, lacking any funds to purchase one. He had done it without a second thought, with the crisp efficiency that came with the experience of dozens of operations. The shopkeeper had emerged from the stockroom with a shotgun only to find that Matthias had slipped behind him. Matthias snorted in disdain as he disarmed the man and cracked him across the temple with his own weapon. He was weakened by torture, and it still wasn't even a fight.

He battled down the anger that raged inside him as he considered what he had been reduced to. The man that his father had raised was not a petty thief, but that man was dead, killed in the Selliar Mountains and in the horrors of the interrogation room. Only this shell of Matthias was left, but Steif willing, it would be enough. Enough to carry out one last task.

He had worked quickly, methodically. He stripped off his prison clothes and stashed them in the stockroom with the unconscious shopkeeper. It would be a waste of time to hide them. The empire would search the road and find the shop empty soon enough, and know that Matthias had come this way. Matthias put on his pants and belt from the mountains, the ones that still surged with the Well's power, burning with anger that matched his own. Then he had grabbed another shirt from the stockroom, the coat to cover it, and the contents of the register for good measure.

Matthias half expected the police to be waiting for him when he emerged from the subway, but he made it up to street level without being hassled. As the crowd jostled him along, he again found himself gawking at the wealth and ostentation of Avali Nova. The Imperial Palace stood just across the street from the subway exit, behind a grand plaza and a fence the spikes of which were tipped with gold. The plaza was replete with statues and fountains, and the sprawling complex behind it seemed to be covered in gold plating from its base to its roof. A round marble arch was the entrance to the plaza, inscribed with the words, "Strength and Virtue Forever." Matthias sniggered as he passed it. He could not remember the empire ever having virtue, and its strength would soon come crashing down.

Matthias followed the crowds down the promenade that led from the palace, a broad avenue lined with trees on either side. The road was another monument to the empire's pretensions, wider than any road needed to be, with space for four two-horse carriages to travel abreast in each direction. No city would grow naturally around this kind of road, but Avali Nova had not grown naturally at all. It had been planned as an imperial capital after the New Empire re-conquered the heart of the Old. Avali Nova was a statement that the empire lived on, that it had never fallen. Until today.

Perhaps a third of a league from the palace, the great road narrowed to fit through a round archway and emptied into a market. At first glance it resembled the markets in the Fringes, but the goods were far more luxurious than most of the Fringes could afford. Fur-lined coats and silk scarves, bracelets and rings of gold and silver. There were rugs woven from Merguisian textiles, spices harvested in Kalid and Accarro, and even seafood refrigerated and shipped in from the Pascuayan coast, hundreds of leagues away.

Matthias retraced his steps to the road, turned right and strode through a series of round arches, each commemorating an Imperial victory. His anger grew with each one he passed. So many battles, so many people brought under the Orastan yoke. The yokes were even depicted in carvings on the arches, images of slaves lashed to carts, carrying the distinctive riches of their lands to the capital.

One arch stopped Matthias short. One of the vanquished was shown strapped to a stool, with twisting ropes drawing his head down into his knees. Suddenly Matthias's back and arms were screaming in pain and the scars around his wrists were burning as though he were back on the ropes himself. Matthias cursed the empire and pressed onward furiously, the torture replaying in his mind. He had been so weak, so impotent. It was too much. It had lasted too long, but no longer.

The arches ended at an open square with an enormous statue at its centre, a man standing with his arms spread, his right hand holding not a sword but a scroll. It was so planned, so deliberate. The man was not some hero of Orastus proper or even of the New Empire. He was Avalinus, the legendary founder of the original Avali, in what used to be the heart of the Old Empire but was now the colony of Orastino. The message was the same unconvincing protest that organized the entire city. Orastus had never fallen. The Old Empire continued, as it had since the dawn of time.

Across the square was the start of the capital's business district, a series of buildings made of stones of different colours. To Matthias's right was a much grander building than any of them, a structure that mimicked the great castles that had dominated this landscape in the days of the Old Empire. It boasted high towers, topped by rounded turrets and fringed with banners of silk. Only the old castles had been made of grey rocks from nearby quarries, while this one was the light brown of sandstone, imported for show from Accarro. The castle, Matthias knew, housed the bureaucracy of the Orastan government, from high-powered functionaries to lowly clerks. He had heard the newsboys in the subway stations, calling out that a tentative armistice had been reached on the Deugan front. No doubt the government would be busy this morning, clustered in this gaudy, defenceless structure, ripe for the picking.

Matthias's destination was to his left, though, across the square from the castle. The building had been a temple back in the days when the Orastans still kept to the five gods of the Old Empire. For centuries afterward it had been left in ruin until a luxury hotel was built on the site incorporating the marble columns of the original temple. The two largest columns were separated by a massive round archway, and within it was a heavy wooden door with brass handles in the shape of mountains. There were no mountains near Avali Nova, but that made no difference to Orastan arrogance. The original Avali was nestled in mountains far to the south, and that was what mattered.

Matthias pushed open the doors and made his way through the lobby to a polished wooden desk. Rugs made of Merguisian fabrics adorned the floors of the hotel, depicting the various lands over which the empire held sway. Matthias was quick to spot his own homeland of Pascuay, dolphins leaping out of the waters off the coast of a quaint fishing village. He wondered idly why the village did not appear to be collapsing beneath roaring flames. That was the way Matthias remembered Pascuay.

Matthias was not nearly wealthy enough to belong amid this luxury, but he had his lie planned. He sauntered to the desk and leaned against it, turning his head slightly so that the hood of his coat masked his face. "I apologize for my appearance," he said in the haughty tones of an Imperial dignitary. "I trust you will appreciate how certain matters require ... discretion. There is a young lady who will arrive later this morning who you will show to my chambers."

The concierge gave Matthias a knowing smile. No doubt this was not his first such request, so close to the seat of government in a place that radiated power. "Do you have a room with us, sir?"

Matthias held out the wad of banknotes he had lifted from the store where he'd stolen his coat. "I would expect so," he replied.

The concierge reached for the money, then hesitated. A lump rose in Matthias's throat as the man's eyes flickered to Matthias's wrist, and back up to his face. Had he noticed the scars from the ropes or the brand? The look lasted only an instant, though, before the man passed Matthias a key. "You will be on the fifth floor. The elevators are around the corner to your right. We will direct the young lady accordingly."

Matthias might have been paranoid, and the concierge may have noticed nothing, but it was too risky to take the chance. Matthias had never ridden an elevator, but he had heard stories of men being trapped. He walked down a different hallway instead and found a staircase. He took the first flight of stairs slowly, making sure to keep his tread soft in case someone in the lobby was listening. When he reached the landing he broke into a run, taking the steps two at a time, then rushing down the fifth floor hallway. He nearly opened the door of his room, then thought better of it. Instead he used the energy to pick the lock of a room down the hall, and upon finding it empty, slipped inside and bolted it shut behind him.

Even that limited exertion had Matthias panting, his back stiffening and his wounded shoulder erupting into pain. The guards had finally extracted the bullet and washed the wound once Matthias started cooperating, but they had waited too long, and Matthias had grown weak. He would never make it to Deugan or Wassia now, not even back to the Fringes. This way was his last, his only chance.

Matthias stacked a heavy dresser in front of the door and pushed the bed behind it to buttress the barricade. He crossed to the window, which looked out on the square below. It was still quiet. As he drew the curtains, he finally allowed himself to relax. He had made it, and he was perfectly placed. The palace, the castle, the business district, the main boulevard, the market, the homes and offices of countless functionaries, all were within a league of this very spot. A smile crept across Matthias's lips, a grim one. Avali Nova and the empire itself were in the palm of his hand.

Matthias calmed his anger just long enough to darken the chamber and draw himself into the map. Then he allowed the rage to surge back through him, to carry him. The belt around his waist had not been touched. It was filled to the brim with the energy, locked there for months, desperate to escape. The pants had been drained in the mountains, but there was still power left in them to serve as his source. Not enough that Matthias would dare try to detonate the belt from a distance, but enough that even in his weakened state, he could funnel it into a bomb that he kept close at hand, strapped to his own body. The highest of Good Steif's worlds were reserved for his martyrs.

He delved in, seizing the energy, conveying it to his improvised bomb. It went, slowly, but something was wrong. Matthias stopped, listened. The energy was tugging at him, pounding in his ears. He took a deep breath and settled into the map, opening his mind to it, blocking the anger. He felt a presence with him, a familiar one. Master Nono seemed to be alone, but the energy was pulling, insistent. Matthias focussed on Nono, tracing the lines of the power coursing through the Master's fingers, of the effects Nono was weaving.

Matthias stumbled backward. It couldn't be. Nono was in the Gateway, but his source of energy was tied to the Wassian Well. It was impossible, Matthias thought, until he felt a burning deep inside him, his entire body on fire at once. It lasted only an instant. Then the sensation passed, and the power beckoned, and he understood.

His years of study under Master Nono had taught Matthias that the feeling he had experienced upon entering his first Well, that the energy was probing him, trying to force its way inside, was frighteningly accurate. The energy implanted itself in its victims, and once it took root, it did not let go. It would leave a Well behind to remain with its host, a parasite, insidious. It was that communion between Matthias and the energy, the sliver of it that always remained in his brain, his lungs and his blood, that allowed him to return to any Well and use its power at will. That was why he did not need to wait an additional twenty-four hours each time for the energy to penetrate. It was already there.

That energy was supposed to be untouchable, though. For Nono to draw on another person's blood and body as a source, to freeze the power inside him, it was unheard of. The energy pounded faster than Matthias's heart. Who was the victim? He had no sooner asked the question than he knew the answer. The energy was agitated, yanking at Matthias, demanding to act through him. There was only one person on the Continent who had earned such loyalty.

Still Matthias resisted. To show the energy that he could. Then he said, in a low murmur, "I'll help her if you help me." He felt the power shift in him and knew that it understood. He smiled as he released it.

The energy moved faster than Matthias could have imagined, bridging the distance from Avali Nova to the Gateway in a blur of light and colour. He was vaguely aware of a crack, a wall collapsing, a pile of rubble. He felt energy rushing to Hallom, and then more rushing to him. Matthias took it and directed it into his belt, the bomb. The energy flowed freely, its anger at him forgotten. Matthias grinned as he whispered a prayer to Good Steif. For once in his life, the one god was truly hearing him.

Matthias felt Hallom entering the map again as he worked, and he threw up a barrier to keep her from his energy. He felt her probe at him, but he gripped the power tighter, and his barrier shimmered and held firm. Then her attacks ceased, and her attention turned to other *acambro* in the west.

Matthias released the breath that he hadn't realized he was holding and watched as Hallom drained the energy from Deugan. She was defusing bombs, Matthias realized. He entertained a moment of doubt. If Hallom was still alive, if she really could save Deugan ... but that thought was useless. Even with a belt of *acambro*, how would he ever reach Deugan, weak as he was, with the New Empire hunting him? Besides, Matthias thought, his anger rising again, Steif had already kept him from the west once. Here, in the heart of the New Empire, this was where his task lay. Where it had always been.

He struggled, bracing himself against the fury of the energy as he led it into the belt, emptying his source. The bomb glowed dangerously around him. He could not say how long he worked, so consumed was he in his task. At one point he heard a commotion in the square outside, and for an instant fear overwhelmed him. Then he redoubled his efforts, seizing the energy woven into the pants, guiding it into the bomb, praying and sweating and pressing. It was almost there.

Matthias heard footsteps thundering down the hall behind him. Frantically he emptied the last of the energy from his pants and hurled it into the bomb with a final, desperate push.

Nothing happened.

Matthias fought to stay in the map, to sense the power swirling around him. It was all in the belt now, trapped, pulsing with energy. It was on the brink of explosion, it needed only a touch more power to set it off, but Matthias's source was empty.

He wanted to scream. He tapped into the energy again and felt it writhing in fury, and something else too. Satisfaction. Matthias squeezed his eyes closed. He was starting to feel sick.

The energy had played him from the start. It may well have

wanted to save Caryn Hallom, but what it wanted more than anything was to be released, and into a Well, not a new belt of *acambro*. Matthias had kept this particular energy imprisoned for months, and he had broken his many promises to set it free. Now he saw the energy's revenge. It had tricked him into diverting just enough power to the Gateway to deplete his source, to doom his bomb to failure.

The footsteps in the hallway grew closer. Matthias heard pounding at the door of the hotel room. He needed to leave, now. The energy may have bested him once, but not forever. Matthias would flee to safety, but he would return to destroy the New Empire, as Good Steif willed. He still had an *acambro* belt and skill with its power. The setback could only be temporary.

Matthias raced to the far wall of the hotel room, yanked back the curtains and threw the window open. He recoiled as he stared into the square below. It had transformed. Empty not two hours ago, it was now filled with Orastan police astride their horses, guns aimed carefully at the building. The square was the most dangerous part, so vast and open. If he could make it to the business district, he could take to the rooftops and disappear into any of the buildings. Some magnates in the capital were even wealthy enough to own horseless vehicles, which could surely outrun the police horses. Nono's rain effect, Matthias thought at once, the mastery of the wind, that was what he needed. An effect that could carry Matthias high above the square, over to the rooftops that would be his salvation.

He heard the door shudder against his barricade. The Orastans would be in here any moment. Matthias focused on the energy, willing it to come to him, pushing it through simple, well-rehearsed motions.

Again, nothing happened.

More pounding at the door. The wood started to splinter. A gunshot passed through it, missing him. Matthias dug deeper into the energy, but it would not respond. He felt only its anger.

He had no time to wait. The power might be furious with him, but it had already taken its revenge, and Matthias needed it now, more than ever before. He begged it, shouted at it, willed it to aid him. He toned his mind to the energy and felt only an icy stubbornness in return. The door of the room splintered again. One more crash might bring it down.

He battled down the panic. He could not force the energy to help him, but he felt it pulsing, straining against the *acambro*. It hated being trapped, even if it hated Matthias more. He thought about the energy struggling, and suddenly he remembered something Nono had told him. He started laughing uncontrollably despite his fear. It was worse than risky, it was utter madness, but Matthias knew how to release the energy now. Another shot rang out from the doorway. There was no time to think, only to place his life into the hands of the one god.

He took a running start. The door of the hotel room came crashing down. A high-pitched ring blasted in his ears, louder than the gunshots. Matthias prayed to Good Steif and seized the *acambro* belt. Fire shot through his hands, and his arms and shoulders erupted in agony, the pain only driving him to run faster. He leapt through the window as the tendrils of flame grasped for his heart.

CHAPTER THIRTY-THREE

The energy was as charged and active as Caryn had ever seen it. It raced and darted, it ran and rolled, it frothed and boiled around her. The very air seethed with it.

The fighting at the entrance was brutal, the Breas crashing the Deugan lines. In the ever-shifting energy Caryn felt flares exploding, energy hands grasping, shields forming and winds howling, the Steffians making war. Behind her, Brenth Nono had coated his legs in the Well's power as a salve against his pain while his drill burrowed a new tunnel a few feet from the one that had collapsed. So many Secrets-users with a source that was unlimited, so many effects darting back and forth at once, and Caryn was in the centre of it, draining the bombs and sealing them, watching the lights in the map dim, fade and vanish.

The energy was making up for the time it had lost when Nono blocked her out. Caryn sealed the last Czemers bomb effortlessly, drained the threats to Tomasburg and nearby Lindau, then turned to Carrak-on-Sea, the city by the ocean she had once called home. Carrak was more difficult, resting at the opposite corner of Deugan, but Caryn managed it delicately, draining its three bombs and reaching carefully across the distance to sew the *acambro* shut. When she finally turned her attention to Stamburg, far to the south, it was simple by comparison.

Nono's tunnel was nearly complete. She saw him working out of the corner of her eye, pressing the swirling light deeper into the darkness, and despite her urgency, Caryn found herself remembering.

The tunnel in Wassia had widened as Jayla and Brenner pressed into it together, the light from their drills cascading brilliantly off the walls of the cavern. They worked without speaking, enraptured by the Well's glory. The green rocks ground into dust, and Jayla felt elated, but she could not ignore Brenner's look. The way his face darkened, the way he set his jaw, the way he refused to look in her direction. He knew, even as she did.

It was the same look Brenth Nono wore now, drilling into a new set of rocks in a new cavern. Reluctantly she ripped her gaze away from him and toward the battle at the entrance. The fighting was turning against them. Nono saw it too. He finished the tunnel, the white light ceasing abruptly. He caught Caryn's eye, then turned sharply away, and Caryn did the same. It was just like Wassia. She had a task to finish.

She was sliding through the map to bring the Brea bombs closer when she noticed a new light flickering out of the corner of her eye. She stepped backward and tried to orient herself. South of the Orastan Well, west of Accarro. She quickly ran through her Orastan geography in her mind. Could that be Avali Nova, the Imperial capital? The light went orange, then yellow, then red, the Steffians trying to detonate the *acambro*. Caryn reached for it and screamed as her mind was repelled by an invisible barrier. She felt her panic rising. She probed at the barrier more carefully. Again it held.

Then the energy was surrounding her, soothing her. Avali Nova shrank in her map, the Brea bombs grew brighter. She took several deep breaths as she understood what the energy was telling her. It had the Orastan situation in hand. She was to focus on Brealand.

Caryn closed her eyes and used her good hand to wipe the sweat from her face. When she opened them, Nono was staring at her. He said only one word: "Go." He was lying on the ground several feet away, his legs still trapped beneath the rubble. At the entrance of the cavern their men were dying, falling back from the trench. "Go," Nono shouted, louder. He craned his neck toward the tunnel. "They're almost on us and my legs are still trapped. Get out of here."

He was right. Every second brought another change to the battle, each worse than the one before. Their lines were struggling to hold together, their men edging further and further backward. The Breas pressed on, massed and brutal. She had already sealed all the *acambro* in Deugan, and the energy had told her Avali Nova was not a threat. She should run while she still had the chance.

Then she thought of Michael Ravencliffe and knew that she never would. Caryn Hallom had not come here to save Deugan. She had come here to save the Continent. Ravencliffe was not the only one who could sacrifice.

That didn't mean that Nono had to. "You go!" she shouted at him. "Dig out your legs, you still have time!" Just shouting it strengthened her resolve. She dove back into the map, scanning it for the three lights that marked Portsmouth, the farthest of the Brea cities. She seized the first bomb and drained it, and followed with the second and the third. She considered sealing them, but a glance at the battle warned her against it. Sealing was careful and delicate work, and the Breas and Steffians were closing in. Getting the energy out of the *acambro* was the priority.

She glanced at Nono as her mind reached for Arlington, the next Brea city along the coast. He hadn't moved. His drill had vanished. "Drill yourself out!" she screamed. "Get out!" The energy leapt to her, the *acambro* emptying, one, the second, the third. Still Nono lay motionless, his face screwed up in concentration. She felt energy moving and shifting without understanding. What was he doing?

Caryn targeted Hastingvale, the capital of the Brea Realm. One, two, three. She pictured Ravencliffe as she drew the power from the *acambro*, his face a careful mask, only the slightest motion in his eyes betraying his relief and his pride.

Their line broke.

Caryn felt it happen before she heard the screams or saw the madness. The Breas had driven a wedge into the centre of the Deugan defenders and now they were scattering, diving to the ground desperately as the Brea wave picked them off. One man came hurtling near Caryn's feet only to be shot from across the cavern and collapse, moaning. Caryn's head was pounding, but she could not let up. Sutton, deep in the interior, was closer to her than the coastal cities she'd defused already. She targeted it and drained it, one bomb after the other.

A Deugan flung a grenade toward the entrance of the cavern and the blast was deafening. For a moment the Breas were thrown into disarray. A body smacked into the wall a foot from Caryn's head and half of a Brea leg splattered the ground near Nono. Caryn looked up at the sound. Nono hadn't moved; his legs were still trapped. His face was solemn, but there was an eagerness that she hadn't seen recently. What was he doing? He could have been deep in the tunnel by now, if only he'd gone. At least one of them could have escaped.

Now it was too late. The Breas had recovered from the confusion of the grenade. The surviving Deugans had formed a new line at a spot where the cavern narrowed, and the Breas were charging them with rifles and bayonets. All around her men fought and screamed and died. Caryn focused on Myerston, the last of the Brea cities still lit with *acambro*. She drained the first bomb with more difficulty than she expected. The city was just across the border, barely farther than Czemers, but Caryn's heart was racing, and the battle made it difficult to think. She forced her mind toward the second bomb, felt it, and with an effort managed to ease the power out of the *acambro*. There was one bomb left.

The Deugan soldiers were falling faster than the *acambro* was. The cavern echoed as much with the groans of the wounded as it did with gunfire. Nono remained in place, shielded from the Brea bullets by the Deugan survivors, his face still screwed up in concentration, and then another transformation. He looked straight at Caryn, and his mouth opened in shock. Staring at him, she thought she saw a tear glistening in his eye.

She emptied the last bomb just as the guns fell silent.

She would never be used to battles. She would never understand the sudden shifts of momentum, the way that calm erupted into madness and madness gave way to calm with barely a warning. She would never be used to the death and horror surrounding her.

Caryn reached into the map, wondering if she could still seal some of the Brea bombs. The Brea soldiers were standing in the cavern, surveying the few Deugan survivors. Several had guns trained on Brenth Nono, trapped beneath the rubble. None of them paid Caryn any attention.

There were at least twenty Brea soldiers. At first Caryn thought that their defenders had decimated the enemy, but then she realized that there must be other Breas in the Well, searching for other Deugan strongholds. There was no way out. Yet still the Breas pointedly ignored her, focusing on Nono as though she didn't exist.

Caryn felt the map slipping away from her, and she let it go. The cavern brightened to orange, and Nono, even with the rifles pointed at him, smiled in satisfaction. Then the Brea lines parted and four new men walked through. Caryn recognized none of them, but a glance at the paleness of their skin told their story. The Master of Secrets had been captured, and the Steffians would decide his fate.

The Steffian leader stepped toward Nono, pistol ready, while the others followed. The leader's gaze was fixed on Nono, but the others' eyes were darting around the cavern. Caryn was certain that one or two of them looked straight at her, but like the Breas, they seemed to register nothing. It was as though she was —

She held her hand in front of her face, and suddenly she understood why Brenth Nono had not escaped the cavern when he had the chance. Tears welled in her own eyes as she understood the sacrifice that he had made for her.

The Steffian leader stopped when he was about five feet from Nono and stared down at the captured traitor. If it disturbed Nono, he did not show it. He merely looked up at the other man, and said, "Rusul."

"Where is she?" Rusul asked. He could not see Caryn, mere feet from where he stood, and no wonder. Looking down at her legs, Caryn could not see herself either. Vividly she remembered a different cavern in a different Well, a ceiling turned invisible and a gorgeous sky beyond it, stars glittering above her and the boy she would come to love.

Nono's look of fear was an act, but perhaps Rusul wouldn't realize it. Nono looked at the gun in the Steffian's hand and pointed behind him. "The tunnel," he said, making his voice quaver, but his eyes flitted to where Caryn was lying, and then to the entrance of the cavern. Telling her to leave, now.

Rusul motioned to one of his Steffians. "Find her." The man crawled into the tunnel. Two of the Brea soldiers followed him, rifles in hand. Caryn rose. She stepped delicately around the body that lay at her feet, careful not to disturb it lest she give herself away. She headed toward the entrance at the opposite end of the cavern.

"Why?" Rusul asked Nono. The Steffians stepped up alongside him. Some of the Breas kept their rifles trained on Nono. Others moved around the cavern to the wounded Deugans, disarming and binding the ones who might survive and giving mercy to the rest.

Nono shrugged. He was buying time for her, Caryn realized, but she didn't want to leave him again. She had promised to go with him, and after what he had done for her, she could not let Nono die. It may be risky, two of them against more than twenty, but she had been prepared to sacrifice herself just moments ago to save Brealand. Of course she would do as much for a closer friend.

Nono spoke softly. "There are things in this life that a man cannot control. The Well's power is but one. When another arose in me, I could only trust it was the will of Good Steif that I follow it."

"You admit that you've betrayed your brothers?" Rusul asked. Caryn stopped, hovering over the rifle of one of their fallen soldiers. She could take it, but wouldn't she be noticed? Even if she were invisible, would the Breas not see a gun floating in the air?

Nono shook his head, as though disappointed. "You are not my brothers, Rusul," he said. "Master Gamoy saw to that."

Rusul did not look surprised. Caryn still hesitated by the rifle, trying to decide what to do. Nono closed his eyes. Rusul levelled the pistol at Nono's head, and before Caryn could react, he squeezed the trigger.

Two men screamed then, but Brenth Nono was not one of them.

The Steffian Secrets-users were collapsed on the ground, clutching at their heads and howling in agony. Rusul stared at the pistol that had failed to fire, and now the nearest Breas shouted as their rifles were ripped out of their hands and spun around against them. Six gunshots rang out at once and six Breas fell, not the ones he'd just disarmed, but others whose rifles clattered to the ground as they collapsed. The Breas had no time to return fire before the rifles shifted, soaring through the air and pressing against six more Brea temples. Their panic was palpable, and now Nono's drill was back, the swirling white light clearing the rubble that had collapsed around his legs, but it was brighter than before, searing, blinding. The Breas could scarcely look in his direction, but Caryn caught a glimpse of Rusul crawling toward Nono before his pistol spun around, un-jammed, and fired into Rusul's stomach. *Nono's not the only one who can use energy hands*, Caryn thought before the cavern pitched wildly and her energy hand dissolved into mist. She felt the Well's power inside her, deep and sinister, more imminent and penetrating than ever before.

The Breas were recovering from their blindness and advancing toward Nono again, and then an image played in Caryn's mind of herself in the doorway, starkly visible against the bright northern sun.

Nono would not be able to keep her invisible for long, Caryn realized, and he was telling her so. He might be able to hold off the Breas and escape into the tunnel, but not while keeping her hidden. If they were both to survive, she needed to move, now.

She went. Caryn inched toward the entrance of the cavern, flattening herself against the walls so that the Breas would not accidentally brush against her. When she finally reached the mouth, she glanced back at Nono. His legs were free, the two Secrets-users were still writhing on the ground, and the Breas were nearly upon him. She felt the energy coursing through her, but she thought it was starting to weaken and felt a pang of fear. She whispered an apology to Nono and ran.

Caryn knew the place she had to reach before the invisibility wore off. She pushed through the Well, but her legs felt stiffer and heavier by the minute. Halfway to the ramp her joints were aching and it was difficult to go on. She forced herself, pausing only when Breas or Steffians ran past her, oblivious. Caryn stumbled, her gait uncertain. Something was happening, something terrible.

The sun beat down on her from above, magnifying the heat of the Well even now in the dead of winter. It had been spring when she made her last escape. Jayla and Brenner had crawled over the dust that had been left when their drills faded, when the sunlight, bright and beautiful, snuck through what remained of the barricade. They paused there, blinking and shielding their eyes. Then they shouted and hugged each other, but soon it ended, and Brenner could only say, "Please don't go."

He'd asked her to go this time, though, and on Caryn pressed. She didn't understand why it was so difficult. The entrance to her tunnel lay just ahead, and she stumbled desperately toward it. Her shoes were starting to come back into focus, she noticed in a panic, and she broke into a run, or as close to one as her leaden body could manage. She saw another team of Breas turning a corner. They hadn't seen her; the effect still had some power, but she had only seconds to spare. She leapt through the gaping hole in the ground, braving the four-foot drop onto the ramp below. The impact of her fall stole the breath from her, and it was all she could do to roll down the ramp, away from the hole and out of sight of the Brea soldiers above.

"You're going to, aren't you," Brenner said.

It was burned into Jayla. How the moment she'd decided that she needed more than comfort, the drill had started spinning in her hands. "I'm so sorry," she whispered.

Brenner stared at the Well, the rock formations and the ridges. Their cavern was one among many here. "It's the energy, isn't it."

How could she answer that? It had been Jayla's decision, but the energy's response to it had confirmed that she was doing the right thing. "Jayla, the energy is not your friend," Brenner said. "It's going to ruin you."

"It won't," Jayla insisted. She was angry now at the way he always turned it back on the energy, as though Jayla were only its pawn. As though she didn't have a mind of her own. She had never noticed it when they were inside the cavern, but after only minutes in the sunlight, it was suddenly infuriating. "I'm going to walk out of this Well and never see or hear from the energy again."

Brenner laughed. "You? You can't give it up." He paced to the edge of the cavern, then back to the spot outside where Jayla was standing. "Apparently you can give me up, though," he muttered.

"It's not easy," Jayla said quietly, and thankfully that silenced him. He had never truly understood her, for all the time they had spent together, but he could read her eyes when she said it, and he knew that she was telling the truth. "I think I need a break from the past. I need to put all of this behind me and strike out on my own, and that will be better for you too. You're my best friend on the Continent, but what if I said that's all I wanted? Friendship? Would you be able to live with that?"

There wasn't even a moment's hesitation. "I want you with me, Jayla. It doesn't matter what we call ourselves. I need you."

"No," Jayla said, not sure where she had learned her strength, the gravity in her voice. "You don't need anybody, Brenner, don't you see that? Don't you know how smart, loving, caring, considerate you are? You can change the Continent, just like Professor Terial said. You don't need me."

"You would help," he said. "Besides, we'll be safer travelling together."

"We'll be safer travelling apart," Jayla said firmly. "The government will be looking for us as soon as they find out we've survived. What would you think if you saw two people looking like older versions of us, together? We'll never get across the border."

"That's not your real reason."

No, Jayla thought. The real reason was that part of her still was in love with him. She was attached to him, and she knew what that meant. Fighting through his mood swings, comforting him in the dark places, drawing him out of his loneliness. All skills she had prided herself on, and nothing for which she had a moment's regret, but with twenty-five years already stolen from her...

"I would hold you back, too," she told him. "We would both be grounded here, in the Well, in what we had together. We would forget that the Well is only a symptom. That we need something to fight for, not just something to fight against."

Inexplicably, Brenner smiled, and that made Jayla even sadder. "You're never going to forget that," he said.

An hour later, Jayla's sack was packed with the meagre belongings that she had taken into the Well and with the gifts that Professor Terial had left her to help start her new life. Brenner had told Jayla of his plan to head to Amim, and although Jayla was horrified — Amim was still under Wassian control, even if it had been recently granted home rule — she bit her tongue. Since she wasn't letting Brenner come with her, she couldn't very well tell him where to go on his own. Instead Jayla controlled her emotions, made her face a mask and slung the sack over her shoulder, feeling its weight like an anchor.

Brenner caught up with her just outside the cavern. "Please."

So much for controlling her emotions. She felt her facade cracking and she nearly ran to him, but there was enough resolve left in her to say, "I'm sorry."

"Please don't go."

Jayla went. Shouldering the sack, placing one foot in front of the other, trying to hold back her tears.

Fourteen years later, in a tunnel beneath the Gateway Well, she tried to do the same. On her first attempt to rise her knee gave out, and she tumbled painfully back to the ground. Scared but determined, she grasped the wall of the tunnel with her good right hand and pulled herself into a standing position. Holding the wall for support, she took one step at a time, willing herself back down the path toward Eolanis satellite and the Gateway Fort.

She was almost at the edge of the Well when she felt numbness in her feet, working its way up through her body. At first she wondered if she had truly damaged her legs, but soon she realized it was just the energy sending her a vision. Nono was in the large tunnel that led north into the mountains. The smaller tunnel he had dug had caved in and collapsed, trapping the Brea army on the other side. He was safe.

Tears welled in her eyes again, and she struggled to find the energy herself to send him an image back, showing him that she was safe too, deep in the tunnel that would lead her to the fort. Then, unconsciously, another image came to mind, an image of Jayla, fourteen years earlier, being helped into a carriage on a dark road in Wassia. Jayla had exited the Wassian Well at its northern end, since the base camps and their watchers were stationed at the east and west. Although it was spring and the days were lengthening, the sun had nearly set by the time she reached the road going northward. After six months in the heat of the Well, the southern evening felt bitterly cold.

The carriage had come hurtling around a corner, pulled by two horses that reared up suddenly to stop for her. In the fading light of day Jayla could see that it was occupied by a couple around her parents' age, which was to say, the age Jayla herself appeared to be. "What are you doing in the road?" the man shouted at her.

"Looking for a ride to Valleda," Jayla shouted back with as much confidence as she could muster. It was the city near the border where the professor's contact lived, the one who could forge the documents that would allow Jayla to enter Deugan.

The couple conferred quietly until finally the man shouted, "We can drop you at the station in Tagras, and you can catch a train from there." Jayla thanked him, and his wife reached down to help Jayla into the carriage. The woman introduced herself as Esga, and her husband as Steno. Then Steno snapped the reins, and the horses took off at their breakneck pace.

For a time Jayla was silent, lost in her thoughts. She still could not believe that she and Brenner had been playing together in the Well that very morning. Now she was travelling on a dark road northward while he headed south. It was starting to sink in that she might never see him again.

"What's your name?" Esga prompted her, when the silence stretched on too long.

For a time Jayla could not answer. She wondered if Brenner had left the Well yet. If he would make it to Amim alive. She wondered whether he hated her, and whether she could blame him.

Jayla paused, swallowed, and forced her thoughts back to the present. She needed to let the Well go. For Brenner's sake, as well as her own.

"My name is Caryn," Jayla said, tracing a bow in the Deugan style. "Caryn Hallom."

CHAPTER THIRTY-FOUR

Caryn Hallom lay on the hard stone floor of the tunnel, trying to fight down the tears. It was dark and suddenly cold. A beam of green light spun behind her as the underground gate locked into place. The heat and pressure of the Well had vanished, and with the energy gone Caryn felt only the injustice in what it had done to her.

Brenth Nono could not have known. What he had done was new and extraordinary. True, Caryn had turned a ceiling invisible years ago, but she was confident that nobody had ever attempted it on a living human being. Nono's desperate measure required the energy to come to her en masse, coursing through her and shaping her. It was complex and difficult, and it had proven too much for Caryn's body to withstand. She had absorbed too much of the Well's poison, and too quickly.

The light was brightest just inside the circular gate. It was there that the yellow and blue from the ground and the orange from the walls and the green from the doorway merged and mingled, and it was there that Caryn had her first good look at her hand and arm. The skin was loose, wrinkled. She rolled up her pant leg, bending down with difficulty, only to see that her skin was mottled and sensitive, the veins blue and prominent. Running her good hand over her face, she could feel the deeper lines around her eyes. Caryn guessed that she had the body of a woman who had spent nearly eighty years in this life. She certainly felt that way.

It wasn't fair. The tears started coming now, unbidden. She had already lost twenty-five years in the Wassian Well. She couldn't afford to lose another twenty-five now, in the space of minutes, because she had stumbled into a power too intense for her weakened body. This life had never been long enough for all the things that she wanted to see and hear and experience, and now, so suddenly, entire decades had been stolen from her. Again.

She wanted to punch the walls. She wanted to scream. Why now, after everything she had gone through? Why, after Nono had nearly sacrificed his life to save her, was she again staring death in the face, not down the barrel of a rifle or the roaring of an *acambro* bomb, but in the harsh reality of an old age come too soon? She had spent only thirty years in this life, for Lessandro's sake! How many years would she have left?

Yet asking that question gave Caryn Hallom the answer. She had more time left than Lana or Hans did. More time than Michael Ravencliffe. More time than any of the boys who had died to protect her and Nono today, or the soldiers who were dying at the Hermann Gap or in the approaches to the Gateway Fort. Nono's intervention might have aged her, but it had also saved her life. When she thought about the sacrifices being made all around her, the sacrifice that she herself had nearly made that very morning, Caryn realized that every day she was granted in this life was a gift. It would be enough for her.

Caryn tried to rise on her ancient knees and couldn't. A few moments ago that might have sent her into deeper despair, but now it only fed her determination. She clenched her right hand into a fist and rubbed feeling into her legs. Then she used her feet and her good arm to half-crawl, half drag herself down the tunnel toward the Gateway Fort.

It was slow going, and Caryn's body ached with every inch she travelled. At times she despaired of ever making it back to Eolanis satellite, but she gritted her teeth, swore at the energy and pressed on. Several times her aging body forced her to stop and rest, but a fire was burning inside her now. Each time she felt like giving up, she would push herself harder, her motivation drowning her pain.

Still, the journey took hours. The tunnel rose and fell, twisted and turned, and through it Caryn crawled, willing herself to survive. She would make it to Eolanis, she told herself, but what would she find when she got there? The Breas had defeated the Deugan force in the Well. By now they may have stormed the satellite forts too, or even the Gateway Fort itself.

When Caryn finally caught a glimpse of electric lighting, she was so overwhelmed that she nearly cried. Despite her aching legs, she forced herself to crawl even faster until she heard the click of a rifle and a harsh whisper. "Who's there?" Clear, unaccented Orastan. Caryn breathed a sigh of relief. The voice was Deugan.

Men were shifting all around her. It was too dark to count them. "Don't shoot," she said in a quavering tone that did not sound like her own voice. Caryn struggled toward the electric light, the touches of it that snuck into the tunnel through the edges of the trapdoor below Eolanis satellite.

Caryn heard gasps and curses as the thin shaft of light fell on her. As her eyes adjusted, she saw that there were a dozen soldiers hiding in the tunnel. None of them seemed to recognize her, but Caryn knew one of them. Gert had been Janusz and Marwin's drill sergeant when they first joined the fort's garrison. Caryn wondered how close the sergeant had been to the two men who had betrayed her. Perhaps it was good that Nono's effect had aged her beyond recognition.

"Who are you?" Gert demanded.

"I came from Varszi," Caryn said, naming one of the villages near the fort. "A few of us went to the Well to hide from the fighting. We didn't know there would be fighting right there. I found this tunnel."

She was about to say more when they heard more footsteps, a member of the team returning to them, and Caryn was forgotten. "What did you find?" Gert snapped at the new man. He must have been sent as a scout, and he must have found another way out of the tunnel without passing through the Well. During her crawl, Caryn had seen one or two spots where shells had brought the tunnel close to collapse and sunlight peeked through the hard-packed earth.

"The Breas have Carmel and Lessandro," the scout reported. "The main gunnery's pounding them, though. Soon those two forts will be demolished like Eolanis here."

"There won't be any satellites left, then," Gert said with obvious dismay. "What else?"

"Sir," the scout said hesitantly, "the Breas — they breached the east wall. They're in the main fort."

There was a chorus of grunts and curses from the assembled soldiers, and Caryn's heart sank. The garrison didn't have the numbers to defeat the Breas in hand-to-hand combat. If the fort had been breached, the battle was lost.

Gert was not ready to give up, though. "We need to get back to the fort," he said. "We've been hiding down here too long. If the Breas have breached the east wall, we need every man we can get inside."

The soldiers stirred, but none looked too eager. It sounded like suicide. What could thirteen men do against the Brea onslaught? How would they even make it back to the fort if, as the scout also informed them, the Breas had captured the moat and the east wall, and were pounding at the main entrance?

Gert knew what his men were thinking. "Do you really think you're so worthless that you can't make a difference back there?" He spoke with the drill sergeant's snarl, but it got the soldiers' attention. "Let me tell you something. You, every single one of you, are fighting men of Deugan, and every single one of you knows the Gateway Fort better than you know your own mothers."

"Not as well as I know Voy's mother," one of the soldiers piped up, and another one shoved him. Laughter helped in times like these.

"We don't have to beat the Breas by ourselves," Sergeant Gert continued. "The Third Army is coming. They're coming for us, and our job is to hold this Gods-damned fort until they get their sorry asses over here. And that, men, is something we can do. The fort is a maze of hallways. Hundreds of choke points where two men can hold off an army. Choke points that we know, that they don't. We can bleed them at every passage, but first we need to get back inside our fort."

This time the groans were gone. Cheers went up around her, the men rallying to their leader. Only the scout hung back. "What about her?" he asked, pointing at Caryn.

"Probably safest here," one of the soldiers said.

Others nodded, but not the scout. "We need all of us with the sarge. We can't leave her alone here."

"You really want to drag her into a war zone, son?" Gert asked. It was as though Caryn had become invisible again. None of them deigned to ask her opinion. *Is that the fate of old women?* she wondered. *To be shunted aside, ignored?* Caryn Hallom was not ready for that yet. She cleared her throat loudly, and said, "I'd like to come with you."

"It's going to be dangerous," the sergeant said. "You're better off here, if you ask me."

"Permission to speak, Sarge?" the scout asked.

"Yes," Gert said, turning to him. "I asked you a Gods-damned question, didn't I?"

The scout swallowed. "She's already in a war zone," he said. "The entrances to this tunnel are behind Brea lines. We can't spare the men to stay with her, but how's she going to reach the medical bay without us? If she wants to stay with Deugan soldiers and take the risk, I say we should let her."

"Do you even know this woman?" Gert asked.

"No, sir," the scout replied at once. "It's just — I thought this was the sort of thing all of us enlisted for. Back when we didn't know any better, I mean."

Gert considered that for a moment. Then he said to Caryn, "Stay at the rear and keep quiet. We'll get you to medical." It wasn't much, Caryn thought, but there was some significance in the scout's memory that their true purpose was not to invade enemies or open trade routes; that their real purpose was to protect people who couldn't protect themselves. There was something in a brief exchange between a private and the sergeant he was not afraid to face down, which boded well for Deugan and democracy.

Two soldiers pushed open the trapdoor. Caryn knew from long experience that it led to an alcove the other door of which was camouflaged into a wall, nearly impossible to find. She blinked as electric light flooded into the tunnel. She was helped up into the alcove, and then the soldiers opened the door to the satellite's sub-basement and rolled a grenade through it. The explosion was not as deafening as Caryn had expected. It was her hearing, after all. Another casualty of age and the Well's power.

Caryn remained behind as the thirteen men pressed into the sub-basement. There were gunshots and another grenade blast, then silence, then another round of gunshots and screams, more furious but more distant. Caryn waited in the alcove, hating her aged body and her helplessness. Finally the scout returned. "All clear," he said. "There were only five Breas, and the grenade scattered them."

"How are our men?" she asked.

"Two down," was all he said, and she could tell he did not want to provide any further answers. He lent her his arm and she leaned on it, following him through the sub-basement. Her knees screamed at the flight of stairs, and the landing was so slick with blood that she nearly fell. She could not remember ever being this weak, even in the worst moments in the Wassian Well when she could barely breathe. Tears welled in her eyes again as she contemplated the years that the energy had stolen.

They made for the underground tunnel linking Eolanis to the main fort. Gert stopped them just outside the tunnel and listened. "Breas," he whispered. "Hiding." The path to Carmel had collapsed, and aboveground the Breas held the moat, the area around the main entrance and the satellites on either side of them. This tunnel was the only route back to the fort. "Let's flush 'em out," Gert said.

They did it with grenades, rolling one into the tunnel at a time, listening to the panic that ensued. The Brea footsteps were moving away from Eolanis toward the fort, and Gert ordered his men forward, rifles blazing. Again Caryn was left behind with nothing to do but listen to the gunshots and the screams. She felt a great relief when the scout finally returned to her. "We ripped through them," he assured her. His uniform was splattered with blood. "When our men at the other end of the tunnel realized what was happening, they jumped in. We took the Breas from both sides."

"Are you okay?" she asked.

"I'm not hurt," he said. It was only a partial answer. "Come on."

Back in the Gateway Fort, they received an update on the battle from the soldiers who were guarding the other end of the tunnel. Here in the basement, Deugan soldiers were scattered in small teams, holding choke points in the narrow corridors. After two large attack waves were decimated, the Breas had mostly given up on trying to conquer the basement and its mounds of arms and ammunition. Instead their enemies were making an all-out push aboveground toward the communications hub, the heart of the fort. The Breas already controlled most of the eastern half of the fort, and at the main entrance to the north, they had pushed back the Deugan defenders and stormed the gunnery. The situation looked dire. The Breas could come at the communications hub from two directions, and there weren't enough Deugans to fight them.

Still Sergeant Gert showed no sign of resignation. "They will never take this fort," he announced. Eight soldiers had survived, including Gert himself, of the thirteen Caryn had met beneath Eolanis satellite. Gert pointed to two of them. "You take our guest to medical," he said. "When you've got her there, head straight for comm hub. The rest of us are heading north of comm hub now. We're going to set our Brea friends an ambush."

The teams split up when they emerged from the basement, and Caryn and her two defenders wandered the hallways of the fort, quiet and wary. Her diminished hearing made her feel almost blind, and she crept forward with difficulty. They had nearly reached the medical bay when Caryn heard the gunshot.

One of Caryn's guards collapsed to the ground as the other shoved her behind him and fired his rifle toward the ceiling. A Brea soldier screamed and tumbled to the floor from the spot above them where he had strapped himself to the wall, waiting in ambush. Two other Breas dropped to the ground and started firing. One of them took a bullet to the chest just as the Deugan soldier was hit in the shoulder, dropping his rifle and shouting in pain. The surviving Brea finished him off, then turned to Caryn, his own rifle ready. Her age would not protect her, Caryn could see that in the boy's eyes. She watched helplessly as he lined her up. He was about to shoot when another gun fired and the Brea soldier crumpled to the ground. Caryn wanted to cry as she pulled herself to her feet.

Hertha was standing protectively over her, a smoking rifle in her hand. The head of the fort's nursing staff was white with a rage that Caryn had never seen in her before. "What kind of monster ambushes an old woman outside a *medical bay*?" Hertha shrieked in fury. She looked around wildly, pointing with her rifle until she was satisfied that there weren't any more Breas nearby. Turning to Caryn, taking deep breaths, she said, "Come on."

Stunned, Caryn followed her. Her knees were still weak and painful, but she hobbled along as best she could. Hertha had told Caryn, back in the Gateway Well, that she had demanded the military teach her to shoot, but Caryn had the impression that the training had been restricted to targets at a range. Caryn did not think that Hertha had ever fired a gun in combat before.

They passed the medical bay, but Hertha continued walking, pointing her rifle ahead of them. "Where are we going?" Caryn asked.

"Comm hub, of course," Hertha said. "The general needs to know what happened at the Well, whether you were able to take out the *acambro* bombs."

Caryn froze in surprise. "You know me?"

Hertha laughed, a shocking, beautiful sound amid the horror of the battle. "Of course," she said, bowing. "My lady. What are a few years between friends?"

"Nothing at all," Caryn said, and then she did start to cry, not from the brutality of battle but from joy. She had not realized until that moment how terrible it felt to be forgotten. Hertha's recognition alone gave Caryn new strength, a way to press against the wall of pain and exhaustion that had been with her ever since Ravencliffe took his life. That was less than twenty-four hours ago. It was difficult to believe with all that had happened since.

"I take it you have the energy to thank for your appearance?" Hertha asked. They were taking a roundabout route to the communications hub; Hertha wanted to approach it from the south, since the Breas were coming in force from the east and north. "The friend and ally you could not bear to let go? Do you still believe the Well must be appeased, whatever the cost?"

"I don't know what to believe," Caryn said honestly. She could not think about the energy now, not when the Breas were storming the fort in force, threatening to undo all that she and Nono and Ravencliffe had achieved. "The energy is what it is," Caryn added. "It's difficult for me to think of it in terms of right and wrong." Hertha nodded, her face expressionless, and pressed onward.

They finally came upon the fort's south entrance. A small team of soldiers guarded it, and they shouted at the women to return to the medical bay, but Hertha ignored them and led Caryn down the large hallway toward the communications hub. They crept slowly, Caryn leaning on Hertha for support as her knee threatened to give out. They had made it only a few feet when the mass of Deugan soldiers came into view ahead of them.

They were retreating.

The Deugans were moving backward, trying to fend off the Brea onslaught. They were well organized, giving ground slowly, but they were retreating all the same, the Breas pushing them back. Hertha grabbed Caryn, taking her useless arm by mistake, but managed to drag her into a hallway out of the way of the approaching armies. Caryn leaned against the wall of the corridor as she struggled against her panic. The communications hub was lost and Deugan was retreating, ever retreating. Soon their soldiers would be pinned against the fort's south entrance, and Caryn saw with horror that the entrance was being opened. She clung to Hertha. The Deugan soldiers hadn't noticed yet, they were too focused on the oncoming Breas, their ranks were about to be taken in the rear —

A horse leapt through the opening doorway, its rider grasping a massive banner on a spiked metal pole. The Deugans threw themselves into alcoves or pressed themselves against walls as the banner hurtled toward the leader of the Brea army, the spike crunching into his throat. Now other horses were leaping through the breach, the infantry and the remainder of the fort's garrison falling in behind them. As the mass of horses and men thundered through the corridors of the Gateway Fort and as the Breas started to fall backward in disarray, Caryn finally registered the device on the massive blue banner. The circle divided into twenty-nine equal slices. The Deugan Wheel.

*

After it was over, Caryn sat with General Freed in his office, listening as he filled her in on the parts of the battle she had missed. The Third Army had taken the Hermann Gap, aided by the New Empire's guns in the Selliar Mountains, before racing northward to relieve the Gateway Fort. The Breas had lost their own mountain guns to a mysterious avalanche, and while Captain Toppel had taken a wound on his mission, he was recovering in a village near Hermannsburg and was expected to survive. The general had released Ralf Danzig and his conspirators for the battle, since he needed every fighting man, and Danzig had died a hero's death holding the east wall of the fort against the Breas. Janusz had survived the battle as one of the last defenders of the communications hub and had fought well during the retreat after it was lost. The battle had very nearly ended in disaster, but the garrison had done its job. They had held the Breas off just long enough.

His own stories finished, Freed leaned across his desk toward Caryn. "Did Nono do this to you?" he asked, anger crossing his face.

"Not on purpose," Caryn said. Now that the fighting was over and she had allowed herself to relax, she felt drained. The emotional pain was hitting her as the physical pain receded. "He saved my life." The more she thought about it, the more she was convinced that Nono really had intended to sacrifice his life for hers. He could not have known that he would defeat the Breas and Steffians, alone against so many. He must have intended to die for her, yet in the end he had let her go. He had directed her out the mouth of the cavern while he escaped through a tunnel at its rear. He must have known then that he would never see Caryn again, and Caryn was starting to realize the same.

"What happened to him?" Freed asked.

It was a difficult question. Freed had been angry with her for lying to him in the past, and she had grown to respect and even admire the general. On the other hand, Brenth Nono had made powerful enemies, betraying the Steffians and causing scores of Brea deaths. He was crawling into mountains that might still be swarming with Steffian operatives and Imperial soldiers, and his age and skin tone would make it difficult for him to disappear in the Range as he'd planned. It might be easier for him if the Continent thought he had perished in the Gateway Well, and Caryn owed him that much.

She cast her eyes down to the floor. "The Breas rounded up a handful of prisoners," she said. "Nobody else in that cavern survived."

"You did," Freed reminded her. He walked around his desk and hesitated before bending down and taking Caryn's good hand. It felt nice. Comforting. "I am so sorry," Freed said. "I know how much he meant to you."

Caryn looked downward again. How much had Brenth Nono meant to her? How could Ernst Freed know, if Caryn barely knew herself? Brenner had been an enigma from their earliest days together, and now that he was gone...

Caryn shook her head and looked up again. Freed withdrew his hand and placed it on his desk, leaning against it heavily. "The bombs?"

"Deugan is saved," Caryn assured him. "All of the bombs in our cities have been defused and sealed. The Steffians' own *acambro* in the west has been sealed too, except for a few strands that we had to keep active because we couldn't tell which ones were Captain Toppel's."

General Freed bowed his head. He was silent, but Caryn knew that he was giving his thanks to the Gods, and she found she did not blame him for it. They all needed their comfort, wherever it came from. A muralled wall, a patient chaplain, a sense, pure and innocent, that there may be wonder yet in the world when the horror finally receded. Caryn had felt that awe and wonder in her own life, in sparkling fountains and endless stars, and in hope for the years to come.

If only Caryn had years to come. The other thing she had realized as the stress of the battle faded was that even if her new body had five or ten years left in it, the Wells could shorten that further — and Caryn was not yet able to leave them entirely behind.

"The job isn't finished," Caryn said softly, hoping not to alarm the general. "If our goal was only to save Deugan, we've achieved it. The Breas will see that the Steffians can't attack us, and I believe they'll accept our peace now. But if our goal was to save the entire Continent, then there's more to do."

The general nodded slowly. He was perceptive, and he understood what Caryn was about to propose. Still, he allowed her to say the words. "We need to seal all of the *acambro* that the Steffians have extracted. The Breas might make peace with us, but the Steffians will keep trying to plant their bombs, again and again. If not against us, against innocents in the New Empire. Besides," she added, "if we're really looking for more than an armistice, if we're looking for a friendship with Brealand, we have to save them from the bombs, too."

"Having those bombs in Brea cities could be useful," Freed mused. "We could train our own people to set them off. Deterrence."

"We could," Caryn agreed, "but should we? Is that the best way forward for the Continent? I still remember the day we met, General, here in this office. You told me that you were here to fight for values you believed in. You named the central satellite fort for Eolanis, the god of justice."

"I do remember," Freed said. "I surprised you. Does it also surprise you now to hear that I agree with you? That I would sacrifice a military advantage to save one enemy from a terrible fate at the hands of another?"

"Not at all," Caryn promised him. "You're a good man, Ern. Even a great one."

Freed shook his head. "I'm just a soldier. That's all I've been, for most of my life." He sighed. "How can an old soldier help the foreign minister of Deugan?"

Caryn had been contemplating that question for some time now.

"He needs to get her into a Well for half a day," she said. "The Brea bombs are already drained. They just need to be sealed. Half the *acambro* in the Fringes has been taken care of, too. It won't take long to seal the rest." Brenth Nono had blown up the Steffian facility that had harvested the *acambro*. Caryn would give instructions to the Foreign Ministry to put the Orastan government on alert. With luck, the Steffians could be kept from building a similar facility ever again, and a new era of cooperation could begin with the New Empire. There could truly be peace ahead of them.

General Freed looked troubled. "It'll be a long time before I can get you to the Gateway Well," he warned her. "After the battle, the Breas fell back on trench lines that protect the Well behind them, and we're in no shape to assault a fortified position. The Third Army is exhausted, the fort's ammunition is nearly gone, and the Breas have been hounding us in the west, too. On top of it, they're still allied with the Steffians for the moment, and their Secrets could wreak havoc on us if they have the entire Well to themselves."

"The treaty says pre-war borders," Caryn pointed out.

"But it may take time to implement, and the Breas might not even sign it at all," Freed said. "Plus, the Steffians won't take kindly to it. Even if the Breas withdraw early, we might still have to fight to get the Well back."

Caryn had feared as much. In a way, she had known all along. "There's Amim," she said, thinking of Nono.

The general grimaced, but she knew he would agree. It would be difficult to slip Caryn into Wassia, where there was still resistance to the Deugan occupation, despite the official surrender. The ink wasn't dry yet on the armistice with the New Empire, and their relations would be chilly for some time. Besides, Caryn's task required secrecy. The Amimi Well, isolated at the frozen tip of the Continent, was the only option.

"You won't return," Freed said.

"I don't expect to," Caryn admitted. "At my body's age, this task will probably exhaust me. Brenth Nono gave me just enough of my life back to finish this job."

It was strange how easy it was after all was said and done. Death no longer scared her, as it had only hours earlier. Caryn Hallom had lived a life to be proud of, and after watching such unexpected heroism from so many others, she was prepared to offer her own.

"You may surprise yourself," Freed told her, forcing a smile. "You've surprised me."

Caryn stood, bracing herself against Freed's desk with her hip. "We should make the arrangements immediately," she said. "I want to set out first thing tomorrow morning. Even tonight, now that the Hermann Gap has re-opened. We don't know when the Steffians might detonate another bomb."

"Fine," Freed replied bitterly. "What's your story going to be?"

"I'm from Varszi," Caryn said at once. "Most of my family lived in Hermannsburg and was killed in the massacre a few months ago. The ones in Varszi have died, either of starvation or from today's battle. My only surviving relative is a nephew who's a dockworker in Carrak-on-Sea." The great Deugan port was still open. All Caryn needed was an excuse to travel to the docks there, and she would be able to arrange a ship to Amim.

"What if somebody recognizes you?" Freed asked.

"They won't," Caryn said. "Most of your men couldn't recognize me, and I've been with them every day for three months."

"That's true enough," Freed allowed. "It's probably for the best. I seem to recall that I had promised to arrest Caryn Hallom and turn her over to the civilian authorities. Something about forged documents? But if Hallom has disappeared..." He smiled, and she smiled back. "I'll have the commander of the Third Army commission a carriage," Freed said. "His men will take you to Czemers and see you safely aboard a train to Carrak. You'll have a letter in my handwriting, telling any ship bound for southern Amim to give you passage."

"Will that work?" Caryn asked.

"I'm the hero who won the Second Battle of the Gateway," Freed said. "They'll grumble, but they'll take you. I promise that." He stopped just long enough to take a breath. "You'll also have cash from me for sundry expenses. What were you thinking of doing with your savings?"

"I'll donate them," Caryn said. "Earmark it for a cause I'd support, I haven't had the time to think it through. Talk to the president. With Hans and Lana gone, you and Georg know me better than anybody in Deugan."

The general was astonished. "Are you certain, Caryn?" he asked. "You would trust me with this?"

"I would trust you with anything," Caryn said. She didn't know where that had come from, but when she said it, it rang true inside her heart.

Freed actually blushed, and he looked away. "You honour me," he murmured. Then he was businesslike again. "You will invent a fake name and some code words, which you will leave with me. If you do survive this and you need any of your funds, you will sign a letter to me from that name with the code words in it, and I will give you whatever you've asked for. It's your money. I will never forget that."

"I know," Caryn told him. "I do trust you, Ern."

Only then did General Freed start to relax. He smiled, his face transformed. "Ralf always said I had a soft spot for you."

She took his hand again and squeezed it. "I suppose this is goodbye."

Freed nodded again. "Thank you, Caryn," he said. "For everything." He stopped and cleared his throat. He looked as nervous as Caryn had ever seen him. "I have to ask one thing, Minister, with my apologies. If this is our goodbye, it would be — an honour to share a kiss, before you left."

Caryn looked at him, surprised. She felt the wrinkles on her face as though they were burning her. "I could be your mother's age," she blurted.

"And I actually am your father's age," Freed replied. "It's a bizarre life we live. But even for an old soldier, that doesn't have to be a bad thing."

He had not always been kind to her, Caryn remembered. Ernst Freed had a quick temper, and he had yelled at her, twisted her arm, insulted her. Caryn had often been drawn to people who treated her that way, she realized. Her own father and mother, and Nono, and Janusz, and the energy, the energy most of all.

Still, she was drawn to Freed, and he had changed since the early days. He had grown to respect her. He was a man she cared for, a man she trusted, a man who had protected her more times than she could count. Caryn thought of what Lana had said about Janusz before either of them knew what he would become: that it was not always wrong to do something stupid and frivolous, as long as you recognized it for what it was. Life was short, and Caryn's shorter than most.

She leaned forward and kissed the general deeply, allowing herself to enjoy the moment of hesitation before their lips met and the sensations that came after. They broke apart almost shyly, and then Freed ushered her to the door of the office, pausing there before resigning himself to the parting that was to come.

Before long her belongings were packed, the papers were signed, and Caryn Hallom was waving to Ernst Freed from the back of a carriage, watching as he grew smaller and smaller behind her. Then the fort disappeared and she was travelling through the night, passing as though through a gateway into the world beyond.

CHAPTER THIRTY-FIVE

When I look back on the Treaty of Hastingvale, I see a monumental accomplishment. The treaty did more than end the Great War. It was a roadmap for cooperation, from the multinational commission to rebuild Wassia, to the trade provisions that forced Deugan and Brealand, however reluctantly, to begin integrating their economies. It's true that the Treaty confirmed the New Empire's right to the Fringes, but that was mostly a political expediency to get it signed. In recognizing Amimi independence and granting full citizenship to the Brea Islands — most of us forget that pre-war, they were called the "island colonies" — the Treaty actually had an enormous impact on the Orastan decolonization movement.

But it's hard to talk about the Treaty without mentioning its architect. The Deugan government has never confirmed it — they insist that foreign policy discussions sixty-five years ago are still "classified" and "sensitive" — but it's generally accepted that Deugan's foreign minister at the time, Caryn Hallom, was the driving force behind the secret negotiations. Whenever the Treaty comes up, I hear the old debate rehashed: Did Minister Hallom actually die in the Gateway, or did she somehow survive?

The problem with that question is that Caryn Hallom herself would never have accepted such a stark dichotomy. She was famously stubborn, but she was also innately creative and able to develop better options. She may have been a Deugan, but she exemplifies the most important lesson that I learned here at O'Keefe College and throughout my career in Brealand. The world is not drawn in solid shapes, with clear borders and outlines. Things do not always have to be just one way, or the other.

Did Caryn Hallom die, or did she survive? Why not ask whether she found another option entirely? She may well have lived through the Second Battle of the Gateway, but that doesn't mean that the Deugan foreign minister survived as such. The experience of war changes people, and I wouldn't be surprised if the Great War touched Minister Hallom more profoundly than any of us have imagined. Just as it touched everybody who was connected to it. Just as it transformed the Continent itself.

— Remarks of Darren Mbenko, Ambassador of Pesaw (northern continent) to Brealand, at his Brea *alma mater* on the occasion of the sixty-fifth anniversary of the signing of the Treaty of Hastingvale (1758).

He was surrounded. Suspended. He was burning like a flame, then doused in water that slowly chilled to ice. Matthias was floating, drifting, out of control.

He saw landscapes and cityscapes, oceans and swampland. He saw flocks of strange birds and jungles of twisted vines. He wondered whether he was seeing Good Steif's other Worlds, but no sooner had the thought come than a stab of pain drilled into his temples, and the images were gone. Matthias was surrounded by mist that coalesced into foam. It relaxed him and he slept.

He was startled awake by a sudden plunge. Matthias flailed but could find nothing to grip. He was plummeting toward the square in Avali Nova, the police and their horses growing larger and closer. Then he was hurtling toward the Kalidi Well, his flesh starting to melt, the power crackling like electricity inside him. Another shift, dizzying, and he was falling toward a tent in the Selliar Mountains. He bent his mind toward that choice, begging the energy for safety, but the mountains faded and the Orastan police were returning to focus. The harder he yearned for the Selliar, the faster he fell toward Avali Nova. He panicked, screamed. The police were closing in, and Matthias knew, with a terrible certainty, that there was nothing he could do to stop them.

Nothing active, at any rate.

Matthias cleared his mind and resigned his fate to the energy. Flashes of light danced across his vision. The dizziness was overwhelming. He reached his arms forward to embrace the ground as it rushed up to meet him.

*

He woke to the smell of cigar smoke and the sound of voices speaking rapidly in a language he couldn't understand. He ran a hand over his face. Something was different, something he couldn't place. He reached for the energy, but all he felt was a loss, a devastating loneliness.

Matthias groaned and sat up. He tried to lean backward, but there was canvas behind him that threatened to collapse. He blinked away the grogginess and forced himself to look carefully at his surroundings. A canvas tent. Cigar smoke. That language. An old memory returned to him, and he said, in a cracked voice, "Rangers?"

A woman's face smiled at him, dark-skinned, middle-aged with lines around her eyes. She felt distant to Matthias, though she was hovering just above him. Everything felt distant somehow. "We in Range, yes," Mila told him. She drew on her cigar, then leaned away from him. "Finally wake, is good."

"How did I get here?" Matthias asked. His voice sounded as dead as he felt.

"My son find you in mountains. He know you were my client. Bring you here."

"How did I get to the mountains, then?"

"Maybe took train?" Mila suggested. "Horse carriage? But no, my son find you half dead on smuggler route. Route that only Ranger know. So maybe Steffian can tell me the answer."

Matthias shook his head. "I'm not a Steffian anymore." He ran his hand over his face again. It was nagging at him. Through the haze that the world had become, he could swear there was something missing —

The scar. The one from the brand searing into his cheek, the one that had marked him as a fugitive. It had vanished. Disappeared, as Matthias had.

Matthias held his hands up in front of his face. They too had no scars, no burns from the ropes digging into his wrists. He ripped off his shirt and stared at his shoulder. There was nothing there, no bullet wound, no infection. The energy had healed him.

Yet he felt no joy in it. There was only foreboding, and beneath it a deep emptiness. The visions were returning, and Matthias was plummeting toward the square again, powerless to resist. How had he persuaded the energy to bring him to the Selliar instead? He hadn't, Matthias realized. There was no persuasion, no dialogue. Matthias had given himself to the energy blindly, just as he had done in Avali Nova. He had abandoned any thought of control or power, and submitted. That was why the energy had allowed him to survive. It had broken him.

Mila took another long puff on her cigar. "Guest not usually taking off shirt in my tent," she said.

"That's a shame," Matthias replied, but the joke fell flat. His heart was not in it. He could think only of the energy, how it had defeated him. How it had trained him to submit and obey, like an animal.

Mila eyed him critically. "No laugh now," she said. "Important to know. Magic bring you here?"

Matthias nodded. There was no sense correcting her wording. The Well's power was magic, truly. It was sinister, and dressing it in names like *energy* or *Secrets* could not mask it. "It brought me here. Then it left me."

"How?" Mila demanded.

"I don't know," Matthias replied. "One moment I'm jumping out of a window in Avali Nova. The next I'm waking up in your tent." Only there was also the awful part in between, the fire and the visions and the falling, and that was just the beginning. He was thinking more clearly as his tiredness receded. He was starting to recognize the real source of the hole inside him. "Why do you want to know?" Matthias asked wearily.

"Is important," Mila said. "Magic coming to Range. Need to understand."

That made little sense. The energy couldn't come to the Range with no Wells in the territory, and surely the Steffians would not be wasting their precious *acambro* here while the New Empire still stood. He was too tired to argue, though. Instead he lay back on the rugs that Mila had given him as a bed and told her what had happened to him as best as he could remember. When he reached the part where the energy had come to him in prison, a weapon handed to him by Good Steif himself, Matthias started to tear up, and it took him several deep breaths before he could continue. By the end of the story he could no longer hide his bitterness. "There was no Good Steif," he said quietly, fighting down the tears that threatened to return. "There was only the energy, and its vendetta."

Mila's look was solemn but sympathetic. "Difficult time, captured by empire, running to escape," she said kindly. "Maybe you not actually sure, no Steif god."

She was wrong. Matthias's certainty was overwhelming. He had felt the energy ripping through his body, scraping at his mind. It had not come from the one god, or from any god. The power was the only deity that mattered. "It Steif existed, he would have let me bring down the New Empire," Matthias said. "He would have let me die in Avali Nova as a hero, not dragged me away to live out a useless life."

Mila raised her eyebrows. "Your bomb would kill hundred thousand people, no? Would kill you also. North gods would not help that. North gods would stop it like your Steif did."

"Your north gods didn't stop the war," Matthias argued.

"Kept Range and North Continent out of war," Mila pointed out. "All of north gods' followers. You should go North Continent. Good place. Big cities, important trade, follow good gods. You will like."

"Mila, I don't want good gods. I don't want any gods."

Mila chewed on her cigar. She seemed to be searching for a way to penetrate the blanket that felt like it was smothering his mind, to persuade him that the hole in him could still be filled. It couldn't. The energy had shown him Steif's Worlds disappearing, and Mila's prying only angered him. "When Rao fell —"

"Rao didn't fall," Matthias interrupted. "It was an earthquake that destroyed the Raolin Temple in Villasud. An earthquake, not a spirit falling on it."

Mila bulled on as though she hadn't heard him. "When Rao fell, most Wassians give up. Raolin religion dies. Nobody remembers. But other Wassians see the fall as a beginning, not an end. They worship god who struck Rao down. They start Steifar, and today is largest religion on Continent."

Matthias only scowled and looked away. He could not bear this Ranger spouting Steifar doctrine at him after everything that had happened. He had been kept from Deugan. He had been kept from defeating the New Empire. Now he was a fugitive in the Range, a backwater of nomads that was defenceless against the looming threat of Brealand. What was there for him here? Without the one god, what was there for him anywhere in this life?

Mila was looking at him curiously. "I am only poor Ranger, not understanding," she said. "You say you put life in god's hand. Should have died, fell to street from five levels. Magic energy should have burned you inside out. Empire police should have shot you. You make test for your god, can he make you live when you should die. But you live! Wake up safe in Range, no more wounds. God passes your test." She shook her head. "Why is this the thing that make you stop to believe?"

Matthias hesitated. He had to admire Mila for cutting through his self-loathing and forcing him to think. He had done so much contemplation before the empire took him, and so little since. Finally he said, softly, "Because faith is ruined when you have to test it."

For a time Mila had no response. Matthias sat, staring past her at the fluttering edges of the tent. He heard birdsong, and human voices too. He wished he could rouse himself to care. Finally Mila said, "Go to North Continent. Nothing for you in Range. There, maybe you find what you look for."

"I don't know of anything worth looking for," Matthias said.

"Good. When not looking is when you find."

"Mila —"

"And passage already paid," Mila added, cracking, for the first time, a mischievous grin.

"What do you mean?" Matthias asked. "By who?"

She crawled to the edge of the tent, poked her head through the flap and shouted some words in her own language. A few moments later Mila's daughter appeared, helping an older man inside. He was too pale to be a Ranger. His body was gaunt, but the haunted look stopped at his face. For the first time Matthias could remember, there was satisfaction in Master Nono's eyes. "What are you doing here?" Matthias asked.

"I could ask you the same," the Master smiled. The energy must have touched him profoundly while he was in the Gateway. Nono looked a decade older than the last time Matthias had seen him. "I discovered a tunnel from the Gateway Well that led to a cave in the Selliar Mountains. From there, I made my way back to the path that Mila took us through last month, and waited. Her daughter found me."

"And that was how you paid Mila for passage to the northern continent?" Matthias asked, confused. He was still trying to recover from the surprise of seeing Nono alive. Matthias vaguely recalled attacking Nono during the battle when he allowed the energy to act through him. He remembered collapsing rocks, Nono being buried. "You told her about your tunnel to Deugan?"

Mila scoffed. "We know this path for centuries. Not use so much anymore, because exit so close to Deugan fort. But Nono does pay us well. He has magic. He give us what we need most at this time."

"He's sold you short, then," Matthias snapped. "The energy is evil. Haven't you heard anything I've been telling you? It's not going to protect you against Brealand, not if it saved the New Empire. You're not getting some incredibly powerful new bomb. Besides, didn't you just say that your gods look down on murdering thousands of people? Why are you smiling?"

Mila looked away, trying not to laugh. Nono put a hand on Matthias' shoulder. "You're still thinking like a Steffian," he said. "Let it go. It's time to move forward."

"Forward where?" Matthias asked, angry that he still didn't understand.

"Mila said that I gave the Rangers what they need most *at this time*," Nono said. "It's winter, Matt."

He suddenly understood. "Winter is the dry season in the Range."

"Rain always was my specialty," Nono said. "I had very little *acambro* left, and it was time to set the energy free. It seemed the fairest way to do it."

Matthias felt numb. What had become of him? Could he really not see past death and destruction? What had the empire done to him? Or had it been the Steffians?

Nono saw the hurt on Matthias's face. Matthias scowled at him, hating his concern, but Nono only moved closer. "Do you think I don't know what it is to lose? Years, friends, love, dreams? I know that better than you do, but I haven't given up. In my entire Steif-forsaken life, I've never given up."

Matthias took a deep breath. Turned back to Nono. "What do you want from me?"

"A fresh start," Nono replied. "Mila's tribe has arranged a ship to take us to Pesaw, on the northern continent. It would be pleasant to have an old friend with me."

Friend. What a strange word, after all that he had been through. Could there really be a fresh start? Was such a thing possible without faith, without plans, without hope?

Mila discarded her cigar and looked at Matthias seriously. "Go," she said. "Staying will make you remember. If you think me wise, take this advice."

"I do," Matthias admitted. "I always have." It was difficult to feel motivated, but he didn't have a better option, and at least he would not be alone. Perhaps Nono was right after all. Perhaps a fresh start was what Matthias needed, and the northern continent would probably better for him than this one. He could scarcely imagine it being worse.

He grimaced and looked away. "I'll go with you," he muttered.

Nono grinned and clasped his friend's hand. Then his face turned sombre. "You are aware, though. There aren't any Wells on the northern continent."

Matthias nodded. Sorrow rose in him, surprising him. For all that he had come to hate the energy, the years were not so easy to leave behind. He squeezed his eyes closed, forcing away the tears. When he opened them again, he spoke with newfound resolve.

"I know," Matthias said. "I'm ready."

*

Caryn sat, shivering, before one of the most beautiful sights she had ever seen. It was blisteringly cold, and despite the heavy parka the wind sliced through her aching body like shrapnel. Beside her, the Amimi guide slowed the sled to give a brief respite to the dogs. She was bundled so tightly that Caryn could see no more than her eyes as she pointed at the scene stretched out before them. "Pilgrim Lake," she said, in heavily accented Wassian. "Almost there."

Caryn could tell. Since disembarking the ship at Port Leyda, she had seen little but shrubs and snow as the dogs guided them along the Pilgrim Way, named for the Steifar who braved the bitter cold to visit the source of their god's Secrets. The tundra had its own beauty in its vastness, but as they approached the Well, the heat emanating from it allowed taller trees to grow, sentinels amid the snows.

The snow was not falling anymore, and overhead, the sun had re-emerged to peek around the clouds. Sunlight danced across the frozen lake before her, the ice glittering majestically. Surrounding the lake, the needles of the evergreen trees clung stubbornly to life beneath the snow that was piled high on their branches. Snow coated the ground as well, pristine and white, undisturbed save for the sled and the tracks of their dogs behind them.

Her guide produced a large metal stake, which she drove forcefully into the ice. Then she grunted, satisfied, and led the dogs onto the lake. Caryn held on to the guide as the sled bumped and jostled, feeling every year of her aged body. She barely minded. All around her the snow glittered like crystals in the sunlight, and Caryn was reminded, once again, of how much wonder and beauty remained in this life after the fighting left it.

They had received the news when they stopped to restock in the northern part of Amim. Brealand and Deugan had signed an armistice, and the Deugan president was travelling to Hastingvale, the Brea capital, to finalize a treaty that would end hostilities for years to come. Caryn allowed herself a moment of satisfaction as she huddled in the parka she had just purchased with the general's money. After a year of suffering, the Great War was over.

They crossed the lake, following the shimmering ice into a hidden cove that Caryn hadn't seen from the other shore. The shoreline here was still dotted with trees, but in one spot they abruptly stopped growing, and the landscape beyond was rocky and bare. The sled pulled them to the edge of the lake, but the dogs would go no further. "Dogs smarter than us," the guide said. "We arrive."

Caryn needed the guide's help to rise from the sled, and then, in the sudden heat and pressure of the Well, to shrug out of the parka and drape it over her right arm. It was frustrating to be so useless, but all the same, Caryn marvelled at the fact that she had made it this far. A long sea journey and a trek through the coldest place on the Continent were perilous even for people much younger than she. In fact, Caryn felt as though the voyage had aged her as much as the Wells had. It would be her last journey, and the woman who stood with her at the edge of the Amimi Well would know it.

Still she said, "I wait for you here, where warm. Only until sundown. Come before then." She pointed at a hut at the edge of the lake. "I stay there one night with dogs. I come back here first light and stay one hour. If you not come then, I go back to base."

"Thank you for everything," Caryn said, still hating the quavering tone of her voice. She pressed some of the general's money into the guide's hand. Caryn had paid her the agreed amount before they'd set out, but Caryn would not need the money any longer, and the Amimi might.

Knees creaking, back aching, Caryn stumbled into the Amimi Well.

There was no need to go far. The energy was present throughout the Well, and she did not want to tax herself, given the job that she had come to finish. She was certain this Well would have caverns like the others, but instead she stopped at an outcropping of rock and leaned against it to take the weight off her legs. She was shielded from view here, but she could still see the sun shining down on her and feel the wind through her hair, warmed by the Well's power.

Caryn waited a time, considering. Then she drew herself into the map, as she had so many times before. The Well grew dark in a small radius around her, and the columns emerged, one by one. The *acambro* lights were blinking too, but there were fewer of them now. Caryn felt the energy coursing through her body, shaping her with its power, corrupting her with its poison.

Her thoughts drifted to Brenner. On the long train ride across Deugan, and again on the sea voyage south, there had been little to do but sit and ruminate on all that had happened. Mostly she thought about the battle in the Well, when Nono had made her invisible and saved her life. She remembered the look of shock on Nono's face as the invisibility set in, and now she could explain it. Caryn had made the ceiling of the Wassian cavern invisible by speaking with the rocks, communing with them through the energy, until finally, shockingly, she had come to know them. To truly know them. To understand.

That was the conclusion Caryn had reached as the ship traced the Amimi coastline. That Brenth Nono had finally come to understand her. While Caryn still had difficulty understanding herself.

She worked deftly, threading the energy through the *acambro* bombs in Breland to seal them, then draining the *acambro* in the Fringes and watching the lights flicker and die. With each effect she produced, Caryn felt the Well reacting with the energy that lived inside her, communing and entangling to broadcast her power to the reaches of the Continent. All the while, her thoughts remained with Brenner at that moment of understanding. Whatever the energy had shown him, it had brought him not only surprise, but a form of closure. He was able at last to leave her behind, knowing that she would be safe.

She finished the last seal and allowed the map to drift away, as her life soon would. The sun was lower now. Caryn closed her eyes and opened her mind to the Well's power, allowing it to flow to her, to penetrate deep into her heart. It was time. Time to see what Nono had seen, to gain that measure of understanding before it was too late.

She saw herself, her features vague and distorted, as though she were made of drifting smoke. Jayla listening to her parents fight, a little girl trying to mediate while her brothers hid. Jayla in the Wassian Well, drawing Brenner out of his malaise, showing him the stars, holding his hands as he leaned in to kiss her beneath a sparkling fountain. Caryn in Carrak-on-Sea, head buried in books, scratching out numbers and sums, trying to survive. Her first internship in Carrak, keeping her profile low, avoiding notice where notice was controversy. Smoothing relations, declining a promotion only to have it forced on her amid angry glances. Her first meeting with Hans, a bodyguard assigned to her protection, for when mediation failed.

Then she saw hundreds of images of herself immersed in her work, first in the Treasury Department and then the Foreign Ministry. The energy gripped her with her own intensity, spoke to her the way she once spoke to herself, telling herself it was for Deugan and for the young women who would come after her. The Sorceress rumours and the death threats as she pressed the Hallom Doctrine on the New Empire. Ranting and ridicule against her anti-war speeches. Rushing through a battle in a vain attempt to save Lana. Sending her own protectors away to fight Breas over the fort's food stores. Putting herself and her friends in the line of fire to allow their raid against the Steffians to succeed. Remaining stubbornly in a cavern in the Gateway Well to drain *acambro* bombs in Brealand. Finally there was an image of Caryn here, ancient and wrinkled in the Amimi Well, sacrificing the last years of her life to finish a job left undone.

It was too much sacrifice, but Caryn had never seen it that way. It had been a source of pride for her, and she had done it without second thought, but there was a part of her, buried deep, that yearned to stop sacrificing. As she had only once before, in another Well in another land at another time, when she had slung a sack over her shoulder and walked out of Brenner's life, desperately willing herself not to look back.

Caryn remembered the thought that had come to her before she'd kissed the general. The way she was drawn to men like Janusz and

Nono, and the way she had labelled the energy as one of them, just as Hertha had done.

The same energy that was with her now, showing her these images, helping her to understand. It was a crutch, she realized with a gasp. Something that she could cling to, something good to emerge from the Wassian Well to justify the ordeal. But wasn't that twisted? Hadn't the energy truly been their enemy, as Brenner and Hertha and even Ernst Freed had said?

There were layers of meaning to uncover, and not enough time to find them. Caryn felt her head spinning as the energy raced through it. She had never blamed the power the way Brenner had. She couldn't. It was a beast, a force of nature. It hadn't chosen to attack her. It was what it was, a source of mystery that would never be explained.

But it was time to leave the energy behind.

It was not a question of fault or blame. It did not matter whether the power was capable of morality, just as it did not matter whether Janusz's betrayal had been for love of Deugan, or whether Nono's assassination attempt was a misguided effort to save her. What mattered, Caryn Hallom realized, was that she needed to stop sacrificing. She needed to seize the life that she deserved.

Caryn felt the power stir then. It moved with difficulty, hesitant, but the image it displayed for her was unmistakeable. Brenth Nono, in the cavern in the Gateway Well, sending Caryn a message to escape where he knew he could never follow. He had loved her too, and Caryn had truly loved him. The energy knew that. It understood.

And so did she. She saw in that moment the sacrifice the energy was prepared to make, the gift it was willing to grant her. Unique, powerful, and even, in its own way, tragic.

Caryn felt the energy that lived inside her, that had flowed through her veins since her first day in the Wassian Well, that had become part of her. It started to warm and tingle. A sign. It was ready. And Caryn knew it.

She drew the energy from her legs, leaving only a strand behind to serve as her thread, to heal her. She felt her legs strengthening, the joints growing limber. With a rush of exhilaration Caryn stood, and it was painless.

She drew the energy from her injured arm. This time the strand remained willingly, soothing the burns, repairing the damage. She flexed her fingers and curled them into a fist. She felt her elbow, her shoulder, felt her arm extending upward and outward. For the first time in more than three months, she felt whole.

She drew the energy from her face. She felt the creases there receding, the wrinkles smoothing.

Then she drew the energy from her heart. It went, sad but assured, flowing into the Well, returning home.

Caryn sat on the ground beneath an outcropping of rock in the Amimi Well and removed her boots and socks, then rolled up her pant legs, the better to look upon the form that the power had left her. Her body, Caryn judged, had spent thirty years in this life. Nearly thirty-one. As she had. Who could say how many years were yet ahead of her?

She had to see, though. She had to know. She reached for the map, as she had hundreds of times before. She tried to overwhelm herself with emotion to send a message to Nono far to the north. She tried Nono's rain effect, the energy hands, even the simple act of driving energy into the ground. There was nothing she could do. The power had disappeared, as though she had never encountered it.

Then it was buzzing around her. The pressure started to build, as it always did upon entering a Well for the first time. The energy attacking its target, striving to force its way in.

Caryn's body was young and healthy. She could resist it for twenty-four hours. She had time yet to linger in the Well, to say farewell to the friend she had known.

But she felt no need. Further north, in the thriving villages of the newly independent State of Amim, a life was waiting for her. People who had known her best friend waited at the edge of dense forests, rolling glaciers, and the greatest beauty the Continent had to offer. The Well was not a place to linger. It was a place to lay old memories to rest. It was a time for new beginnings.

So Caryn Hallom wrapped herself in the parka and began the trek back to the spot where the Amimi guide was waiting. As she reached the edge of the Well she found that it had begun to snow again, adding a fresh blanket to the sentinel trees and the blue-white sheen of the frozen lake. She stepped across the boundary of the Well and stood amid the snowflakes as they drifted and spun around her, each of them unique, small, white and perfect.

She felt, at long last, at peace.

ACKNOWLEDGMENTS

Gateways is the culmination of a childhood dream. I have been inventing and writing stories for as long as I can remember, and it is such a thrill to be able to release a novel into the world. I feel only humility, love and gratitude to all those in my life who have supported me and allowed this dream to come true.

Gateways originated with a non-fiction book, *The Next 100 Years* by George Friedman. Published in 2009, it uses geopolitical forecasting methods to predict major international political trends throughout the 21st century. I found it so interesting that I decided to draw a map populated by invented countries so that I could try it myself. Thus was the Continent born, along with a sketch of its history, its nations and their strategic imperatives – months before I developed actual characters like Caryn Hallom or Brenth Nono.

Along with *The Next 100 Years*, the non-fiction books with the greatest influence on *Gateways* were a pair of great reads about the First World War: *The Myth of the Great War* by John Mosier, and *The Lost History of 1914* by Jack Beatty. Both come highly recommended. In researching the fortresses, arms and tactics of the war, I supplemented these great sources with, I am somewhat ashamed to admit, a healthy (unhealthy?) dose of Google and Wikipedia. In my defence, I was working a more-than-full-time job at the time.

The plot and characters of *Gateways* started to crystallize and I began putting pen to paper (wait, let's be honest: fingers to keyboard) in August 2010, but as late as February 2012 I fully intended to abandon the project. The reason I didn't is that around that time, I decided to send to a friend the ten or so chapters I had written so far. The feedback was sufficiently positive that in the following months, I expanded my group of "readers" to four, sending out my work-in-progress in five- or six-chapter chunks as I wrote them. It was their inspiration and motivation that drove me to finish *Gateways*, and their advice improved the text phenomenally. Trevor Kempthorne, Shannon Refvik, Mark Wilson and Carolyn Sealfon: this novel would not exist without you.

Speaking of reading and giving advice on work-in-progress, I cannot say enough about my editor, Allister Thompson, and his invaluable guidance. The gorgeous cover, as well as the map, were designed by Fiona Jayde, and I think her work is amazing.

My final thank you is for my parents. You nurtured my love for reading and constantly encouraged me in my writing. I would not be the person that I am, let alone the writer that I am, without the confidence that you have always placed in me. Thank you.

ABOUT THE AUTHOR

I've been writing as a hobby since, at the age of four, I penned an epic about my then-favourite sport, the charmingly mis-spelled "baceball." I'm more of a basketball fan these days, but I have kept up my love for writing throughout.

I live in Toronto, Canada, or as we Torontonians like to call it, "the centre of the universe." I'm just joking about that ... mostly. I'm writing a novel at the moment in which the main character hates Toronto, so that's been a bit of a challenge. At one point she describes it as a "frenetic smogscape." To each her own, I suppose.

In my day job, I work as a labour and employment lawyer with Bernardi Human Resource Law (visit us at www.hrlawyers.ca). I practice labour and employment law, which I think is fascinating and covers everything from union certifications to human rights issues, employment contracts to severance packages, and court and tribunal work to harassment investigations.

Outside of work, while I'm less enamoured than I once was with "baceball," I've replaced it with a hobby and passion that I find even more creative, exciting, and easy to spell: swing dancing. In addition to the joy of dancing itself, I have also served in various dance organizing roles, most recently as President of Toronto Lindy Hop, a not-for-profit swing dance organization (www.torontolindyhop.com).

www.ingramcontent.com/pod-product-compliance
Lightning Source LLC
Chambersburg PA
CBHW070352260626
47161CB00001B/115